The Break Line

By the same author

My Friend the Mercenary

The Break Line

JAMES BRABAZON

MICHAEL JOSEPH
an imprint of
PENGUIN BOOKS

MICHAEL JOSEPH

UK | USA | Canada | Ireland | Australia
India | New Zealand | South Africa

Michael Joseph is part of the Penguin Random House group of companies
whose addresses can be found at global.penguinrandomhouse.com

First published 2018

001

Copyright © James Brabazon, 2018

The moral right of the author has been asserted

Set in 14/16.5 pt Garamond MT Std
Typeset by Jouve (UK), Milton Keynes
Printed in Great Britain by Clays Ltd, St Ives plc

A CIP catalogue record for this book is available from the British Library

HARDBACK ISBN: 978-0-718-18623-4
OM PAPERBACK ISBN: 978-1-405-92943-1

www.greenpenguin.co.uk

For Joy

. . . all that mysterious life of the wilderness that stirs in the forest, in the jungles, in the hearts of wild men. There's no initiation either into such mysteries. He has to live in the midst of the incomprehensible, which is also detestable. And it has a fascination, too, that goes to work upon him. The fascination of the abomination – you know, imagine the growing regrets, the longing to escape, the powerless disgust, the surrender, the hate.

Joseph Conrad, *Heart of Darkness*

Prologue: Last Light

Sunday 27 March 1994

It began a long time ago. I was nineteen then and a soldier. Not a killer.

Early that evening, I was called to Colonel Ellard's office. He sent an orderly, who asked me to bring my rifle and follow him immediately. I asked if I was in trouble, and the orderly shrugged and smiled.

'There's a man with him. Smart suit. They're in a hurry.'

We took off down the corridor at the double. The orderly smiled again and hung back, not wanting to be sent on another errand. I entered the room alone. Colonel Ellard was inside with the man who had been watching me all day. He sat at the back of the office behind the door. I couldn't see him clearly.

That morning, when the sergeant major told us to break for a smoke, I'd noticed him standing inside the wire next to the main gate. It was not long after sunrise, and the air was still cold. He had his hands in the trouser pockets of a dark-grey suit and stared at me as I lit and then smoked half a Marlboro. The jacket had a red silk lining that flashed in the breeze and thin lapels that framed a white shirt open at the neck. I ground the cigarette out on a galvanized bin and stared back at him, and he turned and walked briskly towards the officers' mess. He wasn't wearing a coat and he was unshaven, which made me wonder where he'd come from.

Later that day I saw him again, speaking to Colonel Ellard. They were pointing at me as I laid out my kit – rifle, slip, scope, suppressor and a box of twenty rounds – and then he walked towards me while I lay prone on the firing line. Without introducing himself, he knelt down and asked me if I could see the retaining-bolt that held the hundred-metre target in place. I looked up at Ellard, who nodded. Through the scope, I told him I could. The man asked me to shoot it. I did. Then I looked up at him. He studied my face intently, as if looking for something he'd lost, and then walked away.

I stood in the office, at ease. According to the custom at Raven Hill no salutes were exchanged, but you could never quite relax with the colonel. He was so softly spoken that it was hard to hear him on the range, and so patient with us that he made you feel, instantly, as if his entire focus was on you, and you alone. He was the last Irish officer in the British army to come up through the ranks. 'Not from private, but from the pits,' he told new recruits: before he enlisted he'd cut coal on his back in the Arigna mines in County Roscommon. Now Ellard walked tall. He expected, and received, absolute obedience. What we feared was not his wrath, but his disappoint-ment. And, because they worked, we were unquestion-ingly dedicated to his methods. We were, all of us, terrified of him, too – because we liked him but did not understand him. I'd learned quickly in the army that there was no progress of any kind without the fuel of fear.

Sitting behind the walnut desk in his office, Colonel Ellard motioned for me to give him my rifle, so I detached the magazine and pulled back the bolt twice to show that the breech was clear and handed it over. It was his policy that our weapons were always amber: charged magazine on, nothing in the chamber. He placed it carefully on the desk.

'Thank you. You'll find a black Mercedes out the front. Jump in and wait. You're not driving.'

I made to leave. He raised his right hand to stop me and nodded towards the man.

'Max, this is Commander Knight. You are to follow orders from him as if they were given by me. He is your commanding officer until further notice.'

Knight sat behind me and said nothing. I saw his face clearly as I walked out. He'd shaved. He smiled and gave me a curt nod of recognition.

I sat in the front passenger seat. Ten minutes later, Knight stepped outside and put a rifle sheathed in a slip in the boot of the car. He joined me and took the wheel. We drove for an hour and didn't speak. I didn't have anything to say. It was early spring. Dun-coloured hills soaked up the last of the evening light. The clocks had gone forward that morning, and the late dusk was unsettling. We were circling a large village due west of Belfast on a metalled road coated with mud well trodden by tractor tyres and peppered with cow pats. We looped behind the tallest hill and found the moon rising above Lough Neagh.

At a checkpoint below a cut in the road manned by crap hats we were joined by two soldiers in civvies – most probably from the SAS or the Det. No one saluted. They climbed in the back and seemed comfortable with Knight. They must have met before. Fifteen minutes later, we stopped again. I got out first and saw one of our passengers had a SIG semi-automatic pistol stuck in the waistband of his jeans. Knight asked me to take the rifle from the boot of the Mercedes and walk with him off the road, directly up the hill. His accent was from Dublin, sharpened in an English public school, and reminded me of my father's Irish lilt. They would have been the same age, too, had my father lived. The man's brogues found no purchase on the smooth grass, and more than once he stumbled so that he had to steady his ascent with outstretched palms. It had been a hot day in the end, and I'd been burned by the sun; now there was a chill, and the air was sharp and brittle again.

As we climbed higher, I began first to smell and then to hear the village. It was a Sunday. Traditional Irish music tumbled out the swinging pub door and down the hillside. A tang of roasting meat lifted on the breeze off the lake, mixing with the reek of peat smoke and wet grass.

Finally, the climb levelled off on to a broad grassy saddle. We ran slowly and at a crouch to the lee of the hill facing the south side of the village, the straps of the rifle slip bunched in my right hand. I could see the evening dew had soaked into Knight's suit from where he had stumbled. Dark patches spread out from his knees and ringed his cuffs.

Below us, the kitchen clatter that heralded the end of dinner filtered through the half-open window of a stone house. I took a map and a pair of binoculars from one of the plain-clothed operators who'd followed us up and checked the range.

Three hundred metres away, in the failing light, I could see a family of seven lit by a single tungsten bulb, framed by net curtains darkened by smoke from the open hearth. Four children babbled and whooped, whirling round the table, licking grease off their fingers and taking empty plates to a middle-aged woman in the kitchen. She stood, as if transfixed, behind a deep butler's sink beneath a second window. At the head of the table a man sat with another child on his lap, a young girl with long hair the colour of threshed corn. His daughter. Knight crouched next to me and handed me a loaded magazine.

'The man at the head of the table has blood on his hands. Your orders are to kill him.'

'Yes, sir. Understood.'

I eased the rifle from the padded slip. It was my rifle. Despite the bumps and knocks of the journey it would have kept its zero. I clipped on the magazine, adjusted the scope's elevation drum and brought the glass in front of my eye. Inside the house I could see the stains on the man's shirt, the shaving cut on his neck from when he'd prepared for Mass that morning. I saw his daughter's lips moving. Their eyes were the mirror image of each other. I saw his chest rise, watched the rhythm of his breath. The target turned his face to the gathering gloom and stared out of the window, listening to the girl. I fed a round into the chamber. The wind dropped. There were no adjustments to make: safety off; weapon live.

'Sir?'

'Weapons free.'

The horizontal line of the crosshair ran beneath the target's eyes. The vertical bar divided the tip of his nose. He inclined his head, resting his chin on the girl's scalp. Time stopped. Taking the first gentle pressure on the trigger, the pad of my index finger crept to a stop, and then drew a hair's breadth further back.

Nothing.

The clocks restarted. Only the faint dry echo of metal on metal remained above the sound of blood pumping in my ears, oxygen rushing in my throat. I cleared the breech and chambered another round. A flash of brass glinted in my right eye as the dead cartridge spun out in front of Knight's face next to me. I settled the crosshairs. We were alone again, the target, his daughter and I. She touched his cheek. He looked out of the window straight at me, seeming to hold my monocular gaze. First pressure: already I was part of him, following the pin into the cartridge; already I was tethered to the bullet.

Again, nothing.

I gulped a lungful of air and felt the grass-wet palm of Commander Knight on the back of my right hand as I tensed and moved to rework the bolt. And then those three words that still wake me.

'You did well.'

The firing pin had been removed from my rifle. It was the final test in Knight's search for what he later described as a 'legally sane psychopath'.

'Your father,' he said as we returned to the car, 'would be proud of you.'

I

Twenty-three years later

I picked her up at the 360° Roof Bar. She was already half-cut. Her ex-boyfriend was the political officer at the US embassy in Caracas – a crew-cut spy with a face like a potato and a weakness for local women. He'd dumped her the week before, or so I'd been told. I guessed she was either drowning her sorrows or still celebrating. Outside, the city was disintegrating. Everyone was drinking hard.

I bought her a rum and lemon, cracked a joke in deliberately shaky Spanish and sat down beside her.

'How do you know I'm not expecting someone?' she asked.

'Because you've been waiting for me all these years, *corazón*.'

She laughed, and her elbow slipped on the mahogany table. A slop of the sticky dark rum ran over her knuckles. She licked it off.

'Just think how much *more* fun us two blonds could have.' I raised my glass to her. 'Double trouble.'

'Double trouble,' she repeated in Spanish with a wide, sad smile. 'I'm Ana María.'

She held up her glass too and looked at me, waiting.

There we were: a businessman chatting up a local girl

at a discreet corner table on the upper terrace, taking in each other and the view. Except she wasn't a local girl. And I was supposed to kill her.

'My name is Max,' I said. 'Max McLean.'

We touched glasses and both took a long swallow of rum. It seemed like an unnecessary cruelty to lie to her, that dead woman drinking. I was growing tired of being everyone except myself.

Spy fucking is bad for your health in Venezuela, especially for the jilted mistress of the Russian ambassador to Cuba. She was nothing, it seemed, if not consistent in her lousy choice of lover. Now she'd seen and heard enough to get her promoted on to everyone's kill list. If we hadn't got to her first the Russians would have been close behind.

She drank and talked, and I laughed and listened hard. I don't like killing women, and I don't like doing the Americans' dirty work for them. I don't *like* killing anyone. And after another glass of rum I didn't want to kill her. Not because she was pretty, or fun to have a drink with, but because when you're about to kill someone up close like that you watch them very carefully first. Whether you want to or not you get to know them before they are dead. Time distorts. What would normally take weeks – months, even – to pass between two people is compressed into fast minutes; seconds, sometimes. The emotional pressure cooker of near-death evaporates every superfluous detail until all you are left with is the essence of the person you're going to kill.

And I didn't want to kill her because that process of

reduction didn't leave me convinced. Instead, it left me with the sense of something being terribly wrong. None of the details of the brief checked out. Her cover story – that she was a doctor on holiday – was repeated with unnatural nonchalance. Her tipsy banter was light and unforced. She was either an exceptional professional or innocent. And very few people are that good.

I checked in and queried the target. The response was immediate: *Verified. Proceed.*

But it didn't feel right. And it has to.

To kill at point blank, to feel a last breath on you as the light gutters out of their eyes – that is something: something to live with for ever. I've killed a lot of people. Some were holding a bomb or a pistol or a cell phone or a switch; some knew things they couldn't unlearn, saw things they couldn't unsee. Some died for good reason. Others didn't.

That was the purpose of training. That was why I had been sent to Raven Hill. Training ensured you pulled the trigger when asked. No questions.

Most squaddies *want* to miss their target. My job is different. For me there are no misses. Only consequences.

But I have to believe in the shot.

So I didn't take her to the killing place.

Instead I plucked her phone from her handbag and excused myself. I took the lift to the hotel lobby on the ground floor and I checked into the room I'd arranged to kill her in. I ripped the tracker from the hem of my jeans and left it with her cell phone in the bedside drawer. As a precaution I took the battery out of my own phone.

By the time I'd sprinted back up the fire stairs and scooped her up again she'd barely noticed I'd been gone.

Half an hour later, we dropped back down to the parking lot and wove our way through late-night Caracas traffic in a private taxi to a low-rent hotel room at the Garden Suites. We arrived just before two a.m.

Upstairs, I'd held her from behind as we fell on the bed, pushing her mane of dirty-blonde hair aside as she sprawled on the mattress to reveal the point, high on the nape of her neck, where I'd meant to place the muzzle. Then I saw it. Or rather, didn't see it. Ana María Petrova has a scar the size of a bottle top at the base of her skull where the ambassador's Ovcharka took a lump out of her. *This* Ana María didn't have a ready-made target carved on her. Squirming around on to her back, she giggled and hooked her thumbs into the waistband of her panties. She wasn't even a natural blonde.

It wasn't *her* at all.

My stomach heaved. The unease in my guts spewed up into my mouth. I spat bile into the bathroom sink and ran the taps on my wrists, shaking. She'd been very close to never waking up again.

But you knew, I reassured myself, *you knew*.

Two hours and half a dozen Diplomático rums later and we both passed out.

Thump. Thump. Thump.

I could hear the mortars before they landed. The air rips. Long, metallic screeches like sheets of black steel being shredded in the night sky. The first bombs landed in a cluster of three, creeping towards our position: one to the left – far out; one to the right – closer; then one behind – closer still. Rapid, deadly triangulation. Then the first white-hot shards of shrapnel hissed past at head height. Caught in the open. No cover. I dropped and balled up – foetal and braced for impact.

Where was she? Where was Ana María?

Around me, the elbows, chins, boot heels of other men grubbed in the dust. The slightest, shallowest groove you can plough just might make the difference between being shredded or not.

Thump. Thump. Thump.

The reports were hard, flat, close and rapid. Then the bombardment paused, and there was only ringing silence. My ears screamed.

Thump. Thump. Thump.

And then a bright-white burst of light and rush of air and sound wrenched me to my senses like a floodtide ripping shingle from a storm-slapped beach.

Ceiling fan. Slatted blinds. Running water.

Caracas.

Thump. Thump. Thump.

'Señor?'

Empty bed, sweat-soaked, twisted sheets. Alone.

Ten a.m. and already the air was heavy, sticky.

She must have left.

'Servicio de habitación!'

I reached over and patted the low bedside table, searching out the red and white carton and the barrel of a plastic lighter.

Three left.

I drew a cigarette out, lit it and sucked the smoke down. The room pulled into focus as the reality of the dream receded. Sometimes it was Afghanistan, sometimes Iraq. Or Colombia. Uganda. Syria. London.

Almost every day began like that, robbed of clarity by a night of searing dreams. It was easier waking up in the war. Any war. At least I knew where I was then.

Thump. Thump. Thump.

'*Señor?*'

There were hotel staff in the corridor to deal with.

'*Su desayuno, señor.*'

'Yeah, yeah I'm here. I'm just . . . *Esperate.*'

Running water.

The shower.

I hadn't ordered breakfast.

I reached under the bed and tore free the stolen police Glock I'd taped beneath the mattress. Somewhere a Venezuelan cop was being framed for a hit that hadn't happened.

'*Servicio de habitación!*'

A key rattled in the lock. Stopped by a sliding bolt, the door caught with a bang, opening less than an inch. The pressure in the room shifted, sucking at a loose pane in the window which overlooked a garden below.

'OK,' I barked. I dropped the Marlboro into the dregs of her last rum and steadied myself at the foot of the bed, naked. This wasn't going to be easy.

'*Qué tal?*'

I pulled the bedroom door open, free of its restraining

bolt: pistol at waist height; muzzle jammed flat-on against the plywood panelling.

Early twenties. Sunburned forehead. Neat, close-cut brown hair. White shirt, black tie. Black waistcoat. Shiny shoes.

'*Señor* . . .'

His left fist was clenched and held high as if in some mad communist salute, poised to resume his drumming; his right hand was hidden under an unfolded napkin spread out on a service cart.

MI6 peon.

'Can we do this in English? It's been a long night.'

His right arm sagged. He looked deflated.

'And you can take your hand off that SIG, too.' He stared at me, unblinking, alarmed. '*Now.*'

'Mister . . . Mr McLean,' the peon whispered in English as his empty right hand emerged. 'I've got orders to . . .'

'. . . take me to the embassy where I'll receive new orders.'

'Yes, and . . .'

'. . . my current assignment is terminated.'

'Yes, and . . .'

'I'm in deep shit.'

He looked obliquely along the hallway, 'Yes. And . . . Look I'm sorry, but could I . . . ?'

I shut the door on him and hooked the bolt back on. Either they'd let me get away with it or someone had fucked up. Passing out half-cut in bed with Ana María hadn't been part of the plan. By rights they should have had the door off the hinges as soon as I'd walked through it. I listened carefully. No movement outside.

And then I remembered. I didn't have a plan.

She was in the shower all right, planted like a statue under a fountain, staring into a white-tiled void. She turned silently when she saw me in the mirror, eyes widening. I realized I was naked; and that I was carrying a gun.

'*Coño! Max, qué . . . ?*'

I put my fingers to my lips and held up the semi-auto side-on, unthreatening. She turned around properly, and I pushed back the glass splash screen. Her eyes were dilated, carotid pulse fluttering.

'Ana María.' She moved to stop the water. My left hand caught her wrist. 'I have to go. Right now.'

Thump. Thump. Thump.

Her nostrils flared. I let go of her wrist and put my finger back to my lips.

Muffled by the bathroom door and jets of water the knocking outside was barely audible. She heard it nonetheless and relaxed.

'Who's that, your fucking wife?'

'It's complicated. You're not who I thought you were.'

'What? You are a fucking liar,' she hissed in English, her eyes moving between mine and the pistol. Fine spray misted the air between us. It was hard to see properly.

'Wrong Cubana.'

'Wrong Cubana? *Coño!* You are like fucking *unbeliev-able.* You fucked the wrong woman? Eh?'

Then in Russian. *'Idi na khui! Mudak!'* London had got that bit right at least. And I did feel like an asshole.

'Caracas isn't safe.' I replied in Russian. Of the many gifts my mother gave me, Moscow street-slang was one of the greatest.

'Not with *maricones* like you around.' She slipped back into Spanish, which was progress of sorts.

'There are men outside who will kill you if they see you. Stay in here. In exactly five minutes ride the lift to the first floor, then take the fire stairs.' I was whispering in Spanish. 'Leave through the restaurant out the back and into the children's playground. Walk up to the tennis club and get them to call you a taxi. I've taken your phone.'

'You stole my *phone*?'

'No. Well, yes. It's complicated. Don't look over your shoulder and don't come back. Do you understand?'

She didn't.

'Listen. There's money on the table . . .'

Her mouth pursed as if to spit at me.

'No! Not for that. Ana María, please. Get out of the city. Take a week on the beach out of town and then go back to Havana, even Moscow. Take the money and go. They'd kill me too. Trust me.'

I tried to kiss her cheek, but she jerked her head away. I touched the back of my hand to her breast. She didn't move.

'I was supposed to . . .' I could barely get the words out. Training: it helped you to pull triggers and keep your trap shut. I wasn't doing great at either right now.

'People,' I struggled on, 'very dangerous people, *my* people, think you are someone else. And they want that someone else dead.' She stared at me blankly. 'Now you've seen my face. You know my name. That's enough to get you killed, too. For real. I'm sorry.'

'Sorry? Fuck, Max, you know what? So am I. *Coño!*' She pinched the water out of her eyes. 'Get out,' she whispered. 'Go.'

I stopped the shower and turned around, taking a towel off the back of the door to wipe my face as I left.

She stood there shaking and spoke my name again. But she didn't follow me. Her chances of making it out alive were slim. One way or the other I'd likely killed her anyway.

I pulled my clothes on, tucked the pistol into my jeans and opened the door on to my chaperone, pushing him and the service cart he'd hijacked a couple of feet down the corridor.

'Let's go.'

He was staring at the side of my face.

'Sir?'

I looked back down at him as we clicked off down the parquet corridor.

'How did you know I . . . I mean, do I . . .'

'Because your bottom waistcoat button is undone. And please stop calling me "sir".'

2

'Are you carrying?' Jim Jones, the local team commander at the British embassy, looked at me through his Oakleys.

'Stupid question.'

'Fuck, McLean.' He addressed me like a father exasperated with a naughty child. 'OK, *what* are you carrying?'

'Very stupid question.'

We were pulling through Caracas traffic, already close to the safe house.

'McLean, are you, or are you not, armed?' His bald head showed a throbbing vein in bas-relief. I smiled at him as I dropped the black market 9mm into his lap, hamming up my Irish accent for good measure.

'Dere ye go, liddle fella. An' don't ye go hurtin' y'self wi' dat now.'

Jim had spent more time in the SBS lying in ditches in Armagh than he had in boats. He wasn't exactly a fan of my fellow countrymen.

'Prick,' he sighed. He would have had orders to kill me if I'd run.

'And there was me thinking that sergeant majors still call their superiors "sir" in the army.'

'It's a good job I'm in the fucking navy, then, isn't it? *Sir.*'

We both laughed. The MI6 peon laughed too, but stopped when Jim took his Oakleys off and looked at him. We climbed out at Calle el Vigía. The villa was tucked up on the side of a hill, looking down over the inner-city airbase.

'McLean,' Jones cautioned as we turned our backs on the SUV, 'word to the wise before you meet the gaffer. You stink of pussy.' He cracked a broad smile. 'Sir.'

He was clean-shaven now, and his trademark Savile Row suit was a little tighter round the waist, but in most respects Commander Frank Knight didn't seem to have been touched by the years that stretched between the chilly dawn on the firing line at Raven Hill when I first saw him and that sweaty morning in Caracas.

Twenty-three years of sheer, bloody mayhem. I'd seen him grow old; he'd watched me grow up. Without him I'd have had blood on my saddle a long time back. And without me, he was fond of reminding me, he'd have taken early retirement.

'If it isn't the big fella himself.' He took my hand firmly as if to shake it, but just held it fast, gripping the top of my right arm with his left hand as he did so. He looked over my shoulder and then straight at me.

'You fucked up, Max.'

'*I* fucked up?'

'Oh, yes. God damn, blast, confound and *fuck* the Office, but you should have killed her.' He was speaking quickly and quietly. Like everyone else who was in it, he always referred to MI6 as 'the Office'.

'Frank . . .'

'No, Max. No. Do not fucking speak.' His voice rose. 'You had one job. One kill. Not question. Not think. Not fuck. I mean, fuck her and *then* kill her if you must. Christ in heaven! Kill her and then fuck her for all I care. But please do actually kill your fucking target, McLean.'

By the end he was shouting my name, his voice deadened by the soft seventies furnishings that dulled the room.

'It was the wrong woman, Frank. You want a murderer? Then pay a sicario.'

His shoulders sagged.

'You *are* the sicario, Max.'

He sounded tired. But that was the truth. I *was* the hitman. Right woman, wrong woman: obey orders. Boom.

'What happens now?'

'You're going back to London. King is livid, of course.'

Out the window I could see Jones's silhouette circling the SUV, getting ready to chaperone me to the airport.

'Max?'

My eyes flicked back towards his.

'Will I face a court martial?'

'Absolutely not. You will face King. Court martial? Have you gone stark raving mad? You are not a schoolboy going to the headmaster's office. You have just spectacularly fucked up a very black, black op. Which is ironic, because . . .' Frank paused, as if weighing carefully the words that came next. 'Because, believe it or not, King's going to propose you take command of

Raven Hill. Or at least he was. Who knows after this cock-up?' I didn't speak. Frank continued. 'Colonel Ellard should have retired five years ago. Longer, actually. And the truth is, the very bloody *irritating* truth, is that there just isn't anyone else who can do it. But . . . after this . . .' He spread his hands wide as if everything that had happened in the last twelve hours had somehow unfolded in the room we stood in. 'The Yanks are bloody pissed off, of course. And so am I, McLean, so am I.'

'Seems to me that I'm working for a bunch of amateurs.' I shook the last Marlboro out of the pack and struck a match. 'That *we* are working for a bunch of amateurs.' The smoke soothed and cloyed by turn in the thick, wet air. 'You want me to take command of Raven Hill? That's fucking news, isn't it? So tell me, Frank, *please* tell me so I can tell all those bright-eyed boys and girls, how I – *I* – fucked up by *not* killing the wrong woman? I don't know who the madman is here, but right now I'm feeling pretty sane.'

'Because – do I really have to spell this out after all these years? – because she saw your bloody *face*. It's just that simple. Forget everything else. You're *valuable* because you're one of the best damned shots that's probably ever lived. You're *priceless* because you don't exist – at least not outside of our mob.'

We stared at each other across the room, but I wasn't seeing anything but Ana María: her hair wild; her breasts under my palms; the tang of her still on my fingers, mingling with the cigarette smoke. This woman, this unknown woman to whom I'd told my name and who should be dead, still lingered like a ghost on my skin.

'Do you know who she is?'

'Your target. Period.'

'Oh, *do* fuck off. Let me guess: you have no idea and nothing to say other than, "You fucked up"?'

'Yup, that's about the size of it. And we shouldn't be having this conversation. And you know why we shouldn't be? Because she's supposed to be dead. Christ, man, what were you *thinking*?'

He was roaring at me. I drew hard on the cigarette and waited. The colour and excitement drained from his face until he was as beige as the walls that enclosed us.

'King wants to make you a lieutenant colonel. A *commissioned* lieutenant colonel. That's not just rare. It's unheard of.' He spoke calmly. Deliberately. 'There'd be a one-year probationary period. And then Raven Hill would be yours, and with it, if you want it, an identity, any identity. You'd get your life back. A proper life. No more killing. No more running. Fuck, Max McLean would even get a pension.'

'I don't have a life to get back, Frank.' I looked around the room. 'I mean here I am, right?'

He must have known I'd have considered what it would be like taking over from Ellard – not that anyone could ever replace the old man. In fact we'd even spoken about it briefly once after I'd been shot up in an ambush outside Algiers. There would come a point, and sooner rather than later at this rate, when I would have to stop. Maybe letting Ana María go had been my way of putting the brakes on. But then what? Indefinite gardening leave wasn't exactly tempting, or even an option, given how hard it would be to tend roses while looking constantly over my shoulder. No, I knew full well, and had done before I passed out at Raven Hill, that I would either have to be tethered to them for ever or vanish.

I'd disappeared once already. And this is where it had got me.

'Well, maybe you'd better start thinking about what sort of life you do want,' Frank continued. 'It's damned hard to stop being unknown and not get killed doing it.'

'Have you found her?' There was everywhere to look, but at him. I didn't know whether to tell him to shove his job or thank him from the bottom of my heart. My weakness made me angry. Still, it surprised me that my hands were shaking. 'Frank, we've done lots of jobs together. But *this* . . .'

'*This* is what? Murder?' A fringe of sweat was eating into the fold of his shirt collar; a dark-blue, spreading necklace. I looked him in the face, blankly. 'No,' he continued, 'she wasn't the target you *thought* she was. But she *was* your target. And you don't get to choose which targets you kill and which you don't. Most forty-two-year-old assassins have worked at least that much out by now. And if you don't like it, be my guest to try and change it from the top down. But not now, not while you're still bloody operational, for God's sake. This is madness.'

'Have you found her?'

'There are always consequences, Max. Always. And

you know when it goes wrong? Really wrong? When you second-guess what those consequences might be.'

'You haven't, have you?' I permitted myself a smile then, pointing at Frank with the lit cigarette. 'You haven't found her. And you aren't going to. Fuck. You really fucked it, didn't you?' I could see him grit his teeth. He craned his face towards the unmoving ceiling fan as if willing it to turn. Maybe he was searching for inspiration.

'No, Max, you fucked it for me. Congratulations.'

We stood in silence for a moment. He looked back down at me. They must have hacked the CCTV at the 360° Roof Bar and tracked me back to the Garden Suites in real time. Why not kill her then and there themselves? Jim Jones was about as likely to have a crisis of conscience killing a pretty girl as to start whistling 'Danny Boy'. Perhaps dyed-blonde Ana María had been the real target all along, and Frank had wanted her dead. Or maybe he'd had second thoughts, too.

'So, Max,' he sighed, 'I'd be enormously grateful if you'd unfuck it for me.'

'How so?' It was hard not to sneer. It felt like I was winning.

'King is going to offer you another job; and, if you want command of Raven Hill, your *last* job off the books.' Seeing my eyebrows shoot up, he added quickly, 'And no, it's nothing to do with this bloody blonde that got away.'

'Offer or order? And she wasn't blonde. Trust me.'

'Offer. But it's a good one. You'll like it.'

'Sure it will be. Don't tell me, I get thirty pieces of silver for betraying some other poor sap with a kiss and then get to hang myself in the officers' mess at Raven Hill. And to think I actually believed for a moment that you were making *me* an offer. I kill for you, you throw me a bone. Same as it ever was. It's a good job I like you, Frank.'

'And it's a good job I have the patience of bloody Job. Raven Hill isn't a bone. It's the fattened fucking calf. *Jesus.*' Frank sighed deeply, almost desperately. 'It's been a long time that we've worked together – what, twenty years?'

'Twenty-three,' I corrected him.

'Mind if I tell you a story?'

'Knock yourself out. But if you're going to tell me that once upon a time there was a wee Irish lad who pulled the trigger when you asked him to you can fuck off.'

He folded his arms, and then let them hang loose by his sides.

'No. Once upon a time, when *I* was a subaltern, and long before you and I met at Raven Hill, there was a girl. A young girl, mind. Eight? Nine? Dirty feet, scraped-back greasy hair. Up in the hills, during Aden. Can see her clear as a bell. She flew at my mate with a knife as we were searching a bus. It all happened so fast, but the thing was I had my Browning out already, waving the locals off the bus with it. I got a bead on her immediately. I can still see the look on her, screaming above the sights as she ran at him.'

Now Frank was looking out the window. There was no air conditioning. The room was boiling.

'I didn't do it, Max. Couldn't. Just couldn't do it. Not

to a girl, d'y'see? I just stood there like a damned fool not doing or saying anything while she clobbered him.'

He turned back to look at me. His eyes were wet, but whether it was from sweat or tears was impossible to tell.

'She took a chunk out of him, all right. He was lucky not to lose his eye. But it turned out it was just a bloody comb. A hair comb. Not a knife.'

I stubbed the cigarette out on the empty packet.

'And what did he say to you afterwards, this mate of yours?'

'He said, "Next time, shoot the bitch."'

Frank crossed the room and pulled open the door, pausing as it rasped on the deep-pile carpet. An RAMC nurse in civvies followed its slow swing into the room, small black medical bag in one hand, clipboard in the other, ready for my post-operational medical assessment.

'Think about the offer, McLean,' Frank said as he slid into the darkened hallway beyond. 'Much misunderstood, your kind. I'd say right now you need all the breaks you can get.'

3

'Château Musar, 1988. From the Beka'a Valley, no less.'
King, Major General Sir Kristóf King, Director Special
Forces, poured the thick red Lebanese wine himself,
swatting away the hand of the lance corporal who had
the unenviable job of waiting on him.

'You had some . . . *difficulties*, I know, in Venezuela.' A
quick smile tightened across his teeth.

He pressed a heavy glass into my hand and raised his
own without taking his eyes off me.

'Your very good health.'

'Thank you, sir.' I put the cut crystal to my lips,
hesitated and lowered the glass a little. 'And to yours,
General.'

'Please, call me Kristóf.'

I syphoned a mouthful of the near-black liquid into the
back of my throat. King waved his hand almost imperceptibly. With a nod the lance left us alone, his white
serving jacket vanishing behind the heavy sweep of a
teak-panelled door.

'Please, sit down.'

I did, and sank into a two-seater chesterfield that had
been pulled up close to the hearth. It was a cold March.
Slivers of ice still clung to the gutters in Whitehall. Tourists went skidding past the Cenotaph while apple logs

topped with black crystals of coal hissed and snapped in the general's grate. I hadn't seen King for over a year and I'd never been invited for dinner. It didn't bode well. And neither did his first names charade. I suspected that whatever it was that was going to be asked of me was considerably less likable than Frank had made out.

'May I call you Max?'

'Please, do. I prefer it to Paddy.'

'Paddy? Ah, yes, of course. Forgive me. I expect that being a Free Stater was rather amusing for you in Belfast, what?'

Maximilian Ivan Drax Pierpoint Mac Ghill'ean. God rest my father's soul. He'd saddled me with the Anglo-Irish equivalent of 'A Boy Named Sue'. 'Max McLean' the anonymous orphan suited me just fine, and that's how I'd joined the army – in my English name. In the Paras, of course, my accent immediately and inevitably earned me the nickname 'Paddy'.

'It did somewhat confuse the enemy.'

'The enemy?'

'The Sergeants' Mess.'

'Ah, yes, I see. An infiltrator in their midst, what? Marvellous! I bet they all secretly had you down as a Catholic spy.' The quick-flash smile played across his teeth like a nervous tick. It was more grimace than gregarious.

'Not so secretly. Being an Irishman in the Paras, it's a miracle I didn't shoot myself. Sir.'

'*Kristóf*, remember?' His voice hardened into an order. 'Never forget where you're from, what?'

A chipped antique mantelpiece loomed over the open fire – rare salvage from the blaze that had consumed the original Palace of Whitehall centuries before. It was burdened by gilt-edged frames showcasing King's ancestors and children. No pictures of King himself, though. Not advisable in his line of work. Not even here, in his private chambers. Even so, tucked away to one side, half-hidden on a bookshelf straining with green Victorian leather, stood a foot-tall bronze of King as a young man, M16 in hand, right foot forward: a reminder of the days when he commanded G-Squadron SAS and did the trigger pulling himself. One way or another he'd fought hard for his rank, his wine, that statue and the present that betrayed his past. Despite all the *what?* and *I say!* gibberish and despite being at the centre of the Establishment, he remained very much the outsider. Or so it seemed to me, looking in, or more accurately up, from where I loitered on the sidelines.

A black and white portrait of a striking woman in her thirties, all confidence and cheekbones and cradling a Russian sub-machine gun, sat in the shadows on the shelf above the statue. Pinned to the corner was a frayed half-inch of red, white and green ribbon with a hole punched in the centre. It was over sixty years since his mother had fled Budapest as the Soviet Army crushed the Hungarian Revolution, but Sir Kristóf was still in exile. He had her looks, too: black hair and black eyes and a skull too close to the skin. Despite so many decades passing it was unsettling to see that tiny revolutionary flag with the red star cut out of it here, of all places, in the bastion of counterterrorism.

I wondered what King would make of my mother's ancestry. If he or Frank Knight had known who my parents were he might have thought I was the enemy, too. I bit down on a yawn, tired from the flight and the hours of briefings that had bracketed it after everything went wrong in Caracas. Sizing up the almost-empty glass in my right hand, he nodded towards the decanter.

'Don't be shy. The Office has got a couple of cases sequestered for me at Her Majesty's pleasure in the bowels of Vauxhall Cross. Most important materiel they ever got their hands on, what?'

I agreed it must have been and poured a refill. No doubt MI6 loved their headquarters being used as his own personal wine cellar.

'Drank gallons of the stuff at college. Damned tricky to find it now.' He paused and cocked his head to one side. A log cracked on the fire and spat out a shower of charcoal that glowed like a dying flare in the fading light of King's set. It was hard to pick out his eyes beneath his brow; the iris and pupil merged into one black disk. It was like drinking with the Devil.

'I assume Commander Knight warned you about my little proposition?' I inclined my head without actually nodding. 'Yes, of course he did. Good chap, Frank. Reliably indiscreet and discreetly reliable. Well, there you have it.' He paused and sipped at his wine. 'Raven Hill's yours. If you want it, of course.'

'Thank you. It's a . . . it's a very generous offer.' We both smiled. 'You'll give me time to consider it?'

'Of course. Fools rush in, what?'

'Frank, Commander Knight, might also have discreetly mentioned there was a job you had in mind for me.'

'Quite so. Quite so. We'll come to that presently. But first tell me, Max, before the others get here,' he spoke matter-of-factly as he reached over to refresh his own glass, 'why didn't you kill her?'

It was a question I'd been asked repeatedly since I walked down the corridor of the Garden Suites hotel and into the embassy SUV waiting outside the green electric gates. Now King sat expectant, unblinking, perched on the edge of his seat. My mind was racing. Make something up, make a joke out of it, or make it real. In a business where all transactions are conducted with pieces of silver, even a speck of truth is priceless. And perilous. So I told the truth . . . or part of it.

Or at least I began to.

'Kristóf,' I said, cautiously, 'I've killed a lot of people. For you, for Commander Knight, for my men. For my country.' Suddenly I could hear the trace of my Irish accent, hard like so many stones clattering between us. '*This* country.' I looked at the bookshelf, his mother, the ribbon, and shrugged with my hands open. 'But I've never killed for me. I've killed because I've been told to. Sure, sometimes I've wanted to kill. But I never did. I never killed for me.'

King's black eyes stared back at me, half-hidden, unreadable. I held my words, heavy on my tongue. The truth is precious, but dangerous.

'Yes, Max, go on.'

'She saw my face. I told her my name. And that didn't

matter because I was going to kill her. But then, you know, she was the wrong woman. And then the only reason to kill her was because she knew. And *that* . . . that would have been for me.'

I breathed out heavily through my nose and looked down into the dark circle of wine. Both he and I knew full well the question he wanted me to answer was why I'd told her my name at all.

'Never mind orders, what?' King snorted a half-chuckle.

'Quite.' I gathered myself, and went on, trying to deflect him. 'There is a moment, a moment when you either pull the trigger or you don't.'

'The decisive moment.'

'Yes.'

'From which, one way or another, all else flows.'

I looked up at him, pausing again.

'Exactly. And I thought, in that moment, about what might flow from following orders and killing someone I knew to be innocent.'

'*Thought* to be innocent,' King corrected me.

'OK. Well, when I thought about that, it felt like I might drown.'

'I see.' King drained his glass impassively and placed it carefully on the inlaid marble coffee table nestled under the leather crook of his chair arm. 'And now you are treading water in the torrent of shit disobeying that order has unleashed?'

We both smiled.

'Yeah, that's about the size of it.'

It was night-time now, the windowpanes black mirrors revealing nothing but the faint reflection of the fire settling into the grate. Shadows thrown up from the hearth licked across his face like black flames, and suddenly he wasn't smiling any more. I'd come straight to Whitehall from Heathrow in the back of a blacked-out van. I was exhausted.

'You've told me what you thought, Max. What do you think now?'

Without warning the door to King's set sprang open off the latch, inching into the half-light of my interrogation. Voices filling the hall trickled into his chambers. We both stood. King walked towards the door, while I stood awkwardly cradling my empty glass. A white-handed glove rose to salute, the arm hidden by heavy oak. The dinner guests had arrived.

King turned to me, almost entirely enveloped in darkness. I swallowed hard and faced him.

'I think, sir, that next time I'll shoot the bitch.'

4

I straightened up and looked at the faces around the room. Frank was right: I hadn't been summoned to dinner just so King could tear a strip off me, fetter me to Raven Hill or impress me with his wine collection. Along with the other guests I was being briefed on my next job – like it or not.

And what a bunch we were: David Mason, director general of MI6's operations in Africa, whose mission it was; Regimental Sergeant Major Jack Nazzar, a Glaswegian hard-case and one of the most experienced soldiers Hereford had ever seen – he ran the Revolutionary Warfare Wing; Major General King, of course, who had operational oversight for discreet – and deniable – Special Forces operations; and one dead-tired assassin.

'Good evening, Major McLean.' Mason greeted me coolly, no doubt sizing me up in light of the Caracas debacle.

I wasn't even a proper major – that was just an honorific. Only MI6 used it: no one in uniform ever did. Like everyone else who emerged from Raven Hill I'd never been badged, so we never needed to be de-badged for operations they wanted to keep off the books. I was a civilian and had been since the day I left the Parachute Regiment and shook hands with Colonel Ellard. It wasn't possible to be an enlisted soldier, SAS or otherwise, and be truly deniable.

We were known simply as 'the Unknown' – a score or so of ex-SAS, intelligence and other specialist operators tasked by Frank to do the jobs no one else could be seen to do – because we were never seen and did not exist. The army, of course, couldn't cope with anything that wasn't called by a three-letter acronym, so to them we became UKN.

Most of us came through Raven Hill; the rest came from God knows where. Even the Unknown operators I thought I knew, I didn't. Everyone used a pseudonym. That was the point of Raven Hill. The recruits who came from Colonel Ellard's black ops hothouse were orphans, misfits and professional liars to a man (and woman). Raven Hill bred deception and loyalty in equal, terrifying measure.

The briefing was being given by a Captain Rhodes, who introduced herself as being from the Special Reconnaissance Regiment, 'on secondment to the Office'. The only person missing from the scene was Commander Frank Knight – who oversaw all Military–MI6–UKN liaison. Frank was most likely still playing hide-and-seek with Ana María in Caracas. I stubbed out a Marlboro and looked at Nazzar. If the shit hit the fan, he'd be the one scraping it, and me, off the walls.

There was only one question worth asking.

'So who am I going to kill?'

Nazzar smiled, but it was Captain Rhodes who answered.

'You must be tired from your flight, Mr McLean, but if you'll forgive us we'll press on.' She most likely had no idea at all what the job was really about; which at least made us equal.

Most of my jobs were assigned to me by Frank directly, so more often than not I prepped my own trips. If the SAS were involved I'd be briefed in Hereford with Jack Nazzar's troublemakers. Known just as 'the Wing' inside the SAS and 'the Increment' to MI6 – the Revolutionary Warfare Wing was a separate, dozen-strong unit of the Regiment's most experienced operators.

MI6 jobs were run by London and based out of Fort Monckton near Portsmouth. Whitehall briefings were reserved for potential political train wrecks. Everyone was invited so everyone could be blamed. They never augured well. On the evidence available, this one was no exception. MI6 was overseen by the Foreign Office, not the military, and the potential for blowback was always unnerving for the suits who'd deny I'd even been born if the balloon went up.

Like me, Captain Rhodes and Mason were in civvies. Unlike me, they didn't have a bottle of King's wine coursing through their veins. King and Nazzar wore uniform. God only knew what coursed through their veins.

Space was cleared on the old oak table by the lance, who carried away the remains of dinner. When he'd left us, Rhodes popped the lid on a black map-tube which, when inverted, dispensed an aviation chart. It was centred on Sierra Leone, a small – and as the map revealed, a hilly and densely forested – country in West Africa. It had not long emerged from the worst Ebola outbreak the world had ever seen. In the cruellest of ironies the virus had ravaged a country that Britain had saved a decade and a half before from a marauding army of psychopathic rebels who'd slaughtered tens of thousands while plundering its vast mineral wealth. The SAS had seen action there; so had the Paras.

Fixing her glasses to the bridge of her nose with her index finger Rhodes cleared her throat and, almost looking at me, began to spread the expanse of green and blue paper across our now-empty place settings. The yellowed skin creeping along her finger joints suggested a forty-a-day habit. She looked the same age as me, but I doubted she could have been much over thirty. That was skin care by Silk Cut for you. I'd never seen her before. I lit another one of my Reds and exhaled upwards through a jutting jaw, sending a plume of grey smoke towards the chandelier. Someone tutted theatrically. I took another drag.

'Operational precis,' she began. 'The mission is to terminate the command and control capability of a hitherto unknown non-state actor group considered an imminent threat to Her Majesty's Government's interests and representatives in West Africa.' Her voice was throaty, but warm; trustworthy, without labouring to be so. 'Detail,' she continued. 'The group is headquartered *here*, at Karabunda, ten klicks south of the tenth parallel, right up in the far north of the country on the Guinea border. The nearest airstrip is near *here*, at Soron, five klicks due east.' She pointed out the locations on the map as she spoke. 'Karabunda is an old mining out-post. The Chinese abandoned it in 2009. As far as we can tell there was – is – no civilian population on-site. Importantly, the timing of this operation has been brought forward owing to unforeseen developments *here*, at Musala, on the Mong River, nineteen klicks south of Soron.'

'Sorry to interrupt, Captain,' a hard-edged voice from my left butted in, 'but is it no your *job* to foresee?'

'Sergeant Major, if you please. Captain Rhodes is merely –' David Mason was on his feet but was cut off immediately. Sergeant Major Nazzar was on a roll.

'Aye, well, this Captain Rhodes here told us last week – Wednesday to be precise – that this operation would not be green-lit for at least thirty days. *Thirty days*. Meanwhile we've been telling you lot in Vauxhall for weeks to expect a push south by these jokers. Their hit-and-run attacks along the Guinea border weren't meant to take territory, they were meant to capture manpower.'

Apparently unfazed, Captain Rhodes ploughed on between Nazzar and Mason.

'Current planning is to deploy you to Freetown within forty-eight hours.' She looked up at King. Like everyone else in the army she was apparently well practised at managing up. 'It's a bit of a slog up there, but it's a one-shot deal. Neutralize the commander and the –'

Nazzar wasn't finished and cut across Rhodes again, aiming another terse Scots broadside at Mason.

'On the Kabala Road it's a straight shot south to Mak-eni, the biggest town in the north, an' they're rapidly

gettin' the men tae do it. No, what we have here,' Nazzar leaned forward, nudging me to one side, lunging
with his coffee spoon towards the red circle that picked
out Musala on the map, 'is a cock-up. I can tell y' right
now that deploying one man, even if it is McLean here,
is as much use as tits on a bull. For the record, I didnae
authorize it. An' I don't bloody recommend it. You need
boots on the ground before he deploys and that shower
gets to within spitting distance of the capital.'

'Ah, yes,' Mason managed to interject, as Nazzar drew
breath. 'Boots on the ground. You mean like there were
in Benghazi, Sergeant Major?'

Nazzar breathed out heavily. Benghazi had been a
disaster for him. Deployed as E-Squadron SAS with
operators from the SBS, an entire squad of his best men
had been arrested the moment they landed in Libya,
chaperoning an MI6 negotiating team. The Foreign
Office had begged, publicly, for their release. Mason
blamed Nazzar. Nazzar blamed the Special Reconnaissance Regiment. King kept quiet counsel.

'Aye, well, good luck sending him into that lot by him-
sel',' Nazzar retorted. 'Have you got any idea what that
terrain is like, Mason? Or what those jokers can do? *I* do
because . . .' He composed himself abruptly. 'McLean is
valuable,' he said, more quietly, 'too bloody valuable.'
Nazzar was standing right next to me, his now clenched
fist resting lightly on my shoulder. King sat smirking at
the head of the table, carefully threading his napkin
through a monogrammed silver band.

After Benghazi, Nazzar wouldn't commit troops to

Special Reconnaissance Regiment operations unless he was running them personally. But his commitment to UKN was fireproof: the Wing and E-Squadron were our guardian angels. If the job blew up, it wouldn't be Mason – or Frank, for that matter – who came to the rescue.

'An' let's not even mention *Barras*,' he muttered to himself.

I looked at King. There was a stillness around the table. Nazzar sat down; Mason awkwardly followed suit. He was a sharp, angular character: cut-glass accent and personality to match and tipped to take over as the new Controller of MI6. But unlike King he was not the kind of man who bought his own furniture. No knighthood, no Top Brass command – instead Mason boasted a massive inherited fortune and an estate the size of a small country. It was just me and Captain Rhodes on our feet now. She looked enviously at my cigarette.

'I missed *Barras*,' I said, loudly, but to no one in particular. The Royal Irish regiment had got themselves into hot water back in the year 2000. Ten of them and their local liaison officer had managed to get themselves kidnapped by a rebel faction called the West Side Niggaz – re-christened the West Side *Boys* by the politically correct correspondents at the BBC. The operation to rescue them had been code-named *Barras*. In the end the Irish had been saved by Nazzar, fighting then with his old outfit D-Squadron SAS. Most of the rebels were either killed or captured. None of the hostages died. But the rebels' determination to go out fighting had cost the life of one SAS operator. Nazzar never forgave himself. I regretted missing it.

King reached for the decanter nearest to him, hesitated and then poured a small measure of thick, bronze Madeira into his empty wine glass, shaking his head – though whether at the proceedings in his dining room or in disappointment at the lack of liqueur glasses it was hard to say.

'Captain Rhodes, please continue.' Apparently neither King nor Mason wanted to dwell on *Barras* and the past. Nazzar sighed heavily and reached for the Scotch.

'Sir, yes, sir. As I was saying, sir,' Rhodes paused and first glanced at Nazzar, then spoke to me. 'You'll be deployed under natural cover to Freetown on a civilian flight operated by Boliviana from LGW at zero-five-thirty on Tuesday. ETA thirteen-hundred local at Lungi Airport.' She readjusted her glasses and opened a file filled with papers and photographs rubber-stamped 'Secret' on the cover in red. 'On arrival take the chopper shuttle from Lungi to Aberdeen. Your driver, Roberts,' she fumbled for a photo, 'will meet you in this taxi, here. He's local, not military. Good driver. Trustworthy.' I held her gaze for a moment. She wrinkled her nose. 'Very trustworthy.'

'Aye, he'd better be,' Nazzar chimed in.

'He'll take you to the Mammy Yoko Hotel – big international place, run by Radisson now. Famous during the war. We're hiding you in plain sight.' She looked up and smiled at me. I smiled back.

'OK, where do I get comms and tools?'

Roberts will give you this bag,' she fished out a photograph of a Billingham satchel, 'containing a local and international smart phone and a two-way video BGAN sat phone. It's civvie spec, but Inmarsat grants us unit-to-unit comms via the land earth station in the Netherlands. There is no GSM signal where you're heading, but the BGAN will connect directly to the smart phone.'

'So I get video and voice comms from the field back to Hereford?'

'To Whitehall,' Mason corrected. 'All routed through a NATO firewall. It's unhackable. Except by us, of course.'

'Whitehall?' I was looking at Mason. Mason was looking at King. Madeira distractions aside, King hadn't stopped looking at me since the briefing began.

'This operation is being overseen by David Mason, McLean,' King explained. 'There mustn't be any visible UK military involvement. Moreover, we are most keen not to – how shall I put this? – *disturb* our American allies with this operation. Under normal circumstances on a job like this we would, of course, prefer to have you fully supported on the ground, but on this occasion, for reasons I'm sure Captain Rhodes will elucidate presently, you'll be working solo.' He kept looking at me, but spoke to Nazzar. 'My apologies, Sergeant Major, for not explaining that sooner. You are quite right, of course, about boots on the ground. But as you shall see, the exigencies of this operation do not allow it, and we don't consider Freetown to be the rebels' primary objective. We aren't involving or informing the Sierra Leone army in our planning. But I am quite sure they will delight in taking credit for the outcome.'

'Your tool kit will be in two separate drops,' Rhodes went on. 'Your SIG and ammunition will be in your en suite, under the floor tile underneath the, uh, toilet paper dispenser.' We smiled at each other again. 'We're giving you a 229 and match grade 9mm ball, if that's OK?'

I nodded and lit another cigarette as Rhodes turned her attention back to the map on the table.

'And you pick your rifle up here, in Makeni.' She handed me a single silver car key. 'White Merc, parked at the hotel.'

'My own kit?'

'Yes.'

'Great. And what about Ebola? Where do I pick that up?'

'Sierra Leone has been transmission-free of Ebola since January 2016, Mr McLean.'

When we finally got to it, the target turned out to be a white man in his mid to late sixties.

This much Mason and King said they knew: near the remote jungle outpost of Karabunda, way up in the northern hills of Sierra Leone by the Guinea border, a group of rebels (the 'non-state actors', as Mason and Captain Rhodes insisted on calling them) had constructed a camp of some sort, which they'd managed to protect from satellite surveillance under the patchy savannah canopy.

The rebels' motivations were unclear: no manifesto;

no ultimatum; no obvious objective. So far, it was just a rumble in the jungle, but one that had the potential to destabilize the entire region.

King maintained the rebel main force were remnants of the former factions that had fought against the Sierra Leone government, and the British, in the late nineties. 'Still hungry for a slice of the pie', as he put it. A jail break a month earlier by a rebel general who'd run a huge illegal diamond mine in the old civil war lent this idea some weight – even if he'd been found dead in a ditch the following week.

As far as King was concerned Sierra Leone was a linch-pin of international significance: if Sierra Leone plunged into chaos, so would its neighbours. If the war spread as far as Nigeria – one of the world's largest oil producers – the consequences could, he said, be catastrophic. With the Americans playing second fiddle to Moscow on the United Nations Security Council, any sort of peacekeeping intervention would be hard to come by.

As usual, minerals equalled mobilization.

It was from this isolated camp, King, Mason and Rhodes concluded, the rebels had launched a series of successful and unexpected raids initially north across the Guinea border, and then south, seizing the town of Musala – an island of tin roofs and dusty streets in a sea of forest and savannah, clinging to the southern bank of the Mong River. Framed from above by the satellite's lens, it was hard to see why anyone would be interested in it. But from here the Kabala Road wound its way south first to Kabala town, then straight to the major centre of

Makeni and, ultimately, all the way to the capital, Freetown. Even if Freetown wasn't their objective, Makeni linked by road to practically everywhere else in the country worth seizing. All three of them agreed the white man was instrumental to the camp's operation – and the rebels' rapid territorial gains. Nazzar said nothing.

'And you have no idea who this Mr Kurtz is?' I asked Captain Rhodes.

She tilted her head to one side, recentred her glasses and opened her mouth to speak. But it was Mason who replied.

'We think he's ex-Soviet bloc. Probably Russian: 45th Guards Spetsnaz Regiment. Or at least working for them, with them.'

'45th Spetsnaz. That's Russian airborne special reconnaissance.'

'Exactly, Major McLean. Exactly.' Mason filled his glass with the Lebanese red, then mine. 'Formidable, frankly. And that's the crux of it. A year ago the Americans would have been out the gate with us on this operation, both guns blazing. But as General King has alluded to, we all know the regime in Washington is, to put it mildly, somewhat less of an enthusiastic ally against Moscow than they once were. As such, details of your mission will not be raised at the next, or any, Joint Intelligence Committee meeting here, and, as I've made clear, your presence in Sierra Leone will be deniable by HMG – not just to the public, but to all our NATO allies. That means, of course, that there will be no access to US intelligence sources or AirScan imagery. On the plus side, Major McLean,' Mason concluded, 'you will have a clear run in-country without interference from Langley or the Pentagon. On balance US exclusion from this operation should not hinder liquidation of your target's command.'

The room lapsed into silence as we considered the operation ahead. As far as dastardly Russian plots went, it looked like Moscow was returning to form. Proxy wars in Africa had tied the US down for decades before the Berlin Wall came down. They'd cost me a family tragedy, too. But I didn't want to think about that, surrounded by King and his coterie.

'Isn't he a bit old for a field officer? I mean, in his mid-sixties he'd even be giving Jack here a run for his money.' Nazzar grunted. Rhodes laughed and then caught herself abruptly, blushing. Mason took a swallow of his wine – it was only his second glass of the evening – and handed me a photograph. In grainy black and white close-up, many times magnified, it showed a balding white man with his back to the camera. He was saluting while being shown into the back seat of a Toyota HiLux double-cab by a stout, clean-shaven man in his mid-forties.

'That's almost certainly him, your target,' Mason continued. 'The man helping him into the car is Colonel Vladislav Proshunin, 45th Spetsnaz, 901st Airborne Battalion.'

'We encountered him in Kosovo in ninety-nine.' King picked up the story. 'The sergeant major here very nearly interrupted his holiday at Pristina Airport. Mike Jackson

47

calmed the situation down before we engaged. Damned close call.'

'Aye, that's Proshunin all right.' Nazzar shifted his weight in King's Regency upholstery. 'Nasty bastard. Should have slotted him when we had the chance.'

'The image is a crop of this photograph, taken in Kabala by a Global Assistance Committee volunteer based in Makeni. It was collected by our Official at the British embassy four weeks ago,' Captain Rhodes added. 'It's the only photo we have.'

The full photograph showed a primary school decked out with a red and white banner: 'Global Assistance Committee and the Department for International Development – Working Together for a Brighter Future'. The vehicle, Proshunin and the target were on the hard left-hand edge of the frame.

'What's the balance between "almost" and "certain" that he is the target?' I asked Mason.

'We know Proshunin personally drove this man from Kabala to Musala and then returned to Freetown without him; and we have a credible report that there is a man fitting this description at the Karabunda camp, and that his presence at the camp has coincided with the rebels' push towards Makeni.'

That was it. And that was enough.

'What we don't know,' added Captain Rhodes as she passed me the file, 'is whether the man in the HiLux is definitely the man running the camp. But on the balance of probabilities . . .'

'. . . he makes the kill list?'

'Exactly,' said Mason. 'You have a Class Seven authorization from the foreign secretary, effective immediately. Once deployed, we expect your target to be eliminated without delay, and without the, uh, *theatrics* of your last assignment. Is that clear, Major McLean?'

5

A sloppy film of sleet sloughed off the Bentley's windscreen as it hissed along Piccadilly. We dipped down into the Hyde Park underpass, heading towards my hotel in South Kensington. The chauffeur's profile lit up and died back into the London night in an erratic strobe of oncoming headlights. It was cold outside, and too hot in the car. I sat up front in silence, running over the known-knowns of the job so far – which boiled down to this: I'd get one shot, at one man, to stop a war.

The hotel was a good one, discreet and expensive, with a nondescript entrance on Queen's Gate and a fire escape dropping down into the neighbouring church yard. A loaded P238, a clean Canadian passport in the name of Maxwell McLean (a medic from Vancouver) and five thousand US dollars were waiting in the safe. The .380 was for personal protection in London; I'd been promised more cash in Freetown.

I'd be operating under natural cover: the Canadian passport was real, not a forgery, and sanctioned by their government – but for what purpose they'd neither ask nor be told. It would check out online, too: Canadian Max wasn't just an alias, he was an entire social media creation.

Two Hugo Boss suits hung in the wardrobe: one

black, one dark-grey – both forty-two long. Next to them were suspended half a dozen Eton shirts. I wondered if Captain Rhodes had chosen them. Six dressed me better than I dressed myself. On the shelves: jeans, cotton slacks, T-shirts and underwear; on the floor: a pair of gleaming brogues and my battered pigskin walking boots. Slouched on the luggage rack: a red North Face duffel bag, filled with the kit I'd need in-country – all civilian, as usual. The North Face: outfitters to UK Special Forces.

A glass-fronted bar fridge sat humming in the wardrobe alcove, nestled under the safe. I poured both the miniature Johnny Walker Blacks into a water glass, knocked back a Valium and lit a Marlboro. I emptied Rhodes's file on the bed and began leafing through the photographs and maps. The faces around the briefing table snapped into sharp mental focus.

The only evidence – Mason's 'credible report' – actually placing the mystery white man in the camp was from a source code-named 'Juliet', categorized as Ex4x5 in the Intelligence Report:

SOURCE EVALUATION
E – Untested source
INTELLIGENCE EVALUATION
4 – Cannot be judged
HANDLING CODE
5 – No further dissemination: refer to the originator.
Special handling requirements imposed by the officer who authorized collection

The identity of the officer who authorized collection was classified, so gauging their ability to assess the credibility of the source was impossible. So went the blindfolded circle-jerk of the Secret Intelligence Service.

There was something disconcerting about the black and white photo of the two men Mason had produced. I stared at it hard, trying to see into it. The way the older man stood; the crook of his arm at salute; the unsmiling countenance of Proshunin: the scene left me in the queasy grip of a sensation somewhere between déjà vu and disbelief.

Partial identification of a target wasn't unusual. Nazzar's disquiet was. He'd seemed agitated, probably a result of being left genuinely in the dark while Mason and King circled each other. Mason was in charge, and cautiously so. It was a lot of effort and risk for an outcome that could, on the face of it, be much more easily achieved with a cruise missile strike – with or without the US on board.

One thing was for sure: the Sierra Leone army weren't up for the job. Despite nearly two decades of being trained by the British, they'd had their eye wiped by the rebels at Musala: the company sent to secure the town had been annihilated. There were no reported survivors, no witnesses to the battle had escaped, and both cell phone towers had been knocked out. The entire civilian population was missing.

The only account of what happened was from 'John', an unknown bystander – a pastor, possibly – who'd got caught up in the massacre. Before his phone went dead he'd telephoned a woman in Makeni during the attack itself and left a voicemail – which GCHQ had intercepted, hacked and erased, and which Rhodes had uploaded to my cell phone. I pressed play and turned up the volume. Ten seconds of reference tone was followed by the crisp, clear cries for help of a man in deep distress.

'Sista, sista qushe? Na yu brudda John. Sista? Den de na ton, den de kill all man. Le God save we o sista, den de all sai. People den de try fo run but den nor able. We don fashin. De deble den don mek we fashin, sista. Na Satan. Satan de na ya. Na ein. A able see am. Ay mi God wey de heavin. Den de eat we soul. De deble don cam fo we. Satan don cam for eat we. Run sista. Run. You need fo run . . .'

The recording terminated abruptly.

I picked out a dog-eared sheet of foolscap from Rhodes's folder and read the typed English translation:

'Sister? Sister, hello? It's John, your brother. Sister? They're in the town, they're killing everyone. God save us, sister, they're everywhere. The people are trying to run but they can't. We're trapped. The devils have trapped us, sister. It's Satan. Satan is here. It's him. I can see him. Oh my God in heaven. They are eating our souls. The devil has come for us. Satan has come to eat us. Run, sister. Run. You must run . . .'

At the end Rhodes had added a note in her own, spidery handwriting: *Transmission authenticated. Assume Musala CIVPOP eliminated. Proceed with extreme caution.*

Whoever John was, he hadn't made it out alive. No one had.

One thing bothered me more than anything else, more

even than the unnerving language and palpable horror of what John described. It wasn't what was on the recording, but what wasn't: gunfire. The Russians were masters of running Psy Ops and pseudo operations. Whatever they'd pulled in Musala had apparently wreaked havoc on their victims' minds as well, presumably, as on their bodies – and, it seemed, without a shot being fired. There were many seams of fear to tap in Sierra Leone. The terror in John's voice suggested they'd struck gold.

I wiped the audio file and gathered up the papers. They'd be retrieved from the hotel safe after I'd checked out. I stubbed out the cigarette, switched my phone to silent and lay down in the dark.

I doubted King knew what the rebels' true objective was, or what the Russians' involvement really amounted to, despite delighting in an evening-long opportunity to burnish the bright shining lie of his born-to-the-manor authority. Perhaps Mason didn't know either. Perhaps Captain Rhodes knew more than I'd given her credit for, though Nazzar wrote her off as 'just some bloody numpty' when I'd quizzed him in the corridor on our separate ways to and from the bathroom. I'd asked him to find out who she was, anyway.

Once upon a time, as Frank might say, 'perhaps' had been irrelevant; but after Caracas I wanted to *know*. And I knew, too, that was the beginning of the end. Killing people in cold blood without question because I was ordered to might have made me a 'legally sane psychopath'; killing people when I thought I knew they were innocent made me, at best, a sociopath – a sociopath who followed orders. History hadn't judged that sort too well.

Frank had been right about one thing: 'my kind', as he put it, were much misunderstood. Not least by him. Being good at making sheer bloody mayhem was one thing; but sheer bloody murder was another, even for Max McLean. The most enduring thread of humanity I had left to hang on to was wrapped not around any sense of doing my duty, but the certainty that the people I killed were bad people: their guilt served to expiate mine.

But there I was. Alone and unforgiven.

I left home when I turned sixteen and lived in rooms empty of morality ever since: one hotel suite after another, plotting one death after another. As time passed in the army I'd felt better and better about killing. I didn't *like* it – but I grew accustomed to it, and then, inexorably, fell in love with the idea and the strength of it. After my first kill – snatched from nearly a mile away across the wet slate roofs of West Belfast – the younger recruits at Raven Hill began to idolize me. And suddenly I was no longer a grieving child, but a king. It had taken Colonel Ellard years to nurture our talents without making us sadists. What the act of killing paid us, he banked to the army's credit.

Once Frank had said that my father would have been proud of me. For what? Pulling the trigger? Following an order blindly? Proud of me for protecting, for serving, for doing the jobs no one else would do like some fucked-up Irish Dirty Harry? But Frank hadn't known my father.

It was twenty-six years since my father's plane had been shot down by the Cubans over Southern Africa. A brilliant soldier, scientist and mind lost in a blast of smoke and shrapnel in Angola's bright-blue sky on my birthday. When she heard the news, my mother walked into the lake behind our house with stones in her pockets.

And me, I ran.

By the time I arrived at Browning Barracks in Aldershot with a forged letter of consent, no one knew who I was; and I had no idea where I was going.

What would that tall blond reed of a man who never once raised his voice, or struck or humiliated me the way weak men do to wreck their sons, have been more proud of: obedience or insubordination; duty or survival? I took in the tools of my trade, the whisky glass and the pistol. We were supposed to be the Unknown, not the unconscionable. That gentle Adam had raised a Cain. Frank Knight saw that all right, and knew I would, as he put it, 'do well' as his willing executioner.

Ellard had impressed upon us in no uncertain terms that there would come a point in all our lives when the pressure of the job would bring the roof in. 'The question,' he said, 'is which side of the break line will you be on?' I thought of Ana María, the disappointment etched on Frank's face during my dressing-down in Caracas, and the look of relief on King's face when he saw I was still at the coalface. Perhaps letting her live presaged my own collapse.

But you knew, I tried to keep reassuring myself, *you knew*. Whoever she was, she was not the person I'd been briefed to believe Frank said she was. I lay there going round in half-conscious circles until my phone buzzed.

Frank.

The message read:

The quick Red Fox jumped over the lazy brown dogs.

It looked like Ana María had made it out. Havana most probably. Better the devil you know.

Are you in dog house? I asked.

Heading kennelwards soonest, came his reply.

No one at the briefing had mentioned Frank. And someone *always* mentioned Frank. He and King were tight. I typed:

Russian advice?

This time it took a full five minutes for his response to come through. As the Valium pulled me into a downward spiral of empty dreams, the rattle of the phone against the bedside table brought me to just long enough to read his answer:

Go see Sonny Boy.

6

'That's right, sir. And your belt, sir. And the shoes. Any papers, tissues, tickets in your pockets?'

I gave the private security guard a curt shake of the head and stepped into the scanner: hands up; legs apart; staring ahead. With a double swish the sensor passed around me. I caught sight of the edge of the LCD display panel as I stepped out again: green. I got dressed, stuck a sticky-backed name-label to my shirt breast and followed a male nurse out of the thin Norfolk sunlight trickling into visitor reception. We headed through the lobby doors into a grey warren of seemingly endless corridors, stretching to desolate, fluorescent-lit infinities.

From outside the building looked entirely ignorable. Inside, orderlies slipped gurneys silently along polished linoleum that reflected the green-tinged lights above. Here and there, black-clad security men: all private contractors; no serving military in uniform; no weapons in view; nothing to worry about. I could hear my breath as we walked, but not our footsteps. My shoes were locked in a numbered cabinet along with my ID card and pistol. Instead, the nurse and I wore soft rubber clogs. It was like cave diving with no oxygen.

'It disturbs them, some of them, if they hear footsteps. They think you're coming to get them.' The nurse spoke without looking at me, without turning his head at all; his voice was monotone and matter-of-fact.

'Or rescue them,' I said.

We glided left and right in silence into the heart of the facility for a thousand metres, and then stopped abruptly. The nurse punched in a five-digit code on a pad next to a solid grey door and pushed hard. The rush of air the opening door brought with it carried a hint of Dixie jazz and the strong smell of peppermint. A woman in her mid-forties and an ill-fitting business suit sat hunched over a laptop at a table at the far end of the room. I walked the ten paces towards her, and she stood, hand outstretched. I took it, shook it and turned around. The nurse had already gone.

'Mr McLean?'

'Max, please, Doctor . . . ?'

'Crossman. Tina Crossman. And I'm not a doctor. Not clever or patient enough for that by half.' She motioned to one of the plastic chairs orbiting her desk. Please, sit.'

A half-eaten chicken breast and a clump of broccoli languished on a paper plate beside her laptop. A plastic knife and fork floated next to them on the congealed gravy skin. I sat down and opened my palms towards her.

'I'm sorry, I didn't mean to disturb your lunch, I . . .'

She cut me off with her outstretched hand again, this time offering the torn end of a packet of Polos. I raised my palms a little higher and smiled *no thank you.*

'I'm afraid it's what passes for dessert around here.' She loosened a mint from the packet with her thumbnail and put it on her tongue as if she were taking Communion.

'I'm here to see Sonny, I mean *Sergeant* Mayne.'

Crossman bit down hard and crunched her way through the mint, losing herself in her laptop. The jazz faded away.

'Sorry, that's better. Bloody thing has a mind of its own. Yes, Mayne. Sergeant Martin Mayne.' She looked at me quizzically and hooked a strand of greying black hair behind her ear. 'How can I help you with Sergeant Mayne?'

'I'm his friend.'

She looked at me blankly.

'Friend? I see. I'm his counsellor, by the way.' There was a long pause. 'And . . . ?'

'And I'm here to see him. To visit him.' Her mouth opened slightly as if to speak a word she decided to hold on to instead. 'They told you I was coming?'

She turned the packet of mints over between her thumb and forefinger. Her mouth opened and closed again before she spoke.

'Yes, Mr McLean, *they* did.' Her eyes flitted between mine and the computer screen. 'Full visiting rights. Which is unusual.' She sat back, deeper into her chair, adjusted her jacket and looked straight at me. 'In fact,' she continued, 'you'll be Sergeant Mayne's first visitor since he arrived last month.'

It was a five-minute walk to see Sonny Boy. Since entering the one-storey maze of the Brinton Facility I'd walked one and a half kilometres and seen fewer than a dozen people. I'd heard almost nothing. But I'd learned a lot from Crossman on the way to his room. Sonny Boy had been admitted after a twenty-one-day stint at the Royal Free Hospital in London. He was apparently suffering from severe delusional psychosis triggered by an acute post-traumatic stress reaction. Crossman didn't mention any physical ailments. What exactly triggered the reaction Crossman either didn't know or wouldn't tell.

'Fear, Mr McLean,' was all she would say when I quizzed her, 'absolute mortal fear.'

Which was strange, because Sonny Boy wasn't the sort to scare easy: every inch the gentle Irish giant, he'd been in the army for eighteen years, fifteen of them in the SAS – first in D-Squadron with Jack Nazzar, and then with him again in the Wing and E-Squadron. I'd known him half that time. He'd been supporting the Unknown's missions for a year before I found out he'd been given a DSO after his fourth deployment to Afghanistan. The citation remained classified, but it was said D-Squadron's Air Troop owed him their lives – Jack Nazzar included. He was an exceptional shot, and so gifted with explosives it was a perpetual relief he'd joined our army and not the Irish Republicans'.

Military psychiatric cases are handled by the private hospitals of the Priory Group. Brinton wasn't even a hospital. It was, according to Crossman, a 'research facility'. Sonny Boy was neither a patient nor a prisoner. He was a subject. Crossman and I stood in the antechamber to his room, flanked by two guards in black uniforms. Yellow-handled Tasers tethered to their belts were holstered by their sides. They, and an electric security door, stood between me and Sonny Boy. Crossman rolled her shoulders and spoke while looking up at the closed-circuit TV cameras perched above the door.

'Martin is prone to bouts of excitement, Mr McLean; bouts of excitement that can provoke unpredictable responses.'

'Such as?'

'Such as strong *physical* reactions. I'd ask you to be brief, Mr McLean, and not to discuss any of the details of his last, er, deployment. He gets very nervous about that. Very agitated.' Crossman turned to the guard on her left and nodded. The guard entered a series of digits on a key pad on the wall between them.

'You mean in Russia, Counsellor?'

'No, Mr McLean.' She turned and tapped the second part of the passcode into the key pad. The door slid open, revealing a vestibule, a second door with a transparent panel, and beyond it a single bed supporting Sonny Boy's tracksuit-clad hulk. I stepped forward, and the main door began to close behind me. 'Not Russia. Your friend here was evacuated from Sierra Leone.'

Soldiers don't impress me. They get paid to do a job. Either they do it well, or they don't. And Special Forces aren't superheroes. They shit, piss, bleed and grouse like everyone else – including the Queen they serve. But Sonny Boy? He wasn't a soldier. He was a fucking legend. And there he was, sat like Buddha in a soft-furnished hell, hand-rolling a pinch of tobacco. He looked straight through me towards the closing door.

'Long time, Max.'

'Long time, Sonny. How you been keeping?'

'Aw, you know . . .' He looked left and right quickly, dropped the half-finished cigarette into the ashtray and put his crooked trigger finger to his lips. '*Shh.*'

He eased himself off the bed and stood an arm's length in front of me: six foot six and two hundred and fifty pounds of soft-spoken, stone-cold killer. Then, at a half-crouch, he loped towards the far left-hand end of the room. He pointed at me, put his finger to his lips again and stood there, stock still, with one ear pressed against the beige wall. A full minute passed. I shifted my weight, but he held up his hand as if stopping traffic at a checkpoint. Another minute. And another – Sonny Boy unmoving, listening.

'You're all right,' he blurted out, finally. 'It's grand. They've gone. Ha! How've I been keeping? Christ, Max, you wouldn't fuckin' believe it if I told you. You wouldn't believe it for a moment!' He sighed and laughed and sat back down on the bed, hard. 'Sure, you wouldn't believe a single word of it. But there you go.' He looked down at the floor. We grew up a country mile and a world apart in County Wicklow. His accent echoed my own childhood brogue that had been softened in the army.

I inched towards the bed.

'Believe what, Sonny? What's up?'

Without warning a deep, trembling sob spluttered out of him, followed by an awful keening so forceful it made me recoil. He looked up. Tears blurred his eyes. His teeth were clenched, the muscles in his jaw bulging. I put my hand out to him, fingers first, like seducing a wary dog. He said, did, nothing. I put my hand on his shoulder. He flinched.

'Hey, Sonny,' I whispered. 'It's OK. I'm here. It's grand.' I sat next to him, slowly, deliberately lowering myself on to the bed next to him. His hands had fallen into his lap. Tears were falling on them. I took his pistol hand in mine and held it gently. 'It's all right now. It's all right.'

Sonny Boy half-turned to me. His lips were trembling, his jaw slackened.

'You wouldn't fuckin' believe it, Max,' he sobbed, trying to compose himself.

'Believe what, Sonny? Do you want to tell me about it?' Nothing. 'We don't have to talk. Hey, remember that time in Kabul when . . .'

'You're going, aren't you?'

'Going where, Sonny?'

'*There.*'

'What, Sierra Leone?' As soon as I spoke I realized my mistake. He gripped my hand hard and looked me in the eye as if suddenly seeing something for the first time.

'That's why they sent you to see me, isn't it? They're still sending you. That's why they sent *me.*' His voice was quiet, steady. 'Ah, not you, Max. Please, not you.'

I went to reassure him, but it was too late. He lurched into me, twisting and crashing me on to the floor. My hand in his; his face against mine; his teeth at my ear, deafening me with a cry fit to rend my soul.

I went limp, and rolled with him. My right hand was still free. I pushed his head back hard. My thumb gouged his face. There was a wet *pop* as I put his eye out. I rotated my left wrist, and pulled it back to my chest. Both hands free. He lifted a massive balled fist but I hit him first with a left brachial punch. Sonny roared in pain – half-blind, arm paralysed – and collapsed on me, his forearm across my throat. The room blackened. I braced and struck his carotid artery. No effect. My windpipe was collapsing. Blackness. I punched again. He rolled off and found his feet, facing me like an obscene Cyclops. I landed a short jab to his brachial plexus. He swung and missed. I lunged inside his reach, the base of my right palm to the tip of his nose. Blood gushed from his face. My left wrist to his right ear, then my right palm to the bridge of his nose, crushing the cartilage completely. I kept at him. My left elbow to his left ear, hard. He went down. But I was too close and went down with him, pinned under his massive weight again.

Two men in black appeared beside me, electric pistols drawn. Neither fired. My palms found Sonny's temples. His eye hung from its socket on to my cheek. He was bleeding heavily from his mouth, nose and ears; haemorrhaging into his throat and on to my face. The room filled with a woman's voice, and the smell of peppermint and blood iron. I forced his head up, and he looked down through his one dying eye. As my hands began to twist his neck, he smiled and relaxed.

'They're coming, Max. They're coming.'

7

I woke up over the Sahara. At first I thought I could see camel trains winding their way through the dunes. But it was just wishful thinking. We were too high, and all I could see were the narrow outlines of rocky outcrops threading their way across the scorched earth. The slipstream from the engines created the impossible illusion of a heat haze rising off the horizon, and only then did I realize I was cold.

I looked at my phone and reread the last messages I'd received from Frank before take-off:

Sonny didn't make it. Proceed as planned. Don't kill any Russians.

And then in Irish:

Ádh mór ort.

Good luck? I took the battery out of my phone, and the screen went black.

So Sonny Boy was dead.

It had taken me an hour at Brinton to scrub his blood out of my hair, from under my fingernails. I sniffed the backs of my fingertips. Bleach and cigarettes. No Sonny Boy. No Ana María. I didn't even smell like me any more.

I've killed my own kind before: one who went rogue, one who went bad and one who went mad in a petrol

66

station – two weeks back from Afghanistan and he barricaded himself in a service station outside Hereford and poured petrol over himself and everyone else inside. It had been too risky to fire a shot. In the end I'd dropped down from the ceiling with a ceramic cook's knife. No one else would do it.

But Sonny Boy? That was different. And there would be consequences. Sonny Boy was a straight-up hero, and killing a hero, even in self-defence, doesn't go unpunished – one way or another. I'd stopped short of breaking his neck and had been lucky not to have mine snapped by him. When I left the room a crash team was intubating him. His vital signs were wildly erratic, but he was still breathing. The private security men had been scooped up by plain-clothed military police within seconds. Crossman the counsellor hardly said a word. She watched while blood samples were drawn from my forearms, and a dozen shots of *who-knew-what?* were plunged into my deltoids. I asked what they were for. 'For your own good,' she'd replied.

Frank had told me to go see Sonny Boy. But all Sonny Boy told me through his rantings was that he believed he'd been on some sort of recce for my trip – and the thought of that had flipped a switch. But Sonny Boy also believed he could hear things through a sound-proof cell wall and had tried his level best to kill me. Quite who he thought was coming after him was beyond me. Perhaps his brain had been fried in the jungle. But we'd both spent a lot of time in jungles, and neither of us had ever come back that far gone. It was one thing for the local pastor to think the world was ending when the enemy closed in; but Sonny Boy was cut from different cloth.

Mason and King wanted the operation wrapped up inside of a week. If the rebels were as mobile as they believed, then Makeni was already threatened, and so was the capital, Freetown. Mason and King wanted me to get up there and get on with it. I wanted to know what had happened to Sonny Boy. I also wanted to speak to 'Juliet' – the only source who'd placed the mystery white man in the camp. One thing was certain: taking the shot would only be the beginning. Afterwards I had to get out, and get out clean. A week was already looking optimistic.

As we sped our way towards the jungle and eventually the coast, yellow gave way to brown and then green – and then eventually a flash of blue as the 737 flitted over Tagrin Bay before arcing out wide over the Atlantic.

I disembarked on to the apron at Lungi International Airport and wasn't cold any more. It was like stepping under a hairdryer – the sea wind took the edge off the humidity, but the scouring equatorial heat was inescapable. Although the rains were at least a month off, the climate, as well as the terrain upcountry, would be brutal.

My father had spent years of his life in Africa – both in the army, and on long school holidays with me in tow – but I'd never been operational in West Africa. Once through the huge plate-glass doors that helped bake everyone who worked in the arrivals hall into a state of exhausted inertia, there was a momentary rush of enthusiasm from the other passengers to secure pole position at the immigration desk. Soon, they too settled into an extended heat-addled group fidget. But no one hassled me. A man in a limp blue uniform took my Canadian passport, studied my visa.

'Mister Maxwell. Do you have anything to declare?' His accent was soft, as if littered with half-spoken aitches. I told him I didn't.

'Ah, you have not brought your hammer then, Mister Maxwell? So you will not be killing anyone, I hope.' He grinned at me, and chuckled. I froze. The immigration desk is a point of maximum vulnerability. You can't run and you can't fight. If your papers aren't in order or The Man (who is often a woman) doesn't *want* them to be in order you are powerless. This was an entirely deniable black operation. Get busted, and there's no calling the embassy.

The immigration officer held my look, and his smile deepened. I smiled back. Just because I was paranoid didn't mean that London hadn't fucked it up. Again. Then the penny dropped.

'Abbey Road!' I almost shouted. 'You're a Beatles fan, Officer . . .' I peered at his name tag, '. . . Johnson.'

'Bang! Bang!' he said in triumph as he thumped the entry stamps down into my passport. 'Yes! And you are welcome to Salone, Mister Maxwell. Most welcome!'

I tucked the little gold-crested Canadian booklet back into its ziplock bag, and then into the thigh pocket of my cargo trousers, and said thank you to Johnson. In my mind's eye I saw the picture of the mystery white man upriver striding across an Abbey Road-style zebra crossing in the jungle. *Bang bang*, indeed. This Max would make well sure that he was dead.

Defunct air conditioning pipes overhead snaked silently towards customs. Only a whisper of warm air emerged from them. The terminal was new, but it was already collapsing into decrepitude. Sweat soaked into the back of my shirt, clung to my lips, trickled into my mouth. The taste of salt made me thirsty. Anxiety dried out my throat. I pulled the red North Face bag off the stationary baggage carousel and braced myself, hyper-aware of the five thousand US dollars in my other trouser pocket.

But no one in customs stirred, and I strode past their unmanned desks unmolested. It was nearly two o'clock now, and the heat was oppressive. I shouldered my kit and stepped into the light. The sky was razor-sharp. The breeze coming off the Atlantic had stiffened and stirred the fronds of a dozen palm trees standing sentinel outside. The sweat on my back chilled. I pulled a blue Vancouver Canucks cap down over my eyes, scanned and dodged the throng of porters hustling for a tip and struck out for the chopper transfer terminal.

Lungi Airport is separated from Freetown by the Sierra Leone River. Getting into town after touchdown was an unwelcome hurdle to clear. Water taxis, private charter speedboats and an old ferry plied the route in what looked like varying degrees of nausea-inducing sea-worthiness. Fastest – but not for the faint-hearted – was the helicopter transfer. Aged Russian military helicopters piloted by what looked like equally aged Ukrainian crews hurtled passengers to and from the Aberdeen district of Freetown with occasionally fatal consequences: a few years back, one of the old troop carriers burst into flames on landing, killing all the passengers on board.

I found the worn-out Russian Mi-8 humming behind a chain-link fence a short walk from the exit at Arrivals. The service had only just got going again. Given that my father went to an early grave in an aircraft flying over Africa, buying a ticket to climb aboard that rusty Cold War memento didn't sit well with me. I'd have preferred to fly it myself. I stood in line with a dozen equally wary passengers, each of us with our seventy bucks in hand for the one-way, seven-minute Iron Curtain rollercoaster ride. Businessmen, tourists, mining contractors, aid workers, embassy staff and a few wealthy locals – most likely each of us hoping this wasn't the day for an emergency autorotation over the Atlantic. Then the roar of the turbines and the reek of Jet A-1 evaporating in the afternoon sun triggered that familiar adrenaline rush. Fragments of countless chopper flights glinted in my memory as my belt buckle clicked home and the ground fell away beneath us, revealing first the sea again, and then, as we swooped forward, the patchwork ocean of grey and blue and the rust-coloured corrugated roofs of Freetown itself.

Roberts was waiting at the Aberdeen terminal. Five-ten, skinny as a beanpole, with braided hair unravelling at the ends. He looked like he was in his twenties, but I knew he was thirty-six. He was smoking, propped up

71

against an old Nissan with 'God's Gift' scrawled across the bonnet.

'All right, mate. Good flight?' No trace of a Krio accent. Roberts was one hundred per cent south London. I put the red duffel bag on the back seat and folded myself into his ride.

'Yeah, it was all right.' I lit a cigarette.

'Hotel?'

The Mammy Yoko was almost within walking distance of the terminal. We'd flown around it as we made our descent: an expensive white island in a murky wash of green and brown. There were tennis courts and the turquoise rectangle of a swimming pool at the back of the complex fringed by half a dozen women in bikinis.

'No. Let's get a beer. I'll check in later.'

'Cool. I know just the place.'

God's Gift hiccupped into half-life.

'Where did you get that accent from?'

'Peckham.' He smiled. 'Sarf Landan boy, ain't I? Yours?'

'Canada,' I smiled back.

'Yeah?'

'There are lots of Irish in Canada. Trust me.'

'Course there are. What do I call you? Max?' I nodded, and he stuck the cigarette butt between his teeth as he slapped the Nissan's dash in encouragement. 'Come on, old girl. Let's be 'avin' ya.'

'Roberts . . .' I looked around me. Outside, the car was a patchwork of replaced panels, each sprayed with their own shade of grey primer. Inside, the integrity of the Nissan's chassis seemed to rely heavily on strips of gaffer tape and zip ties. 'Is this piece of, uh, premium Japanese engineering going to get us in or out of trouble? I have money. We can get another car.'

'Hey! She's very sensitive! But she goes. And you know her real beauty? No one'll fuck with her. So no one'll fuck with you. You're just one more white man getting ripped off across the town.'

'You got that right.'

Five minutes later we'd crossed the mouth of a long creek that nearly cut Aberdeen off from the rest of Freetown, and were heading into town – driving south and then east. Roberts reached behind him, under my seat, and produced the strap of the Billingham satchel Captain Rhodes said he'd have for me.

'S'all yours. No idea what's in it. And I don't want to.' Which in his accent came out as *Annahdoanwannoo*.

As he drove, he talked. And he was good at both.

Roberts, it turned out, had led a life charmed and desperate by turn. He recounted his story in fits and starts as we bounced along by the coast. Barely eighteen years old when rebels of the Revolutionary United Front poured into Freetown, he'd run away from home and headed straight to the offices of Southern Star, a private military company run by a friend of his dad: an Israeli mercenary who called himself Ezra Black. Roberts wanted to kill rebels. Ezra wanted an untrained kid yapping at his heels as much as he wanted a hole in the head.

'What did he do?' Roberts the skinny, chain-smoking mercenary. It was almost funny.

73

'He shot me.'

'What?'

'He shot me. Right 'ere.' And with that he pulled up his top with his right hand, exposing a knotty lump of scar tissue above his hip bone. 'It bloody hurt. But it saved my life. *He* saved my life.'

Ezra had slapped on a wound dressing, driven him back to his parents' house and then taken them all to the United Nations chopper pad at their HQ: the Mammy Yoko Hotel. The UN were evacuating their staff; Ezra knew the pilots and their military escorts. Roberts – now officially a wounded child in 'critical condition' – was given a UN ID pass and flown to Senegal. From there Ezra managed to get him to an elderly aunt in England. He never saw his parents again. When the war finally ended three years later he was an orphan with a degree in business studies, an English wife and an overdraft the size of a small mortgage.

'Y'know what happened then?'

I didn't.

'Mate, it was fucking mad. No word of a lie. My auntie, yeah? The day they signed the peace accords, she drops dead. Dodgy ticker.'

I looked suitably surprised.

'But that's not the mad bit. The next day – after my auntie died – my missus bought a scratch card.' He paused for effect and looked at me again, eyes wild with the memory of what he was about to recount. 'One hundred large. One hundred!'

She'd paid for a decent burial for Auntie and settled

their debts; he came home, and she came with him. Now he drove a taxi, and she, a former barmaid, ran her own bar – which is where he said we were headed.

'Who've you got left? Here, I mean.'

'Just my grandad. You'd like him. Old soldier, and a proper ladies' man. Always banging on about how great the Irish are, too.'

'Clever man, your grandad. Any kids yourself?'

'None that I know of,' he laughed, and then pulled himself up short. 'Nah, no kids,' he continued more quietly. 'We can't. My wife, she, *uh* . . . she can't have any. You know?' He swerved hard around a peanut seller who'd overbalanced off the kerb and into the road. Roberts changed the subject and pointed towards the sea. A black, red, gold and green bead bracelet with a Rastafarian Lion of Judah dangling from it looped around his bony wrist. The lion's foot was missing.

'That's White Man's Bay over there.' He looked at me and grinned. 'And up ahead, if you keep going, that's Congo Town, where my folks were from. It's come back to life, but during Ebola . . . that was something else. If you weren't scared of dying it's cos you were either crazy or already dead.'

We took a hard right down Wilkinson Road, and the old Nissan thundered south. Women with babies tied to their backs with yards of brightly coloured printed cloth picked their way through roadside markets. Salt, smoke and shit flavoured the moist, hot air that ripped through our open windows.

'I won't lie,' Roberts went on. 'It's been hard, you know? But it's OK now. Better anyway.'

The Ebola outbreak had swept through their lives like a second civil war. Fourteen thousand people had been infected, Roberts reminded me. And nearly four thousand of those had died. The highly contagious haemorrhagic fever liquefied vital organs and caused its victims to bleed uncontrollably from their eyes, ears, mouth, genitals . . .

Roberts had, by his own admission, nearly gone bust. Again. Sitting in a bar is not high up on the list of things people want to do in the midst of one of the most lethal epidemics the world has ever known. But together, he said, he and his wife were just about breaking even again.

'How did you get mixed up with the Brits, at the embassy?'

He gave me a sidelong glance.

'Why? For the money, what else? Let's save "how" for the beer.' And then, leaning across me, he pointed out of my window. 'That's Cockerill, the air base. The South Africans are still there. Anything military that comes in from offshore lands there. Yanks, Brits, Russians. Ethiopians.'

'Ethiopians?'

'Yeah, they send tech crews in to fix the choppers. Cheaper than Russians. And the South Africans insist on it. No one else gets to touch their birds.' He grinned rakishly. 'Not that you'd want to touch any bird they'd been near.'

76

Two large Russian Hind helicopter gunships sat on the apron, blades tied down. They were the same mid-seventies model that I'd trained on in Poland with A-Squadron. At who knew what cost, the British government was financing the Sierra Leone air force to buy gunships from the old Soviet bloc, serviced by Ethiopian crews, piloted by South African mercenaries. With the combined firepower of these choppers alone they probably had enough hardware in place to end the insurgency in the north. Instead, I was supposed to end it single-handed with a single shot. Frank had been right: *One job. One kill. Not question. Not think.* Plausible deniability commanded a high price and a lot of hassle. A cold beer was looking more appealing by the minute.

We'd come round in a steep, narrow loop, hooking around the bottom of the creek and back up towards the hotel along Lumley Beach Road. It ran along a narrow strip of land a couple of hundred feet across, sandwiched between Cockerill Bay to the west and Aberdeen Creek to the east. Roberts pulled up outside a beach bar and killed the Nissan's engine.

'Home sweet home.'

The strip of sand wasn't much wider than the road itself. We climbed out and walked under the shade of the coconut palms that ringed the bar, the Billingham satchel over my shoulder. There were no customers. A tall white woman in a 'Vote Koroma for President' T-shirt presided over the bar, messy auburn hair piled up on top of her head. Roberts kissed her on the lips and turned back towards me.

The woman stretched her hand out over the bar, and I took it. She had a firm handshake and looked me straight in the eye.

'I'm Max,' I said. 'How d'y'do?'

'Pleased to meet you, Max,' she replied in a hoarse south London whisper. 'I'm Juliet.'

8

'Star?'

I nodded.

Juliet prised the crown top off a heavy green bottle of the local lager and poured half of it into a chilled schooner. The wiry muscles in her forearm tensed under the weight. Beads of moisture welled up around the glass as it filled with the amber liquid. We were sitting at the bar. It was getting hotter. Although the palms shaded us, the bar itself shielded us from the small mercy of the breeze blowing in from across Cockerill Bay. A smell of dead fish and rotting vegetation rose as the tide ebbed in the creek.

From a kitchen out the back an old woman produced a plate of fried plantain and grilled snapper. She was sweating hard, and Juliet thanked her in Krio, but the woman didn't speak. When she turned to leave I saw that her right eye was missing. The side of her face was a mass of scar tissue. I looked at the food and I remembered I was hungry. I'd last eaten a meal on the way to see Sonny Boy in Brinton. The plantain took on a reddish hue from the palm oil used to fry it. Salt crystals were scattered over the fish. The skin was blistered and blackened in places by the coals it had been cooked on.

'I think I'm about to eat your lunch, Juliet,' I said to

her. I broke off some of the flesh with my fingers and ate it. It was delicious.

'Oh, it's fine, you go ahead, love. You must be ravenous. Lucy will bring some more,' she replied, looking directly at me. She was beautiful, and hard with it. 'And call me Jules. Everyone else does.'

Juliet. I swallowed her name with a mouthful of beer.

'There is no such thing as a coincidence,' my father would say to me when my seven-year-old mind fretted about why my mother called me in for tea at the precise moment I hoped she'd forget I was outside playing. 'Everything is connected, Maximilian,' he'd chuckle as I traipsed back inside, 'even if we can't see how. Everything. Coincidences are how God and Science shake hands.'

I couldn't see it when I was a child, and I couldn't see it then, either. Never mind shaking hands, it felt like I was being slapped by a cosmic high five.

It was inconceivable that Juliet was 'Juliet', the source – the only source – that had placed my target in the rebel camp at Karabunda. Not even MI6 would have code-named a source so transparently, a source so highly classified that apparently not even General King knew their true identity. Then I remembered what Captain Rhodes had said: *We're hiding you in plain sight*. She was only a captain, but perhaps *she* knew and had hidden 'Juliet' in plain sight, too. Someone other than Mason had to know – if he even knew himself.

What troubled me more was that there was no obvious reason why the source should be withheld from me *at all.* Any scrap of information, no matter how small, could always make the difference between getting to the target or not. I also reminded myself how entirely feasible it was that the source 'Juliet' might not even know they *were* the source: it's possible to positively identify a target without knowing you've done so.

I drank more of the beer and opened a packet of duty-free Reds and remembered too that it was only conjecture that Six had named or renamed the source 'Juliet'. Like so many of the problems that plagued the Foreign Office, it could just as easily have been inherited as created.

'You were going to tell me how you got in with the embassy,' I reminded Roberts. Juliet passed me his lighter as he ran his palms over his braids. The unruly ends curled out from the nape of his neck. They were flecked with grey.

'It was during the evacuation in ninety-nine, like I was saying. When we arrived in Senegal there was this guy, Mike, from the British embassy. He'd flown out with us. He knew Ezra and he needed someone who spoke Limba. I do. They had a defector from up north who they were getting to safety. He wouldn't or couldn't speak Krio, and they wanted me to talk to him. So I did. I got hero points for that, being a kid and shot in the guts and all. Know what I mean? We stayed in touch, me and Mike, and when we came back,' he looked at Juliet, 'well he must have given my name to whoever replaced him at the embassy because they kept asking me to do translating jobs for them. It's good money. Especially when no one's buying Star or needs a ride.'

'Sure, but I thought you said your folks were from Congo Town. Freetown is south. They speak Limba farther north, no?' For the remainder of the flight I'd skimmed – as standard – the latest Lonely Planet guide to West Africa. Backpackers should take some comfort in being briefed as well as most spies.

'That was my mum's family. My dad's folks are from Musala, way up north. There are plenty of Limba in Freetown, but they don't speak it like me and my dad speak it. We're Sierra Leone's only indigenous tribe. He's a *proper* northerner.' He paused and looked down at the bar. '*Was* a proper northerner.'

'Musala, up on the Mong River?'

'Yeah, bright lights, big village. No one has ever heard of it outside of Northern Province. Not even the president, I reckon.'

'Especially the president,' Juliet chipped in.

'I had you down as a fan.' I nodded at her chest.

'What, this guy?' She shook her breasts so the black and white screen-printed photo of President Koroma jiggled about. 'Nah, it's so the punters don't stare at me tits. Ugly bugger, ain't he? Is that where you're going to build the clinic?' I took a drag on the Marlboro and didn't answer. 'Robbie said you're a medic; that you're going upcountry to build a clinic. Is that the clinic in Musala?'

I exhaled and looked at Roberts before I spoke. He was tucking into the plantain and making small pleasure noises while he chewed.

'*Near* Musala,' I corrected her. 'And now I know why

Robbie the northerner here got the unenviable job of carting me around.' I tilted my glass towards him in salute. 'I didn't know your folks were from up there. But I'm afraid I'm not clever enough to build it. That's the contractor's job – if the project ever goes ahead. I'm just doing the needs assessment for the embassy. They want to know they're targeting the right people before they pay for it.'

I hadn't known Roberts's father's family were from Musala. That either made him a tremendous asset or an extraordinary liability. Roberts looked up crossly from his plate and scowled at her. I guessed he wasn't so keen on being called Robbie.

'That's the American clinic, right?' Juliet carried on.

'Max is Canadian,' Roberts said, to her. And then, looking at me: 'Not American. Right?'

'Right,' I agreed, tipping the visor of the blue cap back a little. 'Irish Canadian. English clinic.'

'That explains it,' she continued, 'well, sort of. You don't half sound like that other Irish guy who was here from the embassy.' And then, turning to Roberts: 'You know, that big bloke. Lord, what *was* his name?'

Roberts shook his head. My stomach tightened. I put out the cigarette.

'Hands like shovels,' she went on. 'Ever so gentle, mind. Looked like he wouldn't hurt a fly. He was funny, too. Every time I asked him what he was doing up north he'd just say "You wouldn't believe it for a moment!" God, what was his bloody name? He was here about that clinic, too. Must have been the same one. He made a few trips up to Musala.'

'The big guy, that was probably the engineer,' I said.

'But I was sure it was for the Americans.' She looked baffled and cocked her head to one side. 'He hung out with that bloke Micky from USAID. They went everywhere together at first. Mind you, I think he got fed up with him after a while and came and stayed here for a bit of peace and quiet before he went back up north.'

'What happened to him, the big guy?' I asked.

'Well, that was funny – funny peculiar I mean.' Her gaze was unbroken, and I returned it, trying hard not to steal glances at the president. 'He was supposed to come back here and stay with us again on his way to London, but someone from Micky's office called Robbie on the mobile and said he'd been taken sick and they'd had to fly him home. Malaria they reckoned.' She shook her head at the memory. 'The mozzies are a right bugger up north.'

Roberts finished the last of the plantain and looked wistfully at the door from which Lucy the cook-cum-waitress had emerged earlier.

'Shame, that,' he said. 'He was all right. Someone was supposed to come round and pick up his stuff, but in the end no one showed up. They just told me to give you his bag after all.'

I looked at the Billingham satchel on the floor beneath my bar stool and resisted the urge to reach for it.

'How interesting. I wonder what's in it?' I said to neither of them in particular.

84

Roberts looked at Juliet, and then back at me.

'Search me, mate. Feels heavy, though. Like a camera. Maybe it's his theodolite.' Then a mischievous look flitted across his face, as he lit on a different, better suggestion. 'Hey, if it's gold or diamonds I know a great little restaurant on the beach that's ripe for development.' And then he burst out laughing, and Juliet joined in, and I smiled along with them.

'What do you reckon is in the bag, Max?' Juliet asked me. 'Gold or diamonds?'

'Ah well,' I said, 'it's probably just his sat phone. I'll have a look later.' Then I hammed up my accent. 'But you won't believe it for a moment if I tell you it's gold, sure you won't.'

I took out the black Benchmade knife from the duffel bag, slid the safety catch off and pressed in the small silver stud at the hilt. The blade sprang out sideways and snapped home with a reassuring *thunk*. The tip scored out the newly laid grouting, and I lifted the large oblong brown floor tile clear. Nestled inside the hole I'd uncovered was a small burlap sack about twice the size of a roll of toilet paper, tied shut with a length of nylon sailing cord. I unpicked the knot and carefully slid out the contents, which were further wrapped in ziplock sandwich bags.

I carried everything through to the bedroom, placed the packages on the desk and pulled the curtains to. The room was momentarily plunged into darkness between the sun vanishing behind the thick hotel blackout drapes and the side light blinking into life. Then I extracted the oiled metal of a SIG P229 semi-automatic pistol from one of the plastic bags; two spare fifteen-round magazines and a short silencer from another; and two boxes of ammunition from the third. Each box contained fifty cartridges: premium match grade 9mm full metal jackets. I wasn't a fan of British army issue ammo – made always by the lowest bidder. Captain Rhodes had been as good as her word. The pistol was modified military issue – with a custom flat trigger and no sharp edges to catch on the clothing that would conceal it.

I took some toilet paper from the bathroom, wiped the excess oil from the pistol and ejected the magazine. The slide and action were liquid smooth. The bespoke barrel was threaded to receive the silencer; the threads were protected by a metal cap. I removed the cap and fitted the silencer. It was made from titanium and steel and well balanced. I loaded fifteen rounds into the magazine, inserted it, chambered a round into the breech, ejected the magazine and refilled it so once the magazine was put back in the pistol it held sixteen rounds – which was sixteen rounds more than I wanted to put through it in Sierra Leone. What I needed to do was fire one rifle shot to end a war, not start one with a *pistolero* shoot 'em up.

When we first arrived at Raven Hill, Colonel Ellard warned us that if we ever needed to fire more than five handgun rounds on a job something had gone very seriously wrong, and that we would need more ammunition than we could carry to make it right again. But for this mission the extra bullets were reassuring. As Ellard had also said: 'If you always plan for the worst, you will only ever be pleasantly surprised.' He had fostered in me a chronic sense of unease. His gift, Raven Hill's gift, to all of us, was to eliminate hope and replace it with agency.

I loaded the two spare magazines and put them in the burlap sack with the rest of the ammunition, untwisted the little silencer and put the SIG into a thick hiking sock, and then put the lot into a black North Face day bag. I washed my hands and checked the room safe. The code, always the same, was 1-2-2-3. The door swung open with a beep to reveal a large Manila envelope, which in turn opened to reveal one hundred thousand US dollars in late-series, non-sequential used bills. I closed and locked the safe and turned my attention to the Billing-ham satchel.

Made of canvas and closed with leather straps with brass fasteners, the Billingham was a piece of retro Eng-lish elegance. It looked out of place among the modern lines of a Business Class room in the Mammy Yoko hotel. I turned it over in my hands. No sign of damage or interference. It was supposed to contain a two-way video BGAN satellite phone, a local and an international smart phone. The latter I needed immediately. I'd switched my own phone off once Roberts had picked me up. Ordinarily it shouldn't go back on until I was out of the country.

From what Juliet and Roberts had said, it looked like the last person who'd had possession of the bag before them was Sonny Boy. And the last thing that Sonny Boy had done was try to kill me. I had no idea what was in the bag. What I did know was that Sonny Boy handled plastic explosive like Michelangelo handled marble.

I wasn't in the mood for a surprise.

For a moment I considered taking it to a remote spot on Lumley Beach and firing a couple of rounds into it to see if it went bang. But instead I undid the leather top straps to reveal a double zip secured with a combination padlock which Sonny Boy must have added and which Captain Rhodes hadn't mentioned. That was a good sign, at least. You don't padlock shut a booby trap for which the target doesn't have the code: five combination digits each ranging from zero to nine, and all set to zero. There were exactly one hundred thousand possible permutations, and only one solution. I slipped the point of the knife into the canvas by the lock and worked it along the seam, careful not to push too hard and damage whatever was inside.

There had been nothing to fear.

I put the SIM cards into the phones, switched them on and set them up. Both phones looked completely clean. No trace of Sonny Boy's last moves. Both beeped repeatedly as messages came in welcoming me to Sierra Leone; confirming receipt of a thousand dollars' worth of credit and unrestricted data access; and advising me of the best local numbers to call in case of emergency. The BGAN satellite phone was equally clean, and so was the bag. As usual, Sonny Boy had kept his shit tight. The contents of the bag were exactly as advertised. What was not as advertised was that Sonny had been tooling about with an American aid worker, or someone who claimed to be one. I'd pressed Juliet about 'Micky' as far as I'd dared, and drawn a blank. There were no clues in the phones, either.

Switching them on meant that Rhodes, Mason, King, Nazzar and, of course, Frank Knight would now all know exactly where I was. And where was that? In another hotel room, with the blood not long scrubbed off my hands, which this time belonged to someone I called a friend. I lit a cigarette and parted the curtains an inch. The light was softening. Palm trees in the hotel grounds shimmied in the breeze.

Neither Roberts nor Juliet had mentioned anything unusual happening in or around Musala. We'd talked in detail about Ebola and the civil war, but neither of them had expressed any concerns about a fresh outbreak of either. They were looking to the future and seemed happy enough. I'd walked back to the hotel alone along the Lumley Beach Road, leaving Roberts tucking into a fresh plate of snapper and plantain.

News of Musala falling would soon spread through the Sierra Leone army. The rebels might not have left any survivors, and the town might be locked down, but army rumour mills everywhere operate remarkably well devoid of even the most basic of facts. At the very minimum government reinforcements would have been sent to block the road south from Musala to Kabala. Once the news reached the general population – which could be within hours – pandemonium was possible, at least in the north. That was neither a good thing nor a bad thing. But either way it would change how I operated. For all I knew, Kabala could already have been attacked. The sudden awareness of the enormity of the task ahead made me realize how tired, actually exhausted, I was. In less than a week I'd failed to terminate my target, killed my mate and possibly fatally compromised myself in the eyes of my superiors.

If it was true that you were only ever as good as your last job, I was screwed.

I thought about going down to the bar for a drink but let the curtain fall again. Instead I went into the bathroom and glued the tile I'd lifted earlier back in place. Then I put the glue back in my duffel bag and took out a blister pack of Valium, popped out a ten-milligram pill and washed it down with duty-free Johnnie Walker Black, straight from the bottle. I wanted to go to the bar, to see other people. Maybe talk to someone interesting. Maybe there would be a woman. But who would really be there? Aid workers, assholes and hookers – that's who. And Ana María? She definitely wouldn't be there. So I persuaded myself I didn't want to speak to anyone after all and lay on the massive king-size bed, which was actually just two single beds pushed together, and went to sleep, puzzling about the Juliets.

9

'There's a hundred and six miles to Makeni, we've got a full tank of gas, half a packet of cigarettes, it's dark out, and we're wearing sunglasses.' Roberts turned to me and grinned.

'Hit it!' I humoured him. A happy driver is a safe driver.

After a quick stop for fuel at a one-man pump run by one of Roberts's many cousins – 'the only roadside seller in the city who doesn't water down the petrol' – we'd got on the road again, urging the old Nissan on through Freetown in the pre-dawn dim. We'd clocked up ten miles in good time, Roberts in an old Barcelona top and a battered pair of Ray-Bans, me every inch the respectable Canadian medic – real ID and a real medical kit close to hand. Real dollars, too, which nine times out of ten are more likely to get you out of trouble than a real pistol, which was also to hand.

I'd slept deeply but dreamed relentlessly, waking to fragments of images that told a story I couldn't quite hang on to: my father, leaving the house for the last time; Juliet's face in profile; Sonny Boy giving me the thumbs up as we dropped into the Maghreb, our parachutes opening high and wild above us. The more I chased whatever meaning there was in these dream slivers, the faster they dissolved. Then Freetown melted away, too, as the sun broke free of the hills. Long skeins of shanties thinned out along the road like corrugated spider's webs. Suddenly the city was gone, and there were only individual houses and the occasional village – strung always with the seemingly endless gaggles of children that populated the unfolding conveyor belt of tarmacadam that pulled us east.

I had no plan. My night-time ruminations had left me with no idea if Roberts and Juliet were anything to do with 'Juliet' or what it meant if they were. And I had no way of making a plan other than looking at the lie of the land myself. Someone had identified the target in the rebel camp: I could learn from him, or her, how to get into the camp. The least I needed to know was where I needed to position myself for the shot I was there to make. It would need to be close enough to have no margin of error; distant enough that I could get away afterwards.

In my mind's eye I imagined a sweet spot in the jungle with a clear view of the camp. The nearest designated airport was at Kabala, but it was the airstrip eight klicks by road north-west from Soron that interested me. The Chinese had cut it in the mid-2000s. It was just long enough to land an AN-12. Though the basic satellite imagery provided by Captain Rhodes hadn't indicated any activity, the Russians must have been using the Soron strip themselves. It was in the epicentre of their area of operations, and there was nowhere else upcountry they could land cargo planes or troop carriers. Even if they were just dropping supplies they'd need somewhere at least to land choppers and small fixed-wings like Cessnas, and Kabala was too exposed. There was no way an officer like

Colonel Proshunin – an *airborne* officer no less – was going to drive up to the rebel camp in Karabunda every time he wanted a briefing. He may have chauffeured my target up there once, but my guess was that he'd been a more regular visitor, and he'd be coming in by air.

Getting to Makeni was straightforward, at least.

As we drove, Roberts told stories about the war – some of which he'd lived through personally, some of which were part of the collective folklore of the civil war. The spaces between the villages grew larger and then contracted again as we entered and then cleared the town of Waterloo. In the late nineties, rebels from the Revolutionary United Front had swept through it during their first incursion into Freetown. Safely in the city, his family survived that initial onslaught. No one thought they'd come back.

'But they did,' said Roberts. 'The sixth of January ninety-nine.' He pushed his sunglasses up on to his forehead and kept his eyes on the road. I'd been operational in Central America. But although I'd missed the war, Nazzar hadn't. I remembered his debrief. 'War does not get worse than January six 1999,' he said. And that was from a man who knew all there was to know about fighting, and then some.

Rebels streamed out of the forest and into the city, burning and looting in an orgy of violence unparalleled even in that conflict. Dressed in Tupac T-shirts, women's wigs and even wedding dresses, child soldiers – many high on drugs – systematically rounded up entire suburbs and machine-gunned them en masse. No one was spared: doctors, foreigners, journalists – almost every-one who crossed their path was killed. Just looking at a rebel soldier the wrong way was enough to get a bullet in the head, or worse. Women were gang-raped by the hundred, nuns executed. The names of individual units described the rebels' specialities: as well as the Burn House Unit, Cut Hands Commando and Blood Shed Squad, the Kill Man No Blood unit also ran riot – their method was to beat people to death without shedding blood. Equally macabre was the Born Naked Squad, who stripped their victims before killing them. Hands and limbs hacked off children and babies were hung from trees, or eaten. More than seven thousand people died.

'They killed everyone, everything in their way. Even the dogs, man. They even killed the fucking dogs.'

As well as your mother and father, I thought. I took my sunglasses off and folded them in my hand. As soon as Roberts was on the evacuation chopper his parents headed back into Freetown to get his grandmother.

'Do you know how it happened?' I asked him. 'Your parents, I mean.' He looked sideways at me and then back at the road, unspeaking. For a minute there was only the sound of tyres on tarmac and the judder of air pulsing through the car windows.

'I lost my parents, too,' I said. 'I was a couple of years younger than you were when it happened.'

Another pause.

I hadn't had this conversation for a long time. 'Plane crash. My dad. Then my mum, you know, I guess she just couldn't take it . . .' I trailed off.

'Sorry, bruv. Sorry.'

'Yeah, me too. But it was a long time ago. I don't even think about my dad that often.' It was true, I didn't. The dreams and memories of my father that had been surfacing of late were unusual, unwelcome like an unexpected squall that leaves you soaked and shivering when you least expect it. I had no defence against my own mind other than to subdue it with alcohol and benzos. But some fragment, some shard of him, would always cut through. My mother, though, she was always there, peering in from the perimeter of my memory.

Roberts dipped the brakes as an aging articulated lorry creaked out in front of us.

'Was that in, uh, *Canada*, that you lost your mum?'

'No, it was in Ireland,' I admitted. For a professional liar, even little truths are hard won. I'd never told anyone exactly what had happened.

'I see. Mine . . . God, this is like some fucked-up show-and-tell shit. I raise your mum's suicide with "butchered by kids".' His eyes filled with tears. 'Fucking *kids*, man.'

Yeah, kids with AKs and machetes, I thought. I pictured the scene. It made me sad in that detached way that other people's disasters do.

'They shot my dad,' he went on, 'and then, when my mum and gran wouldn't come out of the house because they didn't want to be raped or chopped up or whatever fucked-up shit those cunts got off on, they tried to burn them out. Except they wouldn't come out. Our neighbour was the only one who survived on our street. She said she could hear them praying together in Krio over the sound of the flames. *"Papa God, we de na evin, na yu wan gren na God."'* He wiped his cheek with the back of his hand. He was angry, and lost. And I expected he always would be. God only knew I was.

'But he's never there when you need him, is he, the Old Bloke upstairs?' he continued. 'Still, here we are, the orphaned black and white survivors roadshow. Fuck me. Beats working for a living, I s'pose.' There were no comfortable words to speak. He smiled and wiped his cheek again, and we drove on in silence.

Dropping down from the high green hills around Freetown, we turned north-west and into Northern Province. Rice paddies flourished in the swamps sandwiched between the sea and the Highlands that rose further inland. The towns and villages and hours rolled past against a backdrop of rich agricultural land. Robat, Masiaka, Mafila – the names were indecipherable, and at once both familiar and meaningless. The vowels sounded European; the consonants seemed always in the wrong place, confusing pronunciation.

There was no breeze here except the cross-draught created by winding the windows down in the old Nissan. Thick grey clouds boiled on the horizon. We stopped to piss, to stretch our legs, to smoke. The air grew heavier. Hotter. We began to sweat and lapsed into long silences; each digesting the other's tragedies. Then we thundered over the mighty Rokel, which downstream becomes the Sierra Leone River and empties into the Atlantic, cutting Freetown off from Lungi Airport. We bought smoke-blackened river fish and spat the bones out the wound-down windows and sucked condensed milk from miniature-sized tins bought at a roadside shop in Lunsar. The road snagged north-east then due east. It was a good road and before we knew it we were pulling into Makeni itself. But the excitement of arrival dissolved in Roberts's recollections.

'Dirty old town.' He steadied the steering wheel with his elbows and lit a cigarette. 'Just darkness and pot holes, my dad used to say.'

'Looks OK to me. Busy. Bit dusty. Roads are all right, though.' And they were. New tarmacadam, new streetlights and scooter taxis everywhere.

'Bloody *okadas*. They're like flies. Put hardworking taxi drivers out of work, they do.' We were crawling down the main drag, past the university, looking for our hotel.

'What's up with you? It's not that bad. It looks like a decent place to me.'

'Rebel town,' Roberts replied. 'Makeni was their HQ.' People crossed the road in front and behind us: men with boxes of supplies of who knew what on their heads; women leading, cajoling, lifting children; students carrying bundles of books. 'And don't tell me this shower didn't roll over at the first opportunity. "Please save us from the wicked president."' Roberts affected a pathetic, whiney voice, before adding: 'Rebel fuckers.'

We pulled up in front of the DJ Motel.

'*O*-K, mister. Easy does it.' We sat in the Nissan, both staring at the motel's tatty Union Jack awning. A couple of teenagers stood in the doorway, smoking. Half of these 'fuckers' weren't even born when the rebels rocked up.

'The war is over,' I reminded him. 'Long time. And you know what that means?' Roberts said nothing. 'That means there is an uninterrupted supply of beer to the north. So shake a leg. I'm buying you a Star.'

The DJ Motel was in fact just a regular hotel with a large car park at the back. It looked decent and clean. There was a dining room, a bar and a business centre – which comprised one ancient PC, a desk, a printer and an office swivel chair. It played host to a man in impossibly pointed leather shoes and a pinstripe suit bellowing erratically into his mobile phone in French.

I checked us in.

We'd been pre-booked into rooms on different floors by Captain Rhodes. Roberts poured the beers and calmed down. We both knew the war would never be over for him. Being orphaned is a permanent condition. So too, it seemed, was war, or the promise of war, looming above this violent coast. Ninety miles up the road yet another army threatened to invade Roberts's hard-won peace. I resisted the temptation to reassure him about a reality he didn't yet know endangered him.

'Your grandfather,' I asked him, after he'd relaxed into his drink, 'you said he was still alive. I presume you're not numbering him among the evil northern collaborators still roaming the streets of Makeni. Where is he now?'

He took a long swallow of beer and let out a sigh of relief.

'Musala. The old man never left.'

10

The motel rose to three floors behind reception, with external staircases zigzagging up above chipped alabaster columns. There was a lift, too. I took the stairs. I let myself into the cool, dark cave of my room. An aircon unit hummed in the wall alongside the bed. White tiled floor. Mosquito net. Ceiling fan. Sink, shower, loo. Third-world three-star. It would do.

All squaddies loved to repeat the bastardization of that old recruitment catchphrase: *Join the Army! Travel the world! Meet interesting people . . . and kill them!* In UKN, at least, . . . *and stay in shit hotels* would have been just as accurate.

I'd told Roberts to get some rest and that I'd see him downstairs at eight o'clock for dinner. I had to pop out and pick up some medical kit from the university, I explained. I hadn't blinked when Roberts told me his grandfather still lived in Musala. He hadn't seen him for a year. I hoped he was still alive.

Collecting the rifle was straightforward. The dead drop was the boot of a white mid-eighties C-Class tucked away in the corner of the DJ Motel car park. I took the silver key that Captain Rhodes had given to me at the briefing in London. The lid opened with a little leap like heavy German car metal on well-oiled springs does.

Lying flat under a tarp inside the Mercedes was a flat, oblong canvas bag with two shoulder straps. A Velcro patch with a red cross in a white circle was stitched on one side, the Canadian flag on the other. The boot clicked shut again. There was no dust on the tyres. The windscreen was clean. I guessed it had been parked that morning.

I walked the bag upstairs and unzipped it on the bed. The canvas peeled away to reveal a soft, custom-made rifle case; which in turn opened to reveal a scoped Accuracy International sniper rifle with a folding stock. Pockets in the case's padded lining held three magazines, a detachable bipod, a sound moderator and a Leica laser rangefinder. I lifted one of the magazines out. It was already charged. I flicked the rounds out and gave them a once-over. Ten Federal Gold Medal 168-grain 7.62mm full metal jacket boat-tail cartridges: commercially manufactured; match grade; consistent. I snapped them back into the magazine. Their report, deadened by the moderator and the forest, would barely be louder than an unsilenced 9mm. That would help conceal my position, but the enemy would still hear their supersonic crack all right.

I'd need to get close before I could pull the trigger. Tree-density, even in the northern savannah, meant there'd be no chance of a long shot: the maximum distance I was likely to get from the target would be three to four hundred metres – and that was pushing it. Taped to the outside of the folding stock was my elevation table for the Federal Golds and that rifle, out to a thousand metres, calibrated to Sierra Leone's atmospheric conditions for early spring. Captain Rhodes had done her homework.

I had all the tools required to do the job. I just needed to find my target, and fast. As soon as news of Musala falling reached the public, the road north would quickly become monitored, treacherous and then impassable. I put the zipped-up rifle bag in the wardrobe, took a step back and caught myself.

'This is ridiculous,' I said out loud. 'It's like trying to conceal a bloody elephant.' I took the bag back out and slid it under the bed. I considered this, and then returned the bag to the wardrobe. Of course, I wasn't supposed to leave the hotel once I'd made the collection – but I had another, unscheduled, visit in Makeni to make before we set off in the morning. I left the room light on, hung the Do Not Disturb sign on the door knob and hoped for the best.

It was the end of the day now. The sun drops fast in the tropics. No lengthy sunsets: just light, and then dark, with a flash of fire above the waves or trees if there are no clouds to mask it. In Ireland the long evening skies in County Wicklow were choked with wild geese harrying the sun westwards. I preferred this sharp transition. The air was beginning to hum with night insects, but it was still just light.

The Global Assistance Committee office was tucked down a side street behind the hotel – sandwiched between the Catholic church of St Francis Xavier and the Jehovah's Witnesses' Kingdom Hall. I guessed they were hedging their bets – and that they'd saved more souls than both of their neighbours combined.

'*Aw di bodi?*' I greeted the receptionist in the first words of Krio I'd learned from Roberts. She looked at me with a mixture of pity and amusement.

'*Di bodi fayn,*' she replied. And then, in cut-glass English, 'And how is *your* body, mister . . . ?'

'*Doctor* McLean,' I smiled. 'Call me Max, though.'

'I see,' she said, grinning in that way that some women do when they've decided you're not worth flirting with but are keen to see just how much of a fool you can make of yourself before you realize it, too. 'And how can I help you, *Doctor* Max McLean?'

I lied and said I was a heading up to Musala, to conduct a feasibility study on a clinic. She introduced herself as Florence, 'from the Nairobi office'.

'Hard though this might be to believe,' I told her, 'I'm new to Sierra Leone. And it's just that I'm heading up to Kabala tomorrow, and my colleague in Vancouver said one of your people had been up there about a month back for an event – couldn't remember their name. I wondered if I could have a chat with them, you know, to . . .' I stopped talking. Florence had stopped smiling.

'Marie Margai,' she said, simply. There was a silence. And then she continued. 'Marie Margai is the volunteer your colleague told you about.'

'I see,' I said, though I didn't. 'That's great. Do you have a number for her? It would be great to talk to her.'

'Well, Doctor . . . McLean, wasn't it?' I assured her it was. 'I don't think you will have much luck on the telephone.'

'Wow, is the cell phone reception that bad up there?'

'No, Doctor McLean, I mean because she is dead.' My back straightened, and my smile faded too. 'Marie died in February. Was *killed*, in February,' she corrected herself, 'on her way back from opening our school in Kabala.'

'I'm so sorry, ma'am. I didn't . . .' I switched from compassionate face to concerned face. 'But how, I mean why? I thought it was safe up there now.'

'That's the saddest thing, doctor. It is. It's so unusual. She was robbed. Maybe her attacker panicked – who knows? – but she was stabbed, and brutally. For what? That little camera of hers. They wouldn't get twenty dollars in the market for it. She was such a happy, lovely girl. It's so sad.'

It was pitch-black now. I left Florence bathed in the green hue of the neon-lit reception. The flush of mourning that passed over her had made her forget that she hadn't quite trusted me. I stood outside in the street. I wanted to turn around and tell her that her friend hadn't been robbed. She'd been liquidated. Instead I cleared my throat and spat into the gutter and lit a cigarette. The air was heady with frying palm oil and gasoline fumes. I could feel the jagged edge of a benzo comedown cutting in and walked back to the hotel. Roberts was sitting awkwardly in the bar next to a punter wearing a shabby suit and an uncombed Afro. They were being teased by two hookers. So I took dinner alone in my room. Fried chicken, fufu and two bottles of Guinness Export.

I ate slowly. The vague feeling of unease that had

bothered me about Roberts from the outset crystallized into a hard, gleaming fear. This was a black operation: dead drops, unknown assets, classified sources, fake identities and me, an unbadged assassin – all working entirely independently of one another; each player able plausibly to repudiate all the others. It looked like the loose ends were being tied up one way or another: first Sonny Boy, then Marie Margai. Who next, Roberts and Juliet? They linked everyone to everything.

If this operation was being swept up as it went along, they were already as good as dead.

Thump. Thump. Thump.

Where was she? Where was Ana María?

Thump. Thump. Thump.

My right hand found the SIG; I was on my feet, feeling my way to the bathroom. No running water. I pulled the cord to the light above the sink. I looked into the shaving mirror, but it was empty. There was no one there. Ana María wasn't there. I wasn't there. Where my face should have been I saw only the reflection of the tiles on the wall behind me. I put the muzzle of the SIG against the silvered glass and squeezed the trigger.

The mirror dissolved into a shower of diamond-white shards blown back past my head. I saw myself then, standing in the void behind the mirror. The screeching stopped, and I could hear – what? My own heart beating?

Thump. Thump. Thump.

But where was she? Where was Ana María?

And then a bright-white burst of light.

My hand on the bedside light switch.

Makeni. Still in Makeni.

Thump. Thump. Thump.

'Hey, mister.'

Empty bed, sweat-soaked, twisted sheets. Alone. Again.

One o'clock in the morning. I stood to one side and put the muzzle of the little black SIG against the peephole.

'Hey, mister,' the voice hissed. 'I keep you company.'

Before I opened the door I wiped the sweat out of my eyes and put the pistol under the mattress. It was one of the working girls from downstairs. Five-five, shoulder-length wet-look extensions, sheer green blouse, black push-up bra.

'Where's your friend?' I asked.

'With your friend,' she replied. She looked quickly both ways down the corridor, lifted the hem of her skirt and tilted her pelvis. She was naked underneath and exposed herself for a second or two. 'Good company. Good massage. No disease.'

She stepped into the room, and I closed the door.

11

We hit the first road block at eleven o'clock.

After a slow start it had been plain sailing for the first hour or so. The Kabala highway was metalled and well maintained. A steady flow of *poda-podas* ran north – minibus taxis carrying people and bundles of goods deeper into the interior. Trucks and cars like ours snaked around them and the cargoes of people and goods they discharged on to the road every few miles.

We both smoked. Roberts hardly spoke. His pursed lips and half-frown hung somewhere between fear and remorse. Distress, I supposed, at the unknown quality of my discretion; shame, most likely, at the sober recollection of how much he loved – and needed – Juliet.

I felt none of those things. Just an emptiness inside.

By the time he'd wound down the window to hand the Sierra Leone army squaddie his identity card it was like sitting in a smoke-filled pressure cooker. I was glad of the change of atmosphere. Roberts and the soldier spoke in Krio. I smiled, nodded my head and tuned the radio to Bintumani 93.7.

The trooper grinned and waved us on.

'What did you tell him?'

'The truth.'

'Remind me again, Roberts, what's the truth today?'
That made him smile.

'You only been here two days and already you're talking like a Limba.'

'You know what they say, mate – inside every Irishman is a Limba trying to get out.' Roberts half-choked and spat out of the still open window.

'Fuck me, bruv. You got that right. I told him you were a doctor visiting my sister in Kabala, and I was hoping to marry you off and get rich.'

It was unseasonably hot for March. Thirty degrees and climbing, and it wasn't yet midday. Five minutes down the road, we passed two SLA armoured personnel carriers mounted with .50-calibre machine guns. The drivers leaned out of their windows, shouting at each other in conversation in what sounded like Krio. A dozen soldiers milled around in British army surplus uniforms, fiddling with their old British self-loading rifles.

'Is this normal?' I asked.

'Remind me again, Max,' Roberts replied, half-serious, 'what's "normal" today?' That made me smile.

'We've only been on the road for a day, and you're already talking like an Irishman.'

'Well, you know what they say, mate.'

The further north we went, the fewer vehicles met us coming south. Heat haze blurred the road. The radio crackled and died. Try as he might to retune it, Radio Bintumani was dead.

'It happens,' Roberts said, clicking off the radio. 'It's the mountains, they kill the FM signal.'

We carried on in resigned, sweaty silence. A palpable whiff of cheap perfume rose off Roberts's sodden shirt. His frown came back. And then, twenty-five miles outside of Kabala, we ground to a halt. All traffic north had stopped. Nothing moved south. The driver of the *poda-poda* immediately in front of us switched his engine off. The battered white shell of the Mazda taxi disgorged a throng of hot, angry passengers. One by one they grasped the futility of frustration like divine revelation and squatted in the shade of a giant mango tree that overhung the tarmacadam.

I looked at Roberts. We both climbed out.

'This is where the highway ends, bruv,' he explained as we straightened up in the pall of heat rising off the sticky blacktop. He turned to me and waved vaguely in the direction of the highway-cum-car park. 'Here on it's just a dirt road to Kabala. There's usually a jam.'

'And it's always like this?' I had a bad feeling. Roberts did too. He sniffed the air and ground out his cigarette in the dust by the side of the road. 'Nah, not always. I bet you a truck has snapped an axle or something. It's a single track. No way round it. I'll go have a looksee.'

We'd stopped in the shade of the tree. Green mangoes crushed by truck tyres filled the air with a sweet smell of decay and fermentation. I sat on the boot of the car, feet still on the ground. Another *poda-poda* pulled up behind me. The driver grinned and gave me a wave. Emblazoned across his bonnet ran the words 'Prayer is the Key'.

My lips worked their way around the Hail Mary,

stumbling over syllables unspoken after years of disbelief. Once I'd asked Sonny Boy why he prayed to the Virgin just before we inserted into a hot landing site. 'The priest says it works even if you don't believe in it,' he'd grinned. And then the night sky lit up with tracer as our boot heels sank into the Afghan moon dust under the chopper. His body armour stopped three AK rounds that night. I didn't know whether that proved or debunked his priest's counsel.

'Well it ain't good,' Roberts sighed. Fine red dirt from the unmade road had collected in his braids. Beads of sweat broke out across his brow. 'Army. Lots of army. Like, more army than I've seen for ages. They've cut the road, and they're out in the bush. You can see them for miles between the trees. Some shit is going down. Serious shit.' I didn't say anything. Roberts reached into the car and took out a bottle of tepid water. He drank deeply. 'No one in our army is going to piss about in this heat unless it's serious.' He wiped the sweat out of his eyes. 'It's fucking March. It's supposed to be *nice* in the mountains. It must be nearly thirty-five.'

'OK, let's go and talk to them. Turn the car around and get one of these taxi drivers to mind it.' I passed him a folded wad of local notes. Roberts swung the old Nissan out from between the two big taxis parked up on the other side of the road, facing back towards Makeni. Then he recruited a lad with biceps like my thighs to stand shotgun over our ride. I shouldered my day bag with the small medical kit and SIG inside. Roberts carried the rifle bag.

The queue of traffic was rapidly lengthening behind us. Up ahead, it was a mile to the front of the line. Roberts had covered the ground fast. It was no wonder he'd come back sweating. A Sierra Leone army major was holding court, pacifying irate truck drivers while overseeing what appeared to be the establishment of a cordon of troops that spread out either side of the road. Roberts had been right. The soldiers spread out for several hundred metres at least in either direction. I could see clusters of camouflage fatigues standing out against the ochre dust in the spaces where the trees thinned out. The major saw me and waved me over. I was the only white person there, and, I guessed, a perfect excuse to cut short his exposure to dozens of disgruntled motorists.

'Hello, sir,' I said. 'I'm Doctor McLean. Heading to Musala. How d'y'do?' I offered him my hand. He took it with a firm, curt shake.

'Well, as you can see, doctor, we are doing only "so-so".' He looked at Roberts, at our bags. 'Musala?' I nodded. 'That, doctor, will be very difficult today. Maybe tomorrow.'

'I see. What about Kabala?'

'That will also be difficult.' He frowned at me from under heavy eyelids. 'May I see your papers please, doctor?' I handed him my passport and circled around him. He was a good six inches shorter than me, and I didn't want him to have to squint into the sun. He thumbed through the Canadian passport, looked at the entry stamp and handed it back to me almost absent-mindedly.

He had a kind face, polished boots and a Browning Hi-Power on his hip.

'You are a team, you two?' He nodded towards Roberts. I told him we were.

'Only a mad dog or an Englishman would want to drive himself around Salone, sir.'

His frown relaxed, and he took my arm.

'Come.'

A beleaguered lieutenant took his place at the front of the queue of complainants and the three of us – Roberts, the major and I – walked twenty paces to a British army surplus Land Rover Defender. We stood in the meagre shade it threw on the dust.

'I am sorry to say that there has been – how shall we say? – an *outbreak* in Musala. It has already spread to Kabala. We are trying to contain it here, Doctor McLean.'

'Before it reaches Makeni?'

'Exactly, Doctor McLean. Exactly. Before it reaches Makeni. You have broken the code.'

I could feel Roberts recoil behind me and heard his sneakers grub in the dirt. I knew what he wanted to ask, so I posed the question for him.

'Ebola?'

The major's drooping eyes refocused on mine. Sliced into the jet-black skin of his right cheek was a thin line of scar tissue that ran from his right ear to the corner of his mouth. Clean and deep, it bore the unmistakable signature of a straight razor.

'No. It is not that devil.' He'd stopped smiling. 'But the government is afraid people will think so and panic.'

'What,' I asked, 'has "broken out", then?' The major pulled the lobe of his right ear and looked down.

'Uh, *cholera*. The government says it's cholera. Bad cholera.' He spoke softly, although no one else was in earshot. For a moment I thought I actually heard Roberts cough the word "bullshit", but he was just clearing his throat.

'Well, that *is* extraordinary,' I said, lowering my voice, too. 'Cholera is my area of expertise, sir.' I patted the side of my day bag with an open palm. 'And I have just the thing to deal with, oh, a couple of dozen cases right here.' The major looked at me again, carefully, weighing up what exactly I wasn't sure. I produced a stethoscope from the kit with an unnecessary flourish, just in case there was any doubt in his mind about our credentials.

'Good,' he said, finally. 'Good. There is something I would like to show you, doctor. I would be interested in your, uh, *medical* opinion.' And with that he ushered us into the Land Rover. Roberts and I sat in the back. The major rode up front. A vacant-looking corporal took the wheel, and we were on the road again.

For ten kilometres or so we drove along the main, unsurfaced, road to Kabala. The beginnings of the town were reaching out to us – a general store, some low-slung houses and even a dilapidated children's playground set back into the trees: 'A Gift From the People of Germany,' announced a rusted sign above the unused swings and roundabout. I was expecting to see no one, but some people were still on the road. A corn-on-the-cob seller was fanning the coals under a dozen or more leaf-wrapped ears in expectation of a lunchtime rush. There were soldiers, too – spread out, but deployed in numbers along the verges, clinging to whatever shade they could find. If they saw the major's Land Rover in time they saluted; but mostly they were oblivious to us until we'd passed them – my white face at the window causing more than a couple of them to call out 'Sah!' with a smile as we sped along.

The terrain became increasingly hilly, and then we turned off the road, heading west and then north-west around the town towards, the major said, the smaller town of Yakala. He checked his pistol and reholstered it. He looked professional, wary.

'Bandit country,' he said, half-turned to me. Roberts caught my eye and shook his head very slightly with a look that said *No it isn't.*

One track gave way to another. The soldiers thinned out, and then, as we entered the outskirts of a larger village nestled between two steep hills, there was a throng of them, standing out in their dark-green fatigues against the dull browns of the village's mud walls and raffia thatch. I could feel Roberts shifting about beside me as we drew to a halt. The major climbed out and opened my door. The driver did the same for Roberts.

The first thing I noticed was the smell of dead bodies. Roberts swore heavily under his breath.

'Wait here, please,' the major ordered, and walked away from us towards a low, grey concrete building. It contrasted sharply to the other houses in the village, and was ringed by sandbags. A flagpole rose up above it, flying the sun-bleached green, white and blue flag of the

Republic of Sierra Leone. He spoke briefly to a sergeant standing by the door and then went inside, covering his face with a spotless white handkerchief as he did so.

'Police station?' I murmured to Roberts, trying my best to smile at the soldiers while not looking like an idiot.

'No. Army post,' he replied, gazing at his feet. 'The north's covered with them, after the war.'

I looked again, more carefully. The roof was peppered with bullet holes: small black apertures which fanned outwards at their edges to make jagged metal splashes reaching skywards. The bullets that made the holes had been fired from *inside* the building. I looked around on the ground. There was no spent brass to be seen. All about us the rising smell of decaying meat grew stronger. On the top of one of the hills that flanked us I could make out a wood and corrugated metal observation post. There were half a dozen soldiers standing there, too, looking out across the hills, towards the northern forests. All of them wore bandanas across their mouths and noses. There were no civilians to be seen anywhere. No smoke rising from the huts. No sound of children whooping or crying. No sound at all except the interminable buzzing of flies and the boots of the soldiers scraping the dust.

Roberts waved away a bluebottle, took a packet of cigarettes out of his jeans pocket, lit one and offered me the packet. I took it and fumbled, letting the last, bent stick drop out of the soft pack. I bent down to pick it up off the ground and saw another butt on the ground next to it. The letters on the paper above the filter caught my eye: they were written in the Cyrillic Russian alphabet. I picked it up along with my own dropped cigarette and slipped it into my pocket.

The major returned, apparently unmoved by whatever he'd gone to look at in the concrete barrack room. I put the unlit cigarette into the side pocket of my cargo trousers.

'If you have a mask, doctor, wear it. It's hot inside.' He turned to Roberts. 'You stay here.' Roberts nodded, thickening the moist tropical heat with a cloud of tobacco smoke.

I squatted down, unzipped the day bag, and took out a simple face mask from the medical kit. I offered it to the major. He refused, holding up his handkerchief. So I put it on myself and then pulled on a pair of latex gloves. I shouldered the bag and reclipped the stethoscope around my neck. 'You will not be needing that, doctor,' the major said and walked towards the building. I followed behind him and stepped into the pitch-black of the unlit room.

The stench of decomposing flesh was overwhelming. The air was hot and thick with flies. Blinded for a moment by swirls of colour and shifting shapes that erupted in the darkness, I stopped still and waited for my eyes to adjust to the gloom after the bright sunshine outside. Slowly, three bodies emerged from the darkness. They were only barely recognizable as human. One lay at my feet, just inside the door. The chest cavity had been ripped open completely, butterflied out to the sides.

Lungs, a heart and yards of intestine littered the floor. Both arms were missing – one of which I could see was lying against the back wall. The neck and lower jaw were intact, but the crown of the skull and upper jaw were missing entirely. I looked at the major.

'We haven't found it, the skull.' He didn't offer anything else. I stepped over the cadaver, took a small LED torch out of my pocket, and squatted down next to it. I realized I had trodden in a pool of congealed blood. Both thighs had been opened at the groin, the femoral arteries rent open. The genitals were missing. I went up and down the body with the torch carefully. The flesh was badly damaged, and decay had already set in, so it was hard to be sure, but there were no apparent signs of gunshot wounds or tearing from blast fragmentation. There *were* unmistakable signs of muscle being cut with a blade of some sort – by a bayonet, perhaps, or a machete. The wounds were too messy to say for certain. What was left of the man's uniform clung to the remains of his corpse in dark matted shreds.

I swept the torch beam across the floor to the severed arm against the wall. A single eyeball gleamed white on the black-red killing floor as the light from the LED rolled over it. I thought about Sonny Boy, and the grievous injuries I'd inflicted on him. The injuries along the arm were unmistakable: bite marks. Human bite marks deep into the flesh of the biceps. The thumb had been severed, connected to the wrist by a single tendon. The deltoid and upper arm were ragged around the humerus, which was intact and looked as if it had been ripped out of the shoulder socket.

I stood up. The major was playing his own torch over the other two bodies. One was sat up against the same wall the arm rested on; it had been cleanly decapitated. The uniform and the rest of the body were more or less intact – except for a gaping hole in the abdomen, punched through the dead soldier's fatigues, out of which the contents of his stomach had been drawn and which spilled into his lap. His rifle was still in his hand, an old British army SLR. Spent brass cartridge cases littered the floor.

The third body was torn in half. Blood, shit and rotting human sweetbread lay decomposing on the floor in a macabre slick of putrefying bodily fluids. The trachea appeared to have been bitten out. But the head was intact. I pointed the torch at his face. The major looked away then, and I saw why. More terrible than the stench of that human charnel house was the frozen look of utter, abject terror etched into the dead man's features. Eyes wide open, mouth still formed into a ragged circle, screaming in terror or pain or both. Flies feasted on his tongue, buzzed in and out of his flared nostrils.

'His name is Musa Sesay.' The major's voice started behind me. 'I knew him. He was a good boy. A good soldier.' He stopped as abruptly as he started. I said nothing.

I've seen a lot of dead people. And I've killed a lot of people up close. But I'd never seen anything like that – not in Syria's torture chambers, nor in the Colombian cartels' killing rooms. It was as if some depraved scientist had created the essence of fear and given it a human face.

I trained the LED on the arm again. The bites were definitely made by human teeth. I recalled the frantic testimony of John, the pastor who'd witnessed the onslaught in Musala. 'They are eating our souls,' he'd said. 'The devil has come for us. Satan has come to eat us.' They may not have been devils, but whoever had butchered the soldiers was inhumane beyond reckoning. More than simply killed, the soldiers had been devoured.

I switched off the torch. Shafts of light spilled into the room through the constellation of bullet holes punched into the roof. They strafed the bodies but illuminated nothing. I turned to the major, who had lowered his handkerchief and was watching me intently. I took off my mask. Sweat leaked down my back, under my arms, into my eyes.

'So tell me, doctor,' he said, his expression hidden by shadows in the stinking gloom, 'does this look like cholera to you?'

12

Fragments of sunshine surged and dissipated across the surface of the pool. An elderly Lebanese man swam gentle lengths in what was left of the morning cool. Two white women spread out on yellow sun loungers. Waiters in gleaming smocks hovered, observing the international flotsam and jetsam washed up on that tiny spit of land and sand jutting into the Atlantic.

When the wind changed, the salt-tang of the ocean and chlorine-whiff of the pool gave way to a heady scent of heat and decay that rolled down from the mountains and the forests that swept and climbed through the interior. Perched there, staring into the blue void of the ocean, it felt like I was sitting on the edge of the world while all the time feeling the hand of an invisible giant pushing hard against my back; the enormous, unseen pressure of the continent bore down, as if driving us all into the sea by sheer force of gravity, or history, or will.

When we had come back to Freetown from Kabala I hadn't checked-in with London. Instead, after Roberts had dropped me off at the hotel, I'd sat drinking at the bar alone, thinking about the charnel house and what it meant.

When the major and I stepped back into the sunlight

he walked me, unspeaking, to a wattle-and-daub hut a little way off the dusty track that ran through the village. He motioned for me to enter. 'It's like this all the way to Musala,' he said and waited outside in the midday heat while I went inside. I opened the rush door, bent down and ducked under the lintel into sweaty, buzzing darkness: the air was as dense with flies as the barrack room had been. The headless body of a baby lay turtle-like on its back by the fire grate. A young woman, its mother, lay next to it, her face missing, arms snapped. Her cloth skirts were piled up around her waist. The join of her thighs was a shredded mess of bone and gristle. Her genitals had been ripped apart so violently that part of her womb had been pulled out along with the small intestine. In a sagging grey amniotic sack the beam of my torch picked out the tiny pale-grey corpse of an unborn child curled up in a pool of thick black blood.

I'd seen enough.

All four soldiers billeted in the village had been killed – three in the barrack room, one on the hill manning the OP – along with all the women and children and elderly men. There were no survivors at the scene; every man of fighting age had been taken. There was no evidence of a firefight. Sure, the soldiers had opened fire. But in keeping with John's voicemail, there was no evidence that they'd been fired *on*, or actually hit anything themselves. This 'infection', the major said, had bypassed Kabala but was ravaging the outlying villages. It was like trying to fence a river. Who knew where it would go next? The trail ended there: the unit that had rampaged through the countryside around Kabala had vanished, and the Sierra Leone army, he said, was not ready to tackle the problem at source in Musala – where I knew the entire local garrison had been wiped out.

'What,' I'd asked him, '*is* the problem? The real problem. I mean I understand what's happening, but . . .'

'Do you, doctor?' The major cut me off. 'As we say in Salone, "The bird that knows is different from the bird that understands." These things you have seen here, they are not *natural*. We are walking through the shadow of the valley of death.' I studied him carefully and we faced each other, unspeaking, for a moment. Then he looked over his shoulder and continued quietly, 'At times like this it's better for soldiers to think what they say and not say what they think.'

After all, the major told me, the army was under strict orders not to speak to the press – but as I was a doctor he could talk to me without disobeying those orders. What I chose to do with what I'd seen, with what I thought I knew, was, he suggested, up to me. I supposed he wanted me to leak the news of what had happened – that an attack, and not a cholera epidemic, was to blame. He accompanied me and Roberts back to where his men had cut the Kabala road. No one spoke.

More politically sensitive than a new outbreak of Ebola, even the *rumour* of a rebel resurgence could be enough to topple the government. So the authorities had settled on 'cholera' to explain why it was no longer possible to travel to the far north. I didn't press him on what exactly he meant by 'unnatural'. It takes faith to engage with faith. One man's devil is another man's rebel. Whatever the actual 'problem' in Kabala, the cholera lie would at best survive the weekend. Both of us wanted to know what we were up against.

'I cannot fight something if it does not exist,' he'd told me as we parted.

Roberts saw the blackened blood on my boots and asked quietly what I'd seen. I told him he was lucky to have stayed outside, and that it was people, not cholera, or Ebola, that had done the killing. He stared hard at the road as we drove back to Freetown, no doubt thinking about the past; I stared into the bush, thinking about the future and the imminent threat of ambush. But no attack came, and conversation between us dried up. I couldn't tell him that what I'd seen was likely proof of what Mason, King and Rhodes had impressed upon me in London: that a new, Russian-backed rebel force was up and running – and heading south. What none of them apparently realized – or at least hadn't briefed me on – was that their tactics made the activities of the rebels in the last war look positively restrained. That the major was reaching to the Psalms and a supernatural explanation was understandable. You can't name what you don't know: and the face of his trooper frozen in horror was beyond anything either of us had experienced.

If the methods the rebels had used to wipe out that village were being applied in occupied Musala – and other towns – the consequences would be horrific. Roberts's grandfather would not have survived.

Sonny Boy had been deeply disturbed, actually driven mad by something he'd encountered in-country. For days I'd wondered what that something could have been. After shining my torch on the face of that dead squaddie, I felt one step closer to finding out. I needed to discover what had frozen his face in mortal terror before it was too late. I had no desire either to be transfixed like that myself, or be consigned to a 'research facility', like Sonny Boy had been.

I couldn't ask Sonny Boy, of course. But if I could find Micky, the American he'd been hanging around with in Freetown, I might get closer to the truth of what was happening up north. One thing was for certain: either London didn't know, or didn't want me to know, that not only didn't it look like an *ordinary* rebel insurgency, it didn't look like a rebel insurgency *at all*. The fact that they'd hit rural villages but bypassed Kabala and Yakala suggested they were probably travelling light – raiding for recruits at the end of their operational range. Taking Musala made more sense: it was the nearest town to their base and gave them access to the Mong River, if that was important to them. But rebels – all rebels, even psychopaths like the old RUF – need at least some of the people to support them. In the civil war Makeni had been full of civilians getting on with whatever life they could manage under RUF control. No civilians meant no food, no shelter and no workforce for a rebel army. Wiping out everything in your path might be desirable in a fully mechanized war: in an insurgency it was madness.

*

The women adjusted themselves on the loungers simultaneously: synchronized sunbathing. The elderly Lebanese continued his laps of the pool. I lit a Marlboro and remembered the cigarette butt I'd found in the village. I fished it out of my pocket and turned it over in my fingertips. Stolichnaya vodka is sold the world over. *Prima Stolichnaya* cigarettes were nearly impossible to find outside of Russia.

London had been right about the Russians at least. I was under strict instructions not to kill any. After what I'd seen I wasn't sure whether that was an order I'd be obeying. What troubled me was that even for Spetsnaz and rebels like the RUF the horror show they'd left behind wasn't just macabre, it was incredibly physically demanding. Hacking off an arm, or cutting open a vagina: easy; tearing out lumps of flesh or limbs from sockets with your bare hands: almost impossible. The Sierra Leone army major was right about one thing: violence like that is not natural.

It was time to start searching for Sonny Boy's American friend. I dropped the cigarette end into the ashtray, picked up my local phone and connected to the Tor browser. So far this job had demanded more of me as a sleuth than a sniper. That wasn't normal. But the more detail I could gather about what trouble I was getting into, the more likely I'd be able to get out of it again, too.

'May I speak to Michael please?'

A bright young Californian assured me she would put me through.

'And who may I say is calling?'

'Colonel Smith, from the WHO.'

'One moment, Mister, er, Colonel Smith?' Her voice rose in an irritating West Coast half-question. Definitely Californian. I stared at the swimming pool, unfocused, still shaking off the buzz of the Valium from the night before. The line clicked, and then hummed gently for a few seconds with a synthesized rendition of 'Purple Haze'. The line clicked again. 'I'm sorry, Colonel Smith sir, did you say "Michael"?' I confirmed that I did. 'I'm sorry,' she continued, 'but we don't actually have a "Michael" working here?'

'Sure you do. Micky, you know? This is USAID, right?'

'Yes, this is USAID, sir. But, er, I'm really sorry, sir, we don't have a Michael in the office?'

'No, Miss, I'm sorry to have bothered *you*. He was here what, three or four weeks ago? He must have gone back Stateside. I'll try his cell phone.' There was a long pause. 'Hello?'

'I, er, it's just I don't believe we've ever had anyone here with that name, sir.'

I hung up.

So there was no Micky at the Sierra Leone office of the US government's aid agency. But Juliet had definitely said he'd worked at USAID. I kept calling. No Micky – or Michael, or Misha, or Mícheál – in their Guinea or Liberia offices, either – and nothing obvious on the web. Then I tried different US agencies. Still nothing. Michael, it seemed, was not a popular name in US agency circles. There were no relevant public listings at the US embassy – neither in Sierra Leone nor along the coast.

Hot coffee arrived on a silver tray. The ashtray was refreshed. Ice water was poured into a tall glass sweating condensation. It was almost like being on holiday.

The one detail stressed most by Mason, and, in a rare moment of unity, agreed to by King, was that there must be no US involvement in the operation. And yet apparently Sonny Boy had been running with the Yanks – or at least *a* Yank.

Not having the Americans on board came at a cost. Not having their intelligence slowed me down. Not having their firepower limited my options. There was no obvious benefit to *not* having the CIA stick its nose in. The Agency had assets and manpower. I was here unsupported and alone.

Almost alone.

Roberts sat down at the table I'd camped out at, shaded by a huge, square sun umbrella. He poured himself a coffee before the white-smocked waiter could reach him and looked around.

'This is mental,' he said, evidently impressed.

'No, it's a swimming pool.'

'I mean sitting here, you know? I haven't been inside since the evacuation in ninety-nine.' He sized up the two sunbathing women, who turned in perfect coordination on to their backs. 'Nice presidents.'

'You've cheered up. I expect they've tarted it up a bit since the rebels tried to book in.' I nudged the packet of cigarettes towards him. 'Amazing they got this far.'

'They spread everywhere, man. Uptown; downtown; through the countryside. Just like Ebola. You don't understand, they were like a fucking virus, bruv, a disease. You could only control it when you took out Makeni. That was their brain, their centre.'

I stood up abruptly, still holding my phone, thumbing the keys.

'Roberts, you are a genius.'

'Of course,' he nodded, with a confused frown. I stepped out of earshot and into the heat of the sun.

'This is the Center for Disease Control, Freetown office. How may I direct your call?'

'May I speak to Micky, please? It's Colonel Smith here at the WHO.'

Pause. Exhale.

'I'm afraid . . .'

'Miss, we have an inbound Class Six biohazard to FNA,' I interrupted her, 'ETA twelve-hundred. I'm with the Global Outbreak Alert and Response Network.'

Pause. Inhale.

'Micky . . . the professor,' she corrected herself, 'is returning to Freetown from Makeni this morning, Colonel Smith. Y'all can try his personal cell phone. He should be landing at the Aberdeen helipad any time now.' She was all sing-song vowels and slurred consonants. A Southerner for sure, from Atlanta most likely, she couldn't be too helpful. I gratefully accepted her offer of his phone number and declined that of further assistance.

*

One by one they emerged from the yellow and white hull. Heads bowed, urgent, hats in hand, they scuttled down the steps and spilled off the flight line into the car park. Some looked disoriented. Others struck out with purpose and direction. Everyone switched their phones on. I watched, waited and dialled. Micky picked up. Six-one, two hundred pounds, black goatee, light-blue jacket, tan briefcase. I killed the call before he spoke. He didn't look alarmed: dropped calls were a fact of life on SierraTel. He was alone. He climbed into a HiLux double-cab in the parking lot; I climbed on to a motorcycle taxi I'd stolen from the hotel. We both headed into town.

At first I thought he was heading to the CDC office, or the US embassy at Hill Station. Instead he kept going and wound his way up towards Regent, a mountainous little town five minutes further on. The views were spectacular. And so was the villa the big Toyota drew up at. I pulled up around a bend in the road in front of another equally impressive mansion and walked back to the gates Micky had now vanished through. The security guard jumped at the sight of an unknown white man turning up unannounced on foot.

'At ease,' I said as I saluted him, walking through the smaller security side entrance and straight past him, counting my steps towards the front door. The HiLux sat burning hot in the courtyard, all glass and reflected heat. 'Tell the professor I'll wait downstairs.'

He worked his mouth, but no sound came out. First his hand moved up to return my salute, then to his radio, then to the Beretta on his hip, and back to his radio again. By the time he'd made up his mind I was already inside.

I met Micky on the stairs. His descent came to an abrupt halt, stopped by the silenced barrel of the SIG semi-automatic.

'Kneel down, hands in the air.' He did as he was told. 'OK, now bring the walkie-talkie slowly to your mouth. Tell the sentry everything is fine and that you don't want to be disturbed ...' He spoke calmly. No obvious code-words.

'Roger that, professor,' came the crackled reply.

'Now throw the handset on to the bed. That's good. Now lie down slowly, flat on your belly, face down, arms and legs spread out like a starfish. OK, good. Do not move. If you move your arms or your legs I will shoot you. Do you understand?'

He said he did.

We were in the villa's master bedroom – the centre-piece of an air-conditioned palace of marble floors and half-finished wiring, all mirrors and ill-fitting hardwood joinery. There were no pictures, no personal effects and, except for the guard at the gate, no visible staff.

'Who are you?' He spoke in a nondescript mid-Atlantic drawl, muffled by the cold stone floor pressing against his lips. 'Colonel Smith, I guess. Huh?'

I wasn't going to get close enough to find out if he was armed. The house was quiet. I stood at four o'clock to his head, SIG trained on his back.

'The very same,' I said. 'But you can call me Max, Max McLean.' Slowly he craned his head up and round to look at me, his palms and insteps held fast to the floor. His face was blank. Not even a flicker of recognition. 'Sonny Boy sends his regards.' His head sagged almost imperceptibly, eyes cast down to the floor. It was an uncomfortable position to hold, looking back at me like that, and purposefully so. 'Sergeant Martin Mayne, to you,' I added in a thicker-than-usual Wicklow brogue. 'He was my mate.'

He kept his mouth shut, quite possibly making the same calculations I would in his position: deny everything or say enough to placate the man with the gun? In the end it nearly always comes down to this: will he kill me anyway? Do I have a chance of killing him first?

'I heard he wasn't so well,' Micky said at last. 'How's he doing?'

'He's dead,' I answered.

'How?' He looked back up at me. The bluff went out of his voice. He sounded genuinely concerned.

'I killed him.'

'You . . . *what*?' He seemed to relax then. He looked away and put his face back to the floor again. 'I don't understand.'

'Me neither. Perhaps we can help each other out. We've both just come back from Makeni. Quite a coincidence. I hear there's a nasty infection north of there. Spreading, too. And you, you work for the Center for Disease Control, right? So you'd know all about infections, wouldn't you?'

All I could hear above the hum of the generator outside was the rasp of Micky's breath on the floor. He exhaled hard.

'You mean the cholera outbreak?'

'Yeah, that one. The "cholera" outbreak that turns soldiers inside out and rips the cunts out of nursing mothers.'

'I don't . . .'

'The same cholera outbreak that drove Sonny Boy mad. Must be pretty scary, eh? Because Sonny Boy Mayne didn't scare easy, did he?'

'I . . . I don't know.'

'I think you do know, Micky. I'm not going to fuck with you. You either tell me what you know right now or I'll kill you, right now.' I cocked the SIG's hammer – which was unnecessary to fire a shot, but lent itself well to the theatrics of threat escalation.

Intimidating someone with a gun is a bad idea. Either draw it and use it or leave it alone – because as soon as you point a pistol at someone you give them the right to kill you. Or to try to. And if you point a gun too close at someone who knows what they're doing, chances are you're going to be looking down the wrong end of your own barrel before you can say 'Hollywood bullshit'. It only works if you're prepared to follow it through to the logical conclusion. If the person you've just drawn on counters with 'What are you going to do, shoot me?' then you only have one option: where you shoot them, and how many times, depends on how much sense you need to get out of them afterwards.

'OK, OK.' He craned his head around again. His face

was taut. He was either well trained and just playing along – or genuinely scared. 'They sent me with him, with Mayne. We went up north together. I have clearance, OK? The army weren't letting anyone go further than Kabala. CDC always has clearance.' He looked at me plaintively. That much was true: agents from the US government's Center for Disease Control have an exceptional level of clearance – I'd met them operating alongside Navy SEAL teams deep inside Syria the year before, investigating a suspected biological weapons attack. 'That's it,' he concluded.

'That's what? Where up north?'

'Man, I don't know, some fucking village.' He turned to look at me again. His eyes were focused. He was playing scared.

'Think harder. Name.'

'K . . . K something.'

'Name. Right now, Micky,' I said. And then his phone rang. A loud, urgent buzzing resonated off the marble floor. It was trapped underneath him.

'I have to answer. Security check-in from the embassy.'

'Where is it?'

'Left-hand pants pocket.'

'OK, slowly. Turn over. Very slowly.'

Getting a call made sense because being almost alone in a remote mansion in West Africa didn't. Whoever he was, someone had to be keeping tabs on him. The gate guard was most likely on loan from Marine Corps embassy security, posing as a local. But one man isn't enough to protect you when you're being hunted.

If I'd had more time I'd have made him strip when we first came into the room – far safer than a weapons search, which I hadn't done either. The buzzing grew more impatient, reaching a crescendo as he raised his knee and dipped his left hand into his trouser pocket. I adjusted my grip on the SIG. He looked at me and saw I meant it. And to *know* I meant it, that meant he *definitely* wasn't scared. He was a pro.

And then the buzzing was blotted out by the flat report of a pistol shot. A hole opened up in the thigh of his trousers, and then with a skidding crack the mirror behind me shattered. The bullet had grazed my left temple. I fired a split second after him, my point of aim fractionally high and right of the hole in his trousers. The *phutt* of the silencer was followed by a sharp snap as my bullet slammed into the pistol hidden in his pocket. The force and shock of the impact spun him sideways and jerked his hand clear. His index finger was blown off at the knuckle; palm and wrist torn open. The phone stopped ringing. A thin line of high white noise hummed in my head. His gunshot would have been heard a hundred metres away or more.

He lay there, staring at his wound, clutching his wrist with his good hand. A thick slick of bright-red blood spread out from underneath him. His jacket was torn at the shoulder. The round had travelled up his arm and exited out of his left deltoid, shredding his radial and brachial arteries on the way to the ceiling. Fine white plaster dust fell on him from where the bullet had lodged above him. He had around three minutes to live. Five at the outside. Freak shots: they never happen when you want them to, and always happen when you don't.

Downstairs, a screen door slammed. I counted slowly under my breath. At eight I took one step back, turned towards the bedroom door and fired twice into the chest of the gate security guard as he entered the room. The Beretta clattered to the floor. I kept my eyes on Micky and walked over to the guard, who was sprawled on his back, and put the lip of the silencer on to his left eye. It twitched. I angled the barrel away from me and fired. Micky hadn't moved.

I walked back towards him, stopping six feet away, SIG aimed at his chest. Hand injuries are excruciating; up there with the worst of them. His face was racked with pain, but he didn't scream. There was so much blood on the floor he must have known he was bleeding out.

'Bad call, Micky – or whoever the fuck you are. CDC or CIA? DIA?' I knew he wouldn't tell me, and it didn't matter anyway.

'Karabunda,' he gasped. 'The village was called Karabunda.' He was still telling me what he thought I would already know. His teeth ground together. His face went grey. He would soon go into hypovolemic shock. And he wouldn't come back from that.

'Why you? Why CDC? There *is* no fucking cholera, Micky. Karabunda's a rebel camp not a fucking hot zone.' He didn't answer. His hand was clamped hard around his bleeding wrist – but the damage ran all the way up.

There are only two ways of extracting information

from a professional suspect: either you buy it from them; or they buy back their life from you. I squatted down, unslung the day bag from my back and took out a tourniquet and a packet of haemostatic gauze.

He twisted on to his side again, rocking back and forth on the floor. The marble was staining red in every direction.

'Why? Why did *you* go to Karabunda?' His face was leaching colour rapidly, fading from grey to white before my eyes. Beads of sweat hung below his hairline. I tossed him the tourniquet and coagulant and walked behind him. 'You've got what, a couple more minutes?' Micky rolled over. He let go of his wrist and fumbled with the tourniquet. 'So you want me to help you with that or what?' He tried to follow me with his eyes, but the pain got the better of him.

'I went to negotiate. To talk.'

'Talk to who, Micky?' I squatted down and cocked my head to one side. I was losing him.

'The Russians. Talk to the Russians.'

'About what, Micky? Talk to them about what?'

'A deal.'

I didn't understand, and we were both running out of time.

'Did you make it to the camp? Did you get to Karabunda?'

'For God's sake help me. Please. I'll tell you everything.' He was becoming incoherent with pain and loss of blood.

'Sonny ditched you, didn't he? He went north again

without you. Why?' Micky's breathing was shallow and fast. The pool of blood had stopped spreading and began to darken and set on the cool floor. 'Why did he go it alone?'

'To break the deal,' he hissed through gritted teeth. 'Dumb bastard didn't understand.'

'How, Micky? Break it how? You need to start making sense. Now.'

'A photograph. He took a photograph.'

'Of what?'

'The scientist. The fucking scientist.'

'You mean the old white man? You saw him?'

'Mayne saw him. Took a photo.'

'By the car? You mean the photo by the car at the school in Kabala?'

'No, at the camp. He got to the camp.'

I asked him where the photograph was. He balled up and shook his head.

'Couldn't find it.'

I looked at his arm. The exit wound was too high to get a tourniquet above it. Saving him wasn't an option. It never had been.

His jaw relaxed, and his eyes defocused. Spittle foamed at the corners of his mouth. Sweat and saliva pooled on the floor underneath his cheek. He smiled and then closed his eyes.

'They're perfect, just . . . perfect.' A long, deep death rattle ebbed and flowed in his lungs as if he was repeating his last words over and over again: *perfect, perfect, perfect* . . .

I leaned over and shot him in the side of the head. Picking up my spent brass wasn't necessary: London and

Langley, Moscow – they'd know who'd done it anyway. I put the medical kit back in the day bag and went through his pockets: one Glock sub-compact 9mm, still useable; one iPhone – locked; one old Nokia on a local SIM – unlocked; and one security pass in the name of Professor Michael Montague. I stowed them all in the bag, too, along with the sentry's Beretta.

Then as I turned to leave the room it hit me. My father had been right. There are no misses, and no coincidences. Only consequences. Never mind the cosmic high five. Sonny Boy – that mad, bad bastard just reached out and slapped me on the back.

'Juliet', the only person to place the white man in the camp at Karabunda, was classified as an 'untested' source in the MI6 Intelligence Report for the same reason that the information could neither be evaluated nor disseminated: because the collecting officer had gone insane, and no one apart from the madman knew what or where the original evidence was.

I'd never have guessed Sonny Boy was either a photographer or a Shakespeare fan. Goes to show you never can tell.

A door creaked behind me. Emerging from the en suite was a young African woman, wrapped in a towel. She startled and started crying as I levelled the SIG at her. She slid down the door frame to the floor.

So that's why he came here alone and not to the office.

She looked at me through her tears and said simply: 'Please.'

13

Roberts rubbed his eyes and peered at me through the morning shadows cooling the beach. The sun was not yet over the mountains, but the sea was already hard blue. I'd spent the night at a guest house across town as the news from the north began to break. Local radio stations buzzed with chatter about a rumoured cholera outbreak. Were the authorities trying to cover up an Ebola outbreak? Why was Musala cut off? Sierra Leone's shock-jocks had questions: no one from the government had answers.

'Where did he sleep?'

'Who? Sleep where?'

Roberts was wrapped in a bright-orange kikoi, which he patted in vain looking for a packet of cigarettes. I offered him a Marlboro. He took it.

'The engineer, the big Irish fella you were talking about the day I arrived. Where did he sleep?'

'He . . .' Roberts dragged hard as I lit his cigarette, '. . . at the Barmoi, on the peninsula.' He exhaled a fog of blue smoke and jerked his thumb behind him, pointing up the beach. The beads on his wrist clicked. 'What time is it?'

'No, here. When he stayed here, where did he sleep?'

'What? Max, man, I don't . . .'

'Juliet said he was supposed to stay here, with you, *again*, but you got a call to say he'd been casevaced.'

'*Cazzie*-what?'

'Come.' I pushed past him into the beach house. Even though it was just getting light on the beach, the darkness inside was disorientating. The door opened on to a living space of rugs and furniture. A long mosquito net cordoned off a sleeping area which made up a third of the room. A palm oil night light burned on a dresser by a low, wide bed. It lit the shape of Juliet curled up like a baby under another circular net hanging from the ceiling. There were two doors ahead of me. I turned to look at Roberts.

'What the fuck, man?' he hissed, and then, after reading my expression, 'On the right. The door on the right.'

I stepped in and found an old-fashioned round light switch – the sort you might have found in England in the 1950s. It clicked a sixty-watt bulb into life, suspended over a shiny poured-concrete floor. Against the far wall was the metal frame of a single bed, the mattress made up with simple white linen. The mosquito net suspended from a metal hoop above it was furled and tucked to one side. At the foot of the bed there was a writing table and chair fashioned from reclaimed wood, and next to that, on the left-hand wall, a brightly painted wardrobe. The centre of the room was marked by a loosely woven red cotton mat. Roberts and Juliet were not rich, but they lived pleasantly enough – or at least, I supposed, she made sure they did.

I stopped still.

The sound of the ocean pulling on Lumley Beach filtered into the room. There was no movement from Juliet next door. Roberts stood beside me. He was breathing hard. He was, I suspected, in the process of realizing that he had no idea who I really was, what I was really doing – or what I could, or would, do. As much as he might not have liked that, he was wound into whatever was happening as much by our disquieting road trip north as by the money London paid him to be my tour guide.

Right then there were only two possible outcomes for Roberts: submission or rebellion. I turned to him.

'It's cool. We're cool,' I reassured him. 'There's something here. Something the engineer left behind. *May* have left behind.' Roberts's shoulders relaxed. He smoothed his left palm over his ragged braids and down his neck. 'I need it, need to find it.'

'What, like now? It's six o'clock in the fricking morning.'

'Yeah, like now. And it's already six-forty-two. You're going to love working with me. Go and put the coffee on. And don't wake Juliet.'

I turned back towards the bed and shrugged the day bag off my shoulders. The door clicked shut softly behind me. How Sonny Boy had ever laid out his six-foot-six length on that tiny single mattress was a mystery. I put the bag down and went to work. I stripped the bed and ran my fingers around the stitching at the corner seams. Nothing. I unfolded the black sprung knife and made a lateral cut the length of the mattress. Foam and springs. No clues.

Then I went clockwise around the room – starting at the headboard. Then the wastepaper basket; the wardrobe; desk; chair; mat. Nothing. Within a few minutes the room looked like it had been hit by a tornado. A cockroach bolted for the door. The drawer split apart with a sharp crack as the hardened steel blade cantilevered the wooden base upwards. If that didn't wake Juliet, nothing would.

But it was Roberts who walked in, coffee in hand.

'What the fuck are you *doing*? Dis is ma fuckin' 'ouse, mate! Seriously!'

He was aghast; and scared.

'I told you what I'm doing.' I was on my knees, sweeping my palms under the carcass of the wardrobe.

And then I saw it.

'Give me a hand.'

Roberts waved the coffee cups around and then, failing to find a flat surface other than the floor, put them down on the smooth concrete. Together we lifted the iron bed frame and turned it over. Submission, not rebellion. Roberts was now an accomplice; part of the enterprise.

'Rest it on its back.'

The bed frame languished in the middle of the room, stranded like an upturned metal beetle. The mesh of springs spanning the frame sagged pathetically. I wondered if it had been defeated by Sonny Boy. The four legs pointed towards the ceiling. Three of them were capped with a disk of soldered metal. One had been sheered open, a dark eye socket staring blankly at the light bulb. I took the torch out of my pocket and shone it down the tube.

Nothing.

I spat on my index finger and gently rotated it knuckle deep around the inside of the bed leg and then withdrew it slowly. Stuck to the pad of my finger was half a cigarette paper, damp with saliva. Shining bright-blue in the glare of the LED beam was one word handwritten in biro: *Juliet*.

I turned around. She was standing there, naked except for a pair of white cotton briefs and a silver pendant glistening at her neck. She covered her breasts slowly with crossed forearms and stared at me, mouth open, realization dawning. She was, simply, beautiful. Which – although it shouldn't have – made everything that followed all the harder.

'Why are you here?' Her eyes darted around the room and then back to me. 'What are you . . . what have you done?' She took a half-step back into the gloom of the living room.

'Don't run,' I warned her. I turned to Roberts. 'Neither of you. Sit down. Both of you.'

'Or what, hard man? Eh? Man, fuck you! My house! In my house! No, fuck you.' Roberts's eyes were wild, but he didn't move. I handed him the cigarette paper. He looked at it and then at Juliet. 'What the . . . ?'

'I said, sit down.' I scooped up the sheet I'd taken off the mattress and tossed it to Juliet. She kept one hand across her breasts; with the other she caught the sheet and pulled it across her chest. She sat down. Roberts followed suit. I squatted on my haunches in front of her.

'Sonny Boy, the man who was here, the big Irish engineer, he gave you something.' She broke my gaze and looked at the floor. 'Look at me. He gave you something. You have to give it to me. Do you understand?'

She looked up, and tears rolled down her cheeks. I could hear Roberts's breathing and the chirp and drone of distant morning traffic creeping its way into the bedroom.

'Now.'

She didn't move. Neither did Roberts. I could feel the SIG in the waistband of my trousers. I contemplated pushing the tip of the silencer into the hollow between her breastbone and her trachea — but unlike Micky, I couldn't shoot Juliet, or even threaten to. I needed Roberts. And she wasn't guilty of anything, except maybe infidelity.

Juliet moved her hands up, slowly, to behind her neck. The sheet fell away. Roberts grunted his disapproval. Looking neither at me nor Roberts she unhooked the clasp of the necklace and dropped it into my palm. I stood up and backed away from them and then turned the pendant over between my left thumb and forefinger. It was a plain, hinged silver locket, about an inch long, engraved with the initial 'J'.

'He gave you this?' Roberts and I spoke simultaneously.

'You said it was from your mum,' Roberts continued. 'What the fuck? It's got your fucking initial on it . . .' He ran both his hands down his face and then held them up as if in surrender. 'Jules, baby . . .' He stopped and looked up at me and then the floor.

'Calm down,' I said, fiddling with the catch, 'it's not her initial. It's probably his mother's, right?'

'Oh, that's fine then, yeah? Like totally fine. Like man-mountain Irish Romeo gives my woman his *mother's* locket? Yeah, that's great, fucking great.' He looked up at me. I touched the SIG behind my back and spoke to Juliet.

'Don't run. Promise?' She nodded. Her hands hovered out in front of her, palms up, fingers apart. Tears dripped on to her breasts. I told her to cover up and she wrapped herself absent-mindedly in the sheet, toga-style, wiping her eyes as she did so. She looked sad and alone.

The locket popped open under pressure from my thumbnail to reveal a recent portrait of Juliet, taken on the beach by their bar. She was looking into the lens, happy, her hair like a mane of fire in the setting sun. I opened the knife again and worried the tip under the photo. It popped out to reveal a piece of folded plasticized paper packed into the recess of the pendant. I handed the locket back to Juliet. She gripped it tightly. The silver chain looped over her wrist. She remained on the floor, but Roberts picked himself up. He was hesitant, calculating possibilities.

I folded the knife back on itself, pocketed it and unfolded the piece of paper that had been hidden in the locket. It was a three-by-two-inch photograph and showed a balding white man – a scientist, Micky had said – walking between two traditional round African huts. His face was deeply tanned. He was in his mid-sixties.

There were other figures in the background, out of focus, some with black and some with white faces. In the bottom right-hand corner of the image was a red, burned-in date stamp: the photograph had been taken five days before Sonny Boy had been evacuated back to England. The image caught the man mid-step, exactly between the two thatched rondels, walking left to right. He was looking down, as if watching his step, face quartered away from the camera towards the line-up to his left. His arm was crooked, as if about to deliver a salute. It was, unquestionably, the man caught on camera with Colonel Proshunin by the school in Kabala; it was, unquestionably, my target.

I turned the photograph over. By now Roberts was standing beside me, looking at the paper. Written on the back in a thin, spidery hand were the words: 'Karabunda. *Cód Súlúch*'.

'Karabunda,' he said. 'That's way up north. My grandad used to hunt there when he was a kid.'

'What's it like?' I asked. 'The terrain, I mean.'

'Hot. Riddled with caves. It's a million miles from anywhere.' He stretched his right finger out and pointed at the scrawl. 'What's that?' he asked me. '*Cod* what? It's not Limba.'

'*Code ssoo-luke*,' I said. 'It's Irish.'

The room was growing hot. Juliet had stopped crying. Beads of sweat swelled at Roberts's temples. We were standing close to each other. He looked at me and asked again what it meant.

'Code Zulu,' I said.

'Right. Great. My missus has been havin' it off with the Jolly Green Giant and now you're speaking gibberish. What does it mean, Max? What does it fucking *mean*?'

'*Maraigh gach éinne*,' I said. 'It means *kill them all*.'

14

I crouched down on the concrete floor again and reached over for one of the coffee cups Roberts had carried in while I'd been dismantling the room. The harsh, bitter kick helped bring the room back into focus. There were only two cups. I offered the remainder of mine to Juliet, but she waved my hand away with a toss of her head. Roberts sat down again, too, and drank from his; we all lit cigarettes.

'Is that a gun?' Roberts said, looking at the bulge the SIG made in the T-shirt behind my back.

'Uh-huh,' I agreed.

'So what . . . If she'd run would you have shot her?'

'Uh-huh.'

Juliet looked at me.

'I wish you bloody had,' she said.

'This is fucked up,' Roberts moved to take a drag on his cigarette but lowered his hand, 'properly fucked up. First you fuck my head up in some weird rebel-cholera mass grave mash-up; then you fuck my house up; and now you're fucking up my marriage.' I nodded slowly and sucked the inside of my cheeks. 'Max,' he said, exasperated, 'who do you think I am?'

It wasn't time to speak yet, so I kept quiet and kept listening.

'All right, I'll tell you. I'm a fucking shit-scared taxi

driver posing as a translator; a professional beer-drinking skirt-chasing beach-brother who got lucky with the girl of his dreams and who's just about holding it together with some magic cash from white boys in suits.' His voice was rising. His Adam's apple started to flutter. 'I've been scared my whole life, Max. I was a scared kid in the war and I was scared shitless by Ebola. I've lost everything, man, everything – over and over again. Mum, Dad, my auntie, my home. Even my fucking country. Everything. Everything except her. And now, and now . . . and now what, man? Now fucking what?' He was crying freely. Juliet was weeping, too. 'I don't want to be scared any more.' He scraped the snot and saltwater away from his nose and eyes with the back of his hand. 'So tell me, man, tell me. Who the fuck are you? And why does your Irish mate want to kill everyone in Karabunda?'

Now it was time to speak.

'I've told you who I am,' I said. 'My name is McLean. Max McLean. That's the truth. I'm a medic.' Roberts looked at me blankly.

'Medic? Are you 'avin' a fuckin' laugh?' Then he turned to Juliet. 'He's 'avin' a fuckin' laugh.'

'No, Roberts, I am not having a laugh. My name is Max. I am a medic. I learned how to be a medic in the British army with that big Irish lad. We're soldiers. Sort of. Or at least Sonny Boy *was*. He died in England after he was flown home. I came here to do a job. I didn't know Sonny had stayed here, or that I was finishing something he started. There's a lot of this that I don't understand, but this,' I held up the photo, 'is helping to make sense of it.'

'Make sense of what?' Roberts croaked. 'For fuck sake! You don't know. You had no idea your mate was here. And you have no idea what that photo means, do you? What is it, a fucking treasure map? Show me, man, show me where X marks the spot where you vanish and I get my fucking life back.' He lunged for the photo. I jerked it out of his way.

'All right, all right. Let's do this one step at a time, shall we?'

Roberts snorted.

'Let him speak, Robbie,' Juliet chided him. Roberts began to swear at her, but I cut across him.

'And let's start right there. Roberts, you need to have a little more faith in your wife. Sonny Boy was many things, but he sure wasn't a Romeo, and sure as hell not to your Juliet. He needed her to . . .'

'Did you fuck him?' Roberts cut me off.

'Man, calm. Let me explain.'

'How the fuck would you know, Max?' And then to her: 'Did you fuck him? Did you? Here? In my house? In my bed?' His voice broke. The tears came again, hard and fast, pouring out of him. He loved her, of that there was no doubt. But he could no more express it than he could shake the uncertainty he felt about her affection for him. Perhaps that's why he went with hookers: not from an absence of love, but in anticipation of the rejection he feared would come eventually.

There was quiet in the room. I didn't know it was his

mother's locket; and I didn't know Juliet and Sonny Boy hadn't slept with each other. Stranger things have happened. But not very often.

'No, I didn't. I didn't fuck him.' Her tears had dried up. She was calm, matter-of-fact. I liked her for that. 'But I did kiss him. Once, here.' She placed her right index finger high up on her cheek, and touched herself lightly. Roberts looked at her slack-jawed. Neither of us knew what was coming next. 'He told me he was going north and that I wouldn't see him again – he said it like he wasn't *ever* coming back, like he thought he was going to die, I mean. He told me not to trust Micky, and then he gave me the locket. You're right, Max, he said it belonged to his mother. I put that photo of me in there to disguise it, like he told me. He said it was funny that we both had the same initial, me and his mum.' She stopped and held my gaze, like she had done the day I arrived.

'Go on,' I prompted her.

'He said I'd know who to give it to when the time came. And I did, didn't I? He gave it to me to give to you, didn't he?' I nodded. Roberts breathed out a long hard sigh of relief.

'Babes, I'm sorry, I . . .'

'It's all right, Robbie. Really it is. I'm sorry. I should have told you. He just looked so . . . *sad*. Giving me that locket, it felt like, I dunno, like leaving a suicide note or something. He said he was a soldier, and I kissed him goodbye is all. Isn't that what you do when soldiers go to war? He was so funny and so kind, and all the kids on the beach loved him, and I thought maybe he wouldn't be so sad if he took that kiss with him, wherever he was going.'

She stretched out her hand to Roberts, and he took it. They sat like that for a minute – neither of them speaking, just rubbing their thumbs across each other's knuckles. I saw then that she had been crying not because she'd been caught out, but because she'd revealed Roberts's own lack of faith in her. In the end Roberts blew his nose into the sheet that she was wrapped up in, and then they both laughed self-consciously.

The room was hot and stuffy. Sunlight trickled in through the doorway from the main room. We were wasting time. Nowhere was safe for them, least of all there. I tried to work out what to do next. But Roberts spoke first.

'What happened to Sonny Boy, then? How did he die?'

'I know how he died, but I don't know what killed him,' I said. 'Something fatal happened to him here, something up near Karabunda tipped him over the edge. It took a long time to play out, but by the time he got back to England he was very, uh, *disturbed*. He didn't last more than a month.'

I thought the nonsense he spouted as he tried to kill me had been his last message to me.

It wasn't. The photograph was.

'*Maraigh gach éinne*,' I said again, out loud.

'Kill who? Why? Is it about what we saw in that village outside Kabala? What you saw?' Roberts asked, and then reassured Juliet: 'I didn't go in the hut. Max did.'

Juliet yawned and freed a strand of red hair from the corner of her mouth.

'Will there be another war?' she almost whispered, as if by saying it out loud she might make it happen.

'No, there won't be. *Shouldn't* be. That's why I'm here. Why Sonny Boy was here. There are rebels, soldiers anyway. Maybe from here, maybe foreign. My job is to kill their leader. You know, "cut the head off the monster". Whatever Sonny saw made him see it differently, though. He went solo, and I don't know why.'

'Some fucking medic you are, cutting people's heads off.' Roberts spoke to me, but had eyes only for Juliet.

'Sometimes the only way you can stop the infection is to kill the host,' I said. 'I'm more of a cleaner than medic.'

What had Sonny Boy seen that he wanted me to mop up? I looked at the photograph. I let them look, too. They were already fatally compromised, and their untrained eyes were fresher than mine. There were two traditional huts – brown thatched mud rondels. Each hut went to the right- and left-hand edge of the frame. In between them, and slightly in front of them and striding left to right, was the white man. It was possible he was walking across the front of them, or he had emerged from the hut on the left and was heading towards the hut on the right. He was wearing grey cotton trousers, a short-sleeved grey shirt with a collar and no epaulettes, no insignia. His hair was messy, his beard unkempt; his European skin was nut-brown and drawn tight on his arms and neck. He was what? Sixty-five? Seventy? I stared at the side of his face, as if by sheer force of will I could make his two-dimensional image rotate and reveal itself. It was just not quite possible to see his face.

In the background a line-up of out-of-focus troops stood to attention. Was the man taking the parade, saluting the men amassed beside him? There were white and black faces. None was recognizable. Their uniforms were indistinct behind the blur, and it didn't matter anyway. You can buy a knock-off Russian uniform for a few quid, or make a Sierra Leone army uniform for pocket change in any Freetown sweatshop.

'Mercenaries?' Roberts asked.

'Impossible to say. Maybe. Probably locals under foreign command. Served any Russians in your bar lately?'

'Plenty,' Juliet grunted, 'pilots and pigs, most of them. Robbie calls them "cabbage monkeys".' I raised an eyebrow at Roberts. He managed a smile.

'What's that?' he asked, pointing to the foreground of the photo. I noticed that his finger was shaking. The actual photo itself was out of focus at the edges – more so at the left and right sides than the top and bottom. I looked hard and angled the matt surface of the print against the dismal light from the bulb overhead. In the same, tiny scrawl at the bottom of the paper was written '300'.

Sonny Boy had given me a location, a time and even the range.

'God bless Mrs Mayne,' I said under my breath. 'May the Lord have mercy on her wicked son.'

I looked up at Juliet. Daylight in the room behind expanded and contracted, creating a brief burning red halo around her head. There was a soft snick of wood on wood as the outer door clicked open and shut in the breeze. She smiled at me, and I smiled back, slowly reaching behind my back. Slow is smooth. Smooth is fast. The short silencer of the SIG cleared the back of my jeans. I brought the barrel round and up, the bead of the sight splitting her eyes. She sat unblinking, staring at me, the smile still playing at her lips. That's how I remember her best, caught between love and fear.

I always know when I've hit the target, when I'm *going* to hit the target. I'm tied to the bullet even before the cordite flares or the trigger is squeezed. The round left the muzzle with a gentle *phutt*, and went in through the left eye. The full metal jacket hit the brain, scooping up the spongy organ in a spreading shock wave, emptying it out the back of the cranium. The air filled with a fine spray of blood and brain fluid, and the metallic chime of the spent cartridge case bouncing off the concrete floor.

I stood up. Roberts didn't move. Juliet's expression hadn't changed. Behind her lay stretched out the corpse of a white man in civilian clothes, still clutching a pistol.

'We need to leave now. Right now. We shouldn't be here. Get dressed, both of you. Juliet, pack a bag. You're not coming back.' They both stood up and took in the scene. Juliet went to speak, but no words came out. 'Move, now. There's no time.' They moved to the door slowly, eyes flitting between each other and the body. 'Just step over him. We need to go now-now. Like now, now, now.'

Juliet's almost naked body vanished into the living room.

I squatted down and ran my hands over the corpse: no sign of life, no other weapons, no wallet, no ID, nothing at all. Whoever he was, he was a professional: surgical gloves on both hands, one of them still wrapped around the butt of a silenced Tokarev: whoever the intended target was, he was expecting them to be wearing body armour. Target or *targets*. If Micky had been above board the whole block would have been locked down and a Delta team would already have been on the roof. If it wasn't the Americans, I wanted to know who *was* trying to kill us.

In the main room I could hear Juliet frantically opening and emptying drawers. Roberts was rooted to the spot, struggling, I supposed, to take it all in. I opened the knife and cut through the dead man's clothes. First the belt, then down the trouser legs and up the torso and along the arms of the shirt. Within seconds the cadaver was naked. Well worked out, no birth marks, no scars . . . but high up under the inside of the right arm, just above the armpit, one tattoo: a tiny black scorpion. It looked like I'd just disobeyed orders. For me, there are no misses. Only consequences.

'What the fuck is that?' Roberts had found his voice again.

'45th Spetsnaz.'

'What the fuck is that?'

'Russian Special Forces. It's their regimental insignia. Idiots. They just can't resist it.'

'Great, so now the fucking Russians are trying to kill you.'

'I hate to break this to you, man, but they're trying to kill *us*. Which is why we have to leave. Now. So for the love of God would you put some fucking jeans on.'

'Where are we going?' Roberts looked stunned again. He swayed on his feet. I led him into the living room. Submission, not rebellion. His temples leached sweat. His eyes exuded confusion. I hadn't known where to go. But when Roberts asked if the men in the photograph were mercenaries, he'd given me my answer.

'We're going to see Ezra.'

15

I went into the light first. Sand, sea, palms and rolling heat. No one on the beach. The air felt hot and heavy. I had my day bag; Juliet carried an over-filled duffel bag; Roberts clutched a packet of cigarettes and the padlocked rifle bag I'd left with him after our trip to Kabala. We looked nothing if not suspicious. Roberts took the wheel and fired up the old patchwork Nissan. I got in the front next to him. Juliet lay down on the back seat with her bag.

We pulled away. There were cars and trucks and *poda-podas* on the narrow road: deliveries to restaurants, people going to work at the hotels. A gaggle of school children in starched white shirts and polished black shoes that shone bright enough to put a guardsman to shame skipped along beside us.

'Your cook, the one with the missing eye. When does she come to work?'

'Eleven o'clock,' Juliet piped up from the back seat.

'Can you reach her? Tell her she has the rest of the week off.' Juliet dialled the number and shortly began explaining the cook's unscheduled holiday in Krio. Roberts navigated the thin stream of traffic and children and headed north to the end of the peninsula. There was only one road in and out at either end. At its southern base, the spit of land that Roberts's bar and my hotel perched on joined Freetown proper. At the northern tip, the city was only reachable by the Aberdeen road bridge, which spanned the neck of the creek like a thousand-foot concrete noose.

'Where's Ezra's place?'

'Near. Wilkinson Road. Other side of the creek, but we have to go around. We drove past it the other day. Just past Cockerill air base.'

'Office or house?'

'Both. I'll call him.'

'No, the phones aren't clean. Leave it.'

We turned east at a huge, dusty traffic circle on to Cape Road. A motorbike slipped in behind us, coming from the Barmoi Hotel. Black guy riding it, messy Afro, blue jeans and a dirty white t-shirt. No helmet, day sack, a hundred and eighty pounds. It was the same guy Roberts had been chatting up hookers with in Makeni.

'Fuck it! Motorbike, twenty metres behind you.'

'Got it.'

'Watch his hands. Juliet?'

'Yeah?'

'Get small. Lie down flat and get small.'

'You want me to gun it man? I'll gun it.' Roberts was coming back to life.

'OK. But not too hard.' Juliet balled up in the footwell behind us. Roberts nudged the Nissan up to thirty-five, forty. 'Distance?'

'Ten metres?'

I looked in my wing mirror.

'I make it eight. Seven. Closing. OK, go to fifty.'

'Can't. Junction coming up. Got to turn on to Aberdeen here.'

'Is it a circle, a roundabout?'

'Yeah.'

'OK, hit it as fast as you can. Go wide.'

Forty-five miles an hour along Cape Road in an old Nissan is like doing a hundred and forty-five in a Jag down O'Connell Street. Pushbikes, children, fruit sellers, even a street preacher – his exhortation to prayer engulfed by our slipstream – sped past us in a blur of juddering heat. Roberts dropped down into third and took the junction at forty. The motorbike stayed with us. Second gear. We curved right on to Aberdeen Road. Back up to third. The reek of burning clutch oil filled the car.

'Distance?'

'He's right on us. I can't shake him.'

'Stay with it.'

Fifty, sixty. Still the motorbike stayed on our bumper.

'OK. When I say, hit the brakes fucking hard.' I checked the wing mirror. The rider was coming up on the inside – my side – one hand on the bars, the other reaching behind his back. 'Now.'

Roberts stood on the brake pedal and heaved the hand brake. I braced against the dash. The Nissan pulled left into the kerb. Metal ground into metal. Smoke plumed off the tyres. Glass smashed. Muscle and bone cracked against the roof, the windscreen, the metalled road. I was out the door, rolling in the dust by the side of the road. I came up and fired twice into the white T-shirt of the rider – now on his knees on the tarmacadam. He lurched to the right, pistol still in hand, firing blindly as he tried to stand. His left arm was open at the elbow from impact. His jeans torn. I fired once more into the ribcage. He fell, face down. I came up on him fast and put the barrel of the SIG into the nape of his neck and fired again. Cars stopped. Children ran. Men backed away, hands up. Blood spread out from under the fallen rider.

Juliet's face was at the window of the stalled Nissan. Roberts turned the engine over, and over. Nothing.

'Engine's flooded.'

I spun on my heels, gun up, scanning sight lines, looking for trouble. Scared faces. The sun. Houses. Shops. Trees. Dust.

'OK, out. Get out. Roberts, grab my bag.' Juliet struggled with her own duffel bag.

'Leave it. Get out now. Go!'

I ran to the nearest car. A red Toyota with blacked-out windows, the door already open, engine still running. SIG at hip height, I reached in and pulled the driver out. A young man in a sharp suit. He scuttled off, head low, hands up. As it dawned on the people who'd stopped to look what was really going on, they too ran for cover. The war might have ended in 2001, but in Freetown people still knew when to hang around and when to split.

'You drive.' We bundled in and took up the same positions we'd had in the Nissan. Roberts bumped the Toyota over the wheel of the smashed-up scooter, edged around an abandoned delivery truck and continued east towards the bridge. Spetsnaz and their military intelligence partners in the GRU were extremely effective at the best of times, and they'd had months to prepare their area of operations. Our cover was blown wide open. They were on to us, and on to us hard. They got to miss as many times as they liked. I'd only get to miss once.

'This ain't right, Max. No traffic. Something's up.'

'OK, slow it down. Juliet, get your head down. Right down.'

There was no oncoming traffic. As we approached the bridge, the sea closed in on either side of the road. Two cops stood in the centre of our lane, waving down the trickle of cars ahead of us. Behind them, a *poda-poda* minibus taxi cut sideways across the road, blocking the entry to the bridge and all oncoming traffic. A small crowd gathered, remonstrating among themselves and with the cops by turn.

'OK, dead slow.' A man was working on the tyres of the minibus, all of which appeared to be flat. A night-club sprawled off to our left. Behind it was a long building with a flat roof. To our right, a tall, unmarked building threw a long shadow over the road. Beyond it lay the bridge and creek itself. 'It's not safe. We need to turn back, but we can't do a U-turn here.' Roberts had slowed the car to a crawl. The cops waved us down.

'Unsafe how? More men on bikes?' Roberts craned his neck around. 'You're the worst fucking fare I ever had, Max.'

'No. Listen carefully. Pull up in front of the cops, but wide, centre of the road. Make sure it's clear behind then gun it in reverse. Hard and fast as you can. When you hit thirty drop the clutch, punch the foot brake and turn the wheel a quarter to the left all at the same time. You'll spin one-eighty. Then bomb it south. We need to get off the peninsula.'

'Fuck, OK. I did something like this on the Old Kent Road once. Let's hope the tyres stay on this time.'

'Don't stop for more than three seconds.'

We drew to a halt. Roberts looked at me, and then in the mirror. I counted under my breath.

One thousand.

The Toyota's gears went from second to neutral to reverse.

Two thousand.

Movement behind me. I turned a fraction.

'Head down!'

Three – the cops lurched away from us as the car leaped backwards – *thousand.*

Tic. Tic. Tic.

'What's that?' Buried in the rear passenger footwell, Juliet's voice was urgent and muffled. Like the sound of the rounds punching through the Toyota's soft steel skin it sounded strangely distant, unreal.

'We're being shot at.' Then to Roberts: 'Keep her steady . . .' We hit thirty. War in reverse. The downed scooter flashed past; but the dead rider was nowhere to be seen; a street kid was pouring gasoline on the dark stain where he'd bled out on to the highway; the crowd no longer cowed – staring, mouthing, pointing. It was as if we were tied to a huge length of elastic that had shot us out to the bridge and was now pulling us back inland through time.

Tic. Tic. Tic.

We'd taken a dozen rounds within seconds. Silver-edged holes opened up like wild punctuation marks in the bonnet. The shooter was aiming for the engine block. Then we lost window glass on the off side. The shots were coming from the flat roof. The Toyota's blacked-out windows saved us. If we'd been in the Nissan we'd have been dead already.

A moment of silence.

Then the windscreen caved in with a pop and a smash. Hot wet air and the roar of the engine rushed through the open cavity of the Toyota. Roberts flinched but held fast.

'OK, spin her.'

Roberts spun the car perfectly on its axis. It had taken me two days at Leconfield to learn how to do that. He was a natural. We stopped for a second. Jagged holes appeared in the rear window glass.

'Go, go, go.'

Roberts ripped racing changes through the gears, right foot flat on the floor, revs off the clock as he punched the Toyota out of second and into third. His face was a study of extreme concentration: furrowed brow, and just the faintest suggestion of a smile at the corner of his mouth. After all the emotion in the house he'd recovered his cool with all the determination of someone who'd lost almost, but not quite, everything.

'Is anyone hit?'

'No, I'm OK.'

'Juliet?'

No response.

'Juliet?' I shouted loud above the engine and turned around.

'Juliet, baby . . .' Roberts craned his neck around, too. We'd hit seventy. Roberts had his Ray-Bans on. With no windscreen it would have been impossible to see at that speed without them. The peninsula was a blur. Sand, bugs, grit were sucked in through the missing wind-screen and stung my face.

'Just drive. I'm on it.'

SIG in hand, I clambered on to the back seat. Roberts braked hard into the junction with Cape Road, which threw me forward, on top of her. I recovered, and lifted her head. Blood spilled from her mouth. I hauled her up on to the back seat and then lost my balance again as Roberts threw a left on to the Lumley Beach Road. We were heading south now, with the sea and Roberts's bar to our right. It was a tight space to work in. I got her up on to the seat, stretched out on her side. I'd turned myself around so I was facing backwards.

Her T-shirt was soaked, the face of President Koroma dyed scarlet. But with blood from where? Her mouth was open. Blood but no blockage. I dug my thumbnail into her earlobe. She opened her eyes: unfocused, con-fused. In the slipstream vortex at the back of the car it was almost impossible to assess her vital signs. I clamped my fingers to her carotid artery and pressed my ear to her lips. Racing pulse; shallow, rapid breathing. I started a primary survey. Head and neck first. Then under her T-shirt. My palms slid over her breasts. They were wet. I looked at my hands. Dark red. I ripped the president's face in two, cleaving the T-shirt from the neck down and found where the bullet had gone in, high up on her right breast, through the pectoral muscle. I put my hands behind her back and ran my open palms down her spine, up her flanks, under her arms. Nothing. No exit wound.

'It's OK,' I mouthed to her. 'You'll be OK.' But she couldn't hold my gaze and grimaced with pain, fighting against my hands.

Roberts looked over his shoulder again.

'Is it bad?' he shouted.

I didn't answer.

Then: 'I need my bag.' It was hard to be heard in the back above the noise of the road. 'Bag!' I roared. 'I need my bag!'

Roberts leaned forward and scooped my day bag off the floor with his right hand. It was heavy with ammunition and cash and he swerved as he struggled to get it clear of the front passenger headrest. It fell down beside me as I ran my hands down her legs, across her stomach. No other obvious wounds. I took out the trauma kit from the front pocket of the bag. As she breathed in, air went into her chest cavity through the hole in her chest. The more it filled with air, the more it pushed her collapsing lung into her heart. Likely result if untreated: imminent cardiac arrest.

I pulled the flat, round packet of the chest seal out of the kit, tore it open and peeled off the backing. Blood oozed from the wound. I wiped it with my left forearm, and placed the sticky plastic valve over her breast. The wound was sealed: air hissed out of the valve as she drew breath and exhaled. No more air could get back in through the wound. She blinked at me. Bloodied spittle bubbled at the corners of what almost looked like a smile. I put my palm to her cheek and cupped her face. There was no way of telling where the bullet had ended up inside her. Maybe she would survive. Maybe she was dying.

'Road block!' Roberts stood on the brakes again. I braced against the backseat. We'd hit the southern end of the peninsula, just as the road bends inland. Dead ahead a jumble of cars and *poda-podas* facing every which way cut the road. Roberts had pulled up fifty metres short. To our right, the Atlantic burned electric-blue beyond the white scum lapping at the shore. To our left, trees, tennis courts and open green fields.

'What's that?' I tapped on the offside window with the barrel of the SIG.

'Golf course.'

'Can we cut through to the city?'

'Maybe. Depends how high the creek is.'

Roberts was shaking. His words came out fast, unsteady. The red roof of the club house was visible through the trees just behind us. We were completely exposed, and there was only one exit.

'Let's do it.' In front of us two black guys emerged, one from either side of the tangle of vehicles that blocked the road. Bent low and moving with cautious determination, the barrels of their AKs were up and on us. 'Go, go, go, go, go.'

As the road block receded through the aperture of

the blown-out windscreen they dropped to a crouch, firing in tandem. The air filled first with the crackle of incoming rounds, and then the *tic-zing-ping-smash* of high velocity steel and copper tearing up the Toyota. The off-side rear tyre popped. Cubes of window glass blew into our faces. A lump of rubber tore off the top of the steering wheel. Roberts's hands jumped up to his face and back to the wheel. He dug his chin down and thrust his head forward as if bracing against a hailstorm.

'Faster,' I shouted. 'Go faster.' Roberts clenched his jaw. You can't order someone not to be scared. And not even a lifetime of training will predict how someone will react under fire. Roberts was keeping it together, terrified but fortified by a near lethal dose of adrenaline.

Juliet was slumped in the back, lying on her good side. From between the seats I squeezed a shot at the shooter on my right. He fell, the AK still firing on automatic, barrel arcing skywards. I swung the silenced SIG forty degrees to the left, tight to the side of Roberts's shoulder. An AK round passed between us, ripping a track through his skin, grazing my right knuckle.

'Fuck! My arm.'

He pulled the wheel left in pain, the back end of the Toyota careering towards the trees just by the golf club entrance, and I lost sight of the target.

'Straighten up. Get her in the entrance. It's fine. You're fine.'

'Fine as fuck!'

Roberts corrected the car and whipped us round hard

into the entrance, boot first. As we curved around the second shooter came into clear vision again, sprinting towards us. I hit him twice in the chest and he fell forward, sprawling in the dust. Roberts brought us to, nose pointing towards the links and gunned the engine. Oil sprayed out of the holes that peppered the bonnet; the chassis lurched, hobbled by the wrecked rear tyre.

'This is going to be short and nasty,' Roberts snarled as he dropped the clutch. We lurched forward. He was right. The Toyota bucked and wheezed as we took off past the club house and followed a dirt track that cut the green in half. Golfers stood in twos or threes, club-stuffed bags to hand, rattled by the noise of the firefight. Some pointed in disbelief; one shouted angrily in Krio; another had stopped his swing midway, still doubled over, club suspended aloft.

'How long have we got? I mean the oil.' We'd hit a crossroads in the track Roberts was grinding along.

'Not long. Ezra's place is dead ahead, over the creek. We can go straight, but we might not be able to cross. Or we can go around, but she might not make it.' Roberts patted the scarred dashboard of the Toyota like he was consoling a tiring horse.

'Go straight. No time.'

Roberts glanced back at Juliet.

'She gonna be OK?'

'She *is* OK,' I said, not knowing if I was lying. She was conscious, but unspeaking. 'But she needs to get to hospital urgently.' After three hundred metres the track petered out between two sand bunkers. 'Drive over the green. Keep going.'

Halfway across the fairway the Toyota sputtered out with a hacking, oil-choked cough. I got out first, gun up. The trio playing an early-morning round in the coolest part of the day went from anger at having their game interrupted to caution when they saw my pistol. Roberts climbed out next. Blood stained the ripped football top at his shoulder, but the wound was superficial. In unison the golfers backed up towards the trees.

'We need to get her out and into cover. I'll carry her. You carry my big bag, and check the rear. OK?' Roberts nodded. I slung the day bag and reached in for Juliet. Her eyes focused and she managed to help herself out a little. She was caked in blood.

'This is going to hurt, OK?' She grunted her consent. I switched the SIG to my left hand, bent down and picked her up, fireman-style, over my right shoulder. She exhaled hard but didn't cry out. 'Let's go.'

I led. Roberts followed, scanning the track behind us. The golfers watched, silently. A hundred metres and we were into the trees. Fifty more and we were at the edge of the creek. The air was heavy with the stench of human excrement. I turned to Roberts.

'There's a slum on the other side.'

'How deep is it?'

'Haven't got a Scooby.'

I looked back through the trees. No one. If *I* were following me, I'd wait for me to break cover. The creek was a hundred metres across – first there was a muddy sand-bar to cross; then a wide island, dotted with scrub; and then, by the look of it, a final fifty-metre stretch across mud and water to the slum on the other side. Taller buildings on Wilkinson Road rose up behind the tin roofs of the shanty. Juliet lay unmoving over my shoulder.

'You go first. If anyone starts shooting, just run and find Ezra. And don't look back.' Roberts didn't look convinced. Neither of us knew if Ezra was even in the country, never mind at home. Roberts was holding his wounded shoulder, shivering with the shock of what was happening to him. 'I'll look after her. I promise. Come on.'

We stepped out into the thick green-brown slime. Roberts first, me following, hard on his heels. We were almost at the end of Aberdeen Creek. We were in luck. It was low tide and navigable. But as we reached the centre of the creek, the staccato *snap*, *crackle* and *pop* of incoming AK fire piped up behind us. Little plumes of sand and water erupted around us.

'Run! Go!'

Roberts hesitated, arms up – half in surrender, half protecting his head. Then he ran – full pelt through the mud and shit and low-tide scum towards the slum and the city. I was completely exposed. I dropped and turned. Juliet came down hard with me. A rise in the island we'd just crossed gave us a foot of cover. I aimed for the muzzle flash in the trees, fifty metres to the right. The firing paused, then resumed in single aimed shots. Whoever was on the right end of that Kalashnikov was well trained. I returned fire left-handed. The shooting stopped, and we were up again. I ran, charging through the filthy water, zigzagging towards the nearest house.

More shots, from multiple shooters. A round clipped

my thigh; another grazed Juliet's back, beside my ear. I dropped again by the edge of the channel. Four men in fatigues twenty metres apart were laying down supressing fire for a fifth man circling to my left in a simple but effective fire and manoeuvre assault. I squirmed down into the mud, legs in the water. Juliet was balled up under me – her pale skin and red hair dulled by creek slime. Her eyes were closed, but her throat fluttered. She was hanging on. We were being strafed accurately and intensively: a dozen shots placed within a hand's width of my head spewed up more sand-spray.

For a fraction of a second I felt cold Irish lake water on my hands; saw hard European sunlight on pale submerged skin, the last glint in her eyes, my mother's eyes, pleading.

This is it, my boy.

I got the SIG up right-handed and put two rounds into the shooter on the far right. He dropped. Then the thud of a grenade exploding in the mud. Grit blew into my eyes, mouth. My head reeled, ears popped, nose bled. I turned towards the *chitter-chatter* report of the second shooter and fired blind. His AK fell silent. I turned further, blinking hard, shaking the creek sludge and memories. Head shot. Third man down. Last round in the breech. I ejected the empty magazine. The fourth shooter was prone now, buried in scrub, firing high, keeping me down. But the guy circling us was on us. No time to reload. I rolled and fired as he dodged. The last round smashed into his left shoulder. I dropped the SIG, twisted hard, up and over Juliet. He staggered and fired, but he couldn't control it and the AK pulled high right. Rounds sprayed the mud between me and Juliet.

I went up fast, body under the muzzle, hands on the barrel, pushing it high. Straight kick to left knee. Right hand up. Closed fist punch to his left jaw. His mouth open, sour breath in my face, eyes wild. I pushed through, hand opening, palm coming down on the top of the AK stock. I pulled down hard and pushed up with my left. The AK arced from ten to two o'clock, rotating on its axis. I pulled back hard. The front sight caught and ripped his ear. Shooter disarmed. He stood paralysed, chest heaving, sweat in his eyes. Jab to face with muzzle. Pistol grip down. Charge weapon. Fire. Two rounds to the chest. Shooter down. Drop.

I lay there covering Juliet, prone, getting small in the sand. Scan. The fifth shooter was moving, firing again. I was up. Six metres and closing. But something wasn't right. The rifle was too light. I fired. The round hit him, went through him. He looked surprised, but didn't drop. I pulled the trigger again. No sound. No recoil. No ammo. Empty.

I dropped just before he fired and then with a single, brilliant, clear *crack* his face imploded behind a veil of bright-red mist. I lay next to Juliet and looked at the sun and then into the silhouettes bearing down on us. It was Roberts. Next to him stood a man with a crooked smile on his face, and an AK in his hand.

'Max,' panted Roberts, 'this is Ezra.'

16

Ezra set down a couple of Cokes and a bunch of small red bananas on the table. An electric fan stirred the heat. Outside, boots drilled and stamped. Inside, the room was filled with the high-pitched whine of blast-damaged eardrums. I was filthy, bleeding and ravenous.

We'd left the city immediately in the back of a private ambulance that the Israeli had conjured up from a side street in the slum. We'd driven up into the hills near Regent, not far, I guessed, from Micky's villa. I worked on stabilizing Juliet with his kit as we climbed east, Ezra shaking off questions with terse monosyllables at the checkpoints that were springing up across town. After forty minutes we emerged not at a hospital or private house, but in a police barracks. 'The training school for the Special Security Division,' Ezra had informed me as we disembarked. With evident pride, he told me that the whole enterprise was funded by Israel, not the British, and was commanded by him. Roberts's arm had been bandaged. Juliet had been carried away at the double to the clinic by men wearing black fatigues and smart red berets.

'He's good,' Ezra said. 'Toufiq. The surgeon. From Beirut. It's a long time he and I work together.' He was looking at Roberts. Roberts was staring at the door. Elsewhere on the compound Juliet was having her chest opened up. 'There are no promises. God willing she will live. But she needs time.' In the way some Israelis shape English sounds, his accent was guttural, almost French, and he littered his sentences with Hebrew words. 'And you,' he looked at me, 'what do you need?'

'A plane,' I replied. 'A Cessna. A 172.' I reached inside the day bag and pulled out the bundles of dollars. 'That's eighty grand.'

'When?'

'Today.'

'OK.' Ezra shrugged. 'Will I get it back again?' I shrugged. 'What else?' he asked. I looked at Roberts.

'He's not coming with me.'

'About this you are one hundred per cent correct.' He smiled his crooked smile. 'There is no possibility whatsoever I will allow him, or her, to go anywhere with you. They are safe here with me. No one will touch them.' There wasn't even a flicker of irony in his speech. 'This,' he opened his palms wide and looked from side to side, to make it clear it was his whole operation he was talking about, and not just the room we sat in, 'is the president's personal project, paid for by the Knesset. It's as safe here as Tel Aviv.' I raised an eyebrow. 'OK,' he conceded, 'safer.'

'Maybe this time don't look after him by shooting him,' I suggested.

'About that,' Ezra smiled, 'I make no promises. Whatever works, eh?'

'Roberts said you worked with the Americans after the war. They're not,' I chose my words carefully, 'on side.' Ezra stared at me. His eyelids drooped over his irises. One moment he looked like he was about to explode; the next as if he were half-asleep. It was too late for talking around it. 'OK, to be clear, yesterday an American tried to kill me,' I confessed. 'Micky Montague. He was with the CDC.'

'That fuck? *Ta'aseh li tova!* No, Micky is not CDC. Or whatever that other *shtuyot* aid agency is.'

'USAID?'

'*Ken,* that one. Micky is CIA. Sure *barur.* Trust me on that.'

'Did you kill Micky?' Roberts snapped his eyes away from the door. I tilted my head in affirmation.

'He tried to kill me. But here's the thing: I shot a Yank spook – and it's Spetsnaz and a bunch of local boyos that come after us.'

Roberts coughed.

'Those *boyos* nearly buried us, bruv.'

It was a fair point. I'd been replaying the chase in my mind during the drive from the creek slum to the barracks. Juliet and Roberts had slowed me down, forced bad choices on me. But I needed Roberts. Left to my own devices, I reassured myself, none of the shooters would have left the woods alive. But lose Juliet, and I'd have lost Roberts. I told myself I needed them both. And then I checked myself. No, I didn't. I didn't *need* Juliet alive; I just *wanted* her to survive. I wanted Ana María to survive, too. But you can't always get what you want.

'Spetsnaz? *Ulai*. You are certain about this?'

'The black guys, no. They were all in uniform, old Sierra Leone army kit.'

'Rebels?' Roberts asked. 'From Kabala?'

'Maybe. They were well trained, that's for sure. But the shooter who came to the house? He had a tattoo, you know, their scorpion.' Now I said it out loud it sounded less convincing. I didn't mention that we knew Colonel Proshunin had been on station.

'Max, how many tattoos do you have?' Ezra asked.

'None.'

'Me as well, I don't have any. It would look good, eh? Israeli Defence Forces right here.' He traced his right index finger down his left forearm. 'Or maybe here?' This time he drew his finger across his throat.

'OK, well I killed a Yank and someone wants me to *think* Spetsnaz is after us.'

'This I agree with,' Ezra shrugged again. 'But so what? They are with God now. It does not matter who they are, or how good they are. You know this. I know this. It matters only how good *you* are, eh?' He took a folded newspaper from his field-jacket pocket. 'This guy, I don't think he was good enough.' Ezra handed me the paper. It was that morning's edition of the *Awoko* newspaper. The headline: 'Cholera in Kabala, Musala: Citizens Told to Stay Calm, Remain Indoors. UN to Take Action.'

'Turn it over,' Ezra said. 'Under the fold.'

Underneath the leader, *Awoko* ran a story titled 'Murder in Makeni'. A British diplomat visiting the Makeni

176

area had been found dead by his car on the road back to Freetown. The hack who penned it concluded the embassy man had been 'mown down by brigands' and his valuables 'looted'. A *Faces of Death*-style photograph of the corpse lying flat on its back adorned the lower right quarter of the page. White man, fifties, slight build, weak jaw. Utterly ignorable. Absolutely MI6. His bloodied white shirt was riddled with bullet holes. His face was serene and untouched, save for one neatly drilled entry wound in the centre of his forehead.

I'd been wondering who next. Though I couldn't know for sure, he was almost certainly the Official – an MI6 officer openly declared to the Sierra Leone government by our government – who'd 'collected' the photograph of Colonel Proshunin and the target outside the school in Makeni. Most likely he'd taken it from Global Assistance Committee volunteer Marie Margai by killing her and stealing her camera. Maybe killing her had been part of the plan. Maybe he'd panicked. Maybe Micky had held his hand. Maybe London had told him to. Now he'd been taken out, too – and in Makeni, where Micky had just come back from.

Maybe, maybe, maybe. But the way I saw it, there was one fact: me aside, Roberts and Juliet were the last loose ends left in-country.

All bets were off.

'This cholera *shtuyot*. This is to do with you?'

'No, it isn't. And it's not cholera. Or Ebola. But there's someone making shit up north and we'd like them to stop. Permanently.'

177

'Ah, it's "we" now, eh? *Mazal tov*. It looks like they are helping you a lot, this "we". Maybe they will find you your Cessna?' The crooked smile was back. There was nothing to say that wasn't untrue and unkind to everyone in London who'd put me here. Myself especially. 'Do you have a plan?'

'No.' I looked at the pips on his shoulder. 'I don't know shit about strategy, colonel. But I do know that no plan survives contact with the enemy. Especially when you don't know who the enemy is.'

'*Bediyuk*,' he nodded, grinning. 'In Israel we say "no plan survives contact with an officer", so it is just as well I don't have one either, eh?'

Ezra raked the bundles of hundred-dollar bills off the table and made to leave. 'I will go and check on your woman now.' He was speaking to Roberts but looking at me. 'Do you need anything else?' he continued. Roberts went to answer. I spoke first.

'Yeah. A clean phone, a Thuraya.'

'OK.'

'And an emergency beacon if you have one, that works off Iridium sats.'

'*Ken*. But careful, eh? With this you will light up the jungle like the Menorah. They will see you from fucking Mars, my friend.'

'Yup, that's the idea. And some det cord in case I need to clear a landing site for a casevac. Oh, and there's one other thing.'

'*Betach*. Anything.'

'Some clean fatigues. I smell like shit.'

'*Ken*, this I also agree with one hundred per cent.'

Ezra left with the cash. Roberts and I sat alone. The room was stuffy, stifling even. Outside, Ezra barked orders first in Hebrew, then Krio.

I sat and scrolled through Micky's local phone. I'd given up on his iPhone – if the NSA struggled to get into them, I didn't stand a chance. The names and numbers were all unremarkable: a mixture of neutral first names and acronyms; Sierra Leonean and international mobiles. All except one: the contact *VX* had a London landline and an extension: 309.

VX: a particularly nasty nerve agent. Hardly remarkable for someone from the Center for Disease Control to have that in their phone. Or maybe V *Cross* – Vauxhall Cross. He wouldn't be the first CIA operative to have a contact number for MI6 HQ.

Fuck it. Roll the dice. I pressed the green key and listened.

'Embankment.' The voice was crisp, clean, confident. I pretended I couldn't hear.

'Hello? Is that Embankment?' I said in my best American accent.

'Yes. Embankment. What extension do you require?' Matter-of-fact. Almost impatient.

'Three-o-nine.'

Pause.

'Connecting you now. Stand by.' I looked up and realized I was holding my breath. Roberts shrugged his shoulders at me as if to say *What the fuck?* I put my index finger to my lip and frowned.

'Three-o-nine.' A second voice confirmed the transfer. Softer this time – a secretary, not a gate-keeper. I exhaled, slowly.

'This is Montague.' I kept up the accent.

'Connecting you now.'

Pause.

'Mason.'

I hung up and removed the battery from the phone.

'Fuck.'

'You OK?' Roberts asked.

'Yeah. No. I don't know.'

'Is it safe, to call out?'

'Fuck no! But it'll keep the boys and girls in Cheltenham busy.'

'OK, whatever. Mate, I can't work out if you really know what you're doing or if you're just making it up as you go along.'

'Fifty-fifty. How you bearing up?'

He slumped forward in the battered old armchair he'd pulled up to the table and wiped the sweat from his face.

'Yeah, I'm OK. If she's OK, I'm OK. Thank you, for what you did back there. I mean, *fuck you* for what you did back there. But thank you, too, you know?'

'Yeah, I know,' I said. And then, pointing at the phone: 'That was bad news. I . . . er . . .' *May as well say it*, I thought. 'I don't know if I'll be coming back.'

He looked aghast and then smiled quickly.

'Well, I'm not going to fucking kiss you goodbye, you cunt.' We both laughed, and for a moment I saw a flicker of the Roberts that had met me at the heliport only four days before.

'Ditch your phone. Ezra will give you a bunch of SIMs with sequential numbers. If I call you, burn the SIM afterwards. I'll call on the next number the next time. Got it?' He said he did, so I took a pen out of my trouser pocket and scrawled Jack Nazzar's cell phone number on the newspaper Ezra had left with us.

'This number belongs to a grumpy old Jock. He's the only person I trust.' I thought about that for a moment and saw Commander Frank Knight in my mind's eye dressing me down in Caracas. 'The *only* person. He'll help you. Don't mention any names. None. Forget any names you've heard from me. Just tell him that all work and no play makes him a dull boy. He'll lead you from there.' Roberts ripped the corner of the paper off and tucked it into his jeans' ticket pocket. Then he took his bracelet off. The black, red, gold and green beads clicked against the little metal lion with its missing foot. He handed it to me.

'For luck,' he said. Worry and fatigue were etched into his face. I put the bracelet on. He smiled weakly, and we lapsed into embarrassed silence. Then I remembered Micky's Glock. I reloaded the little pistol and passed it to him, grip first.

'For luck,' I said. 'It's a double action. Six rounds, plus one up the spout.'

'Double what?' Roberts turned it over to inspect it and squinted along the barrel.

'Just pull the trigger. Put it in your pocket. You'll

know when to use it.' He tucked it away and cleared his throat.

'What *are* you going to do when you get to Karabunda?'

I realized I'd been thinking about little else for days, and with no clear answer. I'd told Ezra the truth: there was no plan. And there never had been. But the solution was suddenly clear. I replied spontaneously, knowing exactly what was to be done. It was as if the thought had always been there, waiting to be spoken.

'Precisely,' I said, 'what Sonny Boy told me to do.'

17

She was old and tired, but she had everything I needed. My day bag was on the co-pilot's seat, my rifle bag in the passenger cabin behind.

There were no ground crew as such – just a couple of pissed-off locals to help wheel her off her backfield plot and run the refuel. It was the hottest part of the day, an hour before sunset. No one wanted to be working.

There was no tower to radio, no clearance to obtain. There was no commercial aircraft tracking equipment that worked anywhere in the country – not even at Lungi International Airport. That was as much in my favour as in the Russians', who Captain Rhodes said had been flying heavy equipment and men up to Karabunda apparently unnoticed by anyone except us for months.

The weather I got from the web: *west wind at eight knots; visibility twenty-three kilometres; high-level clouds; temperature twenty-eight; dew point twenty-three.* There was zero per cent chance of rain: March was dry and searing hot. The route I'd already got from Roberts: I'd be flying VFR all the way – retracing our car journey north from the air, following the road to Kabala, and then due north to Musala and the rebels' operating base. As well as the paper chart, I'd saved the digital maps offline on my phone and punched the coordinates of the only possible drop zone I could identify from the satellite imagery into the GPS. I had two days of phone battery at the outside, not that there was any signal. The satellite phone would be my lifeline.

I opened up the throttle a quarter inch, rechecked the propeller area was clear, started the ignition and adjusted to a thousand revs a minute. Old and tired maybe, but she hummed like a dream. I engaged the autopilot, pushed the controls against it to check it and then disconnected. The familiar *beep* rang out. All good. I ran through the pre-take-off checks by rote, double-checking each one, set the flaps and released the parking brake.

The Cessna taxied into position, and I gave Ezra the thumbs up. He saluted and took a step back. Eighty grand aside, one day he'd be calling this favour in, with interest. Full throttle. The runway pulled me along like a long black line reeling in a metal fish and then spat me up into a gentle climb above the deep-green waterways that wound their way inland from Tagrin Bay. The long shadows of early evening dissolved into clear blue sky. I banked around and headed for the corrugated star of Waterloo town to the south-west – its rusty roofs and glinting windscreens beacons astride the ridge the road hugged before turning north-east to Makeni. I climbed to six thousand feet and held her there, out of the effective range of most ground fire, and engaged the autopilot. I trusted Ezra because I had no choice. If he wanted to have me shot down, there was no safe altitude to climb to.

It was just over two hundred miles to Karabunda. I

took off at eighteen-ten exactly. That would mean boots on the ground at around nineteen-hundred. It was too risky to come in during daylight, and suicidal to come in at night without infrared. Dusk was the only option, and still a poor one at that. This close to the Equator I would have a ten- to fifteen-minute window of last light once I reached the target.

It hadn't been safe to go back to the Mammy Yoko Hotel. Most of my equipment, including the BGAN, had been out of reach from the moment Micky bled out. In my mind I went through the kit I did have, such as it was:

Rifle system and ammo.
SIG, silencer, ammo and a tactical holster from Ezra.
Detonation cord.
Mobile and satellite phones – charged, no chargers.
Paper chart, knife, compass, gaffer tape.
Nearly twenty-five thousand US dollars in cash.
Emergency beacon – also from Ezra – watch, medical kit.
Filtering water bottle, full.
Canadian passport, GPS, two MREs and a packet of smokes.

I closed my eyes, and conjured Sonny Boy from the depths of my memory.

Code Zulu: We used it as slang for situations where the only course of action was to annihilate everything and everyone. It was the nuclear option that left no survivors, like the defeat the Zulus themselves had inflicted on the British at the battle of Isandlwana. As Sonny Boy liked to say in front of the recruits in the mess hall at Raven

Hill loudly and often, 'Didn't those African boys with their spears and their shields hand those English boys with their rifles and their big guns their bloody arses, Max?'

Given that Sonny Boy was six-six and once knocked out the British army's heavyweight boxing champion while the opening bell was still ringing, I liked to agree with him. When Sonny Boy started on his Zulu rants I was definitely more *Irish* than *Anglo*. If he hadn't been out of his mind in Brinton I'd have been hard pressed to bring him down.

Only one person I knew had actually ever put the Code into practice: Sonny Boy himself. Before he made sergeant, Sonny was sold out by his local guides during an anti-narco operation in Colombia. Of the four men in his squad, two were killed and another – a young trooper who'd not long passed selection – was severely wounded. As far as Sonny Boy was concerned the entire village was complicit. What was meant to be an operation against the Norte del Valle Cartel became a paramilitary operation against him, personally.

Out of options and with no escape route, he did what no soldier wants to do, but anyone who wants their mates to survive would do if they could.

Colonel Ellard oversaw the board of enquiry. When they asked me what I'd seen when I finally got close enough to extract them both, I hesitated. It was hard to find the words.

Hauling the wounded private across those broad Wicklow shoulders of his, Sonny Boy had first blasted his way out of the village and then out of the valley. He killed everything in his path for twenty miles. At first with a rifle and grenades, then with his pistol, then a knife and finally with his bare hands: men, women, children – he killed everything and everyone that stood in his way. Like a real-life incarnation of my boyhood hero, the legendary Irish warrior Cú Chulainn, Sonny Boy was gripped by a battle warp-spasm. Consumed by bloodlust, he ripped the life out of anyone within reach. It wasn't until I'd got him into the chopper that he even realized he'd been shot: thirteen times, including straight through both legs.

So I explained Sonny Boy's escape to Ellard the only way I could, the only way he would understand it. I said, simply, 'Code Zulu, sir.'

Ellard promoted him and deployed him to fight pirates in Somalia. General King pondered the things 'that might be achieved with a hundred men like that, what?' and then ordered the hearing's records destroyed. The following month the Americans claimed victory over the Norte del Valle Cartel. As for Sonny Boy, I don't think he ever really recovered. He never spoke again to the trooper whose life he saved. And he never thanked me for rescuing either of them.

I thought about what Juliet had said about Sonny's last goodbye. I have contemplated suicide many times but I have never considered it. And here I was, sitting above that darkening expanse of jungle stretching north-east to the Loma Mountains, about to attempt what, exactly? For the uncounted thousandth time, I saw the pale, frail face of my mother wreathed in floating blonde locks; blue eyes fixed skywards, piercing the clear, cold lake water. Sometimes taking your own life – or giving it up – seems like the only rational act for anyone bereft of mind, or of love.

The truth was that Sonny Boy had already got to the edge a long time before he came to West Africa. It wasn't just Colombia. It was the sum total of where we came from, what we did every day and the eventual realization for all of us that there was nowhere left to go. If you have to kill your soul to survive then there's nowhere left to run to, and nothing left to run for. Fear: it was the be-all and end-all of everything we did. But whatever had sent Sonny Boy mad hadn't just scared him, it had terrorized him into utter madness.

Whether our feet were on the ground or not, all of us Unknowns at Raven Hill were like those proverbial men plummeting from the top of a skyscraper, each reassuring the others as they passed first the hundredth, then the fiftieth, then the twentieth floor: *so far, so good; so far, so good; so far, so good.* Of course it's not the fall that kills you. It's the landing. Sonny Boy fell off the edge in Karabunda and landed at my feet in the observation ward in Brinton. He'd gone back up north to do something, to fight for something, and he'd done it alone. I just had to figure out what, and figure it out fast. Major General King and Frank Knight weren't going to help me; and David Mason looked like he had a tighter connection to Langley than Raven Hill.

*

Eighteen-fifty. I overflew the killing ground outside Kabala. Nothing moved. It was time to go off the edge myself. I spiralled up above prying eyes to fourteen thousand feet and adjusted the flight path to north-east. I set the airspeed to eighty knots. Cabin temperature dropped. The air thinned, but at that altitude I didn't need oxygen. I shuffled over into the co-pilot's seat and slid it back to give myself room. The SIG was holstered on my thigh. I strapped the day bag to my chest. The rifle bag was fastened underneath it, cross-ways. Then I put the parachute on, a skydiver's sport rig from Ezra, over the old jumpsuit he'd thrown into the deal. I lashed the GPS tight to the inside of my left forearm and switched it on. Musala passed beneath the winking red of the port wing tip, clinging to the southern bank of the Mong River.

I double-checked the autopilot. Judging by the amount of fuel left, she'd come down in deep bush over the border in Guinea, somewhere to the west of Marela. I unlatched the passenger door and pulled the D-ring. The door came away with a powerful blast of freezing-cold air. Pressure imbalance rocked the little Cessna momentarily, but the autopilot held her, and she settled down.

Nineteen-fifteen. I stepped out on to the wheel strut and held the aft edge of the open door. Somewhere below in the last glimmer of daylight Karabunda passed to the west. I dropped and released. The silk carried me silently above the savannah. Ten thousand feet. The Cessna carried on, wing tips blinking into the distance, vanishing into the last dregs of the day. Five thousand feet. I watched for movement, half-expecting the hills to spit out bright arcs of tracer. But none came, and the GPS brought me straight over the drop zone. One thousand feet. What I lost in the visibility of a long descent, I gained in accuracy and silence. But if the drop zone was hot, I'd be dead before I landed.

Five hundred feet. The horizon suddenly rose fast, and the rank-smelling hot hum of the woodland floor rushed up to meet me. I pulled hard right over a dark patch between the trees as the last of the day bled out of the sky. I squinted hard into the gloom and saw nothing, no one.

And then my boots hit the ground.

18

Pitch-black silence. I checked my watch. Three o'clock in the morning. The insects, birds, moths, monkeys had all finally fallen silent. It was a simultaneous cessation, a miracle of woodland wild places everywhere. Suddenly the night creature catechism ends, and absolute quiet descends. In two hours the monkeys would rouse themselves, and the cacophony would begin again. An hour after that, first light would fall through the open canopy. Sunrise was at seven. I shifted on to my side, three feet above the ground, suspended in a strip of parachute silk slung between two trees. It was a small luxury, but any fool can be uncomfortable. Sleep in the field is priceless; anywhere off the floor is a necessity.

I'd come down sixteen kilometres north-east of the camp, and just five hundred metres south of the tenth parallel – the absurdly straight line that formed Sierra Leone's northern border with Guinea. Wherever the Cessna had ended up, I hadn't heard the crash. Although the rebels had been raiding north in February before turning their attention south, the Guineans didn't have the manpower to police their own frontier. It could be days – months, even – before the wreck was found, if it ever was. The line on the map that separated Sierra Leone from Guinea was simply that: a cartographic expression that bore no relation to reality on the ground. The savannah and the hills stretched on regardless, unencumbered by the limitations of language and nationality.

I'd neither seen nor heard anyone. It was a harsh, sparsely inhabited place. Almost no one went up there; even fewer people cared who did. The only line on the map that interested me was the one made by the Mong River. It came across the border a few hundred metres to the west and meandered due south nearly all the way to the camp. It would be hard going, but following the Mong would be like sprinting down a race track compared to slogging across hill country.

I made the most of the peace and quiet and went back to sleep. No dreams between the trees. I knew exactly where I was.

It would take all day to cover the ground to the camp. No night movement. No walking in the open. No official communications with London. Not yet, anyway. No one knew where I was, and I wanted to keep it that way for now. The very best that could be said of my briefing by MI6 and Captain Rhodes was that it had been woefully inadequate. Nothing new there, then.

At worst, though, something was wrong – not just on the ground, but in London itself. No one had mentioned that Micky or the CIA were involved, or that Sonny Boy had recced my trip; no one had mentioned that everyone connected with the mission had already been killed – like Marie Margai – or was about to be – like Six's man in Freetown. He hadn't lasted a day longer than my first trip up north – killed, judging by the squeaky-clean tyres on the Mercedes in Makeni, just after dropping off my rifle in the DJ Motel's parking lot. It looked like whoever was cutting the links out of the chain was equally determined to bury me, too.

London had gone to lengths to impress upon me that because the Americans weren't involved there was no high-spec satellite imagery or tracking available. That *might* have been true, but I wasn't going to take any chances until I'd worked out who was trying to punch my ticket, and why. It was time to go off-piste, stay dark, keep tight under cover and remind myself that when I told Roberts that Jack Nazzar was the only person I trusted, I'd meant it.

I was here to do a job that Nazzar had signed off on, albeit grudgingly. That was good enough for me. And the job wasn't yet done. A Russian scientist playing war games with a proxy army? God knew I'd killed for less than that. But if it was murder Frank wanted, that's what he'd get – at a time and place of my choosing.

It was seven a.m. and cool under the trees – when I tested the rifle it needed to be as near as possible to the same temperature as it would be when I took the actual shot. While I waited for the air to warm, I cut out a square of the parachute silk and then squatted down and went for a crap away from the drop zone. I buried my shit along with the parachute rig and jumpsuit. Then I took my mefloquine, wolfed down cold the main meal from one of the combat rations Ezra had given me – beef stew, which looked remarkably similar to what I'd just disposed of – and kept the other snacks for later. As

Colonel Ellard had told us: *in war, take every opportunity to empty your bowels and fill your stomach.*

I checked and holstered the SIG and unzipped the padded case that housed my rifle. I rechecked each piece of the sniper system: rifle, scope, bolt, magazines, cartridges, bipod, moderator and rangefinder. No damage. Everything had survived the jump. I assembled the rifle and inserted a fully charged ten-round magazine. It was my rifle, my scope. If I'd understood Sonny Boy's message correctly I'd be taking the shot at three hundred metres. The huts were approximately six metres apart. Judging by the height and gait of the target he'd likely clear that in six seconds at a straight walk. For a sniper six seconds is like six years, and three hundred metres extremely close. But I couldn't afford any margin of error.

Folded neatly into the pocket from which I'd extracted one of the magazines was a sheet of fifty centimetre square target paper. I opened it up. In the centre was a twenty-five millimetre diamond patch to zero in on. I measured out a hundred metres with the rangefinder and staked the target in position with two spits of dead wood. I walked back to my position, stopped still, closed my eyes and listened.

Nothing human stirred.

I opened my eyes. Slowly I circled three-sixty, trying to see, not just to look.

Again, nothing.

I lay prone, steadied the rifle with the bipod and chambered a round. I set the scope magnification to times seven – the optimum magnification for the human eye – and focused it carefully so the crosshairs stood out sharply against the dull background of the target.

I took two deep breaths to oxygenate my blood and then exhaled slowly, ensuring my point of aim.

Pause. Hold. Fire.

The moderator dulled the rifle's report to a dull *crack*. Deadened further still by the trees, the shot would hopefully be unnoticeable to anyone not close enough to be seen in my perimeter check. The bullet tore the paper open twenty millimetres left of the centre mark and embedded itself into the forest floor. I paused, listened, looked and fired again. The round clipped the same hole, fractionally above. The third shot passed cleanly through the second hole.

I adjusted the deflection drum two clicks to the right and repeated the test. All three shots tore a single hole at the centre mark.

Weapon zeroed.

While I waited for the barrel to cool, I measured out three hundred metres of clear ground – which, owing to the erratic pattern the trees grew in, was hard to achieve – and lay prone again, before adjusting the scope's elevation drum according to the table supplied by Rhodes.

I fired again.

The three rounds grouped around the centre mark – the first a couple of millimetres higher than the subsequent two, which followed each other through the same, expanding hole.

I knew the rifle well. At that range the difference a

cold bore would make to the first shot was negligible. More important was the difference a clean bore could make. The nine shots I'd already fired would make sure those that followed were at least consistent.

I was making too much noise to test any ranges other than the one I thought I knew I needed. I dialled the scope magnification down to times three and set the sights to four hundred metres so that any nasty surprises on the way could be snatched accurately and quickly: set up like that, a shot aimed to the centre of the chest would strike a target between the base of the neck and the groin from a hundred to six hundred metres away. I chambered the remaining round and changed magazines: twenty-one rounds left.

I was good to go bar one final check.

The ringing tone ended abruptly with a terse Glaswegian 'Aye?'

'Good morning, Sergeant Major.'

The line was silent. Then: 'You've got a fuckin' nerve, son.'

'Nice to hear from you, too.'

'This isnae your Office phone. Secure?'

'Not any more it isn't. But we should be good for now.'

'So, tell me . . .' Nazzar and I spoke at once, and then both stayed silent, each of us waiting for the other to speak first. I had to get the business with Sonny Boy out in the open. For all his gruff Scot's stoicism, I knew that Jack Nazzar would have been rocked by Sonny's death. So I continued.

'I know what you're going to say,' I said. 'I know and I'm sorry. But he went for me hard, Jack, wild hard. I had no choice. None. You have to believe that. You'd have done the same.'

Long pause. And then, finally, Nazzar spoke, the hard edge of his tone blunted.

'No, I wouldnae. Sonny Boy was better than me, Max. It would have been me put in a box, and that's the truth of it.'

'Yeah, well. Maybe. He was at the end of his tether, Jack. Properly mad.'

'Aye, so I hear.'

'I'm sorry. I did what I had to, to stop him. But I thought he might make it, you know?'

There was a long pause.

'He was alive?' Nazzar asked.

'Yeah, there was a crash team working on him. It looked touch and go.'

'Ye sure about that?'

'Of course I'm bloody sure. When do *you* think he died?'

Nazzar coughed.

'In the room. Mason said he died in the room. Max, are you sure?'

'Sure as sure.'

'Well that's news. Mason said you snapped his neck in the fight.'

I stopped pacing and stood still. The phone suddenly seemed very heavy, as if the burden Nazzar was imparting weighed down the actual handset.

'No, I didn't. I stopped short. Jack?'

'Aye?'

'It's on film. The whole thing was on CCTV. Multiple cameras, probably.'

'I'll just go and ask Mason for a live action replay, then, shall I? Sounds like a typical Six fuck-up to me. No one knows anything; everyone gets everything wrong.'

'No, Jack. Listen.' I paused. I needed to be cautious – even with Nazzar. *Especially* with Nazzar. My word against Mason's wasn't good enough. If Nazzar was going to be kept onside he'd need details to persuade him. The stakes were too high for him to take anything I said for granted. 'Things here aren't, uh, as briefed either,' I continued. 'There's some weird shit going down. It's not like any insurgency I've ever seen, and everyone connected to this op is being taken out. One after the other.' Nazzar grunted. 'Sonny was working with the Yanks, *a* Yank anyway – a CIA agent going by the name of Micky Montague. His cover was CDC.'

'CDC? Their disease agency? Now that *is* interesting. That numpty captain at the briefing, Rhodes.'

'What about her?'

'I checked her out. She's no SRR, or at least, she *wisnae*. Until last December she was a Tanky, in Falcon Squadron. That's CBRN. But she wisnae at Warminster. She was stationed at Porton Down. An' where d'ye think her last secondment was before being farmed out to Mason for this little shindig?' I told him I had no idea. Chemical and biological warfare weren't exactly my speciality. 'Brinton,' he said, a note of triumph rising in his voice.

'Doing what?'

'No way of finding *that* out without tripping a bloody great wire, son. And call me old-fashioned, but neither of us wants anything going bang down there.'

Porton Down was the site of the British government's most secretive research facility. Run by an executive agency of the Ministry of Defence, it was so impenetrable that even the secretary of state admitted he didn't – *couldn't* – know exactly what research was conducted there. It looked like Rhodes wasn't the numpty Nazzar had thought she was, after all.

I opened my mouth to speak. I wanted to tell Nazzar that Micky had Mason's number in his cell phone. But what you don't know, you can't tell – on purpose or by accident.

There was only one other thing I really needed to know.

'Jack?'

'Aye?'

'Did you know Sonny Boy did my recce?'

The line echoed and clicked, stubble and material rubbed against the mouthpiece at Jack's end. Silence and then the noise of traffic and a car door slamming. He was moving to somewhere he couldn't be overheard.

'Aye. I did. An' if I'd known then what I know now I'd never have agreed to you going. Sonny was supposed to be your spotter. You were supposed to do this together, as a team. But he went a long way off target. The Yanks got him to Conakry, we took him from there. The debrief was a fuckin' shambles, just a load of bloody Mick gibberish about monsters and men. The Office ran it from there, and the job was redesignated UKN only.'

'What sort of nonsense? Anything useful?'

'Ach, no. Just mad ramblings. I've got to go. Keep the heid son, an' gie it laldy. You finish it there, and we'll sort the rest together back in Blighty. And Max?'

'Yeah?'

'Don't fuckin' miss, ya Paddy bastard.'

I signed off with an ironic *Éire go brách!* and hung up.

Hills like giant green knuckles rippled across the border into Guinea. I headed west, under the cover of the canopy, and found the green-brown waters of the Mong River slipping south towards Musala. High above me, the silhouette of an eagle turned a long, languid arc in the morning air. Flanking the banks of the Mong ran an unbroken line of trees. The canopy was low and patchy. I clung to its shade and cover and headed first southwest and then due south. In places the stream narrowed, choked by cataracts of river rubble or dead fall. Tumbled trees made makeshift bridges. No one had navigated it this far north for many months.

Maps recorded the names of no nearby settlements, but satellite imagery clearly showed a village ten klicks from the drop zone, on the far bank of the river: a ragged knot of maybe thirty houses, some with metal roofs, congregating around a path that headed south-east over the river by way of a concrete bridge. I came up on the area cautiously, the first sign of it an abandoned smallholding spread out on the opposite bank. Nothing was cultivated there now; no one worked the land. Then the river made a fifty-metre semi-circular bulge north like a green pimple. I stayed on the inside, my side, under the trees. A hundred metres to my left, the path cut across the bush. And two hundred metres north-west, at the apex of the pimple, the huts and houses of the village spread out under the rapidly rising sun.

I squatted down and shouldered the rifle. The scope brought the southern spread of the village into focus. Except it wasn't habitable any more. Doors had been twisted off their hinges, windows blown out, roofs caved in. Bullet holes scarred the wall of the most substantial building in view – which from the flagless pole in front looked like it had been a police station or army post. Opposite, the mosque stood burned out like a charred skull, blackened windows gaped like empty eye sockets.

In the streets brightly coloured cloths lay strewn about. Empty plastic packets of water, tin cans and a child's bicycle caught the glint of the sun. There was no one there: no guards; no corpses. I scanned the perimeter. No graves, either. This war was like a locust. It consumed everything. Even the dead.

A clump of trees blocked my sight line, so I edged around further.

Seventy-five metres or so from where the track crossed the river, the bridge came into view through the trees. On it stood the single figure of what I took to be a rebel soldier. Five-seven, a hundred and fifty pounds. Camouflage fatigues torn, stockless AK strapped across his back. He faced north, looking upstream, rocking back and forth on his heels. I brought him up in the scope and increased magnification to eight times. His afro was crazy – ragged and laced with strips of red material. Deep cuts criss-crossed his exposed chest. Sweat ran freely down his face, clinging to his beard. No radio. No ammo pouches. No insignia. On his right side hung a machete, fixed to his belt by a twist of blue nylon cord.

I studied his face and adjusted elevation to zero. He was looking across me, so I could only see one eye and two-thirds of his face. But what I could see was enough: he was either deranged or damaged. His gaze was fixed, unblinking; mouth caught between a smile and a grimace. And all the time rocking: back and forth, back and forth. Drugs, possibly. Or battle trauma.

I scanned the village again. Nothing. No smoke in the air, no dust. Birds rose and fell across the damaged roofs. Nothing startled them. A pair of monkeys picked their way through the trash. I returned to the rebel. If I stayed under the trees and kept going I'd pass within a few metres of him, at which point I'd have to break cover. If I went around him across open ground the Man in the Moon would be able to see me, never mind a military satellite. If he fired a shot it would be heard by anyone not deep in the woods. I settled the crosshairs sixty millimetres above his right temple. His eyes remained fixed on the river. But what he was looking at was impossible to say. His arms hung limp at his sides.

Back he rocked, forward he rocked.

I tracked his listlessness through the scope.

Back he rocked.

The faintest whisper of wind came from upstream, cooling the sweat on the back of my neck.

Forward he rocked.

First pressure.

He tilted on to the ball of his foot as far as he could without overbalancing.

The wind picked up. His chin lifted, head snapped straight towards me. He froze, looking directly at me, up on his toes, eyes sharp, focused. His head lifted higher, as if sniffing the air. I'd framed him through the narrowest aperture of leaves and branches. There was no way he could see me.

I shot him between the eyes. He lurched, spun and toppled into the river. The gunshot was quiet enough not to spook the monkeys, and he was close enough to the water not to make a splash that could be heard over their endless chatter. The sluggish current dragged him under the bridge. He didn't emerge downstream. I reset the scope to four hundred metres. Still nothing in the village moved.

I pressed on.

The terrain was rocky. Sparse stretches of barren land spread out – islands engulfed by an ocean of small, densely growing trees. I walked close to the bank under the protection of pockets of gallery forests that sprang up tall in the wet conditions, looking, listening, at times stopping and waiting. There was no sign that anyone strayed off the paths. The Fullah and Mandingo up here were not like the indigenous Limba, who herded the other tribes' cattle and managed their plantations. Roberts assured me with pride that *his* tribe moved through the forest like fish in water. Even in the remotest parts of Sierra Leone, Roberts had told me on our long drive north, the forest was something other tribes feared, avoided and treated with extreme caution. It was a place of spirits and magic and darkness. 'Once upon a time,' he said, 'white ghouls like you emerged from it and stole our children.'

When the bank was too overgrown to navigate I waded into the water, watchful for crocodiles. The sun climbed. I began to sweat, and stink. Maybe the rebel sentinel had smelled me? But still the forest along the riverbank reeked more than I did. Each footfall released a pungent tang of decay. If anyone could smell anything through that they were superhuman. I had been silent, too, and there had been no sound behind me – that was for sure. What's more, the metal of the rifle was dulled matt green to prevent reflection; the scope glass was shielded by a lens shade and honeycomb.

But he'd known I was there, that someone or some-*thing* was there. No question. A second later, and he'd have been moving towards me. It was hard not to be unnerved. I kept on keeping on, silent and slow, moving from shadow to shadow.

Every hour I stopped to drink, filling my drinking bottle with river water. It tasted muddy, but the filter built into the cap made it safe. Green monkeys chattered and whooped in the trees, diving from branch to branch overhead. Where I could see that the river doubled back on itself, and where the canopy thinned out completely, I cut across land, clambering over roots and creepers, through the veil of dense secondary scrub that formed a dusty emerald scum between the trees.

It was hard going.

By noon I'd covered ten kilometres as the crow flies, and walked nearly fifteen. After the rebel on the bridge I'd not seen another soul. The base at Karabunda lay just three klicks to the west. Yet there was no sign of any patrols, perimeter security, or any further evidence of rebel activity. When the sun passed the meridian it would be time to leave the river and cut inland. I needed to find my position, Sonny's position, in daylight. I slowed my breathing and looked and listened: still nothing but the sights and sounds and smells of the forest. But the forest can be deceptive. Sound morphs, deadens, twists between the tree trunks; a man stood still can be as invisible at five feet as a sniper in a city at a thousand metres; an entire platoon can pass within spitting distance of an unsuspecting sentry, unnoticed. The jungle is a weapon. If you fight it, however you fight it, you will lose; turn it to your advantage, and it's unbeatable. But never forget that you don't own it. The forest makes an unpredictable ally.

I'd stopped to eat and rest and sat with my back pressed to a cotton tree, picking through the remnants of the MRE I'd started at breakfast. Hedged in by close-knit vegetation, visibility was no more than six feet. So dense and repetitive was the savannah flora that it was hard at times even to focus on it. I chewed deliberately, surprised at how good the field rations were. I tilted my head and squeezed the last drop of processed cheese into my mouth and swallowed hard. I looked down again and blinked.

I was no longer looking into the tangled void of the jungle, but into the eyes of a child.

19

A girl. Maybe eight, nine years old. Skinny, dirty, with wild, woolly hair. Clothes in tatters. Feet bare. She stood still, just beyond reach, staring at me. Her eyes were bright, focused; her face was taut, scared. I startled and she recoiled but didn't run.

Without breaking eye contact, I reached down and picked out the mini packet of M&Ms from the almost-empty MRE wrapper and held them out to her. She didn't move. I opened the packet, showed her a candy-coated peanut, put it in my mouth, and chewed and swallowed theatrically. I smiled and proffered them again on the palm of my hand, like offering a sugar cube to a pony. She reached forward, hesitantly. I rocked forward carefully on to my haunches. She took the packet and closed it tightly into her fist and stepped back.

'Hello,' I said. 'I'm Max. What's your name?'

No response.

'Max,' I said, patting my chest with my now empty right hand. I pointed at her, and tried again in the shaky Krio that Roberts had been teaching me. '*Wetin na yu nem?*' No response. '*Ah gladi fo mit yu,*' I stumbled on, unsure if I was getting the words right, or if she even understand Krio. '*U sabi tok inglish?*'

She moved her head from side to side almost imperceptibly.

'Where are your parents? Mama, Papa?' I looked around with both my palms turned up as if to say, *over there? Or there?* Her eyes flicked away from mine, and she glanced upstream. I followed her gaze and pointed north. 'Mama, Papa?' She nodded. I gave her a big smile and a double thumbs up. 'Mama, Papa OK?' She looked back at me, and then at the ground. She was still for a while and then shook her head.

I froze, hyper-aware of my rifle and pistol. It was too late to conceal them, and she must have seen them. 'How?' I asked. I spoke before I thought, but she didn't understand. I wondered if she was from the village I'd passed earlier, if the guard I'd dropped into the river had been one of her parents' killers.

'*Watin apin?*' I tried again. Still no response.

It was crass, and I hesitated, but I needed to know as much as I possibly could. I made a pistol with my fingers and thumb. 'Bang-bang?' She shook her head again then without warning leaped forward, mouth wide open, lips back, teeth barred, as if miming a silent lion biting the air. I flinched. She settled.

When I was sure she wouldn't run, I repeated her story back to her without breaking eye contact.

'Mama, Papa . . .' I pretended to bite down on my arm.

She nodded.

'Lion?' I asked, though thanks to the guide book I'd

devoured on the plane I knew there hadn't been any recorded sightings in Sierra Leone for a decade or more. She looked blank. I tried in Limba – one of the few words of his grandfather's language Roberts had managed to teach me. '*Yandi?*' She looked surprised and shook her head vigorously. 'Soldiers?' I asked. No response. And then again in Krio. '*Sojaman?*'

She shook her head again, looking directly at me with an intensity that was unsettling, and drew a circle in the air around my face with her index finger.

'*Dyinyinga,*' she said. She held my gaze for a moment longer, then turned on her heels.

I lurched forward to catch her but stopped myself. She looked back once from the edge of the bush that had screened her approach and then disappeared from view. I looked and listened hard – pulling aside the brush, scouring the shadows between the trees. But there was neither sight nor sound of her, and she was nowhere to be found.

Most operators worth their salt wouldn't have let her leave the clearing alive – myself included, once upon a time. If she raised the alarm my mission was over.

I knelt by the water's edge and smeared first my hands and wrists and then my face and neck with dark-green river slime. Roberts's lucky lion bracelet stuck to me, caked in mud. My black fatigues – a spare uniform from Ezra's supplies – were already filthy. I looked and smelled like the forest – which was to say both terrible and ignorable.

Dyinyinga. I had no idea what it meant. But I did know

this: the cadavers in the village outside Kabala showed clear, unmistakable signs of human bite marks. She might have been a traumatized child, but that didn't mean she was crazy. If her parents had died the way I thought they had, it was no wonder she was petrified. I took out the Thuraya satellite phone, shuffled to the edge of the canopy and dialled Roberts's new number. He picked up immediately.

'Is that you, bruv?'

'Yup.'

'What's up? All good?'

'Yeah, listen. I need a word translated.' I kept my voice to barely more than a whisper. 'Don't mention any names on the phone.'

'You're calling me for a Krio lesson? Classic, bruv. Fuckin' classic. Fire away.'

'It's something like yin-yin-ger. Ring any bells?'

There was a long pause.

'Yin-yin-ger? Are you 'avin' a laugh?' Roberts was *actually* laughing.

'No, as usual, I am not having a laugh.'

'It's d-*yinyinga*.' He composed himself and stopped sniggering. 'Oh, mate. Seriously. You vanish off the face of the earth and call me to ask about *dyinyinga*! What are you *doing*?'

'Never mind what I'm doing. What does it mean?'

'It means, bruv, that you're a long way upriver. The *dyinyinga* are spirits. Like the djinn.'

'The djinn? Muslim djinn?'

'Yeah, sort of. Genies, bruv, they're like genies. Fuck, man, who did you hear that from, for God's sake?'

'I'll tell you later. Second question: these, uh, genies. What colour are they?'

'What colour?' He laughed again. 'M . . .' he caught himself before he said my name, '*mate*, have you been out in the sun?'

'Concentrate. I'm serious. They're sort of like people, right? So what colour are they?' There was another pause. 'The photo. Think of the photo. The men in uniform. What colour are they?'

'Oh! Fuck! OK, yeah, I get it. They're white. They look like white men.'

'Always?'

'Yeah, well. I haven't seen one recently, you know? But you remember the story I told you, about people in the forest being scared of white men, because of the slave trade? That's where it's from. So yeah, the *dyinyinga*, they take the form of white men.'

'And they're bad, these *dyinyinga* genies?'

'Yeah, no, well not always. It depends. My grandad used to say they could be vengeful if they helped you, if you didn't pay the price. Very vengeful.'

'Price?'

'Yeah, your first-born. The *dyinyinga* always demand the first-born son. If you don't pay, they fuck you up. That's why they're too hot to handle. Only the looking-ground man can control them.'

'A what?'

'A looking-ground man. A sorcerer. A magician.'

'O-*K*.' It was a lot to take in. 'Don't take this the wrong way, but did – *does* – your grandfather believe in them.'

'Ha, yeah, course he does. Fuck, mate, *I* believe in them. Every Limba does. You'd be mad not to.' He sounded absolutely serious. I decided not to press the point.

'Hey, man?'

'Yeah?'

'Did I ever tell you that you remind me of my granny?'

'Why, is she gorgeous?'

'No. She left a saucer of milk out for the leprechauns till the day she died. I'll be in touch. Remember, burn your SIM. And don't call this number. Any problems, phone grumpy Jock.'

'All right, take it easy. Good luck.'

'Hey, last thing. Your woman. She OK?'

'Bearing up. Our mutual friend says she'll be fine. Mate . . .' He hesitated.

'Yeah?'

'Would you really have shot her, if she'd run?'

'Of course,' I replied. 'But in a nice way.'

We said goodbye, and I killed the satellite phone.

The savannah was still, and I felt alone and hemmed in, frustrated at my own ignorance of what was happening. I missed Roberts, too. That was the truth of it. Silly, mad bastard. But we'd clicked, and he was cool, and I didn't feel that way often. Or ever. I let my mind wander for a second. An image flickered behind my eyes of Roberts raising a glass of beer and Juliet laughing. Then I saw Sonny Boy's eyeball rolling on his cheek and then I blinked and all there was to see was the endless dirty-green echo of the bushes sprouting between the trees.

It was nearly one o'clock, still too early to move into position. I waited. Perspiration flowed freely down my back, under my arms. Little black sweat bees crawled across my fingers. In the shade of the trees thirsty mosquitos whined and pestered. Half an hour later it was time. I cleared the waypoint of any evidence I'd been there and struck out to the west, and Karabunda.

It takes an effort of will to focus in the bush. The mind wanders. Concentration lapses. It's impossible to stay hyper-alert continuously. Dips in awareness are dangerous, but they keep you fresh, too. The jolt back into the present when the daydream ends makes the nerves fizz with adrenaline, the gut tighten with expectation.

I crouched and listened, and the face of the little girl came back to me, and my mind drifted to her family and the empty village. I tried and failed to reconstruct her life in my head.

There was nothing like encountering a scared child to remind me how unfit I was to be a father, or increasingly, an assassin. As far as conversation went, the best I'd managed was to ask her how her parents had been killed, and letting her go had put my own life at risk. What was it that I could teach a child, anyway? In my head I heard my father whistling 'Jimmy Clay' as clear as the chapel bell on our estate. *When you're gone, mankind follows after you.*

Except no one would be following me. At least, I hoped they weren't.

There I was, creeping through the jungle as carefully as I could to make sure I had the best possible chance of killing someone I didn't know, for reasons I'd probably never understand.

I wasn't special, that much I did know. Jack Nazzar called every operator younger than him 'son'. But he was solid. And whatever the reasons had been why he hadn't told me more about the mission, they would have been good ones. I believed him when he said the job wasn't what he'd expected, either. Nazzar wasn't a concern. He was a comfort. It was Frank that worried me. Right from the beginning he'd been there with me, constantly. Frank *was* the beginning. And now, here, at the end – 'your *last* job' he'd said – Frank was almost invisible. I'd held on to his encouragement and praise for all my life, just like a son hangs on to every word of his father – or at least that's how it was with me and mine. And, just like my father, Frank wasn't there when I needed him most.

You did well.

No, Frank, you did well.

I had no one to do well for.

Fifteen-hundred.

I eased myself over a tree root and squatted down, listening. Nothing, except perhaps the faintest whine of an electrical circuit, far off. It was hard to be sure. Too many shots over a quarter of a century had left me with scarred eardrums and a permanent high-pitched whine of my own. I ran a weapons check, slung the rifle and drew the SIG, silencer on. The slow dance through the trees continued. The river had wound south through a valley cut between seemingly endless, undulating hills.

It had been easy keeping cover. Now, heading across country, it was steeper, harder, but the approach to the base was itself a rough plateau, with hills rising up to six hundred metres around it. Large patches of open ground and rock hindered progress as I detoured to follow the treeline. At least since leaving the river the air had cooled and the mosquitos had thinned. I scanned the horizon for observation posts, but there was no sign that anyone was there at all.

Sixteen-hundred.

It was a Tuesday. According to the time and date stamp on the photograph Sonny Boy had left me, he'd snapped the image at zero-nine-hundred on a Wednesday. The sun was on the white man's face and chest, but raking over his shoulder slightly, towards the camera: he was facing south-east. So Sonny must have positioned himself to the south-west and have been facing north-east. To the south-east of the camp was an open stretch of ground shaped like an inverted teardrop a hundred and fifty metres deep and a hundred metres wide. I edged round it and headed south-west. Sonny had a clear view of the target – near impossible through three hundred metres of trees and scrub. Finding a secondary firing position would be out of the question. His line of sight of the camp must have been directly across one of these patches of open ground.

I say 'camp'. The satellite photos showed a dirt track vanishing into the trees and emerging again on the other side; there was no evidence of any buildings, activity or men. All I had to go by was a GPS coordinate from Captain Rhodes and a photograph from Sonny Boy. Two things were definite: Rhodes was not what she seemed; and Sonny Boy was not the man he'd once been.

I had no ghillie suit, but I needed to break up the black lines of my fatigues. Very few things in nature are black – except for coal, and, perhaps, the heart of a sniper. The river mud and the foliage that stuck to me were a start. I gathered handfuls of grass where I could find them, long thin twigs and leaves, and dried-out palm leaves. The palms I twisted into a headdress; the grass I wove into it. The long twigs and other foliage I poked into the loops and straps of my bag. It was an imperfect camouflage, but my head and shoulders were what counted most, and the outline of them would be softened by the grasses. It would do. It would have to do. I continued walking south-west, through good tree cover, parallel to a larger area of open ground that lay to the south-west of the camp.

Sixteen-thirty.

The camp was four hundred metres due north. I turned north-west, walking back up towards the most south-westerly point of the dead ground Sonny must have framed his shot across. I stepped from tree to tree. Slow. Careful. The wind shifted, picking up and blowing south. It was a relief. Late afternoon was the hottest part of the day. Even here in the hills the atmosphere was still oppressive. With the wind came the chirping of birds and the throb of a generator. Muffled, faint, but unmistakable. It sounded far off, too far for where I had the camp pegged, like the mechanical pulse that emerges from a mine shaft.

Seventeen-hundred.

On my stomach. One centimetre at a time. Elbows forward; elbows down: dragging myself by slow degrees to the edge of the clearing. As the sun dropped behind the hills to my left the temperature fell with it. But where the sun had burned, now insects swarmed and bit. Underneath the bows of a huge tropical hardwood I lay prone, the tip of the rifle barrel a foot back from the edge of open ground. I lay my cheek on the stock, put my eye to the glass and zoomed the scope in to ten times magnification.

There was completely clear ground for around two hundred and fifty metres. A slight rise and fall in the land. Then light savannah scrub began, which reached out fifty metres or so further into the trees beyond. And there, right there, stood two thatched huts beneath the trees with a square of beaten earth behind them. I lined up the mil-dots in the reticule against the height of the hut on the left — which from the ground to the lowest fringe of thatch I estimated at two metres. Six-point-five mils: that gave me a range of three hundred and seven metres. Readjusting fractionally for the approximate height of the hut put me where Sonny Boy must have lain; the only place he *could* have lain to have a clear shot. I rechecked the range with the Leica: three hundred metres exactly. I reset the elevation drum to zero and then dialled in eight clicks clockwise to set the range at three hundred metres.

It dawned on me then. He'd been close enough to take a shot – but didn't. He was more than good enough – so why not? No rifle? No orders? But both Nazzar *and* Micky said he'd gone rogue. From here, there was no way he could have taken the photograph with a camera without using a massive lens. He couldn't have used a rifle scope or a rangefinder, because the calibration markings would have been superimposed on the image. He must have used a simple monocular with a digital camera and estimated the distance – which would have explained the vignette at the edge of the frame. To get this far, to have taken the photograph – he must have had his wits about him. Whatever happened to Sonny at the end of his trip was unknown. But what happened next was as clear as day: he went back to Freetown and left the photograph with Juliet for me.

I scanned the huts again. The light at ground level was failing. And then I realized. Of course he hadn't just *left* the photograph for me, he'd *taken* it for me. He knew this was my job, and that I would finish whatever it was that he had started if he wasn't able to. A month later, and they laid Sonny in his grave while I lay on his mark. There would be no three-shot salute fired over his casket, which was already covered with Mason's lies. Instead there would be one shot fired by me, a silent memorial at dawn. My only hope was that it would be true.

Eighteen-hundred.

Fifteen hours remaining until H-Hour at zero-nine-hundred. A veil of frenetic black wings swept across the hills in perfect silhouette as hundreds of fruit bats dived and whirled towards their roosts high up in the tallest tree tops, searing the darkening sky with their metallic screech-song. Carefully, I laid out in front of me a square of silk I'd cut from the parachute so no dust would be kicked up by the shot to signal my position. I settled the rifle. Serenaded by the distant hum of the generator and the twitchy throb of the crickets, I let my muscles relax into the ground. I emptied my mind and waited for the reckoning.

20

A bright gibbous moon hung over the trees. It shed a white gloom that killed the stars and settled on the crest of the hill rearing up behind the huts where the target was supposed to emerge in the morning. Heat seeped from the earth. Insects swarmed. My hands, eyelids, lips, neck, ears fed ants and mosquitos and all the company of that stinging seething hell which thrives on the forest floor.

I didn't move. I didn't sleep. I had no night optics, no thermal imaging. I didn't need them. I focused my attention on the huts, or rather the clump of trees surrounding them, and waited. There are tricks and techniques to keep alert. But my problem had always been getting to sleep when the job was done, not staying awake during it. Some snipers chew coffee grounds, others tobacco. Before I settled down, I slipped a pebble plucked from the ground under my tongue. It kept my throat moist, and my thoughts anchored.

Seventy-two hours on the gun is the maximum most snipers working alone can manage. Extremes of weather and wildlife can reduce that to a day, or less. Keeping still and staying silent and awake are not the main challenges. Staying focused is. Looking down a scope continuously is supremely, perfectly, disorienting. It eats into your mind and clouds your judgement. It feels like it begins to erode your very soul. Eventually the hallucinations take over. In the early days of the Troubles, Colonel Ellard once spent seven days on the gun, trapped in a house in Derry – a visceral reminder, perhaps, of his confinement in Arigna's shallow coal seams. He could neither walk nor speak afterwards. It took him a month to recover.

Fifteen hours was a luxury.

The moon climbed, banded by drifts of cloud gathering over the high ground. The earth cooled. A light breeze shimmied towards me, shaking night music out of the trees, rattling the grasses woven into my clothes this way and that.

At ground level, between the trees, it was perfect night: utter, impenetrable blackness. To compensate, my brain lit stars and sparks in my eyes that flared and died in the rifle scope. I tried to reach through them with my mind, imagining the target, the distance, the scale. I recalled the photograph Sonny Boy had left for me and then expelled it from memory. When dawn came I needed to see what was there, not what I thought should be there. Both eyes open, lying prone on the gun, I recalled and considered each piece of the mission's puzzle I'd gathered so far.

Nazzar: decent, loyal, misled by command; Rhodes: unknown, professional, and with a worrying connection to chemical and biological warfare – which potentially linked her to Micky Montague, a CIA agent posing as a scientist with the Center for Disease Control.

Careful, I warned myself. Not necessarily posing. Being CDC and CIA were not mutually exclusive. It didn't mean he didn't have a sense of humour, either.

VX the nerve agent stands for *Virulent Agent X*: the most perfect description of Mason you could hope to coin.

And as for David Mason: if Nazzar was telling the truth — which he did, to a fault — then it looked like Mason had lied about how Sonny had died and pinned it on me. Whether Nazzar believed me or not was another matter. So Mason, possibly with Rhodes's help, was running an operation with Micky, which they needed Sonny Boy to execute. Nazzar was misled and co-opted. Sonny Boy freaked out, went rogue and in the process prepared the ground for me. But what made him freak out? And did King know that he and Micky — presumably on Mason's orders — were trying to cut a deal with the Russians? If that was true, why deploy me? Maybe the deal went bad. Maybe Mason was off-piste and covering his tracks.

A lot of *unknown unknowns* as Americans like to say when they're looking for a clever way to cover up a cock-up. The irony of an Unknown operative contemplating his own mission's unknowns wasn't lost on me.

There was another unknown, too: Commander Frank Knight. Absent from the briefing; absent from this job. But Frank was never absent. He was omnipresent. Had he sent me to see Sonny Boy to warn me . . . or to frame me? There was only ever one game Frank played: his own. Genies, Russians, mystery white men and irregular irregulars . . . even a failed hit on a Russian diplomat's wife in Caracas: these were all known unknowns — but only to me. *I* didn't know what they meant, but someone sure as hell did. And that someone was sure to be Frank.

*

Hours passed. And then at the centre of my vision — silently, without warning — light spilled on the ground between the huts. I blinked hard and refocused. A dirty-orange glow spread out, thrown at first by one, and then two, then three and finally four burning torches, each one lit off the other until they formed an illuminated square between and behind the two rondels.

Figures of men hidden by mad metal masks of weird elephant caricatures held the firebrands aloft. In their midst another figure emerged, a tall dancer slipping in and out of the torchlight, a pirate's cutlass in one hand, and what looked like an animal-hair fly whisk in the other. Masked in red cloth, and crowned with dark feathers, the dancer's grotesque facial features were picked out in white shells that glinted like shards of bone erupting through a blood-red wound. In the centre of its forehead one dirty-white eye looked out unblinking into the darkness. It was monstrous. Sonny Boy's rantings seemed suddenly more insightful than insane.

My ears filled with the rhythmic *thump-thump thump-thump* of my heart echoing hard in my head. The beating ebbed with the breeze and washed back over me. Only then did I realize that my heart was pumping in perfect time with the rise and fall of a beating drum hidden from sight by the trees or the huts. It was a big, bold beat — hollow, rich and resonant, as if pounded out of a cavernous tree trunk, and counterpointed by wild, syncopated rhythms made from the clattering of metal on metal, which skittered and chimed in synch with the rise and fall of the shadows cast by the masked men.

And then four more men emerged, unmasked, sweat-drenched, bearing a prisoner between them into the torch-lit square. Tied face down by the wrists and ankles to a bamboo cross, their captive writhed and shuddered beneath the hide of a hyena. His face craned towards the forest. I could see then that his mouth was stopped by a wad of dark cloth. For a moment he leered into my rifle lens with wide, rolling eyes before staring back to earth again.

Details in the night firelight were elusive, diminished further by the narrow aperture of the scope. But through the rifle glass, facts emerged with crystal clarity: the range was exactly three hundred metres; the line of fire was unimpeded; and the captive was unquestionably a white man. Not only that, he was unquestionably a soldier. Early twenties; a hundred and sixty pounds, gym-honed body, close-cropped hair: one hundred per cent squaddie. If I hadn't been told that the area was crawling with Russians, maybe I'd have guessed he was an American. Or a Brit. Or maybe I wouldn't have guessed at all. Perhaps I was just seeing what I wanted, or expected to see: but his round face; fair hair; bony brow all screamed 'Slav' to me. I strained my eye into the scope. If he had a scorpion tattoo it was impossible to pick it out.

The four cross-bearers stopped and hauled the bamboo frame upright, facing me. The prisoner couldn't support his head, which lolled back and forth as the cross jerked to a stop. Nostrils flared, Adam's apple working hard as he retched against the cloth, he looked more bestial than human. The red-masked master of ceremonies paced sideways to face him, his robed back turned to my scope. My heartbeat slowed and fell out of time with the beat of the drum. My finger felt contact with the trigger. My breathing deepened. I began to prepare to fire, even though there was no shot to take.

Not yet.

The drumming quickened, reaching a mad, polyrhythmic crescendo. The one-eyed dancer dropped the cutlass to the ground and, twitching, held the fly whisk aloft. The metal-masked men swayed and jolted, swayed and jolted, over and over, expressing with their bodies a refrain in the music I couldn't untangle. An eerie ululating mingled with the clashing, crashing of the beat and then broke high and free – though whether it came from the elephant men, their master or the unseen drummers I couldn't say.

And then silence.

The torchbearers stood still, and the light settled. The four men holding the cross bowed their heads. But the red-masked man shuffled in the dust still, moving carefully around the dropped cutlass in slow, methodical steps. The black plumes above his head pitched and yawed; held aloft, the fly whisk dipped and flicked. And then with his left hand the grotesque dancer reached behind his back and dipped his hand into a pouch tied to the back of his belt. He stooped slightly and then extended the arm out again with a flourish, pulsing forward four times, until his outstretched palm pressed against the prisoner's chest. Down came the fly whisk, four times in total, across the captive's head and shoulders. Every muscle taut, straining in the torchlight against his bonds, the prisoner threw his head back and roared a cloth-muffled scream into the void. And then he collapsed, hanging limp from his bonds; spent. Slowly, the red dancer withdrew his left palm. Stuck to the prisoner's chest – just above the heart – was a white badge, a cow-rie shell perhaps, or piece of bone. It looked like the Cyclops eye sported by his tormentor. Without warning, the dancer struck the prisoner across the face, so that he revived and looked up and into the white-bone grimace of the red mask. Reaching out once more, the dancer removed the cloth from the captive's mouth and spoke loudly in a language I didn't recognize.

And then, more quietly, he spoke again. The breeze carried the words to me with eerie clarity: '*Vy svoboden.*' *You are free.*

The prisoner's eyes focused and then filled with tears. His jaw worked. The breeze died, and I couldn't hear his reply, but I could lip-read it through the rifle scope in the torchlight.

'*Blagodaryu,*' he said. He was thanking his captor in Russian for releasing him.

The four torchbearers remained still as the men who'd borne him raised their heads and then cut the young man loose. The red-masked dancer picked up his cutlass and held it and the fly whisk aloft. His hands and forearms were daubed with mud or paint. The hem of his red garb dropped all the way to the floor. But there was something unnerving in his gait, the way he held himself, the way he moved.

I felt I knew him, as if there was something familiar about this whole scene – an echo of a long-lost memory. And then I realized: strip away the ceremony and the crazy get-up and standing there was the physical double of the mystery white man in the photographs. That was it. It had to be.

My finger took first pressure.

I felt I was right. But my feelings had been getting me into trouble recently. There was no way to *know*. And what I needed now, what the mission needed, were facts, not guesses. I relaxed my finger, and the one-eyed dancer paced off between the huts and out of vision. The freed man, his guards and the elephant-masked torchbearers followed, so that before long the scene was deserted and the only light that fell into my reticule dropped from the rising moon.

My heartbeat returned to its natural rhythm. I rolled the stone under my tongue and swallowed hard. There were ten hours to wait. I relaxed back into the ground and locked my gaze into the milky black of the forest night. An image flickered behind the scope of Ana María, laughing as we knocked our glasses together for the first time; and then of my mother, looking out over Dublin Bay. I tried to bring my father's face to mind but I blinked again and all the images dissolved.

There was only darkness. Sonny Boy's monsters were gone. And in the morning there was killing to be done.

21

At first it feels the time will never come. You fret because you want it all to happen so that it will be over and you will know what has happened. Then the time draws near. Suddenly it seems too soon and you fret again, because now you want time to stretch. You aren't ready. You need more time. And then when you remember there is nothing left to prepare for, the last minutes expand into eons. You relax and wait. And then, as if without warning, it's happening. The clocks rush and then stop dead. The minutes, hours – days, maybe – of waiting and watching evaporate. In an instant it's you and your target and it always has been. The crosshairs settle with a force of inevitability so profound it's un-noticeable: like drawing breath, the shot is not a climax but a certainty; an unremarkable revolution in the rhythm of everything you are, and all that you have become.

Which is to say, a killer.

The sun rose quickly, as if escaping the chitter-chatter of the monkeys chasing it through the trees and up over the hills. The huts and the trees and the clearing looked different in the morning light than they had in the dusk and then in the glow of the torchlight. The images over-lapped, merged, dissipated. I gently tensed and relaxed my muscles one last time, starting at my neck and rolling down my body to my feet, and then back again. The crosshairs sat in between the two huts. There was nothing in my peripheral vision. And no sign where the dancers last night might have gone to, nor where the white man and his band of soldiers might appear from.

There was no line of sight through the trees left or right of the huts, and the limited satellite imagery I'd seen didn't show any barracks, tents or base of any description. If the Chinese had put up any buildings while they scratched around for minerals, there were none left to be seen. All that I could make out was a thin hunter's path about ten metres behind the beaten-earth square where Sonny Boy had photographed the gathering weeks previously. Perhaps the weird scenes enacted there last night would mean the parade was cancelled. Perhaps Sonny Boy had photographed a one-off event. Perhaps my target was smoking a Stolichnaya cigarette over his morning coffee in Moscow. There was another possibility too, and one devastating if true: if Mason was tying off loose ends after a failed and unauthorized bid to strike a deal with the Russians, perhaps *I* was the target.

Insect bites swelled and blistered around my wrists, ankles. Ants sank their mandibles into my neck. Sweat broke across my back. And then the timbre of the savannah changed, so slight at first it might have been the breeze shifting the grasses threaded around my head. The humming I'd picked up the evening before had resumed. It was a generator for sure, far off or buried. The monkeys stopped. A flurry of yellow birds took off in fright from the boughs above the hut on the left. And then one by one the soldiers emerged from it. A dozen Africans and Europeans dressed in a mixed bag of European army surplus fatigues and civvies. The whites had all the charm of a Moscow bar-brawl waiting to happen; the blacks looked like they'd dressed up as carica-tures of a rebel army – bandanas, juju-charms and amulets, and the usual showing of Disney T-shirts awk-wardly out of place among the guns and ammo: Pocahontas stood dead centre, cradling a PKM machine gun and criss-crossed by two belts of 7.62 that fed it. Lit-tle Chinese hand grenades hung from their webbing; machetes from their belts.

They looked like ragtag comic-book rebels but they were snappy and well drilled. All the soldiers moved together as one integrated unit without trying to do so. They were professionals, and they'd clearly been in each other's company for a while. To the enemy, or from a satellite, they'd look like local troops supported by white mercenaries. But up close they were one hundred per cent Spetsnaz.

They stood at ease. The breeze picked up. The gen-erator continued to pulse; soldiers' boots shuffled on the beaten earth. But that's all the sound there was. Twelve armed men could not have walked through the trees to my left unseen and unheard. Twelve armed men could not have been contained within the walls of the thatched rondel – this morning, overnight or ever. It was too small, and they were too many. No. There was only one place both the troops this morning and the motley crew last night could have come from: a tunnel beneath the hut. The same place the generator was housed too, most likely.

I'd asked Roberts what the terrain was like when we looked at the photo Sonny Boy had hidden in the locket.

'Hot. Riddled with caves. It's a million miles from anywhere,' he'd replied.

I'd taken on board the first bit and the last bit. But it was the caves that were key. That's why there was no trace of the earlier Chinese exploration, and why there was so little trace of anything above ground then: it was all buried. I was on top of them.

I understood, too, why they needed a sniper. Depending how deep the caves went, even a bunker-buster might not penetrate them. Killing people in caves is notoriously difficult. They'd learned that the hard way at Tora Bora. It would have been useful if they'd briefed me on the lie of the land. Spies and their secrets. My career had been like playing a twenty-three-year game of Murder in the Dark with Frank. I never knew if he couldn't, or wouldn't, remove the blindfold; and because of that I never knew if he was driven by duty or friendship. I tacked between those two poles, lost in a sea of blood of my own spilling.

I clicked the little speckled stone against the backs of my front teeth and weighed anchor.

The men stood to attention.

And into the clearing stepped the white man. Walking left to right, stooped slightly, right arm crooked as if halfway to a salute. It was as if Sonny Boy's photograph had come to life. Grey fatigues; weathered, tanned skin. A thin reed of a man bent in the morning sun.

I picked him up and tracked him through the scope as he paced from one hut towards the other, half-turned towards the men, his men. The angle was too oblique for a chest shot. I held the crosshairs in the centre of his head.

One second.

The point of impact would be the middle of the right ear. He looked frailer than the photograph suggested, his hair whiter.

Two seconds.

He moved between the huts as I guessed he would: one metre per second, per stride.

Turn, damn you. Turn. I willed him to look dead ahead. *I want to see your face.* His pace faltered. He slowed. I slowed. But he looked towards the men, arm coming up to salute. First pressure.

Three seconds.

The salute was never made. The arm never raised. No command given. My heart all but stopped, the beat so slow. I was tethered to the bullet, my mind filled with one single certainty. The man was already dead even though the shot was not yet taken. The target's name had already been written in the *Book of the Dead.*

Fractions of a millimetre of steel moved against one another. The trigger travelled less than the width of half a hair. And the man turned and looked out into the trees.

The clocks restarted. Blood pumped in my ears. Oxygen rushed in my throat. But there was no echo of the shot, because there was no shot to take. As I lay prone, I saw my target looking back at me: aged but unmistakable. Pressed between the dark earth and the light sky I saw finally through the rifle scope what had been in front of me all along.

I stared out across the hot African hillside and straight into my father's face.

22

It was him.

No question.

No doubt.

I'd spent twenty-six years trying to forget him. So I remembered him perfectly.

It was shocking. But it was also inevitable. Just as the shot would have been. Of course it was him. There was only one outcome to everything.

And there are no coincidences.

The tension rippled out of my shoulders. My heart rate climbed and then fell again. My neck softened, and my head slumped. I came off the gun and lay my head on the dead leaves and sharp grasses and closed my eyes. As I lost focus, purpose, cramp and nausea set in. The pit of my stomach felt as if it was expanding across the clearing and out across the hillside, as if I was melting into the earth itself. I felt the little good-luck lion Roberts had given me dig into my wrist. I remembered the bullet wound in his side – where Ezra had shot him, to save him. His lucky wound. Sonny Boy had not tried to kill me. He'd tried to save me.

Twenty-six years of forgetting evaporated into the sweat-soaked dirt. I rolled the little pebble around my mouth. Trapped behind the green-red film of my eyelids I tried to gather the floating mosaic of my parents' faces. But only hers came to me.

She'd killed herself because she couldn't bear the pain of losing him – a pain more profound even than leaving me an orphan. But she hadn't lost him. And I was still an orphan.

I came back on the gun and fired.

The round hit him four centimetres above the right nipple. He spun as he fell, twisting around a spattering of his own blood, first looking out towards me and then up to the sky. The bullet punched out of his back, to the left of his shoulder blade. He came down hard, arms and legs akimbo. I took four of the others out at the knees, ankles – wounding, not killing.

Five. Six.

It was as ill advised to fire four shots without moving as it was to fire fourteen. In for a penny, in for a pound. My rounds streaked out towards the compound. I could hear the dull slap of lead on skin; and the sharp crack of bones shearing and splintering.

Three hundred metres is dangerously close. Stand up then and their AKs would have brought me straight back down again. I worked the bolt and kept firing.

Seven. Eight.

Soldiers scrambled to cover my father, lying across him. I dropped the ones at the edge of the clearing first and worked inwards. Slow, but methodical. They writhed and screamed. Blood pumped from arterial wounds arced in the morning sunlight. The dusty parade square turned into a muddy patch of blood-red sludge.

I dropped the empty magazine and reloaded. Ten rounds left.

Time to go.

I rose up on to shaky legs, racked with cramp and the pain of muscles burning back to life. But I ran hard and fast, recovering a flat sprint out of the first stumbles. Shots followed me – the *rat-a-tat-tat* of assault rifles hitting nothing but trees and sky. Pocahontas's foot had come off above the ankle; his PMK stayed silent.

I had to cover five klicks without getting hit, getting caught or getting lost. I was following a hunch, but it felt like a good one. And there was nowhere else to go. Two rounds came in closer, and then a third snapped past my ear. That's the thing about playing at being a rebel: you don't get fancy optics or a decent rifle. It was their last and closest shot. The further I ran, the thicker the trees grew, and although I was slowed by steep ground and underscrub I was out of range and in deep cover before any of the mangled militia drew a bead on me. I ran as steadily as the terrain allowed, retracing as best I could the exact route I'd come in on. I needed to stay under cover. But remaining silent was no longer an issue. Speed was.

Every klick I paused, looked, listened. No dogs, no shots or shouts, nothing in the air. I kept running, stopping, running, stopping. In ten minutes I was at the bend in the river where I'd seen the orphan girl. I crouched by the cotton tree where I offered her the sweets.

No sound. No movement. No sign of her, or that she or I had ever been there. I strained hard above the rasp of air in my throat, the drumming of my heartbeat in my ears.

Nothing.

I searched the foliage that had screened her arrival and her escape. Side to side, then back and forth, prodding with the rifle barrel, staring into every nook and cranny. One metre in. Then two. Then three deep. Within a few minutes I had searched an area twenty metres square.

Nothing.

She just simply couldn't have got further than that without me seeing. It wasn't possible. I went back to the cotton tree to start over.

And then they lit me up.

Boom.

Close contact in the forest is intense. The enemy can be on you before you see or hear them. Noise distorts, your eyes betray you, your senses waylay you. A mortar bomb tore past me, a handspan from my head. With its unmistakable whistle-roar it flew parallel to the ground and exploded into the cotton tree in front of me, sending a shower of bark splinters and shrapnel back towards me. I dodged right and threw myself into the secondary scrub off the clearing. Hot metal nicked my cheek, arm, thigh. It was a young tree. Soft enough that the bomb had gone in far enough to throw most of the shrapnel straight back out past me. Then another went off ten metres to my left; and another to my right. The bombs were high, hitting tree trunks and branches, tearing boughs off in great splintering snaps that were as loud as gunshots. They were small bombs, 60mm most likely, fired by hand by troops on the move. I knew. I'd done it myself.

They kept coming like a deadly waltz.

One-two, three; one-two, three; one-two, three.

The PKMs opened up next, pumping out hundreds of rounds of burning belt-fed tracer. The gloom between the trees flared with a crazy web of high-velocity barium zinging between, through and off boughs like bright-green lasers. Judging from the direction of fire, they had me on three sides. The Mong River bulged out to the west, towards the camp. They were coming at me dead on, and from the north- and south-west. The cotton tree and the area I'd been searching were on the east bank. There was a slight rise in the ground. I got as small as I could and got myself on the gun. Tracer whipped over me, around me. Lines of green-death snapped at my ears. Fortunately the golden rule of sniping is the same as one of the fundamental laws of physics: every action has an equal and opposite reaction. You can light me up at two hundred and fifty rounds a minute, but I can see exactly where you're hiding, soldier boy.

I had ten rounds and made them count. The machine guns fell silent. Then two of the mobile mortar teams. But all the while the bombs still came in from my right flank, low and fast. I got small, ditched the rifle and drew the SIG.

And then I saw them.

Holy God.

Four men – if you could still call them that – broke cover at three hundred metres and ran straight towards me. Two white, two black: all unarmed and dressed in the ragged remnants of what had once been uniforms. Each man carried a traditional fly whisk in his right hand – a wooden grip finished with a length of black hair, exactly the same as the red-masked man had brandished the night before.

And how they ran. A hundred metres covered in seconds.

The nearer they got, the more manifest their hideousness. Every muscle strained, bulged, as if fit to burst, embossed with veins that stood out like tramlines riding across sinew. Their eyes were wild and rolled back, so that their irises vanished into a blur of white-eyed horror. And their mouths – wide open, lips pulled taut – sent forth waves of ululating screeches.

Two hundred metres.

The mortar teams I'd taken out were replaced with rebels firing rocket-propelled grenades. One whistle-thudded into the ground next to me, very loud and extremely close. Molten copper burned me. Shrapnel sliced me. My head sang. Sweat stung my eyes. I touched my left ear. The top half was missing. My hand came back to steady the SIG wet with my own blood.

One hundred metres.

The screams of the men charging me harmonized with the screeching in my head. The forest floor began to burn – magnesium from the spent tracer rounds ignited the leaf mulch. Smoke from cordite hung between the trees, showing up the tracer.

Fifty metres.

I inhaled, drew a bead and breathed out slowly.

Thirty metres.

I put two rounds in the chest of the lead runner. No body armour. A fountain of thick red blood erupted from his sternum. It didn't even break his stride. What were they on? PCP? Ketamine?

Fuck.

Twenty metres.

Single head shot. Down he went. The other three kept on coming.

Ten metres.

Two more head shots. One remained, running flat out towards me.

Five metres.

Everyone else stopped firing for fear of hitting their own man. I squeezed the trigger.

Nothing.

Stoppage. Dirt in the breech.

My left palm crashed into the back of the SIG's slide. I pulled it back, hard. An unspent round leaped out, too late. He dived, I rolled at the last moment. A hundred and eighty pounds of screaming Spetsnaz crashed on to the forest floor next to me. We lay top to tail. I smashed my boot heel into his face. His nose disintegrated, blood coloured his face. I was up, and then down again, his legs sweeping mine from under me. He rolled back, and then sprang to his feet, launching himself upright off his shoulders. I kicked. He caught my boot. He was incredibly fast, and exceptionally strong. I guessed he'd try to catch, lock and break my leg. So I spun and threw my left leg around his neck. But that wasn't his plan. Keeping hold of my right boot, he dropped the fly whisk and grabbed my left, too. I hit the ground again, on my back, staring up at his smashed, crazed face. He rotated each leg in on itself – one clockwise, one anti-clockwise.

He was trying to twist my legs off.

I roared in pain. My femurs began to dislocate from my pelvis. Spit and blood gushed from his mouth; sweat cascaded off him. He looked mad – eyes rolling; mouth screaming; muscles fit to burst, bulging through the ragged strips of his fatigues. I smacked the ground with both arms to brace myself. The hot shards of an exploded mortar bomb burned my skin. My left hand found the recocked SIG. My knees and ankles were about to give way, ligaments stretched to breaking point. I fired blind. The shot tore through his right wrist, shattering the bone. My left leg fell. I twisted clockwise with him, rolled and fired twice more into his chest. The force of the rounds hitting and breaking his sternum sent a shock wave across his torso. He took half a step back, his left hand still latched firm on to my right boot, his right hand hanging from a bloody mess of mangled sinew by his side.

He appeared not even to notice that he'd been shot. Instead of staggering or falling, he threw me. Not a martial arts throw. A monster throw. As if I were a doll in a child's hand he flung me by the boot six feet through the air. I crumpled against the trunk of the cotton tree. I managed a crouch as he set about me again, his wounded arm coming down heavily towards me. Right arm up. I blocked. The force of his swing was so hard that I was pummelled back to the ground and the almost-severed hand sheared off completely, hitting the ground beside us. He carried on, unchecked. He was too close for a head shot. His left hand balled into a fist. I shot it. Fingers blew off; palm flesh vaporized. I rolled, stood and brought the barrel up again, still left-handed. But he was unnaturally fast. A bloodied stump knocked my hand away. Straight kick to the right knee. Nothing. It was like striking concrete. He threw his body weight against me. I tried to sidestep and lost my footing. And then he had me, in an obscene, bloody bear hug. There was no technique any more; just pure, brute force.

When you fight, you should think. And what you should think is: *what next?* And if you're any good at fighting you should know the answer several moves in advance. It's not conscious thought but instinctive anticipation – from a bar brawl to the Olympics, putting down your opponent is a game of full-contact chess. I've spent my whole life fighting, but I didn't know what was coming next.

Arms pinioned, he lifted me off the ground. With no hands left to hold me, he simply squeezed. I felt a rib crack. And then another. And another.

And then it happened. Holding me head and shoulders above him, my heels a good foot clear of the ground, he sank his teeth into the base of my neck. Intense nerve pain shot through me. I felt his bite go deep, grinding against my collar bone. I remembered the dead soldiers in the hut outside Kabala. And then I knew. He was going to bite through my neck. I still had the SIG, but my arms were locked, useless. I pushed down as hard as I could with my left hand, straining towards the ground. As his bite deepened I got my elbow lower than the bulge of his biceps. I crooked my arm, pivoted my wrist . . . and fired.

His brain pan emptied into my face, the bullet grazing my chin as it exited his skull. We collapsed into a bloody heap. I spat out a mouthful of brain tissue and worked myself free from under him. I sat up, wiped the blood out of my eyes and picked a shard of bone out of my tongue. It had gone through my cheek, between my teeth. The wound in my neck was deep, but the bone wasn't broken. The ribs hurt, but everything else did, too. My head rang. My sliced ear throbbed: even the bit of me that had been cut off still hurt. The air reeked with the smell of blood and cordite, and, very faintly, the scent of wild mint, which I thought we'd crushed in the mêlée.

My attacker lay still. Head shots took them out instantly – him and the runners. And thank God. Nothing else seemed to make any difference at all. His arms were thrown up akimbo. On the inside of the right arm, just above the armpit, the tattoo of a tiny black scorpion swam in the blood that drenched him. I scrambled to my feet and looked out from under what was left of the trees. Men in uniform swarmed across the open ground in tight formation. The ululating resumed, and a dozen more runners came into view, sprinting through the lines of troops moving in on me. I remembered with a jolt that I'd just shot my father. Then a rocket-propelled grenade *whoosh-banged* into the undergrowth.

Here we go again.

I ran with my back to the river. But I knew they'd out-flank me. A steady stream of 7.62 snapped beside, above, around me. I kept low, SIG in hand, and dodged trees and branches. Grass burned. Hundreds of rounds ripped up the bush around me. Bit by bit my cover was being obliterated. Training will only get you so far. There comes a time when survival becomes a statistical aberration. I prepared for impact and lunged on as fast as I could, expecting to be floored at any moment.

Another RPG shrieked past, close enough to touch. I hit the ground at the same time it did, only a couple of metres in front of me. I braced for the inevitable shower of shrapnel, the blast wave, the tearing of flesh. But although the explosion was deafening – and unusually so – the ground absorbed the full force of the blast. I put my head up. The grenade had landed in a small thicket of vine-draped saplings. In the middle of them, smok-ing and fringed with shredded foliage, yawned a pitch-black hole. Not a blast crater or a pit, but a hole. Behind me I could hear the splashing of boots in water. The runners were crossing the river. I put my weight on to my hands, drew my knees up, kicked back, and cata-pulted myself headlong into the darkness.

I landed in the mouth of a cave – smoking and torn

up by shrapnel, but just deep and tall enough to navigate at a crouch. I reached up into the sunlight and pulled one of the felled saplings across the opening and scuttled inside. Almost immediately the passage dog-legged hard right, and then after another ten metres or so bore sharply round to the left so that any light from the surface was killed completely.

I moved from daylight to gloom to pitch-black too rapidly for my eyes to adjust at all. I stopped and listened. Two things were immediately obvious: I had not been followed, and I was not alone.

Just audible in the darkness above the singing in my blast-damaged eardrums I could hear rapid, shallow breathing. Something or someone else was there and they were scared, injured maybe – and trying hard, most likely, not to give themselves away. I stared, myopic, into the void and tried to make out any shape or movement. But all I could see was the brightly coloured patterns of night-blindness that wove around my retina. In my mind's eye flashes of the red-masked dancer and the crucified captive sparked and died on the edges of my vision. Was that the breath of another prisoner I could hear? I brought the still-silenced barrel of the SIG up blindly into the blackness.

Nothing moved.

I kept the pistol up and slowly, with my left hand, felt in the pocket of my fatigues for the LED torch. I aimed it along the barrel and clicked it on, ready to fire.

Caught in the beam were the frightened eyes of the girl I'd found under the cotton tree, or rather the girl who'd found me. I dipped the beam of bright-blue light to the ground and holstered the SIG.

My hunch had paid off.

'Hello again,' I said, and crouched down, leaning my back against the wall of the cave. I was filthy, caked in blood and mud and sweat. She didn't blink, wide eyes taking it all in.

There was nothing to say. Nothing I *could* say.

Outside, above ground, the shots and shouts grew fainter – muffled by the trees and the bends in the tunnel and, hopefully, greater and greater distance. I relaxed, and felt immediately overcome with pain and nausea.

I closed my eyes and saw my father fall, cut down by my bullet; the look of surprise in his eyes; his thin frame contorted by the shock of the shot. The tears came then, scoring hot, wet streaks into my bloodstained cheeks. And I cried long and hard. My shoulders juddered, my nose ran, saliva fell from my mouth and pooled on the floor between my feet. I felt the girl's hand press lightly on my arm. I rocked on to my haunches and then down on my knees and rested my head on the cushion of dead leaves on the ground and wept silently in the torchlight with her crouched beside me.

Twenty-six years, and I had never wept for him once. And then I thought the tears would never stop. Engulfed by a flood of memories I barely knew I had, I balled up on my side like a lost child and cried myself to sleep.

23

I woke with a start and swept the passage with the torch beam. Alone. The cave was empty. I looked at my watch. Fourteen-hundred. I'd been out for over four hours. Lying on the ground by my head was a ripe mango and hunk of bread. And next to them stood a little wooden stick man – twigs tied together with twine and a scrap of red cotton wrapped around its head. I sat up and picked it up and turned it over in my hands. The legs were sharpened so it would stand upright. The hands were stumps: on one there was a splinter protruding, like a knife or wand; on the other a wisp of black hair – hers, I supposed. It was crude and childlike but an unmistakable effigy of the red-masked man.

Drawn with a finger into the dirt on the cave floor between where its legs had stood was an arrow, pointing deeper into the cave. I put the figure down and ate the mango, peeling it with my teeth. The bread was fresh – a dense, heavy rye. Soldier's bread. Russian bread. I took the day bag off my back. It had been opened, but nothing important had been taken. She was a curious girl, but not a thief – even though she had every right to be. I drank some water and ate a bar of chocolate.

My senses seeped back to me. I felt ashamed and relieved: ashamed because I had cried neither for my father nor my mother but for myself; relieved because I knew my shot had landed in exactly the right place. No unnecessary pain or suffering. Quick and clean.

But it wasn't finished yet.

I took off my shirt and opened the medical kit. First, I bandaged my ribs, strapping them as tight as I could. Second, I disinfected the wound on my throat, packed it with gauze and taped it up as best I could. Then I swallowed a thousand milligrams of penicillin – who knew what I might have contracted from Super Rebel. Finally I rubbed a fentanyl lozenge around my gums. Instant pain relief. God bless the Medical Corps. Before I put the shirt back on I used it to clean the SIG, which I field-stripped, wiped the dirt out of and reloaded.

The stick-man I left where she'd put it. I wanted to repay her for the bread and mango, but, except for a spare torch, I had little of any use to offer. I put it next to the effigy and then unpicked the lucky lion charm from my wrist and wrapped it around the wooden man. I hoped that might at least make her smile.

Then I taped the LED securely underneath the silencer and rechecked the breech.

Good to go.

The cave was natural: no sign of human habitation, hammer marks or blasting by miners in the granite walls. There were no bats, either, or guano – though I wondered if the colony I saw come in to roost the night before found sanctuary in the hills as well as on them. The air was cool, the temperature stable. I managed to walk at a crouch. Heavy going on the thighs, but I covered ground quickly. After a hundred metres the tunnel seemed to bend off to the left, but it was hard to be sure. What was certain was that I was heading deeper underground, and steeply so. As I descended the scent of the chamber became noticeable. Growing stronger the further I went, a heavy, musty smell filled the passageway. Then the slime-covered walls began to glint, and tiny drops of water hung from the ceiling, which was crested with miniature, milky-white stalactites. I was standing under the Mong River. The floor was wet. I trod cautiously, but there were no pits in the rock floor. A thin fissure above, a fault in the granite, funnelled a steady drip from the bed of the dark-green watercourse above. I swept the floor with the torch beam. Tiny human footprints skirted each side of the mud, this way and that, and vanished on the dry ground that continued on either side.

I pressed on.

The floor became steeper still. The pressure in my ears shifted. I shortened my steps to control my progress. I swept the floor with the torch beam, looking for more footprints, any sign of habitation, but found none. Every few metres I stopped and listened in darkness. The chatter of monkeys and buzz of flies had abated completely. There was nothing to hear but my own breathing coming back to me in the echo chamber of the tunnel.

After a hundred metres or so, the passage divided. To

the right, the floor seemed to climb a little. To the left, the downward descent continued. I ran the beam of light over the walls. Still nothing. No sign of animals, or insects; no markings at all – just unremarkable rock. I stood and listened, the barrel of the SIG pointing downwards. Then in the dirt and mulch of the cave floor, a glint of colour. I bent down and picked up a bright-blue M&M.

Not a thief. A guide.

The sweet was a couple of feet along the left-hand passage. I cut a waypoint in the slime-dirt covering the cave wall, ate the chocolate peanut and pressed on.

I kept on keeping on for five kilometres. The descent levelled out a little, but continued at a slope, downhill and deeper into the bedrock. It took two hours and a small handful of M&Ms before the passage ended abruptly. Perched on a rock up against the wall sat the last sweet, red and incongruous in the black catacomb. There was no arrow. No other sign. I spun around, half-expecting to have been followed, but there was no one there.

'You idiot, Max,' I cursed under my breath, 'it's not a trap. Or a map. It's a bloody *game*. A child's game.'

All this, to end up being caught out by an eight-year-old. There was no plan. And there never had been. I picked up the Judas sweet and crushed it between my back teeth. When you start running, you stop thinking. My whole life had been consumed with tactics, empty of strategy. No thought. Just twenty-six years of flight. And the killing. The endless, bloody killing.

'Don't forget the dead, Max,' I said out loud, 'in case they forget you.'

I swallowed the sweet and sat down heavily on the stone it had rested on. My head spun, the earth turned. The torch beam flashed wildly as I lurched to one side. My feet went from under me. I tumbled through the space of the tunnel and landed heavily, banging my head on the rock wall as I went. I turned round and brought the torch beam to bear on the spot where I'd been sitting but I didn't need it. The passage was now lit by a shaft of electric light. I'd fallen all of a foot on to the floor and ended up on my arse. Shifted by my weight, the stone had rolled aside to reveal a crack in the cave. That's how the light got in.

A roughly hewn corridor stretched out under the burning-hot hillside above. The complex was buried deep, the walls and ceiling of the cave patched with concrete reinforced with steel rods and wire mesh. The drone-pulse of an unseen generator filled the void of the dank stone walkway. Cool air hissed from stainless-steel pipes that wound their way above. At twelve-metre intervals security doors with magnetic-swipe entry panels stood shut against the bright-white light.

I holstered the SIG, slipped the day bag off my shoulders and fed it back through the hole I'd just dropped down from, out of sight. I checked the dressings on my neck and my chest and walked on, singing *'Bayu Bayushki Bayu'* to myself under my breath. Generations of Russian mothers have sung it to their babies, mine included, warning them not to sleep too close to the edge in case the grey wolf snatches them away to the woods.

'*Bayu-bayushki-bayu, nye lozhisya na krayu* . . .' Rock-a-bye baby, don't lie on the edge . . .

Each entry panel glowed red, locked. In each door a security window looked on to a square concrete cell. Through the glass, darkly, the silhouettes of men standing in rows revealed themselves. Listless, naked, heads bowed, bare feet rooted to the spot. Black men and white men, heads shaved, rocking back and forth, back and forth. From above a fine mist dropped on to their shoulders – a grey-green fog pumped from long vents in the ceiling that condensed on the floor and ran in rivulets to a drain in the far corner. No faces were visible, just the muscle-bound backs of ten swaying somnambulists.

'*Pridyot serenkiy volchok I ukhvatit za bochok* . . .' Or the little grey wolf will bite your side . . .

I walked past all five doors. The same scene played out in each. Fifty men clothed in fog and silence, waiting in suspended animation. At the end of the corridor a plastic sign was bolted to the wall. In Russian and English it read:

Инкубатор, Уровень 4. Только уполномоченный персонал.
Incubator, Level 4. Authorized Personnel Only.

Beneath it, a site map depicted Levels One to Five. The layout of the level I was on was replicated immediately above me. That meant there was the capacity for at least a hundred men in the cells alone. There was no indication of what the other upper two levels were for – the armoury, quartermaster stores, a canteen . . . they must all be located somewhere, I thought to myself. What looked like two exits to ground level rose in the middle of Level One – most likely coming out into the two huts my father had emerged from, and moved between. One hut was fed by a lift shaft, the other by a flight of stairs.

My father . . . I checked myself. *What's done is done.*

Inside the cave complex each floor was furnished with stairs at one end and a lift at the other. I'd dropped down into a recess behind the lift that most likely housed the power relay unit for that floor. But what I was looking for was on the lowest level. A bold red cross marked the spot. With any luck the hospital would still be inundated with wounded.

'*I potashchit vo lesok* . . .' And drag you off into the woods . . .

I checked the corridor again. No guards. No sound of footsteps. No obvious cameras. Scores, possibly hundreds, of people above and below me, and the only sound was the rhythmic hum of generators and the fizzing of the fluorescent lights overhead. I reholstered the SIG, leaving the silencer and torch attached, and took the stairs, quickly but carefully, heading down to Level Five.

A stinking, bloody mess, I looked perfect for the part.

My fatigues were ripped. I'd obviously not long ago been in a firefight. And I spoke fluent Russian. Despite the fact that I was missing half an ear and had been decorated with another man's brains, things were working out well: there was nothing to distinguish me from the people who were trying to kill me. Feeling overly pleased with myself, I ran straight into an immaculately turned-out officer at the bottom of the stairs.

'God damn you! Watch where you're going, will you?' he barked in Russian. Then he recovered himself and looked at me properly. My right hand twitched, but the SIG remained holstered. The fire door he'd emerged from swung shut behind him.

'Sorry . . .' I looked at his uniform for rank insignia. One star. Major. I saluted. 'Sir. I mean sorry, *sir.*'

'Name?'

'Ivanov.' Small lies. Always tell small lies to power. We stood a foot apart. Five-ten, wiry, mean as fuck.

'Pass.'

'Sir, I lost it, sir, in the firefight. That motherfucker fucking fucked us. I got separated from my unit. I was told to report to Level Five to get patched up.'

'Huh. OK. Next time take the lift. This is restricted access.' He sized me up. I must have been one of the oldest soldiers in the barracks. I hoped the blood on my face concealed my years. He saluted back. I started to move past him, but he caught my arm.

'Sir?'

'When you're done, see Petrov, the *praporshchik* in

Two-A, and get your pass sorted before some rear-echelon prick really fucks you.'

I smiled and saluted again. 'Sir, yes sir. Thank you, sir.'

He dismissed me with a 'carry on', and we pivoted past each other. I headed through the fire doors and emerged into the hubbub of a cavernous dressing station.

'*Shto?*' The head of a uniformed ward sister popped up from behind a high metal desk set to one side of the reception ward. Behind her stretched rows of make-shift curtained cubicles, a bank of gurneys and a dozen medical staff coming and going from doors on either side. Each exit was marked with the name of the service or facility it led to: *Surgery, Radiography, Diagnostics, La-boratories One* and *Two* and *Emergency Resuscitation.* At the far end one red door, emblazoned with a biohazard sign, was titled in Russian and English: *Quarantine: Level One Infection. Deadly Force Authorized.* The air was scented with antiseptic and sang with the beeping of vital signs moni-tors and the muted urgent conversation that follows an emergency. I turned my attention back to the sister.

'Ivanov.' I pointed to my ear, then my ribs, and winced. 'Major Ivanov.' I didn't fancy my chances of getting away with being a squaddie if anyone looked at me closely enough.

'Unit?' Her accent wasn't Russian. Ukrainian, most likely. She was angular. Matter-of-fact.

Unit? I suspected 45th Spetsnaz wasn't the answer she was looking for. I started to cough hard and retched. The force of it made me cough naturally, but thanks to the fentanyl I felt no pain in my ribs. I doubled over, dribbling saliva.

'Sorry, ma'am,' I spluttered and recovered myself. 'My unit is . . .' I exploded into another coughing fit. I looked up. She'd walked around the desk and stood next to me. A Makarov pistol bounced at her hip. She looked exasperated.

'This is most . . .' And then shouting into the ward, 'Nurse Kuznetsova!' I looked down the row of triage beds. A young nurse stuck her head out. 'Yes, you, Kuznetsova,' she bawled. 'Major Ivanov to Triage One. I'll put Radiography on notice.'

'Thank you,' I coughed again for good measure.

'Can you walk?' The young nurse Kuznetsova touched my arm. I said I could, and she guided me through the centre of the ward to one of the improvised cubicles. We passed Russians and Africans laid out on gurneys and cots and wrapped with bloody bandages. They were attended to by Russian army medics. Weapons and kit were piled up neatly beside them.

'What happened?' I asked. 'I was knocked out cold chasing after that bastard. Mortar, I think. One of ours, must have been. Complete cluster fuck.' She took quick, short steps and locked her knees. Her hips swayed. Her bottom swished under her fatigues. I waited for her to reply and I wondered what it would take to kill the natural impulse to imagine what she looked like naked under that drab green cotton. My grandfather had been so badly wounded in Stalingrad he'd been laid out in a morgue before being evacuated across the Volga. Six days later he woke up in the battalion field hospital bed and proposed to his nurse. They were married as soon as he was able to walk.

We entered the cubicle at the very end, nearest the door marked *Quarantine*.

'More friendly fire,' she answered me quietly, unwrapping a tray of sterile equipment. She was wearing a Makarov as well. Everyone, including the wounded, was armed. 'Two units got in front of the other, yours included by the look of it.' She turned to face me and smoothed the front of her fatigues. She nodded at me. 'You were lucky.'

'*Da*,' I agreed. 'Very. I could have lost more than my ear.'

'*Nyet*,' she countered. 'I mean you were lucky you weren't taking parade, sir. Now please undress. You can sit on the bed.' She turned her back on me and began filling out a sheet of notes. The little pistol was in a closed holster.

'Undress?'

She turned back to me.

'Ah, sorry, your ribs.' She put down the clipboard and picked up a pair of safety scissors and stepped towards me. I let her begin to cut away at my shirt, from the right wrist up the arm. She was strong, her actions purposeful. Her red lips and pretty, pale face belied the determination of a trained, professional soldier. Her head came up to my chest. Strands of blonde hair escaped from her surgical cap. She exposed the arm and brought the scissors down and began cutting away at the torso of the shirt, bottom up.

'Why's that?' I said. 'About the parade, I mean.' She looked at me askance.

'The sniper, sir. Can you believe he knocked out a whole unit, *and* the professor? Poor boys.' Her voice dropped to a whisper. 'Horrific injuries most of them.' She paused while she unsnagged the scissors. 'Not that I give a damn about those apes, mind you.' It wasn't immediately clear if she was referring to the wild men who'd charged me or the African soldiers I'd cut down between the huts. The Russian army was at best prejudiced, and at worst virulently racist.

'Ah, of course, Nurse. Yes, *that* parade.'

She took half a step back. I looked down at her, but she was looking at my chest.

'Oh, I see . . . you've already been dressed.'

'Our platoon medic fixed me up when they found me,' I explained. I swallowed hard. Her eyes remained fixed on the compress that spanned my fractured ribs.

'But these bandages . . . they're not . . .' she pointed towards them with the safety scissors, '. . . ours.' Then she turned my right arm at the wrist, looked at my upper arm and saw. Or rather, didn't see. 'Where is your . . . ?'

'*Prosti menya,*' I said. *Forgive me.* And I meant it.

She went to speak, but it was already too late for her. My hands were at her mouth, throat. I pushed her back on to the bed, covering her body with mine. We pressed against each other. Air escaped from her nose. The veins at her temples swelled. She struggled violently to breathe, eyes wild, pleading, every sinew straining, pushing against me. She tried and failed to reach her pistol and then grabbed ineffectually at my arms. My right hand found the lock knife in my boot-top and I brought the opened blade round to the back of her neck.

'*Shh*,' I whispered. And then, in Russian, 'It's OK. It's nearly over.'

Her lips rasped against my palm. I slipped the point in at the base of her skull. She relaxed. Her muscles gave way beneath me, and her arms went limp across my back. The last glimmer went from her eyes, and it was done. I kept my hand over her mouth for a moment longer to be sure and then turned her on her side and pulled the woven green blanket up to hide her face.

Not having a scorpion tattoo had to have been either a death sentence for me or for her. I made a mental note to tell Ezra about that.

I ripped the arm off the shredded shirt and ducked out of the curtained cubicle. An entire forward operating base had been inserted into the hills of West Africa. The most remarkable thing about it was how unremarkable it felt. Change the uniforms and the accents and I could just as easily have been in Afghanistan as Sierra Leone. Life in the dressing station carried on as normal. Out of sight, I could hear the ward sister at reception berating another medic.

If only Roberts could have seen it. *It would blow his mind*, I thought as I skirted the far edge of the room and kept my head down. I didn't know where I was going, but I knew where I needed to get to. I figured I had ten minutes before Kuznetsova's body was discovered, fifteen at the outside.

Time was running out.

24

I kept my hand on the holstered SIG and continued a slow sweep from room to room. Pocahontas was propped up in bed, leg elevated, ankle stump bandaged, face covered by an oxygen mask. He was out cold, hooked up to a morphine drip and a vital signs monitor. Somewhere in the complex his foot would be packed in ice. I doubted anyone would be sewing it back on out here, though. His PKM leaned nonchalantly against the wall next to the headrest.

I stood still for a moment. I'd done my job: I'd taken the shot I'd had to take. It was the only possible outcome. But that wasn't going to end this war, or any war. Musala was still overrun. And who knew how many more wild men there were out there, laying waste to whole villages, towns. Who knew, too, how many little children there were hiding out in the forest, ignorant of their orphan's life to come.

It felt like I'd already stepped off the line of departure a dozen times on this operation. And then I realized I had stopped. Stopped dead. I was not running. I was not looking for an escape, because there wasn't one.

I was thinking.

I didn't know the *why* of it. But I'd seen the *what* with my own eyes. And that was enough. It stemmed from me. *My* father. I was now outside of orders. And any killing I did would be for me. I'd be sure to let King know that, one way or another. He could stuff Raven Hill down his wine-gorged gullet. One McLean in charge of his own private army had already clearly been one too many.

I was ready; and, finally, I was angry. I stepped out of the cubicle. Another rebel I'd wounded languished next door.

Right area, wrong place.

I continued along the main corridor. It terminated in a metal door covered with a plastic biohazard curtain, emblazoned with the warning:

ВЫХОДА НЕТ
This is not an exit

I checked the corridor was clear behind me, pushed on the bar to open it and backed through a plastic shroud into a pool of red light. I saw when I turned around that I was sandwiched in between two pairs of anti-contamination drapes. I pushed past the second set and allowed my eyes to adjust. Above me a red and white sign in Russian read:

Limit of cordon sanitaire. Emergency exit only. Strictly no contaminated personnel.

I drew the SIG and crept on.

Around me a light mist oozed from ceiling vents like

dry ice, the air conditioning swirling the tiny moisture particles through the crimson-tinged air. There was a delicate hint of peppermint, too, struggling to establish its presence above the stronger, pervasive smell of antiseptic. The corridor was empty and apart from the constant throb of the generators it was quiet. More rooms led off it – all likewise protected with plastic drapes. It felt like a jolt of déjà vu. The red glow; the constant throbbing; the perception but not the feeling of pressure – it was as if I had been transported into the bowels of a nuclear submarine gliding deep beneath the surface.

Like the cells I'd seen on the level above, the doors were also furnished with safety-glass viewing ports. Behind them, men laid stretched out on solid benches which were bolted to the floor. Arms pinioned, heads strapped, feet bound – they were all held fast. It was impossible to say if they were conscious: masks covered their mouths, patches of black fabric their eyes. Every room was mixed between Europeans and Africans: Russians and, I supposed, captured Guineans and Sierra Leoneans.

I turned away from the window I'd been peering through and let the sanitary curtain swish back across it. From down the hall a man in a white coat flew towards me, rubber-soled shoes squeaking on the poured concrete floor as he ran, arm outstretched, cursing in Russian.

'You! Yes, you! What the hell are you doing? Stay where you are. Don't . . .' I cut him off with a shot between the eyes, the gentle *phutt* of the silenced round strangely at odds with the damage it wrought. His legs went out from under him, his broken skull hit the ground with a wet thud. I shot him again and used the pass clipped to his breast pocket to open the door I'd been looking through. I dragged him inside, out of sight of the viewing hatch. A smear of fresh blood dirtied the floor. The smell of peppermint grew stronger.

A European man was strapped down. Shaved head, covered with an EEG headset. Mid-twenties. Younger, maybe. He was tagged with a printed and bar-coded plastic wrist cuff:

Generation 2(iv). Observation Ward 1. Destination Level 3(ii).

Apart from the rise and fall of his chest and seemingly perpetual rapid eye movement he was motionless. On closer inspection the mask concealed an intubation tube, but he was breathing of his own accord. A catheter and colostomy bag collected his waste. A drip fed him. He was connected to a cardiograph. I did a double take: the heart rate was exceptionally, almost fatally, high.

At the foot of the bed a clipboard heavy with computer printouts covered in handwritten notes mapped out his progress over the previous weeks, including dates of infection, when he'd become symptomatic and when he was due to be 'harvested'.

Whatever harvesting entailed, it was scheduled for the following day. His blood pressure was recorded as abnormally low; core temperature a steady thirty-nine degrees Celsius. Most remarkable of all was his EEG reading: brain activity remained almost dormant except for occasional, exceptional spikes.

I put the muzzle of the short silencer between his torso and upper arm and prised a gap between them. There it was, the now-familiar tattoo. As I removed the barrel he opened his eyes. They were crazy, frantic, rolling. He strained against the straps, gagging on the tracheal tube. I stepped back fast but overcame my natural instinct to shoot. Instead, I stood and watched. As much as his bonds would allow, he writhed and fought, desperate to be free. The cardiogram remained constant. The EEG spiked and then remained active. Whoever or whatever he was, he was alive and kicking and fully awake – despite his vital signs indicating that he should be dead or dying.

I approached him again, but he seemed not to be able to see me. I put the muzzle perpendicular to his left knee cap and fired. His joint imploded. Bone, skin and lead were blown through the exit wound. The EEG remained constant; heart rate unchanged. He was trying to bite and retch the tube out of his throat.

Fuck.

He seemed not to notice what should have been intolerable pain. The room hung heavy with the smell of peppermint. As he struggled, the mask worked loose from his nose. His eyes snapped into focus instantly, locking on to mine. His muscles bulged, neck strained, but he was held fast. I put the muzzle against his sternum and fired again. The bullet opened a hole in his heart. A red jet erupted out of his chest. Morsels of flesh and bone and thick arterial blood showered the room. The cardiogram went haywire and flat-lined – but his EEG didn't flicker, and his eyes stayed locked on mine: focused; alert; alive. I put the SIG to his temple and fired a third time. The EEG died. And suddenly I was looking at the corpse of a man, and not a monster.

'Incredible, isn't it?' I swung around, gun up, ready to fire. But my finger hesitated on the trigger steel. 'There's no need for that.' He nodded towards the pistol. 'But you already know that, don't you?' I didn't speak. I had nothing to say. He supported his own weight on crutches, leaning against the doorway. His bandages were fresh and crisp.

'That was a perfect shot. Absolutely brilliant,' he went on. His eyes were etched with pain, but bright and lively despite it. His breath was sharp and shallow. But there was warmth and depth to his brogue.

For the second time that day I'd drawn a bead on my father.

'I knew *someone* was coming for me. And God knows those clowns tried to stop you.' He jerked his head backwards as he said it. The corridor outside was no doubt filled with an entire platoon of clowns of that sort. 'But that's when I knew,' he continued, tapping his chest, '*knew*, you understand – that it was you. No one else could have taken a shot like that.'

'No one else would have wanted to,' I said. And it was the truth. Anyone else would have killed him. 'But they never wanted you killed, did they?' I said. 'There are no such things as coincidences. Isn't that what you always told me? That's why London sent me. The one killer they knew who wouldn't. Couldn't.'

And then it hit me. If London knew, that meant they had to know who I was, too. Who I really was.

He looked at me quizzically.

'London,' he said, 'is not a monolith.' He held out his hand. 'Come.'

I lowered the barrel and my eyes. His gaze was magnetic, compulsive. I reached out and, for the first time in twenty-six years, slipped my hand into his. The skin was looser over his knuckles and the strength gone from his fingers, but they were his hands all right. They held me, his golden boy, like the gentle giant of my childish memory unalloyed by disappointment.

'I have a lifetime to show you, son,' he said, drawing me close, 'and so little time.'

25

He sat on the bed and leaned to one side, taking pressure off the wound. Every movement looked difficult. Even though it was a clean shot and the bullet had passed straight through him it would still have been extremely painful. His lung had collapsed, and was being treated with a simple one-way valve. It was the only way I could have taken him down convincingly that wouldn't have killed him. I'd wanted him alive, and where I could find him: in hospital. For now London – and everyone else – had to think I wanted him dead. If there were eyes in the sky a deliberate miss would have been painfully obvious.

Within a week he'd be almost fully recovered, though whether either of us had that long was doubtful.

'Brilliant. Quite brilliant. Where on earth did you get the idea to shoot me so . . . so *perfectly*?' He looked genuinely impressed.

'From you.' I looked him straight in the face. But it was hard, and my eyes were drawn back to the floor. It was too soon, too raw, to acknowledge him fully.

'Me? How's that? I couldn't hit a barn door with a shotgun. Said so yourself many a time. So did my sergeant major.' We were alone in the room, but outside 'the clowns' – Spetsnaz guards – stood watch. I'd allowed myself to be disarmed the moment I'd lowered the SIG.

Submission, not rebellion.

The fouled observation cell had been sealed behind me and the whole corridor hastily disinfected. Both bodies had been bagged and removed quickly and without ceremony.

'Your henchmen,' I nodded to the door. 'They tried to kill a friend of mine. Almost exactly the same wound. She was lucky. But you're alive on purpose.'

'*My* henchmen?' The thought of the bloody damage done to Juliet stoked my anger.

'Yes, yours. Who tried to kill me, too, by the way.'

'Twenty-six years and the first thing that happens is that we both nearly kill each other. You have to admit there's a certain irony in that. The ultimate blue on blue.'

'It looks more like red on blue to me. And no, it's not ironic. It's fucking tragic.' I looked around me. The ward room was bare, functional. Cold. My voice was loud, indignant. In response he said, did, nothing. I carried on. 'There's no "nearly" about it. You're alive because I let you live.'

'No vengeance, then?'

'Vengeance belongs to idiots.' I pointed at him. 'And forgiveness belongs to the dead.'

'Ah, they did teach you something, then. And better than they taught me, that's for sure.' He spoke evenly, calmly, although his voice was hoarse with pain and lack of breath. 'I miss her, too, Max. With my whole heart. But we don't have time for that. Not now. The soldiers outside, they know what you are, but they don't know who you are. If you trust me you will live. It's probably too late for me,' he shrugged, 'and probably rightly so. But we'll see.' He paused and cocked his head to one side and continued, as if he'd just thought of another possibility. 'If you want to use the time that remains to settle old scores then of course you may. That's your right. But we have time for one thing only. So you choose, Max: the past, or the future?'

He paused again. I kept my mouth shut. Seconds ticked.

'OK. You came here to do a job, didn't you? Eh? Well trust me, my boy. Trust me, and I'll show you how it can be done. Otherwise,' he looked to the ceiling and raised his hands, palms up, 'otherwise all this down here and out there will have been for nothing. All those lives. That would be the real catastrophe, Max. *That* would be unforgivable.'

He was infuriating. His manner hung somewhere between patience and condescension. He spoke in certainties born of an absolute belief in himself that bordered, as they always had, on riddles. For all those years I had clung on to the love and warmth in his voice and the emotional truth it conveyed. But the quiet superiority of it had escaped me.

I stood there like a fool, pointing my index finger at him.

'Think, Max. Why did you let me live?' I remained silent and let him speak. 'You let me live because you want to understand. Correct? And right now that means finishing what you came here to do – even though you don't know what that is yet. Trust me, Max. I will give you the keys to the Kingdom itself. The dead themselves will arise.'

'I'm not in the resurrection game,' I said. Was he mad? Was I in shock? I blinked hard and rolled my shoulders. 'Come on, let's go.'

'Let's go? Max, we're completely surrounded. No,' he soothed. 'There's no fighting your way out of this one. If you can't surrender to me you'll never leave.' I was speaking either to a genius or an idiot: that much I felt as keenly talking to him then as I had as a teenager. 'The commandant knows you are an assassin sent by the British. He also knows you let me live.'

'But why would he let us talk alone like this? Why am I not already dead?'

'Because he doesn't know you're my son, and I've told him you're a double agent. Until he arrives I'm in command, but when he sees what mayhem you've unleashed all bets will be off. Time is short.'

'I see,' I said. And I was beginning to, dimly. 'And that's possible, is it? That the person sent to kill you could actually be on Proshunin's side?'

'Yes, it is. Very much so. London is not a monolith. Remember?'

'So you said.'

'So *you* said. "That's why London sent me. The one killer they knew who wouldn't."'

The plain fact of the matter was that I couldn't get out if he didn't want me to. Right then and there I could no more destroy the bunker than I could bring my mother back from the dead.

'Am I?' I said, as he struggled to his feet.

'Are you what, son?'

'A double agent?'

'I don't know, Max. I really don't know.' He shook his head and smiled. 'You see that all depends on who sent you.'

I gave him my arm, and together we stepped from the warm light of his room to the red glow of the corridor. We were still inside the biohazard area. A dozen armed men lined the way, cradling their Kalashnikovs. He spoke to them quietly in Russian. My mother said it was faultless, his accent perfect, his manner quietly commanding. As a child I found her endless eulogy of his powers of persuasion embarrassing. Suddenly I was glad of them.

'Let's just use the old language now, shall we? Loose lips sink ships and all that. We wouldn't want to drown before we've left the harbour, would we? I never was much of a swimmer.'

'*Mamaí ach oiread*,' I replied in Irish. Neither was Mum. His face was coloured red in the gloom of the passage-way; his expression hard to read.

As a child we'd spoken in the melting pot of Russian, English and Irish that the three of us stirred at home. We were entirely unintelligible to outsiders and quite often only stopped gabbling to each other in the mad patois we'd cooked up when we realized everyone else around us was looking on in awkward, ignorant silence.

He leaned on me, and we wound our way quietly around the warren of caves that fed into the wards and labs. We passed orderlies and doctors, soldiers and nurses – all of whom saluted my father, all of whom ignored me. Whether it was because I was with him or because I looked unremarkably like one of their fighters I didn't know.

'I need my hand,' he said in Irish as we stopped in front of another grey metal door that had been roughly cemented into a natural opening in the rock. He paused for a moment and rasped breath into his good lung. The valve was working well – a simple piece of kit that stopped the chest cavity around the collapsed lung from filling with air. Most likely Juliet was attached to one as we spoke. 'You even missed my rib, you brilliant boy. All this wheezing is just an old man's fondness for strong cigarettes.'

I hovered next to him in case he toppled, but he regained his composure and stretched out his right hand on to the key pad. It scanned his fingertips, and the back light on the panel blinked from red to green. He nodded to the door, and I pushed it open to reveal an improvised but well-appointed laboratory staffed by half a dozen men and women in lab coats and hairnets. They were all armed. They all ignored us. The smell of peppermint was pervasive. Our Spetsnaz chaperones stayed outside, and the door swung shut behind us.

'This doesn't look like the way out,' I said, continuing in Irish, 'or a good place to surrender.'

'Ah,' he replied. 'That's because you don't know what's in here.' He cleared his throat and addressed in Russian the officer who I took to be the senior technician. 'Captain Berezina. Coffee break, please.' She nodded curtly and trooped out of the door we'd entered by, followed by the others, staring resolutely at the floor. As she left I caught a glimpse of the hard cases at the ready outside. I wasn't exactly at the top of my game. But I was pretty sure that with the help of one of their AKs I could make it to ground level in one piece. But outrunning a platoon of the crazies across open ground? No way. I had to find a way of shutting them down before I made a break for it. What to do with any fighters already above ground was another issue entirely.

I looked at my father and did a double take. For a moment it was incredible to me again. Yes, it was him. Really him. *My* father. Twenty-six years of playing the orphan, and now here I was standing next to him. I'd imagined meeting him many times – but none of those fantasies unfolded in a bunker in West Africa. Anger ebbed and flowed. I had no script to follow. But the weirdest thing was that after the shock subsided it felt not only inevitable but *normal*. Of course we were here. Of course he hadn't died when his plane was shot down. Obviously he was a Russian military medical mastermind. Why wouldn't he be? That's what he'd been for the British for years. I went to speak, but no words came. I had no idea where to start and even less of an idea where it would end.

At the far end of the room he unlocked a stainless-steel medicine cabinet and removed from it a transparent per-spex cube the size of my fist. Without thinking, I extended my hand, and he laid the block carefully on to my palm. I held it up to the light and squinted at it. Suspended inside was what looked like a tiny cream-coloured brain, cleaved perfectly in half. Attached and integral to it was a rear, third lobe – shiny black on the outside, pure white inside. It was about an inch by two inches, its weight impossible to gauge in the heavy casing.

'What is it?' I asked.

'It's how this all began, Max.' I lowered the specimen and turned my attention back to my father. 'The reason I am here. The reason you are here.'

'It's a brain. It looks like one, at least. A diseased brain.' I turned it around in my hands. 'Of what? A monkey? It's weird. It looks almost human.'

I'd failed science at school. It was a permanent source of amusement and irritation for my mother and father – both of whom were leaders in their field: my mother publicly at Trinity, my father secretly, for the Ministry of Defence.

'Ha! No. Not a brain.' He was excited, his voice lifting above the pain in his chest. 'But incredible you should think so, Max. Incredible! You're spot on, see. No, it's not a brain, but it is diseased – not that you can see it without a very powerful microscope.' I stared at it harder anyway – as if, by concentrating, what was wrong with it might become clear after all. 'It's a seed, Max. A very uncommon seed. It's from a fruit tree we thought was long extinct, from the *Simaroubaceae* family.

'That sounds . . . prehistoric?' Suddenly I was doing my homework again. All statements were also questions, all questions guarded to hide the ignorance that spawned them.

'Yes! Actually there are plenty of prehistoric plants that survived in Africa, most of them living quiet lives in the equatorial forests, or what's left of them. But this one is the great-great-grandfather – and then some – of the common old ackee. That's probably why it was missed for so long. You see it *looks* common but it's unique because *this* is a seed that grows brains, Max. Can you imagine! This diseased little germ has the power to remake the human brain. And because it can remake the human brain, it can remake the human. It's . . .' he drew himself up and reached towards the cube with out-stretched fingers '. . . miraculous.'

'Got it,' I said. Although I hadn't. 'And this is what makes the men that have been trying to kill me, and everyone else they meet, almost invincible?' Involuntar-ily I touched the ragged edge of my torn ear. 'That's not miraculous,' I corrected him, 'it's monstrous.'

'No!' He shouted and then winced. He withdrew his hand and guarded his chest. Tears welled in his eyes. 'No,' he said again, quietly. '*It's* not monstrous. *We* are.' He hesitated. 'I am.' He wiped his eyes with his palms and composed himself. 'Listen to me, Max. Listen and learn. Not everything is as it seems.' I returned the seed to him. It already felt like a burden.

'OK,' I said. My shoulders slumped. The fentanyl was wearing off, and a deep, tearing pain began to spread across my side. 'We're going to have to do this in Eng-lish, though. My science is shaky enough as it is.'

'Right, yes. English it is then.' He switched languages. 'I take it you've heard of Ebola?'

I clenched my jaw and tried not to sound sarcastic.

'Yeah. I've heard of Ebola.'

It was as if we were both carrying on from where we left off two-and-a-half decades before. The bunker was as much a time machine as it was a military base. But if it was a portal, I had no idea where it was taking us next.

'Jolly good,' he smiled weakly. 'Of course you know about Ebola. But do you really? Or rather, did we? Scientists, I mean. Virologists. No, Max, we didn't.'

'I'm glad I'm not the only one in the dark.'

'You see,' he continued, 'everyone knew all about Ebola except for one crucial fact.' He looked at me expectantly. I didn't disappoint.

'And what's that?'

'Where it comes from,' he said in Russian. He paused then and permitted himself another little smile before continuing in English. 'The Americans searched for the source after the Kikwit outbreak in Congo back in ninety-five. Spiders, ants, birds, beetles – the US military swept up every living thing they could find within miles of the epicentre. They strapped face masks to monkeys, and perfectly healthy people to beds next to the dying, to see if, *how*, they'd contract it. And all they confirmed is what we knew anyway: that apes and duiker deer contract the virus from fruit bats, and that humans contract the virus from them. So bats are the reservoir, the pool if you like, that infects the things that infect us. But where do the fruit bats get it from, eh?' I shrugged my shoulders. 'You can't tell me, because no one can. No one knows. Or rather, no one *knew*.'

'And now you do?'

'Yes, Max, I do. All the clever clogs at the WHO and CDC will tell you that although we don't know for *sure*, bats are not just the reservoir but *most likely* the originating vector, too. But it's not true.' He straightened his back and held up the seed between us. 'This is!' Bats contract Ebola from *this* seed. Actually this *specific* diseased seed . . . and presumably others like it, not that we've found any others, mind you. No one thought it was possible.'

'What, that bats could catch Ebola from seeds?'

'Yes. No! I mean no one thought an animal could contract a virus from a plant. Not just Ebola, but *any* virus. But it is possible, Max, it is. Doctor Raoult in Marseilles all but proved it in 2010 with his research on the pepper virus. That was an amazing breakthrough . . .'

The lab door opened, and a Russian officer put his head around the corner.

'*Vrach*,' he asked, 'how much longer?'

'Calm, calm,' my father replied in Russian. 'All is well. Tell your men to prepare the destination ward.'

The officer looked at me and sniffed.

'*Da*, very good.' He turned and left and the door clicked shut again behind him.

'None of the, uh, *warriors* can be released without my order,' my father explained, and pointed to a fingerprint scanner on the desk. 'My *physical* order. But I digress,' he said, sitting heavily at the nearest work bench. 'Where were we?'

'Marseilles,' I replied, trying hard not to sound exasperated. 'But let's jump to Sierra Leone, shall we?'

'The vector. We were on to the vector. That's right. Now then,' he tapped the top of the perspex with his index finger. 'Fruit bats eat seeds. We've known *that* for years. But *this* seed is different because it's diseased with a filovirus. A very ancient and hitherto unknown filovirus.' He looked to me for affirmation. I nodded. 'It's the progenitor, Max, the daddy of that nasty little triumvirate family *Filoviridae*. Older than Ebola, older than Marburg, older than Lloviu. And do you know what that means?'

'No, I have literally no idea what that means.'

'Well it means that with this, with the original, pure, first-generation vector you can make a vaccine *and* a cure. And more than that, you can make it one hundred per cent effective, and very, very cheaply. True, there are already vaccines. But they were synthesized from a strain of the virus that had already been transmitted and was, by its very nature, already dying. This, Max, this is pure, undiluted primeval dread. Simple, beautiful and powerful. It's one of the oldest organisms alive – over twenty-five million years old! From the Oligocene period, at least. It might even antedate the Grande Coupure. Can you imagine that?'

I told him I couldn't.

'And you can do something else with it, too.'

His mood grew sombre as the excitement of explaining the science of the vector fell from his voice. Finally we were back on to territory I understood.

'You can make a weapon. A very powerful weapon. That's it, isn't it?'

277

'Yes, Max. You could. One could. *They* wanted to.' He inclined his head towards the door. 'Because the virus you can manufacture from *this*,' he tapped the plastic-encased seed again, 'is infinitely more . . . *virile* than the Ebola virus we know. This is the *Ur* filovirus. We've done tests. The cure the Americans synthesized, the vaccine created after the Ebola epidemic here – they don't work. Not on this. Not at all.'

'So unless you have the seed, the vector, you can't make a cure? And of course, if you don't have a cure, then the weapon is worthless anyway?'

'Not so bad at science after all, eh?' He reached out and patted my forearm. 'That's one reason Ebola was never used as a weapon before. We, I mean the Russians, synthesized plenty of it. Even crossed it with smallpox to make it spread faster. But . . . no cure, no weapon. Just like the Bomb, see? Power is nothing without control. Use it, and all you do is endanger your own side. Useless on the battlefield. Useless if you want to *control* territory. Useless if you want to control the number of people it affects.'

'Kills,' I said. 'Not "affects".'

'Yes, that's true. Ebola is survivable. Ebola's parent is not. Fatality is one hundred per cent.' I chewed my cheeks and then chose my words carefully.

'And you, you made it into a weapon?' I looked around, as though expecting to see something that actually looked like a bomb tucked away in the corner or dis-played in one of the glass cabinets that lined the walls.

'Yes. Yes, I did. At least, a weapon is what they got but

278

not in the way they expected. Not in the way any of us expected.' His face relaxed. The last of the excitement draining from his eyes painted him with a mask of detachment. He stood, and reached out for my arm to steady himself and then returned the seed to the cabinet he'd taken it from. 'All will be revealed,' he said.

We walked towards the door, and the guards outside.

'Where are we going?' I asked.

'We are going,' he said, 'to meet Doctor Mac Ghill'ean's Monster.'

26

The patient lay as still and as unresponsive as the man I'd not long before killed in the observation room. I say 'patient': human guinea pig would be more accurate. This time, though, it was an African. Shaved head, statuesque, stretched out like an exquisitely carved block of obsidian. The gentle rise and fall of his chest and the rapid fluttering of his eyes the only signs he was alive. He was separated from us by a glass screen.

'I think I met his friends earlier on today,' I said and felt a surge of dizziness. I realized I had no idea what time it was. I felt detached, almost disassociated from the reality of what was happening.

'I'm so sorry about that. I hear it was quite the unhappy encounter.' He wrinkled his nose as the sharp, clean smell of peppermint was refreshed by a blast of air from the vents above. 'You're only the second person to have killed one of them in combat, by the way.'

'Five of them,' I corrected him. 'I killed five of them. I met one by the river, too. Who else has had the pleasure?'

'You don't know? It was one of your men. A warrior, for sure. Wild strong he was. I've never seen a man fight like that. Crushed its head with his hands. He was lucky to survive, to not be infected. Miraculous, actually.'

I didn't tell him that Sonny Boy hadn't survived.

'I've recalled the original troop. They are incredible,' he said, inspecting the cardiogram, 'but not invincible. Not yet, anyway. But with every generation they grow stronger. Soon they will be indestructible.' He touched the glass with the fingers of his right hand and shook his head. 'My gift to the world,' he said softly. 'Good God.'

I felt physically sick, as if my body was recoiling from the rising realization of what my father had done.

'So what are they?' I asked. 'What's *he*?' I nodded towards the body. My father sighed, but said nothing. We were not alone this time. Two of the Spetsnaz minders had entered with us, and a technician sat at a desk beside the screen, reviewing spreadsheets. My father turned to me. The hard white light from the bulbs that lit the room glared off his pate. The knot of scar tissue on his left temple looked almost blue. Liver spots spread across the backs of his hands. He looked old. But he blinked, and his eyes were bright. They flared and stared at me. Another wave of nausea hit me. I felt disorientated. Cramp began to gnaw at my stomach. How long had I felt like this? I took stock of myself. My heart rate was climbing. I was sweating. Pain, tiredness, the drugs I'd taken in the cave . . . they'd all masked deeper discomfort. I'd been sliding into actual sickness for hours without seeing it for what it was.

'You see, after my plane, uh, came down in Angola . . .'

'Came down? You were shot down. By the Cubans.'

'No, son,' he said kindly, 'that was a lie.' He paused, weighing up what he felt he needed to tell me, and what, perhaps, he owed me, against the time that remained. 'A lie you and I have both lived with. For better or worse it was the kindest lie we could bear to tell you.'

Kind? I thought. *It was kind to tell me you were dead?*

'We?' I said. 'Who was "we"?'

'Your mother, Max. She was betrayed while I was in South Africa. There was no time for her to run. She took the only way out offered to her.'

Betrayed? I let the question fall with the scales from my eyes. Stalingrad had cast a long shadow. But I had never realized just how profound it had been. Of the many things I had both imagined and known her to be, a Russian spy was not among them.

'And you?'

'Me? I became the last defector. I died and was disowned and was reborn in Moscow. After she went and you vanished, there was nothing to come back for, not that I could have come back. That above all was made clear by . . .'

'Stop.' I cut him off hard. Everything was the opposite of what I thought; what I'd always thought. And now there was no time to think at all. 'I don't want to hear any more.' I winced and put my hand on my broken ribs. 'Fuck it. You are what you are. And here we are. Who the fuck is *this* guy? That's what I wanted to know.'

While I reeled inside, my father composed himself and switched his attention back to the man behind the screen.

'This guy,' he said, 'is one of the greatest medical pioneers that's ever lived. We found the vector. *I* found the vector. So naturally I tried to make a vaccine, a simple, infallible vaccine from it. And *this* man, this brave pioneer . . . this . . . *Lazarus* was meant to be the first person ever to be inoculated not only against the virus we found but also Ebola and *all* filoviruses.'

I waited for him to continue. One of the guards cleared his throat, expectantly. My father glanced at the clock and waved his hand dismissively.

'But it didn't work, Max. And good Lord, how I wished it had.' I walked closer to the screen and looked carefully at the man's body. On closer inspection his muscles were sculptor-perfect; but his skin was a patch-work of burned blacks and browns. His face, torso, limbs . . . all were covered with scars that looked like the legacy of infected sores or lesions.

'At first I thought he had died – of the virus, I mean. He exhibited all the gruesome symptoms of Ebola you'll have heard about, and then his vital signs gave out. He was less than a minute away from incineration when I saw his hand twitch. That happened in Liberia, too, and more than once by all accounts. But they didn't come back. *He* did. And so you see,' my father continued, 'out of that, that *failure* rose, well, a miracle. A horrible, bloody miracle. Max, do you remember the stories I used to read to you when you were a boy about the Irish hero Cú Chulainn? Do you remember how on the battlefield he would spin into a battle rage, transformed by a warp-spasm that made him undefeatable?' He was speaking in Irish now, and with increasing passion again, as if the mention of Cú Chulainn was infusing him with the legendary warrior's spirit itself. 'Or the Viking berserkers? Odin's men rushing forward without armour, mad as dogs, biting their shields, strong as bears! Do you remember being amazed at how they could kill with a single blow, and how "neither fire nor iron told upon them"?'

'Yes,' I said. 'I remember.' But I wasn't thinking of the myths and legends he fed me as a child at bedtime. I was thinking of Sonny Boy, and Colombia. And then I did remember. Not just the stories, but the pictures they painted for me in my imagination as a boy. 'Odin, the one-eyed dancer. Last night . . . up there, in the Cyclops mask. That . . . that was *you*?'

'All war is theatre, Max, all victory psychology. You cannot defeat a man unless you defeat his spirit. And you cannot defeat his spirit unless he chooses to be defeated.' His voice rose. His eyes flashed. 'Men are vanquished by what is within them, not what is brought to bear against them. Fear, Max. Fear is the weapon. Not fear of the enemy, but fear of *oneself*.'

He stopped, exhausted. Spittle formed in little white blooms at the sides of his mouth. Beads of sweat pricked his forehead. The bright surgical lights drained his face of colour, rendering him apparition-like in the cool swirl of the artificial peppermint breeze.

He looked, simply, insane.

'Nazis,' I said. 'I remember the stories you told me about the Nazis, too. The evil men like Mengele you despised, the opposite of everything you told me you'd strived for. And this?' I waved my arm in front of the glass screen. I shook my head, and the room span. 'How did you ever convince yourself this was OK? Look at yourself. This is murder, pure and simple.'

'Murder? No.' His voice was calm again; measured. 'You've earned the right to kill me, Max. But not to accuse me. You want to know why you are here? Then look, and listen. The vaccine didn't work because it was too strong, the sequencing wrong. I won't bore you with . . .' he waved his hand again '. . . the detail. Suffice to say it *changed* him. No! No, more than that: it *evolved* him. At first I thought I'd infected him with the original virus because it was a live vaccine. But I hadn't, and the consequences were as spectacular as they were unpredictable. Spectacular, and very valuable. Chasing discoveries less than this has made fortunes and bankrupted nations. And I knew immediately they would try and take it away from me, pervert it for their own petty politics.

'Are you following me? They happen, mistakes like that. Especially out here, in the field. Usually these tests take years – decades even. And look at this place, just look at it. The chemistry sets I bought you as a kid were better equipped.' He clenched his fists and his eyes flashed. 'But here, right here, in this dank little cave and against all the odds I created something, Max, the likes of which the world hasn't seen for a millennium!'

I struggled to focus. I was losing my bearings in the madness of his brainstorm.

'I created a berserker, Max. An actual, human berserker. Not just a wild fighter but a shapestrong, an *úlfhéðinn*, a shapeshifter, a *hamrammr*. In Russian I call them *Spyashie*: Sleepers – men waiting to be awoken. Do you understand, Max? This man, this ordinary man, was transformed, *re*-created, changed utterly, and by what? Accident? No, Max, this is *fate*: a pure, biddable warrior who fights without prejudice; without malice; without *opinion*. So no, not an evil man, but a weapon, a super-human weapon. Controllable by his creator but fundamentally and unthinkingly *neutral*. He follows orders in the same way a bullet follows the barrel: perfectly.'

My vision was blurring, sense of space and balance faltering.

'You unleashed them? You experimented on live human beings and then you unleashed them? Have you seen what they do?'

The face of the dead soldier in the village outside of Kabala was etched into my memory. And now I knew: it was not as if *some* depraved scientist had created the essence of fear and given it a human face – it was my father who had done it. 'You know, don't you? You *do* know.'

I was speaking in English. Behind me I heard the guards adjust their rifles. The technician looked up and studied me carefully. Sweat dripped from my brow; the remnants of my tattered fatigues were soaked through. My teeth began to chatter.

He replied quietly, carefully.

'Yes. Yes, I've seen the horror they wreak. Of course I've seen it. I've seen it and I've lived it. And so have you. But I've seen something else, Max. I've seen the living you leave behind, those your government condemns to a living death, the survivors whose mothers live without their sons; the bereaved for whom the sun never rises. You can't hide behind your guns, Max. They don't fire themselves. But,' he turned to face the cataleptic behind the glass, 'he is pure, as a new-born is pure. *Re*-born – without fear, or regret, or judgement. His mind may seem uncommunicative, but it exists. He thinks. They all think. They are cognitive beings. They may not speak, but they have language. I said I evolved him. But that's not true. I have achieved something even more remarkable. I regressed him, *devolved* him into an original state, *our* original state. They stand on the threshold of free will: still obedient to their creator; unconscious of good and evil; ignorant of guilt. It cost half a million Russian souls to defeat the Nazis in Stalingrad. It would have taken just a few hundred of *him* to have crushed them.'

I doubled over and tried to focus. Sweat rolled off me. An intense, grinding pain awoke behind my eyes, blotting out thought. I heaved and vomited bile. My ribs felt like they would cleave from my chest.

'So what do you think I called him, Max, this man, still a *man* you understand, who is unrestrained by his own humanity?'

'I don't know,' I said. But my answer was as much a general statement to everything around me as an answer to his question.

'The only name worthy of a true prelapsarian, of course!'

I fell to my knees and spread my hands on the floor to steady myself. I vomited again. A string of bloody mucus forced its way up my gullet. The smell of iron fused with the reek of peppermint.

'Adam!' he said, triumphant. 'I called him Adam.'

I collapsed on to my side. Blood seeped from my nose. Then I understood.

'You're all immune,' I said. And they had to be. No one wore masks. No one was decontaminated as they entered or left rooms. There was freedom of movement in the whole of the biohazard area. Everyone in my father's perverse Garden of Eden was immune.

Everyone except me.

I remembered the mouthful of brains I'd spat out earlier, the puncture wound in my cheek and tongue from the rebel's shattered skull.

The guards laughed and walked over to me and bent down to pick me up. They'd taken my SIG, but they hadn't found the little black lock knife. I balled up and drew my knees to my chest, and my right hand found the handle tucked into my boot-top. My thumb pressed the silver button by the hilt, and the blade swung out and locked. I drove it sideways into the nearest guard's ankle. The point went in below the bone, glancing backwards. It severed his Achilles tendon and he buckled. The second guard lurched for me, but his wounded partner fell and crashed down on top of me, face up. I let go of the knife, which was embedded in boot leather and tendon-gristle, and drew the pistol from the open holster on his belt. I fired two rounds into the side of his torso and a third into the other guard as he fumbled for his rifle. He fell. I twisted and got to my knees. The room slid away from me. I spat blood and tried to stand. I raised the pistol and fired into the fallen guard again, found my balance for a moment and then lurched hard into a wall cabinet. A bottle fell and smashed. Stainless steel instruments clattered to the floor. I steadied myself and wiped blood out of my eyes. The echo of the gunshots rang in my ears.

The technician stood up clutching a syringe. My father cautioned him to wait.

'No syringe,' I coughed. I aimed at the technician. 'What . . .' The words in my head would not form in my mouth.

'It's all right, Max,' my father said. 'This man is going to help you.'

'No.' That was all I could manage. The technician threaded his way carefully between the bodies of the dead guards. 'No!' But he kept coming. I shook my head and vomited again, a stream of pure blood this time. When he was within touching distance he reached out with the syringe. I fired as he did so. The bullet went through his throat. Arterial blood erupted from the wound. He dropped first to his knees and then keeled over on to the floor. I bent down and scooped up the plunger and needle from his hand and stumbled towards my father. His back was pressed to the glass screen that separated us from 'Adam'. He had nowhere to go.

The lab had been turned into an abattoir.

I caught him around the waist in a clumsy, bloody grapple. He gasped as I knocked the wind out of his bullet-damaged lungs. I could sense the door opening behind me. Boots on concrete. Metal moving against metal. I clawed my way up him, pushing him hard against the window on to his first patient's resting place. My eyes filled with blood. My brain throbbed with pain so acute that I could see colour pulsing and exploding in my head around the smooth black mask of the original berserker who remained undisturbed by the struggle playing out across the divide.

I brought the barrel of the pistol up under my father's jaw and dug it into the top of his windpipe. Men were shouting behind me in Russian. I leaned against him, exhausted, delirious. I brought the syringe up too, gripped in my fist, thumb on the plunger. My legs began to give way. My forehead smeared against his. I looked him in the eyes. Blood cascaded from my nose, drenching us both. I could feel myself fading into a confusion of pain and disassociation. My hands were alien to me. My legs absent. Cramps tore at my stomach.

My father wrapped his hand around mine, enclosing my thumb and the plunger. The needle tip dug into my chest. My cheek pressed against his.

'Why . . .' I rasped through the blood in my throat, 'am I here?'

'This,' he said in Irish as the needle went deep into my chest, 'is why.'

His hand contracted. The serum forced into my muscle. I looked at the fading image of the man behind the screen. The lights of the laboratory flickered. I squinted into the glass and saw the reflection of my own eyes staring back at me. I swallowed hard. The room went black, and my feet gave way from under me.

As I lost consciousness the voice I heard was neither my father's nor those of the men closing in around me but the memory of General King pondering the things 'that might be achieved with a hundred men like that'. It was a brutal, searing truth: Sonny Boy hadn't lost his mind because he'd been infected; Sonny Boy lost his mind because he'd gazed upon the face of the enemy and seen not a monster, but a mirror.

27

Nothing.

Pure, absolute void.

No shadow.

No echo.

An eternity of emptiness in endless grey.

It's not that I can't remember. I haven't *forgotten*. I was neither unconscious nor dead.

I just simply *wasn't*: being without agency.

Perhaps that's how we live in the womb until we are ripped into the world, awoken by human voices, drowning in the oxygen of existence.

Sound first.

The last sense to leave; the first to return. And I heard, as if it were the noise of thunder, a rolling, rhythmic drumming.

Thump-thump, thump-thump, thump-thump.

The noise came from within me; from around me. It went through me; wrapped me tight and held me fast. Deep, resonant vibrations that began where I ended and circled around to end where I began.

I struggled to get free. And as I struggled I knew there was a division. There was me, and there was everything else.

My eyes were open. But I saw nothing.

Silence.

Back into the void. No struggle. No memory.

Pain.

Bright, crisp, clear pain. Pain like noise, rising and falling with the ebb and flow of my heart.

Shape and form, too. Light, building and dying. Shifting. Pulsing.

I *was*. My hands, feet, outstretched, tied. I worked my jaw, but it was blocked.

And then a rushing of air in my mouth as if my throat had been uncorked. The taste of blood. And the weakest, faintest trace of peppermint.

The void again.

I opened my eyes. Above me a silver light drew into focus. A focal point in the vacuum which expanded into the blackness above and beyond it.

A laboratory ceiling? The hospital? No – the moon. A lopsided, ill-formed moon, bright enough to navigate by.

More lights – flickering dirty, orange flames that sent shadows licking the ground beneath me. I was suspended above the ground by my own limbs. I tried to lift my head. Someone was screaming. A deep, guttural howl. I lifted my chin and felt the force of the cry. It was me. I was screaming. I tried to choke it back, to swallow the noise. My head snapped back and forth. Around me faces ebbed and flowed in the firelight. Four beasts swayed and stomped. Feet beating time to the wild, rolling thunder ripping through me; through us. Grotesques in the half-light ululating through mad metal trunks.

I clenched my jaw, and the scream stopped.

I shut my eyes and saw the memory-print of the scene

around me. The void had vanished. And then I remembered: the cross; the drum; the one-eyed dancer. A sharp blow caught me across the jaw, and I opened my eyes. He was there, his bone-mouth grinning, mad eye flashing in the half-dark. The elephant men stilled. The dancer held aloft the fly whisk; the cutlass already dropped to his feet. As the red-masked man shuffled a dusty two-step around the rusty blade he brought the horsehair whisk down across my head and hissed in Russian: '*Vy svoboden.*' You are free.

His mud-smeared hand reached up to my chest and pulsed hard four times against my heart. I screamed. And I saw.

The world came back into sharp, unforgiving focus. My mind filled with thought and feeling and memory like a valley engulfed beneath a burst dam; the grey void of nothing flushed away by a flood of being.

My father's hand fell away from my chest. I spoke without thinking.

'*Blagodaryu.*' Thank you.

The four men who had carried me cut me loose. I was wrapped in the skin of a hyena and layers of pain: my neck, my ribs, my head. It felt as if someone had taken an axe to my skull. I doubled over and dry-heaved into the dust – whether from the pain or the infection I neither knew nor cared.

No blood. No bile. I retched again and straightened up.

My father stood there, unmasked now, robed head to

foot in red, mud daubed on his arms and feet. The cross-bearers had gone, the elephant men too. It was just me and my father. He held a single torch that both lit us and blinded us, deepening the black of night so that not even the moon could penetrate the gloom around us.

'You wanted to know what your mission was, Max'. I nodded, coughed. Words formed but stuck in my throat. The echo of the drums still pounded in my ears, my chest. 'One man sent you to kill me; another to save me.' He looked into the gloom and waved the torch from side to side and shuffled in the dust. 'But that was not your mission.'

He reached out and put his hand on my shoulder. The ceremony had exhausted him. Even in the ruddy glow of the torchlight his face was ashen. His features were drawn tight, his breath short, but his eyes flashed as he spoke, filled with inspiration, insanity.

'All these years I wanted to do what was right. Your mother, too. We picked a side. We fought. And we were wrong. What Russia was and what Russia became: that was the greatest betrayal of all. It was a poor excuse for losing her, an even poorer one for leaving you.' Tears clogged his eyes. His breath rasped short in his lungs. 'By God, I'm sorry. I'm so sorry. Not a day passed that I didn't regret every choice that took me away from you. But the fight was all I had. It became everything, the only thing that remained. And now, now there's a chance.' He gripped my shoulder hard. 'Now there is something truly worth fighting for. I was never the mission, Max. You are.'

I stared at him, uncomprehending.

'I don't understand,' I said, forcing the words out. I reached across my chest and took his hand from my shoulder. 'We just need . . . to go.'

'There is nothing to understand, Max. It is finished. The terrible, unforgivable, beauty is born, and I have given it all to you.' He freed his hand and laid it across my heart. 'Here. In you, in your blood, is everything you need to create Adam, and to destroy him. I have perfected the virus and the vaccine in secret. For forty days they will remain live. These greedy fools underground,' he stamped lightly in the dust of the parade ground, 'and those fools in London are ignorant, stupid people, interested only in what my creation can do for them. But you, my boy,' he brought his hand up to my face, 'my beautiful boy, are the future. The house, the money, the title — use everything I left behind and use it to fight. Fight for what is left to save and make your mother proud. Use your *fearúlacht* and do what she and I never could. Fight, but fight and *win*.'

I shook my head.

'No. Come. Come with me. You and me, together. Please. We can talk later but we need to leave now.' I spoke softly, cautiously. I thought of the girl in the cave, and the disconnect between his night-time ceremonies and the absolute devastation his creations unleashed. And I thought of Raven Hill, too, under my command, and the spectre of controlling an ever-expanding army of perfected, indestructible Sleepers.

'No, son, my time is done. Use my warriors. But

remember, they are not monsters, Max. They are men. Never forget that. There is only one monster, and it is time he bade you farewell.' I stood and watched him as he walked to the open doorway of the hut. He turned to face me, smiling in the flame-light, hand raised in farewell.

'Make wars cease to the ends of the earth, Max. Break the bow and shatter the spear. Burn shields with fire! Who creates the warrior, controls the warrior!'

He let his hand drop, pulled the Cyclops mask back over his face and vanished into the darkness.

28

I found her where I last saw her.

She was asleep in the first antechamber of the cave, balled up as I had been when last she'd seen me, head on her hands. A makeshift palm-oil lamp threw a weak yellow light across her. The tiny coiled wick held the smallest of flames, just enough to pick out Roberts's bead bracelet tied around her wrist.

I shed the hyena skin and shook her awake gently, keeping at arm's length. She woke slowly, awareness flooding back to her as it had done to me an hour earlier. Wary, but not scared, she sat up and blinked at me.

'*Aw di bodi?*' I asked.

She stretched and shrugged her shoulders and then pointed to the wound at the base of my neck.

'*Mi bodi fayn,*' I said. She looked nonplussed. I gave her the thumbs-up and smiled. 'OK,' I said. She smiled, too. There was no sign of the stick man, but the torch I'd given her was on the ground next to her. I picked it up, switched it on and handed it to her. As she swished the beam around the cave I blew out the lantern and removed and coiled the wick. I hoped it would do. 'Let's go.'

She led me first to the muddy patch under the river. We paused. She retraced her footprints so as not to leave more, and then I followed on behind her. The navigation marks I'd cut in the walls were enough to guide me, but she knew the caves even in the darkness. She was the best guide I could have hoped for. She moved fast, too, unencumbered by height in the low passages. Within an hour we'd reached the point where I'd dropped down into the base, and where, crucially, I'd left my bag. It was still there, untouched. I picked it up and fished out a couple of hard biscuits. Both ravenous, we stood and ate them on the spot, washing them down with gulps from the water bottle. When we'd finished, I plucked a fentanyl lozenge out of the medical kit and ran it around my gum line. The painkiller kicked in immediately, but the rush was disorientating, like slamming half-a-dozen shots of tequila. I steadied myself against the wall. She put her hand out, thinking it was a sweet. I shook my head.

'Medicine.' I slung the bag over my shoulder. 'OK,' I said. 'Let's go,' and made to leave by the way we'd come. She shrugged her shoulders and raised her eyebrows. 'Yeah, go.' She looked at me and shook her head. In disbelief, not refusal. 'Trust me,' I said. 'I know what I'm doing.' She shrugged again and in reverse marching order we began the long trudge back through the cave complex.

We stopped where the floor grew muddy. I pointed to the ceiling.

'*Riva?*' She nodded and sat down, exhausted. We'd been walking through the tunnels for over two hours. I gave her the water bottle and went to work quickly.

I took the day bag off and fished out the detonation cord. It was enough to bring down a forest tree. Whether it would be enough to crack open the cave ceiling was another matter entirely. Designed as an explosive fuse to detonate other explosives with, det cord could also be used as a primary device in its own right. The SBS used heavy cord to cut through harbour piers underwater. I'd used it to blow the handles off locked doors. It looked like a length of washing line and was endlessly versatile.

It might just work. All I needed to do was open the bedrock a fraction. If the fault ran along the break line in the roof of the tunnel the weight of the water would do the rest. Carefully I packed a double strand of the cord into the fissure in the rock above me, taping it in place as I went along with gaffer tape from the day bag. It was hard going. With my arms fully extended I could just touch the ceiling. Reaching up pulled my ribs apart, but the fentanyl masked the worst of it.

The blast needed to be tamped upwards. It was no use if the force of the blast was dissipated into the empty space of the cave below. It doesn't take much to direct an explosion. I rummaged through the bag. Folded up inside was a copy of the *Awoko* newspaper that Ezra had shown me in Freetown. I flattened it out and then folded it again, this time into a vertical strip. I put a crease along the length of it, filled it with mulch and dirt from the tunnel floor, and taped it up hard over the cord, leaving the detonator fuse exposed at one end. Finally, I unwound the oily wick that had lit the girl's lamp. I tied it in a slip knot over the fuse, and carefully let it hang down into the cave.

In the side pocket of the day bag I found a crumpled

packet of Marlboros and my lighter. I thought about lighting a cigarette but looked at the girl and thought twice. Instead, I just lit the fuse. Palm oil burned hot and slow. I had no idea how long the wick would take to burn down. Long enough, I hoped.

The girl looked at me. I pointed to the ceiling.

'Boom!' I mimed with my arms the cascade of water that I hoped would follow. She looked up, wide-eyed, at the little yellow flame eating its way slowly towards the rock roof.

'*Dyinyinga*,' I said, while mimicking washing my hands and flicking my fingers towards the floor. 'Finish.'

She looked up and down and smiled, and together we walked out into the night.

I gave her the remains of the MRE, took a moment to get my bearings and then pointed her due east towards the small town of Bindi. It was about five klicks as the crow flies – the same distance from the cave as it was due west to the entrance to the huts that masked the base's entrance. I made a sign for walking legs with my index and middle fingers. She turned around and said nothing. I gave her the thumbs-up, but she looked down and wouldn't meet my eye. I squatted down on my haunches and held her shoulders lightly.

'I can't help you,' I said. 'You have to go. You'll be OK. Everything will be OK.' I turned her around to face the direction she'd have to walk in and patted her back. Her cheeks were wet with tears. 'Please,' I said. 'Go.'

She walked off into shadows, carefully threading her way through the trees towards Bindi. I had no idea if the town had been sacked or not – but she stood a better chance there than she did staying with me, that was for sure.

When her silhouette disappeared from view I headed off in the opposite direction, keeping under the trees, moving as fast as the terrain and the darkness would allow. The moon was dropping now, but its brightness was a godsend. Without it, I would have been blind. Dawn was not far off, and when the sun rose I would be painfully exposed. But for a while longer I could remain hidden and move unseen through the silver shadows of the ragged savannah woodland.

I kept up a steady jog, all the time waiting for the noise of the earth giving way and the deluge that would follow it. I hoped that at least the bottom level would be wiped out and the science to replicate my father's experiments with it.

I stopped and listened. Half an hour had passed since leaving the cave, but all was silent.

Up ahead the two thatched rondels were clearly visible. I had no weapon, not even a knife this time. But I didn't need one. I crouched beneath an ackee tree at the edge of the clearing and took the emergency beacon that Ezra had given me out of the bag. It was a civilian specification personal locator beacon. It was my only failsafe. If the bomb in the passage didn't work – this might. I pulled out the aerial, lifted the anti-tamper seal, rested my thumb on the *on* button – and stopped.

If I pressed it I might never know for sure whether my father was a Russian agent, a double agent or simply a madman. But one thing *was* for sure: my mission was wide open from the start. The Russians had known I'd been on the ground almost immediately, and my father knew Sonny Boy was one of my men. Kristóf King, David Mason, Frank Knight: who wanted my father dead, who wanted me dead, and who wanted my blood?

There was something else I knew, too. My father died in a plane crash in Angola. Whatever he or my mother had once been or later became, they had both died for me, then and there. My mother was not his puppet. That masked madman was not my parent.

And yet he was.

'Fuck it.'

I pressed the button.

Nothing around me changed, but Ezra was right: the powerful satellite signal it sent up notifying urgent need of emergency rescue would be visible to anyone and everyone. It was as if I had painted the entrance to the base – and everything and everyone inside – in bright-white light. The location of their secret base was now public knowledge.

I covered the unit under a pile of rotting ackee fruit skins by the base of the tree. It was just eight kilometres north-west to the airstrip at Soron and the possibility of hijacking a plane to Guinea, or at least walking north across the border.

I paused and then stepped away from the base and back into the trees. As I did so a voice in Russian barked at me.

'*Ostanovis!*'

I stopped as commanded and turned around slowly with my hands spread open. I peered into the darkness and found myself squinting across the top of a raised pistol and into the unsmiling face of Colonel Proshunin.

29

'Sergeant, take him down.' Proshunin barked orders in Russian. Boots kicked the backs of both my knees. I crumpled, twisting on to my side as I fell to protect the broken ribs I thought were going to get a beating. Half a dozen AKs were trained on me. 'Alive.' Proshunin ordered. 'Inside.'

At first they hesitated. And then one of them searched me. I lay prone. No weapons to find, they cut the back pack off my shoulders and emptied it in front of me.

'OK,' one of the men said in Russian. 'Clear.'

They picked up the empty bag and forced it over my head. What little light there had been was extinguished: one shade of darkness replaced by another. Hands grabbed my arms and hauled me up. My wrists were bound with my own gaffer tape. A rifle muzzle jabbed into my spine.

'*Davai, davai,*' the solider grunted. I moved forward tentatively only to be shoved onwards. '*Skoreye!*' I walked faster.

It was hard to hear clearly under the makeshift hood, but it didn't sound like they'd found the beacon. I was hot, breathing hard. Sweat ran into my eyes, which I strained for any glimpse of detail through the fabric of the bag.

Nothing.

Was this what it had been like when I was . . . what, unconscious? I had no memory of it at all, except a vague recollection of thick, grey fog. I remembered that I couldn't remember. That was all. If I had done anything, killed anyone like the other Sleepers had, it was lost to me. In the couple of hours or so since my father had set me free the pain in my head had faded – though whether that was due to the virus losing out to the antidote or the fentanyl was impossible to tell.

The soldiers pushed me on. I felt a change in the atmosphere. Stripped from the waist up, my skin had to guide me now that my eyes couldn't. We'd stepped inside one of the huts and started to descend. This was it, then. No escape now. If the charge was going to blow it would blow at any moment. Just like Sonny Boy, I'd be trapped on the wrong side of the break line, after all. I tensed at the memory of lighting the fuse and then exhaled.

Of all the ways to go, I thought, *I didn't see this coming.*

The air cooled as waves of air conditioning wafted up to us. We dropped three flights of stairs before passing through another doorway and emerging into a corridor. From my memory of the site map on the wall below decks we were on Level One. Proshunin told his men to take everything they found in the bag to the laboratory.

'Crack the phones. I want the information now.'

'Sir, yes, sir. And the prisoner, sir?'

'Level Two. The observation room.'

The group split. Half a dozen men stayed with me,

Proshunin included. His boot-step was short, his breathing heavy. I couldn't see him, but I could sense him. We dropped another two flights and wheeled sharply to the right. The pressure changed again. And with it, permeating my senses as the hood was removed, came a sharp tang of peppermint.

Blinding light. The room was lined entirely with white plastic sheets. Dead-centre sat an examination chair, complete with sprung metal head, arm and leg restraints. On a metal trolley next to it a woman in a lab coat was laying out swabs and syringes. Dental drill bits and a bone saw had already been removed from their sterile wrappers. This was going to get rough.

'Bit high-tech for you, isn't it, Colonel?' I said in Russian. 'I was looking forward to a good punch-up.'

'On the contrary,' he replied in heavily accented English. 'There is nothing high-tech about Captain Tarasova's methods. By the time she has finished with you, not even your own mother would recognize you.'

My eyes adjusted properly to the room. Twenty feet square. Low ceiling. One entrance, behind me. Four of Proshunin's men had come in with us: two that I could see; two that I could hear adjusting their rifles.

'One last thing, if I may. Please do not trouble us with your name and rank. We already know them.'

'Is that a fact, Colonel Proshunin?'

'Yes, that is a fact, Major McLean.' It wasn't Proshunin who answered. Captain Tarasova unwrapped the last of my torture implements and pivoted sharply on her heels. She'd already washed all the dye out of her hair, and the lab-coat uniform bit hard into her identity. But she was unmistakable.

'Don't you know,' I said, 'that gentlemen prefer blondes?'

'*Mudak!*' she sighed.

It was her all right. Ana María had got out of Caracas.

Two of Proshunin's men came from behind me and pushed me towards the chair. As they spun me around and then cut the tape from my wrists, I saw the other two aiming their AKs directly at me. To have resisted would have been to die then and there. I've always been suspicious of anyone who says they want to go out fighting. Once you're out, you're out. I was planning on staying in the game as long as possible.

While my limbs and head were bound to the examination chair, Ana María busied herself with what were apparently the tools of her trade. She was just at the edge of my vision, and I saw her as a blur in the corner of my eye. It was, frankly, hard to know what to say. Had she known who I was in Caracas? I certainly had no idea who she was, who she worked for, or even if she had escaped or Frank had let her get away. Suddenly David Mason and General King didn't look like the prime candidates for fouling my mission – whatever it was, or whatever they thought it was. My father had said it depended on who sent me.

Other people might have ordered it. But Frank sent me.

'You know my name,' I said. 'What's yours?'

Nothing.

'You're going to kill me anyway. Or if you don't, he will.' I strained my head in the direction of Proshunin, who was now out of sight, but my head was held tight. 'That's not asking much, is it? To know your name.'

She spoke then, but to the colonel, not to me.

'Permission to begin, Commandant?' Her Russian was hard and fast. A native speaker for sure.

'*Da*, carry on, Captain Tarasova.'

She moved closer to inspect me and leaned down into my face. As she did so the two guards who'd covered me stepped forward so I could see them too. Their rifles were still trained on me.

'I'm not fucking Houdini,' I muttered under my breath. She shone a light into both of my eyes, examining them as she did so. I remembered the fuse and imagined her floating underground in the flood that I was powerless to stop. A wave of claustrophobia choked me.

'Ana María,' I murmured under my breath, trying not to let Proshunin see or hear what I was saying. 'If we stay here, we die,' I said in Spanish. 'Trust me. We have to get out.'

In one movement Ana María brought her left fist down into my groin. It was a perfectly executed punch that connected fully with my genitals. My testes expanded against my pelvic bone under her knuckles. I blacked out momentarily, coming back around as a wave of nausea rolled up my gut. My stomach muscles went into spasm, forcing the biscuit I'd eaten earlier back up into my gullet. I was caught in the perfect body-shock of total pain. Of all the methods devised over the centuries to incapacitate a man, hitting him in the balls remains the purest and simplest way of causing undiluted agony.

'My name is Captain Ana María Tarasova,' she said, cracking the wide, sad smile that had disarmed me in Caracas. 'I am a medical doctor, so you can be confident that you will die exactly when Colonel Proshunin wishes it.' She scooped my bruised testes into her palm. 'Which will not,' she continued, 'be soon.'

Her fist closed.

Sparks of red and yellow flashed across my vision. I roared with pain so deep and loud that blood vessels in my throat burst, and the taste of iron filled my mouth again. I clenched my jaw and swallowed the scream. Encouraged by the effect, she grabbed harder still, and I opened my eyes to look at her.

I saw her standing there, calm, professional, detached, monitoring her effect on me as a biologist might assess a frog before dissection – or how I might assess a target through a scope before termination. Barely a flicker of exertion showed in her face. I closed my eyes again, trying to breathe through the pain. And there she was, naked under the shower, pinching the water out of her eyes in the hotel bathroom. Proshunin's voice brought me back to the torture chamber.

'Enough entertainment, Captain. The serum. Let us find out what kind of agent Major McLean really is.'

'Of course, Colonel. Of course.' The overhead lights flickered as she relaxed her grip. But the pain persisted. Through a wide-bore needle she drew a syringe of colourless liquid from a glass phial retrieved from the trolley. 'Open your mouth.'

'Can I have it on a sugar cube?' I forced a weak smile.

'Open your mouth,' she repeated. 'Or these men will open it for you.'

'Nice of you to offer *me* something to drink for a change. I don't suppose you have any ice and lemon, do you?' Her face remained impassive. Beautiful, but unmoved.

'No,' she said. 'Just a little remedy to loosen the tongue. I am going to enjoy our conversation, Max.'

SP-117. No taste. No colour. No side effects. The Russian Biological Weapons Department 12's most effective truth serum. It had worked on Litvinenko. And it would work on me. She closed her free hand on my testes again. The pain was indescribable. 'Or would you prefer me to inject you with it?' she said as she began to crush me again. 'Here.'

I opened my mouth.

She leaned towards me again, serum in hand. As the feeding-needle touched my lip the room shook, rattling the torture tools on the metal trolley. The bright-white lights flickered and died, and in their place security lamps lit the room in red. From vents in the ceiling a cloud of peppermint-scented vapour billowed into the room. Proshunin spoke, but his words were lost beneath the wail of an emergency alarm.

Ana María straightened up, the serum undelivered. The guards lowered their rifles and looked at each other and then to her for an explanation. An automated voice in Russian commanded all non-immunized personnel to assemble on Level One immediately.

Proshunin shouted orders into his radio. The only words I could make out were *'obshchiy vypusk'*: general release. The door to the interrogation room opened, and the sounds of barely suppressed panic filled the air.

The charge had blown.

30

The wick held up.

Thousands of gallons of water from the Mong River were flooding the underground base from the bottom up. I struggled in vain against the restraints. Proshunin was already out the door, his voice fading as he barked more orders along the corridor. The four Spetsnaz guards followed him. I'd never seen Russian Special Forces operators so rattled. Perhaps they knew what was coming.

'Ana María!' I bellowed. 'For God's sake, please! Ana María!'

She'd stepped out of my limited arc of vision and left, I supposed, with Proshunin. I strained with all my might. It was pointless. The room was filling with peppermint vapour – huge swirls of it expanding under the dull-red safety lights. Over and over the automated warning instructed everyone who was at risk from infection to congregate on Level One.

I closed my eyes and conjured the image of Roberts and Juliet sitting at their beach bar the first day I met them, the girl in the cave heading towards Bindi.

'I hope you make it,' I whispered to myself. That would be nice, I thought, if one decent person made it out of this. I didn't number myself among them. 'Don't sleep too close to the edge,' I reminded the girl as she trod the moonlit savannah in my mind's eye, 'in case the little grey wolf bites you.'

The door to the interrogation room swung shut, muting the noise of pandemonium spreading outside. That was it, then. One way or another it looked like I was already in my coffin. There were no great thoughts. No regrets. Nothing except for a calm resignation to the inevitability of it all. That, and a wonder at the stupidity of ever imagining the world could be different just because you wished it to be so. In my mind's eye I saw my father don his mask and disappear into the hut that one last time. If only I'd had another chance to bring him round, I thought. If only I'd followed him. Maybe, just maybe, I might have saved him. Saved myself. No possibility of that now.

I relaxed and found the words came to me more easily than I would have imagined.

'Holy Mary, Mother of God . . .'

The door to the room opened and closed. For a moment echoes of alarm filled the space again. Like pressing a sea shell to your ear and releasing it, the tide of panic outside flowed and ebbed around me.

'Pray for us sinners . . .'

Then I heard the unmistakable metal *click-clack-snap* of a Kalashnikov safety catch being released, and the breech charged.

'Now and at the hour . . .'

The barrel pressed into my skull at the base of my right ear.

'. . . of our death.'

I heard a spring release; metal freeing itself. My head vibrated from the shock, and I was free.

'Amen,' hissed Ana María into my ear. The metal restraints had sprung clear of my forehead, wrists, ankles. The AK barrel still bored into my head. 'A life for a life.' She spoke in faultless English.

'Thank you,' I said. She withdrew the muzzle and threw me the rifle. I tried to sit up. It was excruciating.

'On your feet,' she ordered. Everything hurt: my ribs, my head, my ear, the wound on my neck, and now my balls. 'Get up!'

I inhaled, stood and rolled my shoulders back. She shook her head dismissively as if to say 'pathetic'. I checked the magazine in the AK. It was fully charged.

'OK, let's do it.' I exhaled hard. I moved to the door and peered out of the observation window. The main lights had failed in the corridor outside, too. Everything was lit by the eerie glow of red security lights. In their ruddy hue the ordered military veneer of the underground base dissolved into what it was: an abandoned mine that promised to become a tomb.

The main generator, or at least the relay, must have failed. I guessed that was also in the lower level.

'What have you done, Max? What's happening?'

I ignored her and stepped away from the window glass, looking around the room for anything that might help get us out.

Fuck, I thought, *it's 'us' now, is it?*

I slung the AK over my shoulder, scooped up a

handful of ampoules from the table and zipped them into the cargo pocket of my fatigues – except the one marked морфин, whose thin glass neck I cracked. I drew a few mils of the clear fluid out into an empty syringe that Ana María had laid out on the trolley and injected myself in the thigh.

'What are you doing?' she shouted above the constant automated order for anyone at risk of infection to assemble on the level above us.

'Treating your handiwork,' I replied. The effect of the morphine was, fortunately, almost instantaneous. It was a low dose and went to work on the pain just enough that I could function, without knocking me out. I clicked the fire selector on the Kalashnikov down to single shot and looked out into the corridor again. Uniformed soldiers, nurses and a ragged collection of 'rebels' ran left to right, heading for the exit to Level One. A lone figure stood out among them, head down, radio in hand battling his way against the tide. It was Proshunin, heading in the opposite direction. I jerked clear of the window as he passed.

'Can they get out?' I asked Ana María. 'The creatures in the cells below?'

'The Sleepers? No. Only if they are released.'

'OK. How are they released?'

'The professor,' she replied, 'only the professor can release them.' We were speaking in English now. 'That's what Proshunin was ordering. A general release.' There was a subtle change in the room. She looked around, and then up. 'Shit!' Her face tightened. She looked suddenly scared.

'What? What is it?''

'The neutralizer. It's stopped.' I looked up too. There was nothing to see. I shrugged. 'The vapour. The peppermint gas,' she shouted, exasperated by my lack of understanding. 'It neutralizes them, makes them docile, easier to control. The pumps must have failed.' She looked at me, eyes wide with fear. 'Max,' she asked again, 'what have you done?'

'I blew the main gen set.' There was something I needed to know. 'Ana María, the Sleepers . . .' She looked at me, horrified.

'Yes?'

'Can they swim?'

The penny dropped.

'You flooded the base? *Mudak!* But that won't stop the professor. His lab's airtight, because of the experiments. The Sleeper cells, too. But if we don't get out before the emergency power fails, we'll be trapped.' She swiped her pass against the lock and opened the door, and we stepped out together. The noise of the announcement was louder. Distant shouts in Russian added to the cacophony, but the stream of people had eased off to a trickle of individual stragglers. She made to go right, towards the exit, but the stairs were jammed with evacuees. I caught her wrist.

'The professor,' I said. 'I need him alive.'

As she looked at me, the faintest glimmer of a smile played at the edges of her mouth.

'Professor Mac Ghill'ean,' she said. 'He's your father, isn't he?' I nodded. 'The hut where you came in, there's a blast door there. If it's sealed we'll be trapped. And so will the Sleepers.' I gave her back the AK. She hesitated, and then gave me her pass.

'OK. Give me ten minutes and then seal it,' I told her. 'First sign of the Sleepers, lock it and run.'

'The first sign of them is already too late,' she said.

I put my hand to her cheek for a moment and then turned to face the emptied corridor. I didn't think it mattered if she sealed the door or not; if she was on my side, theirs or just hers; or whether she'd known who I was in Venezuela or not. I was already on borrowed time: unravelling who she was, or wasn't, was a luxury I couldn't afford. As I broke into a jog I heard her shout after me.

'Good luck, Max McLean.' And I felt something then, the same connection I'd felt in Caracas and the same shock at losing it.

I kept moving towards the lift at the far end of the level. I glanced into the rooms as I ran: all empty. No sign of Proshunin, and no sign of how he'd got out. But if I was risking my life to reach my father, then I bet the colonel was, too.

At the end of the corridor the doors to the personnel lift were shut, and the floor indicator lights above them were dead. Then the tannoy system gave out, and the bunker was plunged into an unsettling silence. I swiped Ana María's pass over the scanner beneath the call button.

Nothing. The main system had lost power, and the emergency back up wasn't enough to run the lifts.

I put my fingers against the lips of the doors and tried to prise them apart, but to no avail. Wherever Proshunin had gone, he hadn't used the lift.

Beside me the last door along the corridor opened. A soldier in battle dress appeared, panicked, buttoning his trousers. He turned to look at me as my right fist caught his windpipe. He collapsed and I caught his head, twisting it under the weight of his own body. His neck snapped easily. I took the 9mm pistol from his belt, cocked it and tucked it into the waistband at the small of my back. I took two hand grenades from his webbing, too – but right then it was his bayonet I needed most.

I put the point between the lift doors, banged the blade home repeatedly with the heel of my palm and then pulled hard to the left. The door opened enough to get my fingers into. I pulled again and felt the strain on my broken ribs as the doors inched apart. The gap was just enough to squeeze past.

I put my head through first and looked down. Dim red lights lit the shaft that fell away beneath me. Electrical and steel cables vanished into the gloom. Down the right-hand wall hand grips had been set into the concrete to form an improvised ladder. It looked like the Russians had just refitted the old mine lift.

I looked up.

The car was suspended above me, abandoned on Level One. That meant there was clear passage all the way down. The lift could take at least twenty people and the chasm was vast. I listened hard. From far below the sound of gushing water echoed up the vertical chamber.

The complex was flooding, but slowly. Either the charge opened only a small fissure, or the tunnels and caves underground were sucking up too much water.

I forced myself into the gap I'd made between the doors and pushed. They opened enough to attempt a standing jump to the ladder from the lip inside. I made the distance easily, but the sudden jolt of grasping the hand-grip tore hard at my ribs. My fingers slipped on the metal. My knee bounced off a lower grip and spun me into the wall. My right shoulder grazed concrete. I was falling fast. My head smacked against another grip. I flailed with my right hand, desperately searching for a hold. My fingertips found purchase but under the speed of the fall my own dead weight snapped them free.

I was dropping too close to the wall and risked knocking myself out and drowning. Skin friction-burned off my upper arm. I pushed out hard with both hands, grazing palm flesh. Spinning out into the middle of the shaft, I folded my arms across my chest and pressed my ankles together.

A rush of red-tinged air. I relaxed for impact, and the soles of my boots hit the flood. The boom of exploding water cracked in my ears and then bubbled under with me, transmuted into a torrential rush-roar as the river water swallowed me.

I brought my knees up and spread my arms to slow the descent, and my feet found the floor. The water was dark but not opaque. The security lights persisted even underwater, making the outflow of the Mong River look like a stream of thin, transparent blood. I kicked my way to the surface.

The floodwater had reached the bottom of the lift doors for Level Four, where the cave tunnel had first led me into the bunker. From behind the doors came a pounding rush of water. I held on to the lift cables to steady myself for a moment and then dived back under.

It was five metres down to the bottom and Level Five. The weight of the pistol and the grenades helped sink me into the well. The lift door had already been partly opened. Through the gap a pale arm waved in the current. I fed it back through to the other side and braced against the doors as I had at the top of the shaft. They were stuck fast. I tried again. The doors were rigid.

Snipers have an unfair advantage holding their breath. Lowering our metabolic rate and slowing the heart is a trick of the trade that steadies the shot and means we can go for longer than some underwater, too. I could manage five minutes at the outside. I breathed out a little air to relax my diaphragm and pushed again. The doors opened another hand-width. Just enough. In the dark water of the corridor beyond hung the limp cadaver of the Ukrainian ward sister. Somewhere down there would be the body of Nurse Kuznetsova, too. Any pang I may have had at killing her dissipated into the water around me. They were all dead now anyway.

I surfaced and drew breath. From above, the timbre

of the shaft had changed. Above the rushing of water came the rapid thumping of what sounded like distant drums. It was a crazy, offbeat rhythm, but its depth was different to the drummers who kept time at my father's night-time ceremonies. The echoing patter rippled up and down the height of the complex like an endless loop of hands thudding against metal.

Shit, I thought, *the Sleepers*.

With nothing to neutralize them in their cells, they'd come to.

I dived again and swam out of the lift well and into the passage. I pushed past the ward sister, and stared into the red hue of the abyss ahead. Bodies emerged from the gloom. Patients still hooked up to bags of intravenous fluids; soldiers weighed down by weapons; doctors with the billowing white wings of their lab coats spread out behind them: all were lifeless.

I oriented myself, and tried not to think about the people I'd killed in the flood. That kind of pressure can crush a man.

One minute.

The hospital level was flooded to the ceiling. Making two-minute forays into the tunnels before coming back up for air in the well wouldn't give me anything like enough range to search properly. There may have been air pockets here and there, but finding them in the dingy glow of the security lights was impossible. I had an idea of how to do it, how to keep breathing underwater, but it was a gamble. I kicked my way along the submerged hallway.

Two minutes.

Crunch time: turn back, and live – at least for the moment; or continue – and if the gamble failed I'd be dead in a couple of minutes.

I pressed on.

Three minutes.

The layout of the level was unfamiliar. Last time around I'd come in from the other end, by the stairs. Even more confusing was that the layout was different down there. Whereas the upper levels were all laid out following the same pattern, the hospital was cut up into smaller, isolated wards and labs. I could feel the flow of water, the river current, dragging me along. I swam along a dead end and doubled back on myself, cursing the lost seconds.

Four minutes.

My chest was tight, my neck strained. I breathed out a little and pushed through a fire exit into a junction between two wards. Packed tight with bodies, the people who'd worked on that level had taken refuge there en masse, maybe hoping that the heavy metal door would save them. It hadn't.

I forced my way through them. Dead hands stroked my face. Tresses of hair unloosed from a nurse's missing cap snagged in my fingers.

Five minutes.

Dead man swimming.

I emerged into the intensive care unit. Pocahontas hung upside down, the bandages on his ankle stump unravelling into the river water. My chest heaved, eyesight dimmed. I breathed out involuntarily. The last of the air in my lungs bubbled up and along the dead man's body as I pulled him towards me. Water rushed into my mouth, up my nose. I tore the oxygen mask from his face and pressed it to my own, kicking downwards as I did. My left hand reached the valve on the cylinder anchored by his bed as my throat opened and my lungs dragged in a stream of pure, cold oxygen.

I was alive, but my time was up anyway. As I drew heavily on the sub-aqua lifeline, Ana María would be sealing the blast doors. I breathed deeply through the mask and set off again, propelling myself through the biohazard area.

Everywhere was darkness. And then up ahead, at the end of the walkway, a single bright light shone out through the window of the last laboratory on the row. I fought my way towards it, a drowning moth ploughing towards a sunken moon. I reached it and pressed my face to the glass and drank in the scene before me.

Bone dry in his perfectly insulated office my father stood holding the perspex block that encased his life's work. In front of him, the green-lit glass of a thumbprint-sized scanner blinked rhythmically in time with the sound of my heart beating in my ears. I slammed my fist against the window over and over again, but the feeble sound was lost down there, washed away with the running river.

Carefully he set the seed down next to the scanner and slowly, deliberately, crossed himself. From a drawer under the desk he produced a hand grenade. I rapped on the glass with my knuckles. And then, in silence, I watched his fingers curl around the detonation lever. I realized then what he was going to do. The blast would obliterate the vector, and the scanner. The Sleepers would be trapped and destroyed along with his life's work – leaving me the sole inheritor of the project he'd perfected in secret.

He picked up the seed again and held it close to his chest, tight to the grenade. He straightened up to face me with his eyes closed and with a wince of effort he pulled at the pin.

'Look at me!' I roared underwater. The sound carried hardly any further than the bubbles that leached from my mouth.

He bowed his head, and the detonation lever spun free, his index finger wrapped around the pin. His body jerked. His eyes opened wide in surprise and he saw me.

'*Dia dhuit*,' he mouthed in Irish. *God be with you*. And then bright-red blood spilled from between his lips.

He collapsed to reveal Colonel Proshunin standing behind him – who saw the grenade and lunged forward. He grabbed my father's right arm by the wrist, and forced his thumb down on to the scanner.

The colonel looked up at me and sneered. From the ceiling behind him hung the open door to the escape tube he'd scuttled down.

I closed my eyes, braced for impact.

But it's impossible to prepare for devastation like that. And when the blast came I felt nothing.

I opened my eyes, but all the light had gone. Instead

of a brightly lit beacon, the window was now a dark square, painted red from the inside. My mission had been completed for me; my father hoping all the while that I was completing his for him. I turned and swam, lungs straining for lack of breath, as the vibrations of metal security doors being flung open juddered through the bunker.

Proshunin had opened the gates of hell.

31

I beat my way through the water, stopping at Pocahontas to replenish my lungs, to the well of the lift shaft. I broke the surface of the water to the sound of metal ripping. Mad howls and ululations filled the air. Above me I saw the lift doors begin to open. Level Three was first. Barely distinguishable in the gloom, arms emerged from the forced opening, silhouetted against the security lights. A figure jumped. And then another. They leaped from the lift doors to the car cables and climbed, effortlessly swinging their way up to the exit I'd made for them on the floor above. Dozens of them followed suit.

Then the doors on the levels below were wrenched apart – less than eight feet above my head. I could hear them in the tunnel right next to me, at the same level the river emptied out into. I dived down hard and clung on to the hand-holds to keep myself under. The doors came apart, and a rush of cold water was released into the well. Immediately above me the watery outlines of the Sleepers streamed into the lift shaft and scaled the walls to freedom.

There was no backlog, no hold-up. They were getting out. Ana María couldn't have sealed the hatch. I only hoped she'd got clear before they emerged into the world above.

Five minutes. Twenty, fifty, a hundred of them had poured out of their cells and headed to the surface. My lungs heaved in my chest. Carefully I put my lips above water. My face broke the meniscus, and I gasped. Above me the silhouette of a Sleeper spread out, arms and legs akimbo, plummeting towards me. He screamed as he fell, a wild tearing shriek that peeled and bounced off the walls as he accelerated through the air.

I pulled myself under just before he hit the water. Two-hundred and twenty pounds of what had once been a Russian squaddie ploughed through the red water next to me. As his face passed mine his hands shot out towards me. I pressed myself flat against the wall as his flailing arm swiped at and missed my stomach. I'd already lost half my ear to one of these monsters. I didn't intend to lose my guts, too.

As his descent slowed I grasped the Makarov concealed behind my back, bringing it round at the last moment, as he surged towards me. His arms reached up to me and I kicked myself towards him, pistol outstretched. As he grasped for my hand I fired at point-blank range into his face. The life went out of him instantly, and he fell back to the bottom of the well, obscured by a thick bloom of his own blood.

But the shot had betrayed me.

I surfaced again to see the Sleepers were no longer climbing. They had stopped still, peering into the steadily rising water below them. The pistol had recocked. I fired at the heads of the nearest three, towering over me now less than a body's length away. The rounds opened up their skulls, and they fell into the water next to me, spent.

The howling stopped. The creatures looked at one another. And then from the top of the lift shaft I saw one of them let go of the cables and jump towards me. I dived furiously to the bottom. By the time he hit the water six others had jumped with him, plunging down in pursuit.

In the seconds it took them to steady themselves I clawed through the gap I'd prised open in the submerged lift doors, pulling the pin on a hand grenade as I squeezed through and letting it fall behind me. Four seconds to get clear. I fought my way along the corridor as they dived down to find me with speed and determination. The little Russian bomb went off as the leader tried and failed to force his way through the narrow aperture in the lift shaft behind me.

This time I felt it.

The doors took the brunt of the explosion, as did the floor of the well, which bounded the blast back up at them and away from me. The water boiled, and the concussion wave rolled over me, punching into my lungs. Blood seeped from my nose, ears. I spat out air and spun head over heels.

The blast wave ripped through the Sleepers, compressing the gasses in their altered bodies – rupturing lungs, shredding internal tissue. All that they could withstand: but what they could not survive were the massive brain haemorrhages the blast inflicted. They sank, defeated. Obliterated.

I swam back into the shaft through the slick of blood and body parts that clogged the doorway, coughing and spluttering to the surface. The last of them were out of their cells, climbing the cables and using the hand-grips to pull themselves up. The water was halfway up the entrance to Level Four, where I'd originally come in down the cave tunnel, and where the river was pouring in.

More of the monsters looked down at me. I took the last grenade from my pocket and held it fast. In the absence of a plan, rank hubris and repeating the trap I'd just sprung was all I could manage.

I was out of the game.

'Come on, you bastards!' I yelled at them. 'No retreat! No fucking surrender!'

One after the other they dropped down the shaft, whooping as they fell.

And then the earth moved.

A huge, body-racking tremor rattled not just the lift shaft, but the whole of the old mine complex. Next to me the bodies of the Sleepers bombed into the water. But I didn't dive. The surface rippled and swelled, and through the half-submerged, half-opened doors next to me a deep bass rumble erupted into a deafening rush of water and splitting rock. As the hands of the underwater warriors grasped at my legs, the dark void of the passage beside us filled and burst with a solid wall of surging water.

The granite bedrock had given way completely. The Mong River was cascading freely into the base. Funnelled into the lift shaft, water exploded upwards, rolling and tumbling me in the midst of a gigantic water spout towards the top of the base. It was useless to hold on. As the water rose it engulfed everything in its path. The Sleepers were ripped from their cables, footholds. Bodies washed out of the corridors. Papers, uniforms, hands, faces flashed past me in the washing-machine ride to the surface. I oriented myself in time to see the bottom of the lift car stuck at Level One approaching rapidly. I got my head above water, took a last gulp of air and kicked ferociously to the edge.

The escapees had widened the crack I'd forced between the doors, making it easier to pass through. The pressure of the rising river banged me hard against the top of the opening, which grated against my spine, tearing the pistol free of my belt. I pulled my legs up under me and kicked on. The flood rolled me along the corridor faster than I could have hoped to swim. I twisted and turned, enmeshed with the arms and legs of dead soldiers and live Sleepers, until I found myself at the stairs. The water rose fast, scraping me up the steps that Proshunin had marched me down, hooded, not long before.

The colour of the water changed from red to darkbrown to light-brown as the security lamps gave way to the pale glow of daybreak. The power of the surge ebbed, and there, not far above me, the outer blast door yawned open. My mouth found fresh air. I breathed hard and deep, tearing myself out of the water, pushing my legs up the final flight of stairs, two at a time. I let the grenade sink into the abyss below as outstretched hands clutched at my ankles.

As the blast ripped through my pursuers the heavy hatch slammed down. I rolled aside, out of the little thatched rondel and on to the stamped earth of the ceremonial ground. The sun was just clearing the ridge, raking everything with the long shadows of dawn.

I struggled to my feet and ran a few steps, blinking into the blinding light of a perfect African morning. As my eyes adjusted, one thing became crystal clear: I was still surrounded.

The Sleepers had fanned out into the trees ringing the square of flat earth between the two huts. Rocking back and forth, they sniffed the air and locked their eyes on me. Here and there soldiers and medical staff stood or lay between them. Some were injured, others just exhausted. Most were armed.

They all had one target.

I looked around for Ana María, but she was nowhere to be seen. As one, the Sleepers stepped forward, naked and wild-eyed, muscles straining. A low growl rose from their ranks – deep and resonant, like the throbbing of the generators I'd destroyed below me. Metre by metre the circle tightened. The Spetsnaz fighters stayed back, rifles up. I raised my hands, slowly. I had no weapons, nothing to fight with, nowhere to run.

After they killed me, a hundred monster men would

stream into the bush. They would infect others to swell their ranks. Within weeks cities would fall. And then whole countries. It had taken less than a thousand rebels to overthrow Charles Taylor's government in Liberia. The fighters massed around me would alone be enough to bring West Africa to its knees. As far as mission failure went, it was catastrophic.

Mixed with the low groan of the advancing Sleepers came the dirt-dance shuffle of their feet on the move. I knew what was coming. I looked down and stared at the curved patterns my father's deliberate dance steps had carved into the ground. My boot came to rest on a little mound. As the Sleepers' feet slid nearer I dropped into a crouch to scoop a handful of the rust-brown earth into my palm.

Remember that you are dust and to dust you shall return.

But as well as dirt, my fingers found steel. There, half buried, lay my father's ceremonial cutlass – dropped the night before, when he'd set me free.

I seized the hilt and stood up, holding the rusty blade aloft. The Spetsnaz men kept their eyes on me, but the Sleepers looked up in unison.

'Stop!' I yelled. 'I order you to stop!'

Eyes fixed resolutely on the blade, they continued their death march, moving ever closer. If I'd reached out then I could almost have touched them, the circle so tight that I was engulfed by a crowd of the Africans and Europeans, the metal of whose souls my father had smelted into the gold of his ambition.

A failsafe. There had to be a failsafe, a means of

controlling them. But there was no fingerprint scanner here, no mask, no hardware except the cutlass.

Control.

Roberts had said that only the looking-ground man can control the *dyinyinga*. Hands reached out. Fingers grasped at me. They would tear me limb from limb. Then I understood my father's final message: *Who creates the warrior, controls the warrior.*

He'd quoted from the Bible.

Psalm 46: 'Break the bow and shatter the spear.'

I was out of options, and struggled for the words.

'Be still!' I shouted. Their hands laid upon me, unstopped. My left arm, my throat were clutched hard. Fingers crushed into my flesh. I brandished the cutlass and roared in Irish with everything my lungs had left.

'*Éistigí!*'

The hands stayed their grip and then fell away. I looked them in the face, these men who would be like you and me if only they could have conjured the thought of it. Their eyes rolled. Their bodies swayed and rocked. And to a man they sniffed the air around them, picking up my scent like a pack of hunting dogs.

I pushed through them towards the rifles of the Russian soldiers.

'*Ubey yego!*' shouted an unseen trooper. *Kill him.*

As the squaddie facing me adjusted his aim the front rank of Sleepers sprinted past me, over me. The burst went straight into them. Bullets hammered into bone and muscle. Over it rose the battle song of their ululations. The trooper vanished into a haze of red mist. His limbs scattered; skin sloughed; intestine popped. Before anyone could react there was nothing but a bloody mess where the young man had stood.

The other soldiers backed off, weapons up, fingers tensed on trigger steel. In front of me the Russian Sleeper who'd absorbed a dozen rounds to his chest brandished the head of the eviscerated soldier and shrieked a gut-wrenching call to arms.

'When I sharpen my flashing sword and my hand grasps it in judgement, I will take vengeance on my enemies,' I bellowed in Irish, pointing into the Russian lines with the cutlass, 'and repay those who hate me!'

The Sleeper tossed the severed head into the ranks of uniformed men facing him, barking a peal of victory howls. In response, the Spetsnaz operators opened fire to a man. A phalanx of Sleepers formed a shield around me as assault rifles and machine guns emptied into them. From every direction hot metal erupted into the living wall of muscle. Green tracer whipped through them. Grenade shrapnel tore ligaments, shattered bone. Smoke, heat, light filled the air in a burning rush of cordite fog. The earth lifted beneath our feet and rained down on us from above. A ricochet grazed my neck. An explosion knocked me to the ground and the sword from my grip.

Fizzing with adrenaline and understanding, I stood, and exhorted them in Irish.

'*Fúmsa an díoltas!*' I roared. *Vengeance is mine.*

32

The Sleepers pulsed like a concussion wave, expanding into the ranks of Russian Special Forces that surrounded us, sweeping them into the trees, catching them in a tidal wave of single-minded destruction. I saw it then, the genius of it. The pure, unadulterated power of what my father had created. I saw too what King had seen in Sonny Boy and why he also craved an army of men like that.

But Sonny Boy was just one man – unique, possibly. This was more than a weapon, more than an army, even: it was a *force*. Individually they were brutal curiosities; as a unit they were unstoppable by anything other than massive explosive firepower; as a totality they were practically invincible.

Some of them fell lifeless, shot through the head. Others were cut in half, or floored by severed legs. But they were the tiny minority. Those of them mortally wounded by normal standards stayed in the fight. My father had made sure that the dead no longer saw the end of war.

They were fast, precise and ruthlessly efficient. No man could outrun them. And once they had your scent, no man could hide from them. Synchronized by instinct the entire group coordinated without the need for spoken language. They were perfect hunter-killers. Scavenging rifles from the dead they left behind, they armed themselves as they went, although the only weapon they needed that morning was their own brute strength. I stood still and watched them fan out, reducing the remnants of the conventional army they'd once supported to bloody pulp.

Perhaps that is what Gatling or Nobel or Oppenheimer felt: awe at the power of their invention surpassed only by their disgust at its creation. Maybe that – what, remorse? – was what my father had felt, too, when he gave me the means both to create and destroy the work that consumed him. At least, I hoped it was. It's one thing to build a bomb; quite another to re-engineer people into weapons. My father had crossed the line from enquiry to obscenity. And there I was: protected by it and profiting from it. What had repulsed me in Kabala rescued me in Karabunda.

I bent over, and my guts heaved. I was dehydrated, faint from lack of food, riddled with virus and physically broken.

One last push, Max.

I had to get clear, and fast. Depending on who had picked up the emergency beacon signal – and what they could see with their eyes in the sky – a cruise missile strike could be imminent. I was in danger of being killed by my own plan. I figured the airstrip at Soron was my best bet. If there was no plane there then I could jump the border into Guinea. Without orders to follow or an enemy to kill, I hoped the Sleepers would stay still long enough for me to figure out what to do with them – or *to* them – if no strike came. None were nearby now.

The cutlass had been knocked out of my hand. As I stooped down to look for it, the ground rose up to meet me, and I fell to my knees, retching.

Come on, man. Get a grip.

I spread my hands out on the ground to steady myself and looked around for something – anything – to drink. I needed water more than I needed a weapon, but there was none to be had. As I perched on all fours, summoning the strength for the last stretch, a shadow crept up behind me.

'You made it, then?'

Her voice had lost the hard edge of the interrogation room. In its place was that familiar sadness. I turned around and tried to stand but collapsed back into the dirt. I looked up at her, but the sun was bright behind her. There was blood on her face and a pistol in her hand.

'Yeah,' I said. 'Seems so.' There was nothing but death around us. Already a gyre of vultures twisted up into the sky above. I looked at the hut. The blast door was still closed, but I could hear movement. The Sleepers trapped inside were trying to get out.

Whoever Ana María was, and however handy she was with a semi-automatic, it seemed inconceivable that she could have survived the onslaught.

'How?' she asked.

'I swam. You?'

'The same way Vladislav went down.' For a moment I was lost. And then I remembered. Colonel Proshunin,

Colonel *Vladislav* Proshunin. When my father was shot, Proshunin's hands were empty. No pistol. My father's body would have taken the brunt of the blast. I looked closely at her fatigues. They were torn, and she bled from shrapnel wounds in her arm and shoulder.

'You,' I said. 'You were in the room.' She stepped to the side, and I was blinded by the sun. I shielded my eyes with the back of my hand. 'You shot him. You shot him in the back.'

'He was a traitor. Faithless, like father like son.' I opened my eyes and squinted at her silhouette. She pointed the barrel of the pistol at my chest. I spat into the dust. Blood and saliva clung to my unshaved chin. 'But he delivered to us what we need. What you both would have destroyed.'

'You think Moscow gives a fuck?' I laughed. 'They tried to start a war. They failed. They'll try again somewhere else. So it goes. No, you're on your own, sweetheart. I turned them, and you can't escape them. They'll find you. And they'll kill you. It's over. Whatever this was, it's finished. You're finished.'

'Oh no, Max. We've only just begun. Colonel Proshunin was a patriot, a true Russian martyr. You didn't stop him, Max. And you never could have.'

She was starting to sound like my father. I wasn't going to be able to reason with her any more than I could with him.

'Bullshit,' I sighed. 'The science is blown to bits, and those fucking monsters will tear you to pieces. We'd make it, you and me. You don't stand a chance on your own.'

'You and me?' She rolled her shoulders and adjusted her

grip on the pistol. '*Coño!* You were right about one thing in Caracas. It *was* you I'd been waiting for all these years. Your father's work is pumping around your veins. Your blood is the price of our victory, Max. A life for *life*. Your life.'

'But why here, why now? Why not in the room, in the chair?'

She laughed then. A sad, arrogant laugh that evaporated in the gathering heat of the morning.

'You understand so little about something for which you have risked so much. The code, Max. The code. With your blood we can create the virus and the vaccine. But we can't control them. We *couldn't* control them – not when they first awake. He would never have told us how; and you didn't even know that you knew it. Colonel Proshunin released the Sleepers to fulfil his mission. And now that I have fulfilled mine, you will die like the mercenary dog you are.'

'I am what I am.'

'Your father created the greatest weapon the world has ever known. And you gave us the trigger. Remember that, Max McLean, when you stand before your God.' She cocked the hammer on the 9mm. I clenched my fists.

'You know,' I said, 'Frank's mate was right,' and turned my eyes up towards the heavens. 'Next time, shoot the bitch.'

I blinked as the *whip-crack* of the pistol report lashed across me. I felt no impact, no pain, just the echo of the shot in my ears. I opened my eyes to see Ana María fall, toppling to earth in a graceful sweep of bloodied curves.

From beside the hut a figure stepped into the heat of the day, pistol in hand.

'Is she dead?' Roberts's voice shook with fear and exhaustion.

'In your own fucking time.' I smiled at him and reached up. He grasped my wrist and heaved me to my feet, staggering backwards as he did so. Sweat ran freely from his braids. He was breathing hard. I pulled him towards me, and we embraced in the heat and the dust, arms locked hard around each other's necks, steadying each other there on the killing ground.

When we separated he looked immediately at Ana María's body. I prised the little Glock I'd taken off Micky's dead body in Freetown out of his fingers. His hands were trembling.

'I said you'd know when to use it.' I smiled again, but his expression was lost in a mess of anxiety. 'Roberts, how . . .' I began to ask the inevitable question, but there was no point. Not then. He was there. I'd learn the why of it soon enough. What it meant was clear: if Roberts could get into Karabunda, I could get out. But first I needed him to concentrate on me, not her.

'Is she dead?' he repeated. He was straining for breath, struggling to take in the enormity of what he'd done. I saw that his cheeks were wet not only with sweat, but with tears, too.

I kneeled beside Ana María and rolled her on to her back. I pressed my ear to her lips, and my hand on her chest. Nothing at all. I chased the memory of the person I'd held, who I'd felt something for. But all I saw was another body.

'Yes,' I said, straightening up. 'She is.'

341

He covered his mouth with his palm. Words failed me, and then I understood what to say. I put my hand on his shoulder, and he focused on me.

'You did well,' I said. 'Your father would be proud of you.'

In the distance the familiar *whump-whump-whump* of an inbound chopper sliced the air; from inside the hut came the sound of buckling. The blast door was being wrenched free.

'Roberts,' I barked at him, 'if we don't get out of here we're dead, too.' He froze, trying to calculate what he'd done; what could not be undone. 'Now, man, we have to go *now*.'

I made to move. He blinked and seemed to remember where he was as his mind made room for anything other than the consequences of killing.

'But you have the code,' he said frantically. 'She said you have the code. I heard her say it.'

'Yeah, but I don't have the sword.'

'Sword? What fucking sword? You need a sword?'

'I don't know,' I said, 'and I'm not going to find out.' The growl of the chopper grew louder. 'Move,' I shouted at him. 'Now!'

I grabbed Roberts by the back of the neck and propelled him into cover under the trees. We ran through the human remains the Sleepers had left in their wake, pounding blood into the dry dust.

'Down, down, down.' We fell to the ground as the chopper cleared the ridge, the rotor-roar suddenly deafening in the clearing. It was a Russian Mi24, loaded with rocket pods.

'What are you doing, man?' Roberts wrestled free of my grasp. He was coming back to himself.

'Saving your ass,' I barked back, picking up a discarded AK. 'And mine. We can't outrun a gunship any more than we can those freaks underground. Now shut up and get small.'

But Roberts didn't get down. He got up and ran back into the clearing.

I made a grab for his ankle and missed. Within a moment he was out by the huts again, standing near Ana María's body, waving his arms. I shouted a warning after him, but my voice was lost in the din of the helicopter's motor. The big metal bird turned to face us, nose down, blades flaring. The twin-cannon on the front would shred him as surely as the Sleepers. I checked my flanks and looked behind me and sprinted at him. I caught him around the waist and brought him down hard. His face hit the ground, his lip split; bloodied soil from the ceremonial ground matted his dreads.

Bundled up together on the ground we yelled at each other simultaneously.

'What the fuck?'

The rotor wash fanned us. Flying grit stung my face, temporarily blinding me. The sheer force of the down draught turned even the smallest stone into bruising shrapnel. Huge swirls of dust fanned out behind the fuselage, spreading into the ragged wings of an angel of death. Roberts picked himself up and lunged forward, bent double.

'Come on!' he mouthed, beckoning me on. 'It's OK!'

I got up too and ran behind him, head down, into the dust storm. The pilot brought the chopper round. The side door was already open. Standing there, one hand outstretched, the other holding his AK, was the unmistakable figure of Ezra Black.

He hauled us up, and Roberts rolled on to the deck of the flying metal tank, suddenly jabbering from the adrenaline rush and the sheer relief of survival – though about what exactly was impossible to hear over the din of the rotar.

I looked up at Ezra, who was scanning the landing site as the bird pulled skywards. He pointed to a headset. We lurched to the side, but I managed to stand and steady myself by the open door. I put the headset on.

'This is costing some serious money, my friend,' I laughed, and he looked at me, eyes wide with sincerity. 'Seriously, eh? These South Africans are *meod* expensive.'

'Hey, bru, you fly with the best, you pay like the rest.' The pilot's voice crackled through the headphones. I spoke into comms loop.

'This is Max McLean.'

'Howzit, Mr McLean?' The pilot's hard-edged Afrikaans accent was tempered by the detachment of combat concentration. Underlying the nonchalance of most pilot chopper-chatter was a razor-sharp focus. 'Flight Captain Jan Van Vuuren at your service. Good to have you on board, hey.'

'Thanks for the ride, captain. Her Majesty's government is good for the money.'

'*Ja*, the way I hear it, you owe a little Scotsman a lot of whisky.'

I looked at Roberts. But Ezra spoke.

'When you make this call to London from my base, it stirs up a lot of shit, eh? Six of Micky's CIA *idiotim* try their luck. Roberts gave me the number for Nazzar. He's a good guy. We fucked up a lot of rebels together during *Barras*.'

'*Ja*, we gave those clowns a *moering* for sure.' Van Vuuren cut in. 'But now *hier kom groot kak*!'

Down below, the remaining half-dozen Sleepers had made it through the blast doors and were sprinting out of the hut. Bereft of orders, they sniffed the air and ran to the trees.

'Fuckin' zombies, man, actual fuckin' zombies.' Roberts had got his headset on, face pressed against the viewing port, transfixed. 'This is *insane*.'

I looked at Ezra.

'What can I say?' Ezra shrugged. 'I had him covered. He was supposed to stay with the chopper. But even me, I couldn't shoot him twice. He knows the terrain. And *no one* knows this terrain, not even my guys in Freetown.' He looked at Roberts. 'Next time someone gives you a gun maybe you tell me, eh?' But Roberts was too absorbed in the tableau playing out beneath him to pay attention.

'Yeah, well we're not clear yet,' I said. While Roberts marvelled at the walking dead on the ground, I braced myself for what was to come. I hoped Van Vuuren was up to it. I pressed the mic to my lips. 'There's unfinished business on the deck, captain.'

'It's your show, McLean. We're on auxiliary tanks. Enough juice for one pass, no BDA. Are there civilians down there?'

'That's a negative, captain. This is a rebel area.' I scanned the bush below.

'Negative on civilians copied. Just like the bad old days, hey Colonel Black?'

The Israeli smiled and stowed his AK.

'What's in the tubes, captain?' I asked.

'Eighty mil frag and fuel air good to go.'

He banked wide over the hillside, lining up for his run. Fresh air pulled through the vortex of the open door. Ezra moved to the port door gun and racked a round into the GPMG. Roberts strapped himself in, stunned and fascinated by turn at the horror unfolding around him. As we gained height, the reality of the country below receded. The Mong River kept on rolling, a slight swelling at the breach the only sign of the havoc her green waters had wrought below. The broken corpses of the doctors and technicians, soldiers and scientists looked surreal – scattered stick men thrown from the little rondel huts, dotted between the circular blooms of perfect little trees. Ana María lay still in the dust, fatigues ruffled by the mechanical breeze of the Russian gunship.

The Sleepers stood motionless, clustered together, necks craned skywards, salvaged weapons hanging ineffectual by their sides. Their mission completed, their enemy vanquished, they simply waited. They had been ordered only to wreak vengeance, nothing more, nothing less. And that is exactly what they had done. The headset buzzed back into life. It was Van Vuuren again.

'Fire control order.'

I looked at Ezra, and Roberts, and then out of the door at the ground. This would be the only chance to stop them. Caught out in the open, they would not survive the barrage. The fragmentation rockets would cut them to pieces, render them immobile. The fuel air explosives would vaporize everything in their path. As the accelerant ignited, the firestorm would create vacuums on the savannah. Bodies would implode; the blast doors sealing the bunker would be ripped clear. The tunnels and corridors and lift shaft near the entrance would collapse. Scant trace above ground that anything had ever happened would remain, except for the black scar of a bush fire. And deep below, unseen and untouched, my father would be entombed, sharing an underwater mausoleum with Colonel Proshunin for ever.

The men that my father had condemned stood listless in the African sun, waiting. There was nothing left for them now but betrayal and obliteration. And monsters or men, I knew at that moment their deaths would be on my conscience until the day I died.

'Code Zulu,' I replied into the headset. 'Kill them all.'

33

'Where have you travelled from today, Mr Schwartz?' I
rubbed the sleep out of my eyes and managed a smile.
Say what you like about him, Ezra Black had a sense of
humour.

'From Tel Aviv,' I replied, and then after an expectant
pause added: 'via Brussels.'

The UK Border Force officer entered more data into
the console in front of her and scrutinized the Canadian
passport. Unlike the documents I'd flown out on, it was
a fake; unlike the British, the Israelis were expert for-
gers. She sized up the unshaven and unsmiling deadbeat
in the photograph against the unshaven and unsmiling
deadbeat in front of her. My hair was brown, now; my
beard, too. I did a double take every time I looked in the
mirror. Fortunately the immigration officer didn't.

'And have you visited West Africa in the last forty
days?'

I shook my head.

'No, I flew from Toronto to Tel Aviv direct.'

MI6 had put out a phoney Ebola alert via the FCO –
screening for me, I guessed, while appearing to look for
the non-existent virus. Jack Nazzar had sent Ezra
enough bitcoin to buy me a new identity; Ezra had pulled
enough strings to bring it to life. Over a secure line in

Freetown, Nazzar had made one thing clear: he was as angry about Sonny Boy's death as I was.

He'd agreed to help bring me home on my terms because he knew it was the only way he could learn the truth of who sold out who, and why. Ultimately, I was expendable – even to Jack Nazzar. One man always is. Sonny Boy had been, too – which is why we'd been sent in the first place. But as units, E-Squadron and the Increment – and the UKN they supported – weren't. The cock-up in Benghazi had proved that much. If we were being betrayed from the inside, it was his men that would suffer most.

If Mason was hanging me out to dry – and that was a big 'if' – it hurt Nazzar as much as it did me. Until I knew for sure one way or the other I wasn't just on the run, I was on the loose.

'And you're on holiday, sir?'

Nazzar had made something else clear, too. If I was for the high jump, so was he. 'Fuck it up, son, an' it's no just ma pension that'll go bang.' He'd given a dismissive snort and hung up. There was nothing more he or Ezra could do for me. I was on my own.

'Mr Schwartz?'

'Uh, yes, sorry,' I replied. *Focus, Max. Focus.* 'Just for a few days. I've always wanted to see Westminster Abbey.'

'A pilgrim, then?' she smiled.

'Yeah, you could say that.' I smiled back, and she stamped the passport.

'Welcome to the United Kingdom. Enjoy the sights.'

349

I had no bag to reclaim, no taxi arriving; and, I hoped, no one waiting for me. I pulled the baseball cap I'd bought at Ben Gurion down over my eyes and headed out of the airport into a cold spring day. The ground was wet from a recent shower, and the tarmac flared bright white in the low sun. I stared at my feet and took a series of buses into central London.

No one stopped me. No one spoke to me. No one tried to kill me.

So far, so good.

The safe house was on Russell Square – an apartment in a mansion block opposite the Morton Hotel. The corridors were deserted; the constant traffic outside muffled by thick carpets and brass-trimmed fire doors. I stepped through the main door and took a sharp right up the stairs to the second floor, straight to apartment 201.

A discreet keypad enclosed by a black metal cover released the door lock. No keys, no porter, no trace – because UKN did not exist, none of its assets did either. The fact that my head was so far above the parapet was a rare exception thanks to Frank, and the jobs he gave me.

The locations of the safe houses, the real identities of the operators, the provenance of the money that fuelled them, were all off the books. MI6, the secretary of state, Director Special Forces – they didn't know, and they didn't want to know: what you don't know, you can't be held accountable for.

An en-suite double bedroom, kitchen diner, and a hall

with a separate loo. I opened the wardrobe in the bedroom and found what I was looking for. I keyed the same entry code into another pad – which this time unlocked a squat metal safe. Inside, a SIG 226 9mm pistol, two charged magazines, five thousand sterling in used bills and the keys to a Mercedes AMG Estate parked in the underground garage. I pocketed the keys, checked and loaded the pistol, grabbed the bundle of fifties and headed back downstairs.

If you support your house with a fifth column, don't be surprised when it collapses on you.

I stepped out into the square.

Thump. Thump. Thump.

Between the flowerbeds and trees I see the Sleepers running, swarming, spilling out into the city streets. A policeman is eviscerated. Cars stop, their drivers panic-stricken as the monster men cleave metal and drag them, screaming, to awful deaths. Mothers run after crying children. And everywhere is blood.

I shut my eyes.

Thump. Thump. Thump.

The rotor-wash is pulling at Ana María's hair. Rockets are streaking through the golden light of a West African morning. Clouds of vapour ignite; trees combust; the air burns. Amid the flames, the Sleepers stand still, waiting, uncomprehending. And everywhere is blood.

Get a hold of yourself, Max.

I blinked hard and found my feet.

I walked along Bayley Street and then dog-legged on to Percy Street. As I turned north up Charlotte Street, a rain shower thinned the pavements of office workers, who scuttled under awnings or into restaurants, looking for refuge.

I put my hand to the clean dressing on my throat and then ran my fingers along the ragged top of my ear. I felt like a tourist coming home still dressed for the beach: dislocated, neither here nor there, as if I was lagging behind myself. Being back in London after a job was always the same. Like resurfacing after a dive, it took time to depressurize, and while you waited nothing seemed quite real. Coming back from *this* job was like still being trapped in the diving bell. I had no idea what sort of world I would surface into.

But as I walked I began to remember who I was.

The Fitzroy Tavern stood at the junction with Windmill Street. There were two renovated Victorian saloons on the ground floor – divided by polished-wood walls. I made my way around to the long bar on the left and ordered a glass of Guinness.

'I'm sorry, mister, we've no Guinness.' The barmaid wore an apologetic smile. Five-two, blue hair, pierced black eyebrows. Skinny as a rake. I shrugged. She put her hand on one of the draught taps. 'They do their own stout, you know? In fairness it's not bad. And the Guinness tastes like shite over here anyways.' A Dubliner. No doubt.

'OK,' I nodded. 'You're the boss.'

'A glass was it?'

I nodded again, and she slipped a little half-pint jug under the tap. It filled and clouded and settled, and she topped it up, fielding orders from either side of me as she did so. I offered her one of the fifties I'd taken from the safe. Her hand moved towards mine and then faltered.

'No, you're grand. That's on the house.'

'No, really, I'm sorry I don't have anything smaller.'

'Don't be daft. First one's on the house today. You look like you're a long way from home.' What I looked was nonplussed. 'Happy Paddy's Day,' she said. March 17th. Of course. I raised the glass to her.

'*Sláinte.*'

She went to ask me something but got distracted by another customer, so I took the drink and perched on a barstool at a high table at the far end of the counter. I faced the door, back to the wall. It was a large space, sparse, with seats around the edge and plenty of room for standing. There were toilets downstairs and a restaurant above. I was going to have to do this somewhere. And here was as good a place as any. If they were going to find me – which they would, eventually – then they would find me when and where I wanted them to.

I took a sip of the stout and wiped the head off the moustache thickening across my lip. She was right. It tasted OK. From inside my jeans pocket I fished out a pay-as-you-go cell phone I'd picked up at Heathrow. I composed and recomposed the SMS to Frank half a dozen times.

In the end I kept it simple:

Fitzrovia. 20:00hrs. Location to follow.

There was no point giving him any other instructions.

Frank, as usual, would do only as he pleased. He'd consider coming mob-handed or early or not at all. But he'd know I'd know that too. Frank had overseen my transition into a professional escape artist, and we both knew that in the end he'd buy a ticket to this show or risk missing the final act for ever.

General Kristóf King's number I'd got from Nazzar. Good luck trying to squeeze a drink in with any other top brass at short notice on a Friday night. But Director Special Forces has an Achilles heel: if you have his emergency number, you can always reach him, day or night.

Three rings and then muffled confusion as the strings of a Hungarian violin were cut short in the background.

'King,' he barked into the receiver.

'It's McLean,' I replied. Pause. 'Max McLean.'

'Ah,' he said without missing a beat, 'the prodigal son returns, what?' I kept quiet. He filled the void. 'I hear you've progressed, Max.'

'From what to what, sir?' I asked.

'From not pulling the trigger at all to pulling it rather more than anticipated. Where are you?'

'London. We're going to meet tonight. Fitzrovia. Eight o'clock.'

'Eight o'clock? I say that's . . .'

'I'll see you then, General,' I interrupted him. 'I'll call again at seven forty-five.'

I hung up. King's motivations were unknowable. Whether he came or not would tell me almost everything I needed to know about him anyway.

Next I punched in the London number I'd memorised in Freetown.

'Embankment.' Same matter-of-fact operator.

'Three-o-nine.' I replied like for like. No niceties given nor expected at Vauxhall Cross.

'Stand by.'

To let me know I hadn't been cut off, the line sang with an easy-listening classical music track. After ten seconds Mr Matter-of-Fact came back on the line to tell me I was being connected. Hold music again. And then: 'Major McLean, I suppose.' Clipped Queen's English. David Mason had picked up the call directly. That was a good start.

'I've got what you want,' I told him. He paused before replying.

'Got what, McLean?'

'Your pound of flesh.'

'I . . .' he hesitated. 'I'm glad you've decided to come in, Major McLean, but . . .'

'Fitzrovia, eight o'clock sharp. I'll call you back.' I hung up and took the battery out of the phone.

On our first day at Raven Hill Colonel Ellard once told us that every course of action begins with one decision: do something or do nothing. When I was sixteen I'd chosen to do something: I ran. And all else followed.

I pressed the middle three fingers of my right hand into my left wrist and felt the radial artery pulsing beneath the skin. Now I was a forty-two-year-old state-sanctioned killer, and I'd chosen to stop running. I believed in what I did. Like my mother and father, I'd picked a side. And like them, my side betrayed me. I'd been allowed to live a lie, sold out and then turned into a weapon.

Colonel Ellard had taught us something else that day, too: never forgive, never forget.

The barmaid worked her way around the room, clearing tables, balancing a stack of glasses. She moved confidently – pivoting between the punters, deflecting banter. Detached and determined. What was she, twenty-five? Younger maybe. She was pretty and, I hoped, poor.

I drained the glass of stout and put a fifty pound note under it as she approached.

'*Go raibh maith agat*,' I said. *Thank you*. Now it was her turn to look confused. She lifted the glass and stared first at the red note and then at me. '*An ndéanfá gar dom*,' I said to her.

'I'm from Dublin,' she said, 'not feckin' Donegal. I hardly have a word of the Irish and I've no time for a lesson.' She stepped back. I pushed the note towards her.

'I need a favour,' I said again, in English, but amplifying my Wicklow accent for all it was worth. 'Nothing weird, like. I'm coming back later with a couple of English yokes. Proper posh. Know what I mean? I need to loosen one of them up a bit. Just a bit of fun. You know, relax him so he has a good time.'

'Whether he likes it or not?'

I reached for her hand, as if to shake it. She drew back further, but when she saw what I had to give her she let me take it, and I palmed her a bundle of notes.

'Exactly,' I said. 'Whether he likes it or not.'

When we'd finished talking, I walked down the stairs

and scoped out the toilet. A corridor led under the bars above and up a flight of steps to a side door on to Windmill Street. I pulled the baseball cap down over my eyes and circled round the block along Rathbone Street, cutting up Percy Passage and into the Charlotte Street Hotel, just across the road from the Fitzroy Tavern. Escape and evasion didn't get any more basic, but under the circumstances it was the best I could manage.

I booked into an attic room on the fourth floor. The window looked down on the pub on the corner of Charlotte Street and Windmill Street and over the rooftops beyond. I'd know soon enough if the barmaid called the cops or if anyone else called the cavalry. I killed the lights and lit a Marlboro.

There was nothing left to do but wait.

34

King was the first to arrive. He stepped out of a black cab immediately in front of the Fitzroy Tavern and vanished inside the main bar on the left, as instructed. Mason was next. He was dropped off in what looked like an official car – unmarked and unremarkable, distinguished only by tinted windows and a suited chauffeur. He was wearing black tie. They were both on time. They'd both picked up immediately when I called at seven forty-five. Neither of them had said anything.

Frank was late.

I peered down hard on to the sodium-lit pavements. He hadn't replied to my text messages. I scanned the streets, scrutinized the taxis.

Then I saw him.

He was walking down Windmill Street, straight towards me. His suit jacket was open, and the rain had soaked his hair and shoulders. He was walking fast, head down and determined. I wondered where he'd come from. The windowpane fogged under my breath.

'OK,' I reassured myself, 'let's go.' I took off down the stairs at the double, jumping two or three steps at a time.

As I stepped out into the drizzle Frank stepped into the pub. I was as sure as I could be that the barmaid hadn't called the police. But whether she'd lost her bottle remained to be seen. I was also sure that no nasty surprises were waiting for me on the roofs that fanned out beyond the hotel window. What I didn't, couldn't, know was whether anyone had been positioned on the roof directly above me.

I braced myself and headed for the same door Mason and King had used. I walked briskly enough for the March weather, but not so much as to stand out. It took me three seconds to cross the street. I reached out for the handle and pushed.

No shot came.

If they'd found me and wanted me dead, they wanted to know what I knew before they killed me.

The door closed behind me, and the warm fug of beer and banter drew me in. Frank had crossed the bar in front of me and was making his way around a pair of already tipsy customers. A shock of blue hair flitted behind the bar and then disappeared from view. I followed Frank. King was at the far end of the bar, leaning on his hip. He saw Frank first and then me behind and straightened up. The room was more brightly lit than I'd imagined it would be, but his eyes were still lost in the shadow of his brow. It was hard to read him. He nodded, and Frank turned around to greet me.

'If it isn't the big fella himself.' He grinned at me and held out his hand. He looked genuinely pleased to see me, and I realized I'd had no idea what to expect from any of them. I could feel the SIG nestling against my spine in the small of my back. We shook hands. He touched my shoulder as he did so, making sure, it seemed, that it really was me. 'Thank God you didn't pick the *Archway* Tavern,' he said. 'I haven't been able to drink in there since 1983.'

I grinned back, freed my hand and touched my temple in a light salute to General King. He kept his hands in his coat pockets.

'Sir,' I said. 'Thank you for joining us.' He shot Frank a quick glance, and Frank gave a half-shrug, as if to say, 'Don't look at me.'

'My pleasure,' he snorted. 'Quite the surprise, what?' He studied me and wrinkled his nose. 'Please do call me Kristóf, though. We look ridiculous enough as it is without bloody well saluting each other. I suppose you invited Mason?'

I nodded. King raised his eyebrows. Frank swore under his breath. Mason emerged up the stairs from the toilets. His fingers were wet, and I could see that he'd washed his face. He didn't offer to shake my hand.

'Ah, Major McLean. I see you corralled the other . . .' He paused, agitated, unsure of how to refer to King and Frank in public.

'Wise monkeys?' King interrupted.

'For God's sake,' Mason sighed, 'this is a bloody farce.' He carried on, unperturbed, his voice rising. 'An *absolute* bloody farce. You can't really believe you're going to get away with this, can you, Major? Whatever your . . .' he hesitated again, '. . . *game* is, you'd better pack it in and start helping us to unravel the unholy mess you've left behind.'

360

'Get away with what, exactly?' I asked him. 'Murder?'

The four of us stood in a semi-circle around the bar, facing each other off. If he expected the other two to back him up, he was mistaken. King just stared at him. Frank looked around the room.

Two of the other tables were occupied with drinkers – giggly students attracted by the cheap beer and a couple of lads attracted by the students. Punters tripped to and from the door down to the toilets. No one looked at us twice. Mason started to speak again but was silenced by the barmaid.

'What'll it be then, folks?' The Dublin accent of my blue-rinsed accomplice turned all of our heads. 'And before you ask, we've no Guinness.'

'No Guinness? Some Pat's Day drink this is, Max.' Frank squinted at the draught taps. 'I'll have whatever that stout is and do my best to pretend it's proper.'

'Good man,' she encouraged him. 'To be fair, it's not bad at all. A pint is it?'

'Uh-huh,' Frank nodded.

'Make that two,' I added. She plucked another glass from the rack and looked up at King and Mason.

'Gents?'

Mason ordered a tonic water, King red wine. The barmaid stopped the tap on the first pint and switched glasses as the first settled.

I looked at the three of them. I had one shot, at one target. And it had to count.

I put my hand in my pocket. Frank reached inside his jacket. He could have been going either for his wallet or his pistol. I beat him to it and put a fifty on the counter top. His hand fell away, and he grinned at me again.

'*Go raibh maith agat*,' he said.

'My pleasure,' I said. 'Next round's on you.'

I angled the note slightly away from myself.

'Right you are. Take a seat,' she said, taking the money and counting out my change. 'I'll bring your drinks over when they're ready.'

We sat at a low table furthest from the door. Mason had his back to the wall. Frank sat to my left, King to my right. Each of them had the effect of calming the others down, sizing each other up as much as they were me. The atmosphere was not so different to a mission briefing. And, as usual, no one knew who held the cards.

As we settled into our seats, what little chat there'd been between us evaporated into awkward silence. King kept his coat on. Mason adjusted his bow tie. Frank smoothed his rain-wet hair and looked at the faces around the table. He wasn't smiling any more. It struck me that he'd been grinning not because he was glad to see me, but in anticipation of Mason and King's discomfort at seeing me.

'Well?' he said.

I opened my mouth to begin, but this time it was I who was cut off.

'Here you go, gents.' Ring-wrapped fingers transferred two pints of stout, a tonic water and a small glass of red wine from a circular bar tray to the middle of the table. 'Enjoy.'

I lifted my glass. My ribs smarted. Frank raised his glass, too.

'*Sláinte*,' he said and gulped a mouthful of the strong black stout. He swallowed hard and nodded his approval at the English drink.

'*Do shláinte!*' I replied.

'*Egészségünkre*,' King sighed to himself. I looked at him, and he tightened a quick smile across his lips. Mason said nothing, and sipped his tonic. The bar was getting noisy. Another table filled up next to the students, who were attracting admirers like moths to a flame. Before long I'd have to raise my voice to be heard. I swallowed another mouthful of stout. Everyone else drank, too, as if that would conclude our business more quickly.

'Right, then,' I said. 'Let's cut to it. Sorry to be blunt, but I don't have much time.' Frank looked at me quizzically. I pressed on. 'You know what really interests me, gentlemen?' No one answered. 'OK,' I continued. 'I'll tell you, then. It's not that you all came this evening. I expected that. It's that none of you told the others you were coming. Isn't that fascinating?'

'Indeed,' said King. He leaned back in his chair and relaxed. 'And painfully so.' He paused and seemed to make his mind up about something. 'I like you, Max. Let me be clear about that. And let me be clear about this, too. You're an asset. You were sent to do a job. You were given limited information for your own good, and for the good of the mission. I know you know this. Everything we do is secrets and lies. Falsehoods that serve a greater good. I imagine Colonel Ellard already gave you this lecture at Raven Hill, however many years ago.'

'Twenty-three,' I reminded him.

'Well, there you go. Twenty-three years. You're a professional, not a rookie. So tell me. Tell *us*. Why are we here? Because right now all *we* know is that you killed an awful lot of people, apparently including a senior GRU officer *and* a CIA agent, and all hell broke loose. Mason is right, Max. It's an unholy mess – and we still don't have the first idea *why* it is.'

'And how do you know I killed a CIA officer?' I asked him. 'Because Vauxhall told you so?' Mason folded and unfolded his arms. I ploughed on. '"Never forget where you're from." That's what you said to me, isn't it, General, two weeks ago, when I got back from Caracas?' King inclined his head in agreement. 'Well, the reason we're here is because I never knew where I was from, and one of you three has forgotten which side you're on.'

'Max,' Frank rolled his shoulders and looked up to the ceiling, 'as far as we can tell, you did your job. The target seems to have been terminated. If it was a shit job, then I'm sorry. But before you carry on,' he took another mouthful of his pint, 'remember that what you say now cannot later be unsaid.'

'I know, Frank, but you mustn't worry.' I looked at Mason and softened my tone. 'You see, all I want is a friendly chat.' Mason undid his bow tie. 'A heart to heart, if you like.'

'That would be nice.' Mason murmured so softly that it was hard to hear him. I leaned across the table towards him. The SIG bulged at the back of my jeans. 'A nice, friendly heart to heart.'

'What?' said King.

'Yes, a nice heart to heart.' Mason spoke up, his voice warm, but strong. 'It's so good to talk, isn't it?'

'Is it?' King frowned and looked at Frank. Frank looked at me. I was still looking at Mason.

'It is,' I said. I reached out and laid my hand on top of Mason's. 'It really is. May I call you David?'

'Oh, please do. Surnames are so formal, hmm?'

'So, *David*, you see there's something I'd really love to know, something special that I think only you can tell me.'

'Of course, Max! Of course. What would you like to know?' He took another sip of his drink and licked his lips, sitting forward in expectation of my question. Frank had moved closer too. King sat up and pushed his wine glass away from him. I took a deep breath and hoped I was on target.

'You see, David, it's just that Colonel Proshunin knew I was coming. He knew my name, and why I was in Sierra Leone. How is that possible, David? How do you think he knew that?'

Mason yawned and looked me straight in the face.

'Because I told him.'

Frank put his pint down and straightened up.

'What did you say?' he asked. Mason turned to Frank.

'I said I told Colonel Proshunin that Max was coming.'

'And why, David, did you do that?' King spoke slowly

and carefully, perhaps fearful of what might be said next. Confused where to turn, Mason looked at me.

'So that he'd kill Max, of course.' There were tears in his eyes. 'I'm so sorry, Max. Will you forgive me? *Please* forgive me. It's so good to be able to talk about all this at last. It's been such a burden.'

'It must have been,' I said. I withdrew my hand carefully and hooked it around the back of my chair within easy reach of the SIG. 'And why did you do that? Try to have me killed, I mean.'

'Because I wanted to broker a deal. And so did the Americans. It's very simple really.'

'A deal with who, David?' I asked him. It had felt anything but simple to me, trapped underwater with my father's monsters.

'With Moscow, naturally. We'd let them keep the virus and save their professor from, well, from *you*, Max.'

'What was the deal?' King asked. 'What did you want in return?'

'Influence, Kristóf.'

'Influence?' King backed away slightly.

'Yes, influence. You're so old-fashioned, Kristóf. You can't stand the Russians, and all because of something that happened in Hungary when you were just a silly little boy. I bet you don't even remember it, not really.' King let him continue. 'Lies, you said. Lies and history. And do you know what comes between them, Kristóf? *Ideology*. Once upon a time the Russians were just an irritant we defined ourselves in opposition to. But now they're the future. Our future. The Americans know it,' Mason turned to Frank, 'but we're being left out, held back. *Corrupted*, fooled by fools into giving up gladly the very things we should be fighting to keep. This isn't about left or right any more, Kristóf. The core has crumbled. The *idea* of Europe, of democracy, of everything – *everything!* – you fought for,' he looked around the table, 'that *all* of you fought for, has failed.'

The three of us listened in silence. Beads of sweat formed on his brow and upper lip. He sipped from his glass and turned his full attention back to King.

'Do you think Washington or Moscow will give a damn about us while we despise ourselves, wringing our hands at the memory of how great we once were? No, Kristóf. We need to act. The game's afoot, and God damn anyone who thinks otherwise. It's the strong who will survive – strong men and strong nations. This mission was about only that: our survival – building a strategic partnership with people who understand their destiny, not serving the traitors in Westminster who fight against ours. You break one set of rules only so that you can follow another. But the Russians know there *are* no rules. They've seen it first and seen it clearest. And you, you are just blind men groping your way in the shadow of a giant.' Frank put his hands under the table. I sat back a little. 'It was a unique opportunity,' he concluded. 'And I took it. With access to their virus we could have done anything together. Anything and *everything*.'

'So you made sure the operation was set up to fail all along,' King said. It was a statement, not a question. No one spoke for a moment. I didn't have long left.

'Yes. Rather clever, really. Max gets just enough rope to hang himself, and we get, how did they describe it? The keys to the Kingdom. We save them from Max – a threat that we created – and they're eternally grateful. That's all espionage is, you know. An international extortion racket.'

'And Sonny Boy,' I pushed on. 'Sergeant Mayne. He messed it up for you, didn't he? He knew what you were up to and tried to stop it himself because he found out about the virus, what it could do.' Mason nodded. His cheeks were wet with tears, but he was still smiling through them. 'Is that why you had him killed?' Mason nodded again. 'And the others? Marie Margai? Your Official in Freetown?'

'Yes,' he sighed. 'All of them. And that counsellor, too. Crossman, was it?' He yawned again. 'Last week. Poisoned her in her own office. Brutal business. So good to get it all out in the open.'

I sat back in my chair. Mason wiped his eyes and nodded at me. Frank and King looked at each other and then at me. I reached inside my jacket pocket and took out my cell phone. The voice recorder was still running. I pressed stop and then send and Jack Nazzar, wherever he was, received an email of the audio file.

Mason rested his head against the wall and closed his eyes. As King went to speak again, Mason slumped to one side and slipped into deep sleep. There were so many questions, but it was a narrow window and the curtains were already drawn. I put the phone back in my pocket and reached over to check his carotid pulse.

David Mason would wake up in a few hours with a head-ache and no recollection of our heart to heart. All he'd remember would be falling asleep suddenly in a London pub.

From my jeans I produced the glass ampoule that the barmaid – already well on her way to who knew where – had given me back with my change.

'SP-117,' I said to King. 'Courtesy of our Russian friends.' He held out his hand, and I dropped it into his palm. 'It's what they call "the remedy that loosens the tongue".'

'How did you know?' Frank said. 'It could have been me. It could have been the good General here. How did you know whose drink to spike?' He put his hands back on the table, in clear view.

'A number in a cell phone,' I said. 'Confusion over when someone died or who killed them. The enemy who knows your name. All bullshit. Interesting bullshit. But still just bullshit. Depending how you look at it, it can mean anything or nothing.'

'OK. But you *knew*, right? You always bloody know. So how?'

I stood up and looked at them both. King tilted his head back, and for the first time I saw his eyes. They weren't black. They were brown.

Probably just like his mother's, I thought.

'Proshunin didn't just know my name,' I said. 'He knew my rank, too.' I picked up my glass and tilted it towards Mason. 'You're both military. Neither of you would have told him I was a major, because I'm not.'

'That's it?' said King.

'Nearly,' I said. 'There was one other thing, too.' I looked at Frank. 'The scientist, my target.' Frank looked me straight in the face. His eyes widened almost imperceptibly. 'He served in Aden, didn't he?'

'Yes,' he said. 'I believe he did.'

'That was a nasty scar he had, on his temple.'

'Indeed it was.'

'He had a run-in with the locals, I believe. On a bus,' I said. Frank spread his fingers out on the table.

'It's a good policy, I find,' he replied, 'not to ask too many questions to which you already know the answer.' He looked at King. 'It gets boring for other people.'

'Sure,' I said. 'But how did *you* know it was him?' Frank cleared his throat and turned his attention back to me.

'Because Sonny Boy came back covered in blood. Drenched, but not infected. We ran the DNA. There was only one match. Whatever it was the professor was doing, Max, he embedded his own DNA into it.'

And mine, I thought. The virus and the antidote, the new, final strain was made with *my* DNA. I felt my heart beat in my chest, my ears. Blood surged through my veins. His blood. Bad blood.

'Commander Knight, I'm not sure I entirely understand,' King stood. Frank remained seated next to Mason.

'What are you going to do now, Max?' Frank asked. 'Raven Hill is still an option, if you want it to be.'

King nodded his consent.

'There's something I have to get out of my system

first,' I said. I swilled the remaining stout around the bottom of my glass. 'I'll be in touch.'

I turned my back on them and started towards the exit, but Frank called out over the building din in the bar.

'Ana María made it out of Venezuela.'

'I know,' I replied, 'she made it back to Karabunda, too.' I saw it clearly then. I wasn't the only one who'd mistrusted MI6. 'You knew she was involved. You switched out my original target for her at the last moment, didn't you? So Mason couldn't stop it.'

'Maybe I did,' Frank said. 'One thing's for sure, though: if you'd killed her in Caracas, we wouldn't be here now.' He gripped Mason's shoulder and smiled. 'You did well.'

'So did you, Frank.' I walked to the door through a throng of green wigs and tricolour T-shirts and stepped out of the heat of the pub and into the freezing night air. I stopped to drain the last of the stout before heading off. The whole city was coming to life around me. In front of me, the bullet had already left the barrel.

I didn't hear the shot.

You never do.

The glass sang with a bright, clear *snap* as the round exploded into a handful of jagged shards. They'd heard what I had to say all right; I supposed they were going to make sure I didn't say anything else. I looked up into the open door of a blacked-out van and the face of Jim Jones.

He lowered the silenced barrel of his pistol and climbed out. The bullet had missed me by a whisper and embedded itself into the wooden frame of the door behind me.

'Grumpy Jock liked your email,' he said, pushing past me into the bar. 'Happy Saint Patrick's Day. *Sir.*'

I breathed out hard.

It looked like Mason was going to have a rough night.

Epilogue: First Light

Monday 20 March 2017

The driver set me down at Oughterard. I watched the tail lights of the bread van disappear into the pre-dawn gloom and then walked the last two kilometres north up Glann Road to Baurisheen. The silver-black expanse of Lough Corrib stretched away to the east. I stood for a while, letting my eyes adjust, breathing in the wind and waves and wildness.

I'd abandoned the Mercedes at Holyhead and boarded the ferry on foot. My cell phone was at the bottom of the Irish Sea. The last message it received was from Roberts and Juliet.

Heading up to Bindi, bruv. Wish us luck.

They were looking for the girl with the broken lion bracelet. If anyone could find her, it was them.

Over the weekend I'd walked and hitched across country from Dún Laoghaire. I hadn't gone home. Maybe I never would. It was twenty-six years since I'd walked the halls and gardens of our old house; our family home. All that could remain was an echo. The voices, *their* voices, were long gone, distorted by time.

Who was it that went to my mother that day and gave her the choice to take her own life, or have it taken from

373

her? I hadn't asked, because I hadn't needed to. It would have been someone like me, and the only person I knew like me was Frank. When she was gone and my father vanished, I became his penance, his project.

Mason had set me up to fail; Frank had set Mason up to fail; and King didn't care who failed as long as the Russians didn't win. I crouched down and stared at my reflection emerging in the dark lake water.

It was hard to see what winning looked like.

At the end of a small spit of land I found the boat I was looking for, a blue and white skiff pulled up on to the beach. I unhooked the painter from the cinderblock anchor and left on top of it, secured under a heavy stone, the price of a month's rental in cash. I threw my bag in and pushed off.

In Holyhead I'd dropped an insulated envelope containing another small glass phial into the post. As the rising sun chased the shadows off the hills in County Galway ten millilitres of my blood would drop on to the doormat of Captain Rhodes at the DSTL laboratory in Porton Down. If the Russians had managed to get the virus to Moscow, she'd be able to stop them; if King wanted to create an army, I'd be able to stop him.

I pulled hard at the oars and set my course for the wilderness of the lake islands. My little boat beat against the current. Forty days, my father had said – after which I would get back to doing what I did best.

Killing was my life.

Anything that happened before or after was just waiting.